SECRETS FROM THE PAST

"I was having multiple affairs, wasn't I, Paula?" Amanda took a deep breath. "I mean . . . I was . . . promiscuous . . ."

"What a funny question," Paula said, shifting uneasily.

"You're my best friend. Tell me the truth . . . stop shielding me from myself."

"I'm not . . ."

"Yes, you are. And I love you for it. But the game is over. The past is no longer a sanctuary if it starts haunting a person. It's time you helped me put some of the ghosts to rest . . ."

"Well, you didn't exactly hide the fact that you didn't think your marriage to Brent was . . . ah . . . enough. And then there were the men. They openly lusted after you. And you encouraged their chase . . ."

"Was I sleeping around?"

"Yes," she whispered, wincing at the pain that flashed across Amanda's face. "I mean . . ."

"Thank you," Amanda nodded. "It's all right."

Amanda stared at the horizon. The sun had risen and the day was bright and full of promise. But she hardly noticed any of it, her heart heavy with regret and confusion.

"With whom, Paula? I need to know. The men, who were the men . . . ?"

SHATTERED ILLUSIONS

LINDA RENEE DE JONG

ST. MARTIN'S PAPERBACKS

SHATTERED ILLUSIONS

Copyright © 1991 by Linda Renee DeJong.

ISBN: 0-312-92578-6

Printed in the United States of America

St. Martin's Paperbacks edition/November 1991

10 9 8 7 6 5 4 3 2 1

To my mother—
    for believing in me
To my son—
    for putting up with me
But most of all,
    for his constant support, his encouragement, his love—
    my Inspiration, my best Friend, my Lover,
    the Man of my Dreams, the Love of my Life,
    —to my husband.

And, last but not least—
    to my editor, Jennifer Weis,
    whose continued enthusiasm for this book
    and valuable input and support
    have made it a riveting, more exciting read.

Prologue

THE MUSTANG TURBO SKIDDED AS IT HIT A DEEP FLOOD pocket, spurting fountains of water up into the streaming rain, its speed only momentarily deterred. Grazing the deserted roads along the outskirts of Barrington Hills, barely missing a curve, it roared through the black night, mindless of the raging storm that swept across northwest suburban Chicago. The sound of screeching tires was drowned out by the howling October wind and rain battering the windshield. Visibility was at zero.

A log suddenly loomed in the hazy beam of the fog lamps, barricading most of the road. The car swerved dangerously, its left wheels spinning in the muddy side strip, right rear bumper scouring against a sharp tail end. Skidding, it hurled itself back on the slick asphalt, and without reducing speed, went into yet another curve. The Mustang thrust through the darkness with hellish recklessness, its right wheels perilously scraping the edge of the gaping ravine lurking below.

Oblivious to the danger, the young woman behind the wheel shifted gears and pressed her foot farther down on the gas pedal. A sob escaped her and she bit her trembling lip—hard, then harder, tasting the blood that mingled with the salt of her tears. A silent scream welled from deep within and for a split second she felt her chest constrict. She shook her head, again and again, her hands gripping the steering wheel with a force equal to the raging wind while trying to blink away the stubborn tears that streamed down her face.

Angrily, she fumbled in the dark for the knob of the defroster. Yet as minutes passed, nothing happened and, frantic, she used her left hand to wipe the dense moisture off the inside of the windshield. On the outside, the windshield wipers worked at full speed. But the gushing rain was no match for them and, blindly, the car plunged forward.

Another ragged sob tore from her ashen lips. A man's voice rose above the roaring storm; a harsh voice, uttering even harsher words, but it was their meaning that haunted her—"Looks like, little lady, you might've botched up your own future here. Pinching money isn't always a savings, you know. Like I always said: you get what you pay for."

She shook her head in anguish, desperately trying to block the hollow echo . . . So what if he was a doctor? That didn't make him God! She bit her lip again, hard, wanting to feel the pain. It wasn't fair; it couldn't be happening to her. The man was wrong, dead wrong. He had to be. Why, tomorrow she would go and seek out a second opinion, and a third if she had to. Impatiently she brushed away the hot tears, but they kept coming and she couldn't seem to stop them.

Out of sheer frustration, she wiped the fogged windshield again. Damn! What a time for the defroster to break down. Peter was right, she should have had the car checked weeks ago. It was way overdue for its annual inspection. She groaned inwardly. Peter was right about so many things. If only she listened to him more often.

A sudden glare of light leaped at her. She threw the wheel to avoid a collision. The shrill wail of a horn whined past her as the Mustang swerved, sliding off the road, ramming the edge of a bush and heading into a sharp curve. Ahead was a second pair of blinding lights. She gasped, and threw the wheel again. Her heart pounding into her throat, she could hear the tires screech as she hit the brakes, but the road was too slick and the turn too sharp. She could feel the car skid and frantically tried to maneuver it, to hold it onto the road, but the Mustang had gone out of control, and as she took her foot off the brakes, she knew she had lost control of the wheel.

The driver of the blue Volvo swerved to avoid the oncoming car, which seemed to directly torpedo into him, and he felt the car make a complete spin before it hit a tree alongside the road. He cursed vehemently, but in the midst of his strong language, his eyes widened in horror. In the beam of his bright lights he watched his assailant go off the road and over the bend. Forgetting his rage, he quickly opened the door and ran toward the spot where he had seen the other car disappear.

The headlights were still on. In the rain he could just make out the dim outlines of the car and knew it had rolled over onto its side. Crawling backward, careful not to lose his footing, he scrambled down, scratching his arms on a couple of sharp branches along the way. Finally his right foot touched the vehicle. He turned and cautiously felt his way around it. Finding the door, he reached for the handle. Thank God, he thought, it was the driver's side, and it was not locked. The inside light came on when he opened the door. He peered inside and frowned. The woman behind the wheel was unconscious, her head slumped against the dashboard. What good is it to have the seat belt on when it isn't tightened? he grumbled. Well, at least it had held her body in place. He launched her head upward and out the door before he fumbled to loosen the belt.

The car suddenly weaved. God, the rain must have soaked the ground to mud! He moved with feverish speed, concentrating on hauling the woman out of the car, and just as he had managed to drag her next to him on the muddy slope behind the vehicle, he heard the car door slam shut. Keeping his grip firmly on the motionless figure beside him, he turned around just in time to see the car tumble over, once, twice, and down the dark ravine. He heard a dull thud, almost immediately followed by a burst of flames.

A sudden wave of nausea threatened to overcome him. He closed his eyes, desperately holding on to the unconscious body by his side. After a while the world stopped spinning, the bile in his throat subsided, and he slowly opened his eyes. He shuddered, and it was not just from being drenched.

Chapter 1

SOUNDS OF VOICES, AS IF FROM A DISTANCE, FLOATED
through her hazy subconscious. Hushed voices, the words
unclear. A curious odor penetrated her senses and she
stirred. The voices suddenly stopped, and another sound
reached her—a rhythmic, monotonous beeping sound.
Slowly she tried to open her eyes. They felt heavy and it took
sheer willpower to force them to open. Blurred images appeared and again she willed herself to focus her vision. A soft
rustle came closer and she felt a warm hand gently lift her
arm.

She could not see the face, her vision still blurred. Vaguely
her mind deciphered an image in white. It spoke to her; still
the buzzing in her ears prevailed and she could not distin-
guish what it said. She tried to speak, but the words never
reached her quivering lips. Finally, defeated, she closed her
eyes again and sank back into the safety of oblivion.

The man in white felt her pulse, comparing it to his wristwatch, and nodded. Gently he lifted her eyelids, and a sigh of
relief escaped him.

"She'll be all right now, but keep a close eye on her." He
nodded to the nurse and picked up the chart to make an
entry. When he finished, he looked at the still face in the bed,
disbelief in his eyes. She looked so young, so fragile under

that transparent oxygen mask and the white bandage around her head. An ugly bruise marred her left cheek.

"Unbelievable," he muttered underneath his breath.

"Excuse me, Dr. Rossiter, did you say something?" The head nurse looked at him, suppressing her irritation. These damn doctors, why did they think that being a nurse qualified her to understand their mumblings?

"Sorry, Liz." Philip Rossiter smiled. He had noted her irritation and knew only too well her opinion of doctors. But she was the best in her field and it would not do to be on her enemy list.

"I was only thinking out loud. Lucky girl, damn lucky. From the reports, she should have been dead, burnt to a crisp. Yet here she lies, virtually unscathed, with only a concussion. Severe, perhaps, but nonetheless just that. No broken bones, no crushed skull, not even a facial disfigurement." He waved her unspoken protestations away. "That bruise on her cheek will fade. In a few weeks she'll be as good as new. Amazing, isn't it?"

Liz Stephens scowled. "Amazing is the man who rescued her. Not too many like him around these days, risking his own life, and for an irresponsible hell-driver!" She pressed her lips together, suppressing the harsher words that came to mind.

"Indeed. He deserves a medal for his bravery."

She threw him a suspicious glance, yet the expression on his face was that of genuine respect, and she turned away, still not quite sure. Philip Rossiter was a skillful physician, but she disapproved of his dry sense of humor and found his sarcasm misplaced; more often than not, it assaulted her sense of propriety.

"Call me when there is any change, would you, Liz? I'd like to have a stern word with the reckless young lady." He handed her the patient's chart and with a fleeting smile mockingly saluted her and walked out of the room.

The hospital cafeteria was crowded with early lunchgoers, mostly staff members of the first shift. Carrying his tray, Philip Rossiter made his way to the nonsmoking section and glanced around for an empty seat. His eyes lit up as he spotted a man in white seated by the window, talking to a strikingly attractive redhead. A wry smile curled his thin lips and, detecting an empty seat behind them, he strode in their direction.

"How's it going, Daryl? Hello, Sally, early shift this morning?"

"Hi, Dr. Rossiter." Sally rose and picked up her tray. "You're in luck, I was just leaving." She threw both men an alluring smile and walked away.

Rossiter put down his tray and turned his head to watch her swing her well-proportioned hips as she headed toward the exit. He puckered his lips and sat down.

"I hope I wasn't interrupting anything?"

"Damn sure you were. As usual, your timing is lousy. But then, you never could accept the fact that women, good-looking women that is, find me more attractive than you." Daryl Wills leaned back in his chair, his eyes laughing.

Rossiter grinned and poured ketchup on his hamburger. "You're married, thus a challenge to a fun-seeking redhead."

"Wrong, you're too finicky, thus you'll never find your Juliet."

"When you find me a double of your wife, I'll let down my defenses, but only then." He bit into the hamburger. "Pass the salt, will you?"

Daryl handed him the bottle.

"I should be going. Time for my rounds."

"Are you very busy?" Philip took a sip of his milk.

"Nothing special, why?"

"Didn't you work with amnesia victims at Lutheran?"

"Skokie Valley, years back. I was 'on loan' there, right after my residency." He watched his friend, his curiosity aroused. Philip was not one to make small talk where patients were concerned. "All right, spit it out, Phil. What's on your mind?"

Phil took another sip of milk. "I think I've got one on my hands. She was brought into Emergency four days ago. Car accident."

"Go on."

"She doesn't seem to remember anything about herself or her life before the accident. Doesn't know who or what she is, where she lives, nothing, a total void."

"No ID?"

Rossiter shook his head.

"The car crashed into a ravine and went up in flames. And everything inside with it."

"What about family, next of kin?"

"The man who brought her in claims he'd never seen her before in his life. He said he managed to get her out of the car before it went down into the ravine." He looked his friend straight in the eye. "I've worked with an amnesia patient only once, when I was a resident. You've seen more of them. Do you mind looking in on this one?"

Daryl shot him a pensive look.

"You think it might be faked?"

"Not necessarily. She's suffering from a severe concussion, so it could be temporary."

"So what's the problem?"

"I can't put my finger on it. There's something . . . in her eyes . . . some hidden pain, or perhaps it's fear. Anyway, will you come?"

"I'm not an expert in that field, Phil," Daryl said.

"Maybe not, but you know more about it than I do."

"What are we waiting for?" Daryl rose.

Rossiter finished his milk and stuffed the last bite of hamburger into his mouth. Then he quickly picked up his tray and followed his colleague to the exit.

Supported by pillows, she was seated in the bed, her small face almost as pale as her surroundings, the mop of short coppery curls in sharp contrast to her colorless lips. She was not beautiful, but there was something infinitely more catching about her than good looks, Rossiter thought as he entered the room, something far more arresting. Perhaps it was her eyes. Deep-set and wide, set far apart, they seemed to fill her entire face. And those cheekbones, delicate and definitely an asset. She reminded him of a frightened young doe, lost in the woods, forsaken by its peers.

A sharp gasp made him jump and he looked at his friend with surprise. Daryl's eyes had widened, disbelief and bewilderment battling for first place, his face as pale as the woman's.

"Amanda? My God, Amanda, it's you!" It sounded like an accusation. "Why, it's really you!"

There was no hint of recognition in the young woman's eyes, only confusion and a touch of fear at the stranger's exclamation. Daryl approached the bed, his face contorted by intense emotion.

"It's me, Daryl. Daryl Wills, remember me? Your brother-in-law. Where have you been all these years? We'd given you up for dead."

The woman raised her arm as if to defend herself. Still, there was no sign of recognition or acknowledgment. Her eyes went to Rossiter for help. Remaining in the background, Philip started to open his mouth to come to her rescue. Then, thinking better of it, he closed it again and solemnly watched the drama before him unfold. But no matter what he said, Daryl's pleas fell on deaf ears; the woman's reaction remained the same—she did not know him. Finally, she began to cry, the fear in her big eyes now quite evident, and Philip stepped forward.

"That's enough, Daryl. She needs to rest."

He pressed the call button and Nurse Stephens entered the room. She took one look at the distraught patient and all but threw the two doctors out, mumbling indignantly.

"That wasn't just a performance in there, was it, Daryl?" Philip watched his friend's face. He had never seen him so shaken before.

"Hm, what?" Daryl ran his hand through his hair and looked up.

"Is she really your sister-in-law, or were you just testing her?"

"Testing? Are you crazy? That woman is Amanda Farraday, or my name is mud!"

"Farraday? As in Brent Farraday?"

"One and the same. His wife." He glanced at his wrist-watch. "Look, Phil," he said, "give me five minutes to make a phone call. Yes, yes, I know you want to hear more. I've identified your Jane Doe for you, haven't I? Five minutes, and I'm all yours." Before Rossiter could utter another word, he was gone.

The doctor's lounge was deserted in the afternoon. Most of the medical staff had already left the hospital and the resident doctors had just finished their afternoon break and were back on duty. Daryl Wills picked up the phone and dialed an outside line.

"Hi, Bambi, did you give Dr. Farraday my message?"

"He's in surgery right now, Dr. Wills, and yes, he knows that you called. Three times."

He frowned. "Surgery? At this hour?"

"It was an emergency, trauma case."

He sighed, suddenly exhausted.

"He must think I'm in heat if he never bothered to call me back," he growled.

"He did call you back, but you didn't answer your page."

Daryl's hand went to his beeper, and he grimaced. Damn, he'd forgotten to turn it back on since last night. One of these days I'll get myself into trouble over this, he thought.

"Never mind," he spoke into the phone, "tell him not to leave the hospital until I get there. Better still, tell him I'll drop by the house, his house, tonight. Tell him it's important. Oh, and Bambi, get yourself a dozen roses, and put it on my tab."

"I'll tell him. And Dr. Wills, the name is Fawn."

He laughed as he put down the receiver. Great girl, that Fawn. Great legs and a nice sense of humor. Excellent nurse, too. He missed the nurses at Lutheran General. Sometimes he wished he had stayed on, but his father was co-founder of Barrington Memorial and he had an obligation to fulfill.

"Dr. Wills, Dr. Daryl Wills, please report to 418 immediately."

The voice over the hospital communicator sounded crisp, almost ominous. Even after all these years, he hated being paged this way. It never failed to remind him of the days when he was called into the principal's office, invariably for some misdemeanor. He sighed and left the lounge. He had hoped to call Karen at least, but that would have to wait for now.

Chapter 2

"ARE YOU SURE?" BRENT FARRADAY REACHED FOR A CIG-
arette, his face taut, his firm jaw twitching.

It was past eight o'clock before Daryl and Karen had
shown up, only because Karen had insisted that they wait
until after dinner and closer to the children's bedtime. Daryl
had given in, recognizing the good sense in her suggestion. It
would have been awkward to discuss this matter with the two
youngsters around.

"Absolutely," he affirmed.

"No doubt whatsoever?"

"None."

Brent lit the cigarette, his hand trembling.

"Couldn't she be a look-alike?"

"My dear man, how many women on this planet have
Amanda's eyes, hm? You must admit, she has the most extraordinary eyes, wide-set, and of the most unusual color.
Tawny with green specks." Daryl leaned back in the sofa and
crossed his legs, meeting Brent's speculative gaze with indulgence. "Besides, she's a bona fide redhead." He suddenly
grinned. "It's not out of a bottle, old boy. I checked."

He watched his brother-in-law get up and pace the floor.

"Why would she, after all these years, suddenly show up
like that? I did everything to find her, everything."

Daryl nodded and ran his hand through his thick brown

hair. "She didn't 'just show up,' she had an accident. Chances are she didn't know where she was, or was on her way somewhere else. And remember, she doesn't recall anything."

Brent glared at him.

"How can you be so sure that she's not faking it? Perhaps she did recognize you and decided to pretend the amnesia. I wouldn't put it past her. She was, after all, quite theatrical the last time I saw her." His voice had an edge of bitterness.

"This one is genuine," Daryl insisted. "Phil Rossiter wanted my opinion on her condition, so she was already suffering from loss of memory before she even saw me."

Brent furrowed his brow and resumed pacing the floor, his jaw working. Lighting another cigarette, he followed the rings of smoke as they rose and dispersed before reaching the ceiling.

"God, four years. Four long years. Mandy was only four then, and Josh . . ." He sighed. "Josh was still a baby, barely two and not even potty-trained." He strode toward the bar. "Can I fix you something to drink? I know I need one."

"Me, too." Karen entered the room, a warm smile on her face. The look she gave her distraught brother displayed open affection.

Their resemblance was remarkable—both tall, both blond and gray-eyed, and both with that touch of class and grace that earned them many an appreciative glance. But where Brent carried an aura of solemnity about him, Karen was all feminine charm and her smile was as soft as the angora sweater draped around her shapely shoulders.

"Those are marvelous kids you have, Brent. You can be proud of the way you've brought them up." She had volunteered to put them to bed, indulging in a gory bedtime story, which was her nephew's favorite kind.

For the first time that evening, Brent smiled. "Don't worry, you'll soon have your chance." He handed her a glass of wine. "Are you sure your doctor would condone this?"

She grimaced, stroking her rounded belly. "A little wine now and then won't harm anyone." She took a sip and glanced at Daryl. "Right, Daddy?"

Daryl grinned, knowing the "now" was triggered by his news. Karen had not touched the stuff since her first days of pregnancy.

"I never did understand why she left four years ago. No

note, no phone call, no explanation whatsoever." Brent handed Daryl a glass of Scotch and sat down again, gulping his own drink. "We hadn't even quarreled. If the housekeeper hadn't told me she saw her leave with a suitcase, I would have thought Amanda was kidnapped by aliens from outer space. Even the police couldn't trace her."

"What do they know? All they're interested in are the tickets they can hand out to unsuspecting citizens, both on the road and in parking lots." Daryl laughed, recalling Karen's indignation when she had come home with a parking ticket last week. She had gone to the grocery store just to get milk and had illegally parked in a handicapped space. When she came back, a policeman was standing behind her car writing out a ticket. She had argued that being seven months pregnant qualified her as handicapped, but he had not seen it that way.

"Why don't you come with me tomorrow and see her? Maybe, just maybe, she'll recognize you. If nothing else, the shock might snap back her memory," he suggested.

Brent emptied his glass and stared at Amanda's smiling picture on the mantelpiece. He felt a wave of bitterness engulf him each time he looked at the picture, but for the children's sake, he had kept it there. They were young, they needed to remember their mother.

"All right. I have a surgery scheduled for nine o'clock. I'll drop by after that." He got up. "How about another one for the road? No, not you, little mother." He grinned as Karen stuck her tongue out at him. Pouring the drinks, he became serious again. "When will she be released?"

"I'll have to check with Phil. She's suffering from a severe concussion. As soon as that is licked, I would assume you can take her home."

"Provided she is Amanda." Brent handed him the glass.

"She is Amanda."

A hush fell in the room, each absorbed by his own thoughts.

The man hesitated, shuffling his feet uncertainly. He suddenly felt awkward, and he instinctively hid the bouquet of pink carnations behind his back. But just as he thought of leaving, the young woman in the hospital bed looked up from the book she was reading.

"I . . . I just came to see how . . . how you were, eh, do-ing . . . ," he stammered.

A nurse pushed the door wide open and all but forced him to enter the room.

"Why, Mr. Collins, what beautiful flowers," she exclaimed. "Mrs. Farraday will simply love them. Here, let me put them in a nice vase for her." With a warm smile, she took the bouquet out of his hand and went to the patient's bed to remove the tray on the table next to it. "I'll be right back."

The woman in the bed stretched her hand out to the hesitant visitor, whose face was now flushed with embarrassment.

"Mr. Collins, please do come in." She gestured to a chair by the wall.

"It's so nice of you to drop by. I must thank you for saving my life." Her voice was soft and melodious, her tawny eyes warm. "Please take a seat. I don't get many visitors."

He cleared his throat, and approached the bed. He grabbed the chair, turned it backward and straddled it.

"It was nothing. Anyone would have done the same."

She shook her head, and smiled.

Why, she is beautiful when she smiles, he thought, astonished at the change. It was like a sudden burst of sun rays had broken through a gray cloud, and the dimples in her cheeks brought a hint of gay mischief to her small face. She was younger than he had expected. The woman he had carried into the emergency room less than a week ago had been smeared with dirt and blood, her hair drenched by the rain, and he had not paid particular attention to her face, but she had worn a dark expensive-looking suit, the kind a career lady would wear. He had estimated her to be at least in her early thirties. Yet this woman was barely in her twenties, and not at all like the career woman he had rescued.

"No, not too many people would have done what you did —risk your own life to save a stranger's. It was very coura-geous, and very noble indeed."

He shifted uncomfortably, embarrassed by her praise.

"I'm sorry I can't offer you anything."

"That's okay. I'm glad you're doing so well."

The nurse came back with the vase of flowers.

"There, you see. It brightens up the room tremendously." She smiled. She handed the patient a book. "I found you another one. Let me know when you're finished, I'll get you more." With a friendly nod to the visitor, she turned and left the room again.

The young woman smiled sheepishly.

"Nurse Talbot feels I should broaden my romantic horizons. This is only the fourth romance she has given me to read." She held up the book in her hand. "I don't have the heart to tell her that my favorites are mysteries." She looked at Collins and they both burst out laughing.

"What were you doing, racing through the night in that dreadful weather?" He saw her wince, and instantly regretted his inquisitiveness. "Sorry, you don't have to tell me. It was rude of me to be nosy. Forget I asked."

The happiness in her eyes had disappeared. A cloud had fallen over her face and she looked almost frightened. Her reaction puzzled him. Had he touched a sensitive chord, he wondered, or was she merely hiding something?

"They say that the car . . . my car, was burnt up. Did you . . . see anything . . . when you got me out? Before it rolled down the hill?" She was barely whispering.

Collins shook his head. "No, why?"

"Oh, nothing." She turned away and stared at the window, then down at her hands in her lap. "Just that . . ." She bit her lip and looked up. "Was my purse . . . ?"

Collins gaped at her for a split second, dumbstruck.

"Lady, I was lucky to get you out. That car was wobbling and I had to move fast, or we would've both gone down with it. So, no, I didn't get a chance to rescue your purse or even look for it. To tell you the truth, it was the farthest thing from my mind."

"Please, I didn't mean . . ."

Her gaze shifted from his agitated face to the tall man in the doorway. He had entered noiselessly, his penetrating stare fixed unwaveringly on her flushed face. Mesmerized by his almost hypnotic stare, she returned the look, her tawny eyes wide and unblinking. She felt helplessly drawn to his presence, suppressing the urge to get out of the bed and run into his arms, touching the thick blond wavy hair, the strong jaw, the stern lips.

"Hello, Amanda." His voice was deep and cultured.

Collins turned around, his expression bewildered. Slowly

the tall blond stranger approached the bed, his gaze locked on the woman.

"Aren't you going to introduce me?"

The man in the chair got up and extended his hand.

"The name is Collins."

"Ah, Mr. Collins, it's a pleasure to meet you. I'm Brent Farraday, the husband." He shook Collins's hand. "Thank you for saving my wife's life. I'm truly indebted to you, sir." He turned back to the woman in the bed, ignoring the stunned expression in her eyes. "How are you feeling, darling? You look rested and, I must admit, quite attractive without all that makeup."

Collins shuffled his feet, wiping his hands on his jeans. "I'd better be going now. It's good to see you're doing good, Mrs. Farraday. Nice to have met you, Mr. Farraday."

"Thanks again, friend. The world needs more brave men like you, believe me." Brent shook the departing man's hand again and watched the door close behind Collins.

"Well, aren't you going to say how glad you are to see me?"

His sarcastic tone puzzled her, but it was the bitter note in his voice that stung. He did not seem particularly happy to see her. Whatever she had done, it must have been pretty bad for him to be so cold toward her, especially when she had barely cheated death. Was she running away from him that night, she wondered? It must have been quite an argument for her to drive as recklessly as they said she did. Only a fool would speed on slick winding roads on a dark stormy night—a fool, or a distraught person after a heated quarrel with a lover . . .

"Phil Rossiter says you're well enough to go home next week. I haven't told the children yet, just in case you decided to go back where you've been all this time."

He walked over to the window and split the blinds with his forefinger. Suddenly he turned around to face her, his fierce eyes flashing.

"Where the hell have you been, Amanda? For God's sake, it was bad enough to disappear, but not to let me know that you were even alive? Did you think I wasn't going to worry? And what about the children—*your* children too—did you think they wouldn't miss their mother? Do you ever think of other people's feelings, *our* feelings?"

He hardly noticed her wince at his outburst, all too wrapped up in his own pain.

"Answer me! Where have you been these past four years?"

Four years? What was he saying? What on earth . . . ? She shook her head, trying to shake away the overwhelming confusion.

"I . . . I don't know . . ."

"Don't toy with me, lady. You can drop the pretense now, the game is over."

"I . . . really don't remember . . ."

Brent slowly relented. Her bewildered expression was too real, too convincing, and he had never known her to let him yell at her without lashing back. He took a deep breath. God, he needed a cigarette badly.

"All right, we can discuss all that later. Are you coming home next week?"

She looked at him for a moment, her hands rubbing her bare arms.

"Well?"

"Am I . . . are you my . . . husband?" It was barely a whisper.

"The last time I checked. Want some identification?"

"You said . . . children . . . Tell me about the children."

He hesitated for a moment, then reached inside his jacket and took out his wallet.

"These are their pictures, taken this summer."

She studied them in silence. They were both blond, the little boy a miniature of the man before her, the girl more like herself.

"Mandy is eight now, Josh six. They don't remember you, but I left your picture on the mantelpiece in the living room for them to know what you look like."

She looked up, a hint of tears in her big eyes. "They're lovely," she whispered. "May I . . . keep these?"

Brent frowned, then nodded. "For what it's worth, they need a mother, preferably their own."

He shoved his hands deep into his pants pockets and walked away from the bed. For a moment he stared out the window, then turned and strolled back to the silent figure, his expression closed. He saw her mouth quiver at his approach and he looked at the full sensuous lips, remembering with a sharp pang how he had ravished them and how pliable they had been, trembling beneath his hungry touch. He dug his nails into his clenched fists, and when he spoke again, his voice was harsher.

"You really don't remember anything, do you?"

Her eyes suddenly filled with tears.

"If you hate me so much, why do you want me to come home?" Her eyes echoed the pain in her voice.

"I told you, the children need you."

"But you don't?"

He looked at her coldly.

"Don't flatter yourself. I've lived for four years without you, thinking you dead. I can learn to live another forty the same way. Trust me."

She cringed visibly, but didn't lower her eyes. Four years, he had said. Not just one week.

"Tell me, was there any reason for me to leave you?"

"You tell me."

"I mean, were we having a . . . a problem?"

Brent sighed. God, she really didn't remember a thing.

"We were having problems since the day we married, Amanda. I guess we never should have. We were just too different, in too many ways."

"And yet, you want me to come home."

"Well, perhaps we can work things out. Besides, where would you go? And what better way to regain your memory than raking it up, dirt and all?"

He watched her turn her face from him, and catching a glimpse of the agony in her eyes, something within him broke. She had not looked this vulnerable since the day her parents died. Brent took a deep breath. It was the shock of seeing her again, he told himself, the shock of seeing her alive. Nothing more, nothing else. The little bit of feeling he had left for her years ago had died the day she left.

Deep inside his pockets his nails dug into the flesh of his fists, and the sensation drowned the pain in his chest. He turned around so she would not see the expression on his face.

Chapter 3

THE SILVER JAGUAR SMOOTHLY TURNED THE CORNER and made its way up the wide street. The homes on both sides of the street were big, mostly Tudor style, surrounded by luscious lawns, green even this late into the fall, and gardens that would be colorful in the spring, well kept and tastefully landscaped in keeping with the neighborhood. Young healthy trees flanked the pavement that formed a border between the lawns and the street. Slowly, the car approached a cul-de-sac that marked the end of the road, and drove up a curved driveway, stopping in front of a closed garage door.

Brent turned to the silent woman in the passenger seat, a pensive look in his eyes. She appeared distracted, as if quietly absorbing the new impressions thrown her way. The bright afternoon sun threw a glimmer on her hair, bringing out the fire in the unrestrained curls that danced against her delicate cheekbones and around her ears. He quelled a familiar urge to reach out and touch it, and turned his head.

As if sensing his uneasiness, she turned her head to look at him. The ride from the hospital had been uneventful, almost relaxing. Still, it felt like a new experience to her, as did everything that had happened since the day she had opened her eyes in the white hospital bed. Each event, each development was yet another piece in the gigantic jigsaw puzzle that was her life—the life she had no memory of, a life that was as alien to her as her surroundings.

It was like starting over, from scratch—only, partly in reverse gear, and without any clues to guide her. And it was scary. As she glanced at his profile she wondered about him —this man who claimed he was her husband. How did she know that he really was just that? Or that she was the woman he and Daryl Wills said she was? Or even . . . Just then Brent turned his head, and at his mocking gaze, she blushed.

"Are you all right?" He seemed less hostile today, his gray eyes slightly less cold.

She forced a smile, unconsciously wringing her hands in her lap, and looked away. *If we were having problems, why does his presence have this effect on me?* she wondered, bewildered at the tingling exhilaration she felt at the sight of him. Had she felt this way four years ago, or was this, like everything else, a new experience?

"Come on, let me show you the house before the kids come home." He glanced at his watch. "School is out in about an hour. I briefly told them about you, that you had come back, but I didn't tell them when you'd be home. That would have been too much excitement for them, and I wanted them to get through the week as normally as possible." He opened the car door and stepped outside.

Her eyes lit up. So that's why he had chosen to get her released on a Friday. She quickly opened her side of the car and saw that he was waiting for her.

As Brent opened the massive front door, a smiling, silver-haired woman greeted them.

"Welcome back, Mrs. Farraday. You certainly chose a mighty fine day to come home. I'm Mary Flynn, the housekeeper." She spoke with a heavy brogue, but it sounded warm and friendly, and Amanda smiled back.

"Thank you, Mrs. Flynn," she said softly.

She took an instant liking to the tall, bony housekeeper with the face full of wrinkles and her wavy white hair tied in a loose knot at the nape of her neck. Mrs. Flynn's warm smile extended to the gentle gleam in her cornflower-blue eyes, and in that moment as their gazes locked, she knew she had found a friend.

Stepping inside the marble entry, Amanda halted, and

stared. The unexpected openness overwhelmed her and she held her breath as she took in the enormous space that stretched before her.

At first glance it was but one huge room with small clusters of furniture in separate corners. But as the groupings began to make sense, she noticed the sunken living area around an open brick fireplace on the left, a slightly raised formal dining area in a semi-alcove on the right, and a leisure corner at the far side with white wicker chaises and a grand piano. A breakfast nook housing a white wicker dinette set completed the room. Glass windows and doors from floor to ceiling extended over the entire far end, with a full view of the cemented semicovered patio and the enormous back yard. An arched opening angled between the formal and the leisure dining areas, allowing a glimpse into a sunny kitchen connected on both sides by open tiled counters.

Amanda expelled a long-drawn-out sigh as her wide eyes caressed the furniture. Apart from the white wicker pieces, the tone was contemporary touched by European simplicity, and softened by subtle shades of mauves, plums, and deep purple. The color lent an aura of exotic luxury to the place. The off-white velvet sofas looked soft and comfortable, the smoky charcoal dining chairs bold and sensual, balanced by smoked-glass tables and ultramodern black and white lighting fixtures and lamps of unusual shapes. And everywhere, as if by casual afterthought, were huge live plants. No curtains, no sheers, no blinds. Just light, an abundance of light, from outside.

She lifted her gaze to the high vaulted ceilings, and gasped. There, high above them, lay the secret as to why the room was bathed in so much light: a circular string of tinted glass domes grinned down at her from the ceiling. Excitement and exuberance filled her; she suddenly felt alive, real. For a moment she held her breath, swept by a strange emotion, so strong it threatened to overcome her. A jarring flash, a sensation of familiarity, a jagged glimpse . . . *My God.* She closed her eyes, trembling. *I've seen this all before.*

Brent glanced sideways and saw her flushed face. A pity she didn't remember—he could still recall the aghast expression on the contractor's face when she told him about the skylights.

"What?" The man had almost panicked. "With the winters here? This is Chicago, lady, not California!"

But she had been adamant, and when she threatened to use another contractor, he had thrown his hands up in the air, and she had won. Later, pleased with the result after all, the man had added—at no cost, because she had been the first customer to widen his horizon—automatic shutters to protect the glass from ice and snow, ingeniously activated by the single touch of a button.

Brent lit a cigarette, still watching her. He had to admit he had not been too thrilled in the beginning—with everything, the house, the skylights, the interior, the design, the bill—but the finished product had won his admiration. And he had been proud of her when friends and neighbors hailed her brainchild, calling it innovative, original, and behind her back, bizarre. Yes, she had talent all right, unique and exceptional. He only wished it was confined to interior decorating and architecture . . .

"Are you ready for the upstairs tour?" he asked coolly.

Amanda started. She had forgotten his presence. Slowly, she turned.

"There's another room on the other side behind the guest room. Sort of a family room, if you will. The children like to play there. You can take a look at it later."

"It . . . it's fabulous . . . truly exquisite . . . ," she murmured, trying to regain her composure.

"So it is—thanks to you," he said dryly.

Her eyes widened.

"Me?"

Brent nodded. "It was your idea, your creation."

For a moment she did not move, the expression on her face frozen. Then, with a deep sigh, she turned toward the wide, open stairs next to the marble entry.

"Yes, I'm ready," she said.

The doorbell rang. She could hear Mrs. Flynn's warm voice and then the excited chatter of children's voices. Amanda gripped the kitchen counter trying to steady herself. She could feel her heart pounding in her chest, the nagging ache at the back of her head suddenly unbearable. Despite herself she looked at Brent, and as if this were the cue he had been waiting for, he left his place by the window and strode out of the sunny kitchen.

Presently the chatter stopped and the little bit of courage she had left evaporated with it. She knew he had told them. Involuntarily, she shivered. The sunshine that poured through the kitchen windows did not warm her and she began to tremble. *Why did I agree to come home? I deserted them, God knows for what reason, but to reappear like this . . . ? If I don't even know who I am, how can I expect these children to . . . ?*

Brent's tall, lean frame appeared in the arched doorway, his blond head almost touching the top. In front of him, two small figures reluctantly dragged their feet. Their faces somber and guarded, they watched the silent woman by the counter. Instinctively, Amanda smiled. Her clenched hands relaxed. Slowly she felt her panic ebb away and a feeling of guilt begin to surface as she sensed the fear behind their hostile masks. *My God, what have I done to them?*

She stretched out her arms to them, her voice soft and warm.

"Don't I even get a hug?"

The children did not move. Not that she had expected them to.

"Guys, this is your mother." Brent gently pushed them forward, but they kept on staring at the woman they had only known from pictures.

Undaunted by their lack of response, Amanda slowly approached them. Why, they look exactly like us, she thought, bewildered by the resemblance. She had studied the photographs Brent left her in the hospital over and over. Still, the shock of seeing the children in real life threw her. Josh was the image of Brent, only his hair was as red as her own, just curlier. Strange, she mused, in the picture it had looked quite blond, and she had not been prepared for the revelation. His eyes, though shaped like Brent's, were more blue than gray. And Mandy—she must have looked that way when she was her age—wore her long wavy blond hair in a fashionable thick French braid held by a single ribbon, her green eyes wide and set far apart in her elfin face.

She swallowed the lump in her throat and willed herself to keep on smiling. *Please,* her eyes implored, *I'm just as scared as you are, won't you help me a little?*

"Hi, you must be Mandy." She held out her hand, but the little girl did not take it. "And you must be Josh." Not making the same mistake, she touched the boy's cheek, and winced as he jerked his face away from her touch. Helplessly, she looked up to Brent, a silent plea in her big eyes.

"Come now, guys, you were so excited to hear Mommy was coming home. You could at least give her a hug." Brent put his hands on their shoulders and gently nudged them.

Josh took a step backward.

"Mothers are supposed to love their kids, not leave them," he mumbled.

She cringed at his bitter reproach, but did not say a word.

"Now that's enough!" Brent said sharply.

"No, he's right, and I'm sorry." Amanda hastened to intervene, sensing impending punishment, or worse, a forced apology. Which certainly would not endear her to the boy. Absentmindedly, she brushed a rebellious curl from her eyes.

"Daddy said you don't remember much." Mandy's voice was cool, but not unfriendly like her brother's.

"I . . . he told you the truth. I don't even know who I really am."

"Then how do you know you are our mother?" It sounded like an accusation, and she blushed.

"I . . . your father identified me."

"What's 'identified' mean?" Josh wanted to know.

"It means he recognized her as our mother," Mandy explained, without for a second taking her eyes off the woman in front of her.

"What if he's wrong?" Josh persisted.

"I'm not wrong, she is your mother," his father said.

But the boy was not convinced. "If she is really our mother, why did she leave us?" He glowered at her, shuffling his feet.

"I . . . I don't know the answer to that . . . ," Amanda said unhappily. Then, seeing the hurt in Josh's eyes, she hastily added, "But it was not because I didn't love you. Both of you. Of that I'm sure, very sure." She saw the boy's defiance waver.

"Very, *very* sure," she repeated firmly. Kneeling before him, her eyes misty with suppressed tears, she dropped her voice to a husky whisper. "Please, darling, believe that."

Josh stopped his shuffle, yet his little face remained grim. "If you don't remember anything, how can you be so sure?"

Amanda sighed and smiled through her tears. "I'm blessed with a superintelligent son," she muttered. Ignoring Brent's appreciative chuckle, she maintained eye level with the boy and simply said, "I just know. As your mother, I know, and I'm sure."

Dear God, she prayed, *let it be so, let this be the truth.* The knot in her stomach tightened and she could hear her own heart thump against her temples. But she smiled, outwardly calm, and as she looked at both children a warmth filled her, and her thumping heart began to quiver with a joy that threatened to choke the very breath from her. The feeling was overwhelming and she felt giddy, exultant, and relieved. How could she not have loved them? Slowly she rose and turned to Mandy, her eyes pleading.

"I need help to remember everything, learn who I am, be your mother again, the kind of mother I should be. Will you help me?"

The girl only stared. Then, suddenly, a small smile broke through.

"Josh and I will both help you, won't we, Josh?"

The boy did not reply, his little face still surly.

"Won't we, Josh?" Mandy raised her voice slightly.

Josh shuffled his feet. "Do I have to?" he mumbled.

Mandy nudged him, her green eyes flaring a silent warning.

"Oh, all right, but only a little," he grumbled.

Mandy stepped forward and held out her hand.

"Welcome home, Mother," she said.

Amanda's lips began to tremble and she held out her arms, but before she could reach the girl, a huge white-haired dog ran toward her, barking loudly as it jumped up against her. She staggered at the impact and grabbed the edge of the kitchen counter, but her right heel slipped and she spun around, losing her balance and sprawling across the clean floor. Mandy gasped, her hand flying to her open mouth.

"Kavik, here, Kavvy. Here, here, boy," Josh shrieked.

Instantly, the Samoyed released her and jumped against the boy, licking his face with sheer delight. Brent stepped forward and offered her a helping hand. "Take that beast outside. You know the rules. How did he sneak inside anyway?" he snarled, glaring at Josh's sheepish face. But Amanda waved him away and made a face, rubbing her behind as she tried to get back on her feet.

She promptly landed back on the floor. The dog barked at her, wagging his white bushy tail and trying to pry himself loose from his little master's frantic grip. This was a new game for him and it looked like such fun. If only his little master would release him; he would show them how to really play.

Suddenly Amanda, still seated on the floor, started to giggle, and Mandy's startled eyes widened even further. Then, cautiously, she made a sound that resembled a chuckle and shyly glanced at her father's scowling face. The giggles from the floor turned into laughter and, encouraged, Mandy began to laugh, too. Before long Josh joined in.

Brent's frown deepened, but the expression in his eyes softened. He watched the laughing woman on the kitchen floor, tears streaming down her cheeks, and his indulgence changed to a growing curiosity. Finally, Amanda stopped laughing and tried a second time to stand up. As she weaved, Brent's firm grip on her arm steadied her and held her up, and this time she gave him a grateful smile.

"Josh? Did you hear me? I said take the dog outside where he belongs," Brent ordered.

"He only wanted to play. He really didn't mean to hurt you," Josh said defensively, his eyes guarded.

Amanda smiled and held out her hand. "Of course he didn't. I never thought otherwise." She gently patted the dog's head, and Kavik grinned, clearly enjoying her gentle strokes. "I'm glad you two are such good friends."

"We are, very. Kavvy is my best friend. Can he sleep with me tonight?" Josh pleaded eagerly.

"Josh!" his father warned, but Amanda kept smiling.

"We'll talk about it," she said and her eyes met Mandy's. She pulled the girl into her arms and kissed her head. "And you? Are you Kavik's friend, too?"

"I'd rather have a cat, but Daddy won't let me." The girl nestled her head against her newfound mother as she shot a look of triumph in her brother's direction. But Josh ignored her, content at having the dog beside him.

Amanda glanced at Brent and she knew he was waiting for her to ask him about the cat. She smiled again and said nothing.

"How about some refreshments?" Mrs. Flynn interrupted. She had witnessed the entire episode from her corner in the kitchen, wisely keeping her silence and extremely pleased with the turn of events, and especially warmed by Amanda's reaction.

"Sounds like a splendid idea." Brent clapped his hands. "Okay, wash your hands, you two, and take Kavik outside, Josh."

"But, Dad . . ." Then seeing his father's stern look, he sighed and obeyed.

Mandy looked at Amanda questioningly, and received a reassuring nod. When the children had left the kitchen, Brent faced his wife.

"If you're going to nag me about the cat, you can forget it," he began, but Amanda only smiled. His irritated reaction amused her.

"I wasn't," she said and turned to take her seat at the kitchen table. "At least, not now," she muttered under her breath. But if Brent did not catch it, Mary Flynn did, and the housekeeper chuckled. Amanda just looked up at her husband and smiled, ever so sweetly.

Chapter 4

HER EYE FELL ON THE PICTURES ON THE MANTELPIECE, and fixed on the one of herself. Her hair was much longer then and somehow it seemed straighter, the waves perfect, not one curl out of place.

"That short hairdo becomes you. Makes you look younger, more innocent." Brent watched her put down the picture.

He could not help wondering if she had deliberately cut it to spite him. He had always preferred long hair on a woman and when he had first met her she wore hers past her tiny waist, full and billowing and bouncing around her like a cape. Even when later, after Mandy was born, she had worn it shorter by a foot, it still fell down her back. He had loved the feel of its velvety softness and he had touched it often, allowing his fingers to ignite the sensation that never failed to fan his then insatiable desire for her.

"They are good children; you did a fine job raising them." She ran her finger across the top of the television set and looked at it, but did not comment on the dust she had picked up.

"It wasn't always easy, and some of the credit goes to Mrs. Flynn. She's more than just a housekeeper, she's our stronghold." Brent hid his surprise; he had noticed her gesture—the Amanda of four years ago would have said something catty.

"And you—from what I've seen, you're a good father. They adore you." She managed a smile. "I doubt that they actually missed . . . their mother . . ." The word burned and she bit her lip.

Brent had put them to bed a half hour earlier, and she had declined taking part in their bedtime ritual, feeling instinctively that the gesture would be too much for the first day. And when she heard their happy laughter float down from their bedrooms, she knew she had made the right move.

"Give them time. It was quite a shock for them to meet you after thinking you were dead all these years. But they're young, they'll adjust in no time, you'll see."

She nodded and walked to the other side of the fireplace.

"Why did I leave, Brent?" She did not look at him, staring again instead at her own picture. Why was there none of them together? she wondered. A lone portrait of her all by herself—as though she were an outsider, as if she did not quite belong. There was a picture of Josh and one of Mandy, one of the two of them, and a snapshot of them on a boat with Brent, laughing. But there was no family portrait of the four of them, none of her as part of the family, not even a picture of her and Brent.

"I was hoping you would tell me," he answered levelly.

"You mentioned we were having problems . . . What kind of . . . problems . . . ?"

He sighed and studied her for a moment. "We were having problems shortly after we got married. And it went from bad to worse. But certainly not awful enough for you to skip town. Or so I thought. Evidently I was wrong."

Amanda shivered at the coldness in his voice. She could not bring herself to look at him, sensing his intense hostility.

"You said earlier that you had thought me . . . dead. Why didn't you remarry?"

"Let's just say, I learn from my mistakes. Besides, I never did find the right stepmother for the kids."

"But there is someone?"

Brent watched her wearily. "If you're asking if I have been celibate, the answer is no. But there is no one seriously linked to my name at the present time." He walked to the bar and opened a cabinet. "How about a drink? The usual?" Without waiting, he poured two glasses. "I'm sorry, but I don't feel like concocting martinis tonight. Do you mind?"

He walked over to where she stood and handed her a glass of cognac. Amanda took a sip and choked. Brent frowned. "You used to take that stuff every night as a nightcap." He took the glass away from her.

"What else did I use to do?" She coughed and swallowed.

"Lots of things. It'll take more than an evening to update you on the gory details. For starters, we never talked. You found that boring. This is by far the most we have ever said to one another."

Startled, Amanda glanced at him and, seeing the cool expression in his eyes, turned her head quickly.

"If you're not happy to see me, why bother bringing me here?" She bit her lip at her own bitterness.

"I thought that was obvious. The children, of course. They deserve a mother, even if it is you. I thought I explained all of this at the hospital." His frown deepened.

She lowered her head and again bit her lip. Of course, how ignorant of her to ask. He adored his children, as much as they adored him, and he was willing to sacrifice his own feelings for their needs. Why else? How could she, even for the slightest moment, have dared to think otherwise?

"Look, I know you're anxious to fill in the gaps and you want me to do it for you. But quite frankly, I don't feel up to it right this minute, or any other time for that matter." He took out a cigarette and lit it. "Besides, it wouldn't be fair. I'd only be biased and you'd be far better off taking it from here. For both our sakes. That way, perhaps, this family stands a chance to piece things together—at least until you've regained your memory."

He watched for her reaction, but she did not respond, her head still lowered, intent on examining her neatly clipped fingernails. Her silence irked him, yet at the same time it puzzled him; he had expected her to at least challenge his motives and her lack of any outward emotion left him with a void that was both awkward and a deliverance. He turned to walk to the bar and missed the look of anguish she shot in his direction.

"Why don't you go upstairs, get some sleep. It's been a long day and tomorrow will come soon enough." Brent took a sip of his cognac and lit another cigarette. "I'll be along shortly."

Amanda threw him a furtive glance. He wants to be alone,

she mused, he needs time. Time to be by himself, to get a grip on the situation, time away from her. And as she watched him inhale the cigarette, she instinctively knew that he would not smoke in the bedroom.

Bewildered, she looked down on the enormous amount of tiny pots and bottles in the drawers. What was she doing with all that makeup? How could anyone have use for so much? She picked up a bottle of perfume and sniffed it. She grimaced and quickly put it back. Perhaps it had been a gift.

She closed the vanity drawers and looked around. Like the rest of the house, the master bathroom was spacious, with ample room to dress and a wall-to-wall mirror that stretched along the entire vanity counter. She slowly sauntered to the louvered closet that separated the dressing area from the marble bath and the elaborately tiled shower stall. Opening the doors, her eyes widened and a gasp escaped her.

It was a walk-in closet the size of a hidden room. A light automatically switched on as the doors opened, revealing an abundance of clothes, racks and racks of them—on the left shirts, trousers, jackets, suits; on the right, dresses and gowns for all occasions—long, short, ordinary dresses, glittering evening wear. She wandered around in a daze, now and then examining a dress, touching the fine materials. God, she must have been mad to buy all of this!

Opening the built-in dressers at the back of the closet, Amanda frowned. There were more clothes, sweaters of all colors, T-shirts, tops of all shapes, flimsy negligees. My God, wasn't there just one decent nightgown in those drawers, she wondered, viewing in disgust the sheer lot she found. For a moment she pondered if this was Brent's taste, or whether she had felt he needed enticement. It was odd, he seemed so reluctant to talk about the problems they were having— could they have been centered around the bedroom? Finally, she chose a silk lilac print, slightly less see-through than the rest, and grabbed a dark purple robe from a peg on the wall.

Back at the dressing counter she sat down and began to brush her short curls with angry, impatient strokes. She had hoped to find something familiar in all of this, yet nothing brought back even the hint of a memory. It was like walking in a dream, only there was no light at the end of the tunnel.

The afternoon had passed amicably. At five o'clock Mrs.

Flynn had smilingly taken her leave; a niece had picked her up and she would spend the weekend with her sister and her family. Amanda had a suspicion Mrs. Flynn arranged the visit to give them a chance to celebrate their reunion, alone. And with the help of Mandy and one of the many cookbooks, she had concocted a decent meal. Brent had been quite civil, almost friendly, although she attributed his good behavior to the presence of the children, and even Josh loosened up as time went by. Once in a while, he even forgot to be hostile and acted like a normal six-year-old, especially when she had shown interest in his stamp collection.

She stopped brushing, and smiled. Perhaps it was not so bad after all. They were two lovely children, and she really enjoyed their company. Even their petty bickering seemed pleasant. She suddenly looked forward to the weekend. It would give her a chance to win them over. Already she felt she had found an ally in Mandy.

"Amanda?"

Brent's voice startled her. A blush colored her cheeks as she wrapped the robe tight around her body, her heart thumping at the sound of his approaching footsteps.

"Hi, may I come in?" His tall, lean figure filled the archway that linked the master bedroom with the dressing area. She watched him in the mirror, conscious of his insolent stare. "I see you found your way around the closet," he mocked.

She resumed brushing, trying to hide her sudden anxiety at his presence, and saw him take something out of his pants pocket and frown as he stared at the object in his hand.

"The hospital gave me this. You were wearing it when that man brought you in."

It was a pearl drop earring. Just one. She looked at the lonely piece in the palm of her hand, wondering if the other half of the pair had gone up in flames with the car.

"They apologized that they had to throw away your clothes. They were torn and smudged with grease and mud beyond salvage." He checked his pockets for more and took out his wallet. "Peculiar. No rings, no other jewelry, just the one earring."

Pulling open a corner drawer in the vanity, he put away his wallet. "You handled them very well." He began to unbutton his shirt without taking his eyes off her, a gleam of amusement in his eyes as her brushing became more rapid.

"Who?"

"The kids. In another week or so they'll be eating out of your hands. Good move, Amanda. I'd say you haven't lost your touch."

The brushing halted. Slowly, she put the brush down and looked at him in the wall-to-wall mirror. Why was he repeating his reassurance? He had said it all downstairs. Then, seeing the odd gleam in his eyes, she relaxed. His expression was glassy and she wondered how much more of the cognac he had gulped down before he had come up. Suddenly she felt better. *Why, he's as nervous about all this as I am,* she thought.

"You make it sound like I'm on trial, sort of like a stepmother, or some woman you just brought home," she said lightly, deciding to play along.

Brent raised an eyebrow. "Well, in a way you are. They were babies when you left them, they've never known you as their real mother. If it hadn't been for the pictures I keep around the house, they wouldn't remember you at all."

He pulled the unbuttoned shirt out of his trousers, exposing a muscled bare chest, and smirked when she turned away.

"They're lovely children. You can be proud of them. And they adore you." She got up, clutching the robe, and wondered if he would notice that she had said that before, too.

"Of course they do, what did you expect? After all, I've been both father and mother to them, the only parent they could cling to these past four years." He strode past her to the walk-in closet and opened it.

"It's a relief to see that you haven't changed a bit, your figure, I mean. It would've been a shame to start another collection."

"Collection?"

"Your wardrobe. You'll find it all in here, waiting to be worn again."

Amanda flinched, then, slowly, straightened her shoulders. "Did . . . did you keep all . . . of that?"

"To tell you the truth, there were times I was tempted to give it to charity."

"Was I . . . did I . . . It would take years to go through . . ." Her eyes went to the racks and racks of dresses.

"Not you, Amanda. You never wore an evening dress twice, and the others . . ." He reemerged from the closet, and wrapped a dark blue robe around himself, his eyes taunting her. She turned her head, but his hand caught her chin. "Feels a little like Cinderella, doesn't it?" he said softly. She lifted her eyes to his and began to tremble. Slowly she pried her face loose and stepped aside, brushing her arm against his in her haste to get away.

"I've never known you so anxious to get to bed, my dear."

Amanda paused in front of the king-sized bed. Frantically she looked around the room. There was no other place to sleep but that big bed in the middle of the bedroom. She took a deep breath. Stop being childish, she told herself. After all, he is your husband. And what was he going to do, rape her? With butterflies in her stomach, she crawled into the bed and switched on the light above the nightstand.

His dark blue satin robe now loosely draped atop pajama pants, Brent walked over to the bed and picked up a pillow. Amanda watched, puzzled.

"Sleep tight, princess. And if you dream of Travis, give him my regards."

Travis? Who the hell was Travis? Brent pulled a blanket out of the decorative trunk at the foot of the bed and glanced at her, his lips curling slightly at her bewildered expression.

"You must remember Travis. Your lover, or did you think I didn't know about him?" The coldness in his eyes matched the tone in his voice. Then, without another word, he turned and walked away.

"Where . . . where are you going?" she whispered.

"In here." He gestured to the raised boudoir off the main room, separated by an open oak railing and furnished sparsely with two chaises longues in front of a small open fireplace flanked by a small desk at one end and a bookcase at the other. Rich velvet curtains of a deep plum shade flanked the bay window covered by white and lacy sheers, and the cushioned bench at the far end of the area. In her nervousness, she had not noticed that part of the room. "I think we should keep up appearances, don't you? Or would you prefer I sleep in my den downstairs? Better still, would you like me to keep you warm? It might be fun after four years."

Amanda did not reply. She reached to switch off the light

on the nightstand beside her and slowly slipped underneath the covers.

Brent chuckled in the darkness. He had seen the relief on her face, and for a brief moment, he felt like changing his mind and shocking her by crawling next to her in the big comfortable bed. Then, as he turned to peer at her through the dim shadows of the room, he relented—she looked so lost, all curled up in the huge bed, more like a frightened doe. He shrugged and went up the four stairs that led into the boudoir.

Glancing around him, he grimaced, remembering how he had ridiculed her the first time he had seen this alcove. Amanda had insisted on this sitting area—a corner of romantic privacy, she had called it—essential to every married couple's bedroom, a place where they could rekindle their flame of passion. Right. As if a bedroom were not that kind of a place. As if a king-sized bed was not enough.

They had used this cozy private corner exactly twice, and both times they had been engaged in a heated discussion that developed into an explosive quarrel and ended up in separate night moves, with him being banished to the downstairs guest room. Some romance. He could think of better ways to fan his passion.

He sighed and spread the blanket over one of the chaises-longues. Damn! He had forgotten to get clean sheets. But his head spun and he desperately needed to unwind. With a suppressed snarl, he stretched out on the chair, cursing as he found his feet sticking way beyond it. He got up and pushed the second chair closer, then grabbed the blanket and bundled it around his tense limbs.

The outside light danced inside the room, and for a moment he wondered if he should pull the curtains, then decided against it. The shimmery night did something to him, and tonight he cherished the dim light sneaking into his corner of the room. He needed some light in his life, even if it was but a hazy glow. He could close them later; right now, he would indulge in the silvery glimmer. With a deep sigh, he snuggled his head against the corner of his improvised bed and stared into the darkness of the night.

Chapter 5

SHE OPENED HER EYES, FOR A MOMENT NOT KNOWING where she was. Then, remembering, she relaxed and turned her head to the spot next to her. It was empty. Stretching her supple body, she squinted her eyes at the alarm clock on the nightstand, and made a face. Ten past eight. The room was cloaked in semidarkness, the heavy curtains keeping out the sunlight.

Slowly, reluctant to leave her warm nest, Amanda got out of bed. Making sure Brent was nowhere in the room, she headed for the bathroom and took a quick shower. After a brief hesitation, she chose a simple black skirt and a beige angora sweater. One look in the mirror brought a smile of satisfaction to her small face. Her hair was still damp, making it curlier, and more coppery. She opened the drawer and looked at the tiny makeup bottles. Finally, she put a light touch of moss-green coloring on her eyelids, instantly highlighting the green in her eyes.

Three blond heads looked up when she entered the kitchen, and she suddenly felt awkward. There was curiosity in Josh's eyes. How odd, she mused, with the light a certain way his hair looks more blond than red, just like in the photograph.

"Good morning, darling." Brent sounded cheerful, almost too cheerful, she thought wryly. "Come join us for breakfast."

He signaled Josh with his eyes and the boy scurried out of his chair and hastened to seat her, receiving a warm grateful smile that set his impish face ablaze. Brent got up and walked to the small oven between the big oven and the microwave, and took out a plate.

"I hope it's not too dry by now." He put the plate in front of her. The pancakes looked perfect, light brown and plump. "How do you want your eggs?"

"It doesn't matter, let me—"

"Oh, no. Weekends are my days to cook. I'm quite good, really. Right, kids?"

Josh made a face, but Mandy smiled. "He really is," she said.

"You used to like them scrambled." Brent waited for a response.

"Scrambled is fine."

"Scrambled eggs coming up. Pour your mother some coffee, will you, munchkin?"

Mandy jumped up immediately and shortly returned with a mug of hot coffee.

"I knew you would come," she said softly, the expression on her elfin face solemn.

Amanda smiled and took the girl's hand in hers. "Did you?" She did not have the faintest idea what the girl was hinting at.

Mandy nodded, her eyes very green and bright.

"She dreamed it," Josh said, licking the syrup off his fingers.

"Our Mandy is quite psychic." Brent brought the frying pan to the kitchen table and filled her plate with scrambled eggs. "How about some bacon? Mandy prepared that. She's a great little helper, our Mandy is, aren't you, munchkin?"

Brent put the empty pan back on the stove and returned to the table with a fresh mug of hot coffee. "How are the pancakes?" He waited for her to swallow a piece.

"Quite good." Amanda nodded, and took another bite.

"Mandy dreams a lot," Josh said and grinned when his sister kicked him under the table.

His father threw him a look of stern disapproval. "She told us last month that you'd be back." He nodded at his embarrassed daughter and smiled.

And you didn't believe her, Amanda thought. She took a small bite of her eggs and turned to the girl.

"Tell me about your dream," she asked gently.

"I saw you walk into this house. You had short hair, just like this. And Daddy was very angry that you had cut your hair."

"I'm sorry. I don't know why I did that."

"I like short better," Josh said.

"In that case I'll keep it this way for awhile." Amanda glanced at Brent, then concentrated on her pancakes. "You know, these are delicious. You're a good cook."

"Wait until you taste his spaghetti." Josh emptied his chocolate milk and pushed the glass away from him. "Can I be excused, Dad? I'm done." He glanced outside longingly.

"Not just yet. You haven't seen your mother for a long time."

"But she'll be here for the rest of my life."

"Joshua!" Brent glared at him.

"Well, he's got a point." Amanda smiled. "And I'm a slow eater. Perhaps if he promises to come back in fifteen minutes?"

Outside Kavik barked and Josh shuffled restlessly in his chair.

"Oh, all right. Fifteen minutes," Brent called after the disappearing boy. "I must say, this is a good beginning. Or is this your way to win a little boy's heart?" He rose to refill his mug of coffee.

"Mother? Do you really not remember anything?" Mandy eyed her solemnly.

Amanda swallowed and took a sip of coffee before she answered. "I'm afraid not. If your father hadn't come to the hospital, I would not have known who I was."

"I always hoped you'd come back to us."

"Well, munchkin, now she has." Brent lit a cigarette and walked to the window. Outside, on the wet grass, Josh frolicked with Kavik, shrieking with delight as the dog jumped over him and playfully tugged at his clothes and licked his face. He opened the window. "Josh, that's enough. Come inside and dry yourself."

"It's not fifteen minutes, yet," Josh rebelled. But he stopped the frolicking and came back into the house.

"You're just in time to see me dance." Mandy smiled, her green eyes sparkling.

"Dance?"

"Ballet. I'm a bud who turns into a flower girl. Aunt Paula made my costumes. They're so pretty. Do you want to see them?"

Without waiting for an answer, she dashed out of the room and returned with dainty green and pink costumes.

"Oh, ugh!" Josh wrinkled his nose at the sight of them.

"Mother is going to see me dance," Mandy said triumphantly.

"Yeah? How about my award presentation? Will you come with Daddy to see me?"

"I'll come to both, if you want me." Amanda brushed the curls from Josh's clammy forehead and smiled warmly at Mandy. "What award is this, Josh?"

"Computer ex-excel—"

"Excellence." Brent came to his rescue. "Josh is a computer whiz. He created a new program and for that he won an award from school."

Amanda's eyes widened with admiration. "Well, that sounds quite impressive. You must be very good to get such an award."

"Oh, I am. Come on, let me show you." Josh jumped up from his chair and ran out of the kitchen.

"Modesty is not one of his virtues, and I'm afraid I'm mostly to blame for that." Brent grimaced.

"Blame?"

"I've encouraged his self-confidence. It does carry over once in a while, but I've never bothered to dampen his enthusiasm, or tone down his achievements for that matter."

"Praise does wonders for the ego." She smiled. "He's only a child. He needs to be encouraged. How else will he flourish?"

Brent looked at her with surprise. An odd gleam crept into his guarded look and a hint of a smile curled around the corners of his mouth.

"Mother, are you coming?" Josh shouted from the other room.

"Why don't you show your mother the den, munchkin?" Brent said.

Mandy quietly obliged, and taking Amanda's hand, she led

her to the den next to the downstairs guest room where Josh awaited them impatiently, his computer ready for the demonstration.

Totally engrossed in Josh's computer wizardry and mesmerized by the little fingers flying over the keyboard, transforming images on the monitor, Amanda did not hear the doorbell ring. Neither did she hear Brent enter the den, and when he spoke, his voice startled her.

"Amanda?" She looked up, surprised to see him in the doorway, his face impassive. "There's someone here to see you." He waited for her to pass him.

"Me?" She was suddenly nervous. Why didn't he just tell her who it was? Why the secrecy?

Seeing the policeman in the living room, Amanda paused, turning to Brent and hesitating.

"Mrs. Farraday?"

"Yes?"

"I'm sorry to bother you, ma'am, but we found this in the ravine and we thought it might be yours." He handed her a sparkling object. It was a gold pendant, half of a mizpah. Instinctively, her free hand went to the gold chain around her neck. She stared at the piece in the palm of her other hand.

"Where . . . where did you find it?" she whispered.

"At the spot where your . . . ah . . . the car first went under. It must've gotten loose when your rescuer hauled you out."

She kept staring at it, wondering at its significance, then looked to Brent for help. Receiving none, she again turned to the man in uniform.

"What . . . what makes you think it belongs to me?"

The man shuffled uncomfortably, taken aback by her defiance.

"May I see it?" Brent finally spoke. He took the pendant from Amanda and turned it around, then put it back in her hand, facedown. "Yes, officer, it belongs to my wife." He nodded at Amanda. "It has my initials on the back, and the date of our first anniversary."

Amanda's eyes widened—B.F. 14Feb79.

"You had it made for us. My half, with your initials, is in the drawer upstairs."

The policeman breathed an audible sigh of relief. "Well, that's it, then. Just sign here for it, Dr. Farraday, if you please, and I'll be out of your hair, sir." He handed Brent a logbook. "Have a nice day, folks."

She was still staring at the gold mizpah when Brent returned. Standing very still, she marveled at the chances of the cops finding such a small trinket in the bushes, or even in the dried mud. What were they looking for in that ravine? An odd feeling stirred within her. Here was something she had had on her before the accident—another piece of identification?

"Amazing," Brent murmured. She stared at him, puzzled. "You weren't wearing your wedding ring, yet you kept this little trinket. Really amazing." He pouted, his eyes mocking. "Pity you can't tell us why."

They stood facing each other for a moment, the question suspended between them.

"Mother? Are you coming back?" Mandy's small voice broke the tension, and with a deep sigh, Amanda turned away and swiftly walked over to the child.

The day went by fast. Brent kept himself in the background while Mandy and Josh competed for her attention, and willingly Amanda gave it. She was eager to learn about their lives, their interests, the things they loved and the things they hated. Their enthusiasm took away the bitter edge, the uncertainty, and slowly the dense fog cleared and the shadows began to take shape. By the end of the day, Amanda knew she was home, and even Brent's aloofness could not shatter her happiness.

He was not unfriendly or nasty in any way, but the undercurrent of suppressed hostility was palpable. He remained reserved and detached toward her, as if she were a stranger visiting his home and entertaining his children, and accordingly he was courteous and cautious not to display any emotion. Once in a while she caught him looking at her with an odd curiosity, and when she said or did something that made the children laugh, his eyes would flicker almost imperceptibly, and she would wonder why he should act so surprised. Especially when she allowed Kavik to come into the house and play with Josh on the living room carpet, laughing at the two wild puppies rolling around the floor.

In the evening they went out for pizza. Mandy and Josh both agreed it was their favorite.

"Do you like pizza, Mommy?" Mandy asked.

Amanda looked at Brent helplessly. "Do I?"

"Not really. But this pizza place has other Italian favorites too, and you did like lasagna."

She had eaten the pizza, and loved it.

That night, Amanda helped put the children to bed.

"I'm so happy you came home," Mandy whispered in her ear, clinging to her neck as she tucked the girl underneath the blanket.

"I'm so glad to have such a beautiful daughter," Amanda whispered in return, and kissed the girl's forehead. "I'm sorry I didn't come back sooner."

"It's all right. You're back now, and that's what counts."

At the doorway, Amanda turned and blew the child a kiss, then switched off the light.

"Mother?"

"Yes, sweetheart?"

"You're here to stay, aren't you? I mean, you're not just passing by, or visiting?" She could hear the dread in the girl's voice.

"No, darling, I'm here to stay. For as long as you want me."

"Forever and ever."

"Then forever it is. Sleep tight and pleasant dreams."

She closed the door behind her and jumped. Brent's tall figure loomed at the end of the hallway, his face expressionless, his eyes cool. Without a word, he brushed past her and walked into his daughter's bedroom.

"What can I fix you?" Brent opened the cabinet above the bar and took out a bottle of Scotch.

"The usual?" She was suddenly weary, wishing she could excuse herself and go someplace alone. She needed to be by herself, to relish the upbeat emotions she had accumulated that day. He was such a contrast to the children and his coolness threatened to ruin her happiness.

"One vodka martini coming up."

But when she tasted the martini, Amanda made a face. "Did I like this stuff?"

"You never drank anything else, unless you count cognac."

He paused as a thought struck him. "Would you rather have a gin and tonic? I seem to recall that you had switched to those a little while before you took off."

But Amanda shook her head and put the glass on the table before her. Brent lit a cigarette and sipped his Scotch.

"The children really took to you today. Try not to be bored with your new game too fast."

"What makes you think it's just a game?"

"You used to thrive on games, my dear."

Amanda picked up her glass and looked at him. She hated the taste of the martini, but she needed to hold on to something. "Perhaps I have changed."

"A leopard changing his spots? Now that would be interesting, and a first in the history of human psychology."

"Perhaps I really like the children?"

"Is that why you've stayed away all this time?"

She looked down at her hands and studied her nails for a moment. "Can't we call a truce, Brent? Whatever I have done to you in the past, can't we bury the hatchet and start afresh?"

He did not answer her and, emptying his drink, walked over to the bar to pour himself another Scotch.

"You barely touched your martini."

"I . . . it's too strong."

He looked at her for a moment, then took out a new glass. "Here, try this one."

Amanda sipped the drink.

"Hm, better. What is it?"

"Highball. Bourbon and Seven-Up."

"I like it."

"You used to hate it. Said it was unsophisticated."

"Is that why you fixed it for me now?"

"You liked the pizza tonight." He lit another cigarette. They were silent for a moment, then Amanda threw back her head and brushed a couple of mischievous curls from her forehead.

"Why did I leave, Brent? What kind of problems were we having?"

"Too long a story for one evening. Like you said, let's call a truce and bury the past. Perhaps that's best for all of us."

She did not press him. She saw his jawline tighten and sensed instinctively that to push him now would be futile.

Besides, she felt like enjoying the evening. No point in hurrying; she had a whole lifetime to paste the pieces together.

Sunday came and went and they spent it in harmony. In the afternoon it rained, ruining Brent's plans to barbecue hamburgers and hot dogs on the garden grill. So they settled for White Castle burgers, which Brent and Josh picked up while Mandy and Amanda made salad and dessert. And they played Disney movies from videos and snacked on buttered popcorn.

Toward the evening the rain stopped and they went to the Red Lobster and Amanda enjoyed their exquisite strawberry daiquiri. And all that time she was aware of Brent's watchful eyes, scrutinizing her reactions, yet careful to keep his expression cloaked. It was as though he were waiting for her to make a wrong move, and it made her uncomfortable.

Trying very hard to ignore his presence, she busied herself with the children, laughing at their jokes and listening to their adventures. As the rum began to take effect, she managed to shake off the feeling of being watched and gradually she stopped caring if her actions met with his approval. Soon she even involved him in their conversation, and by the time their food was served, the tone had lightened up and to their fellow diners they looked like any other happy family enjoying an evening out.

When they were finally alone that evening, Brent suggested she go to bed early. It had been a full weekend and she looked exhausted.

"You're a big hit. They simply adore you."

"It's just a novelty. Wait until they find out that a mother is not always fun and games."

"It was hard on them not having one. Especially Mandy. By the way, why did you cut your hair?"

Amanda looked at him with surprise.

"Never mind. I keep forgetting that you don't recall these things." He lit a cigarette and blew out the smoke. "I'll be up in a little while. Don't wait for me, it might get late."

"Are you . . . going out?" She bit her tongue. It was none of her business what he did. She could not waltz back into his life and expect him to pick up where they had left off years ago.

"No. I'll be in my office. I make it a habit to study each case one last time before I go into surgery in the morning." He had noticed her embarrassment, and for a second his eyes flickered, but there was no mockery in his voice when he explained his actions.

Amanda rose, blushing now. "Good night, then," she said softly.

"Good night." Brent watched her head for the stairs, noticing her trim ankles, mesmerized by the graceful swing of her slim hips. He remembered that walk of hers. It had never failed to catch his attention, and even now it did something to him. His expression softened.

"Don't grow your hair," he drawled. "It looks good on you the way it is."

She turned around briefly, smiled, then quickly went up the stairs, her tread light and carefree.

Chapter 6

IT WAS SIX-THIRTY A.M. BRENT SMOOTHLY MANEUVERED the sleek silver-gray Jaguar out of the garage and lit his morning cigarette. The drive from Lake Forest to Park Ridge was uneventful, routine. Yet he still missed the convenience of living closer to the hospital.

When he had first taken the post at Lutheran General, they had bought a house in nearby suburban Glenview. It had been ideal, even when later he joined the staff, part-time, at Skokie Valley. So central, so accessible. Especially with his practice in Niles, which was literally halfway between the house and the hospital. But Amanda had wanted a better neighborhood, and she had her heart set on more prestigious pastures—like Lake Forest. As his practice flourished and his reputation grew, she had gotten her wish.

Then, after she'd gone, he had contemplated moving back to Glenview, but the hope that she might return and the fear that she wouldn't find them had kept him from doing it. After a while, he'd gotten used to the distance, even enjoyed the long drive before and after an exhausting day. It offered him a chance to think, to sometimes come up with a simple solution to a problem case. And when Paula and Matt had moved practically next door, he gave up the idea of Glenview altogether.

Paula was a godsend. She took care of the children like a

mother, bringing them to her home after school—and with a twosome of her own—and making sure his house was run smoothly. Because of her and Mrs. Flynn, his home and family stayed intact and lacked nothing. Soon Amanda had become a memory, a vague gnawing, somewhere in a dark corner. Or more like a shadow hovering about, not quite forgotten, but not quite real enough to feel its impact. And their lives had settled in. Besides, the children had been too young to really remember her, and he . . .

Brent lit another cigarette. A sudden twitch of pain contorted the left side of his mouth. Yeah, what about him? Had it been ego that made him pursue young Amanda Hartley, sought-after debutante at the age of nineteen? Every red-blooded young male in Cook County at least knew of her; why, she had been Miss Teenage Chicago and Miss Teenage Illinois by the time he'd met her, not to mention reigning Rose Queen of the exclusive Winnetka Country Club—eligible only to the offspring of its revered members—twice in a row, running for a third term. And there he was, a struggling resident at St. Joseph's with high surgical aspirations and a massive dose of dreams to make a name for himself in the medical world.

That Mr. and Mrs. Hartley had approved his pursuit of their frivolous daughter, recognizing his drive and ambitions, and hoping the eight-year age difference would provide the mature, stable hand she needed, had not been revealed until the day after their death. And they had died horribly. In a plane crash in the Mediterranean. It was during the funeral that Jed Hartley, Amanda's uncle, had told him of his brother's hopes, and Amanda, too distraught to care, had clung to the solace of his attention. Six months later they were married.

Funny, he thought, the pain returning, he had never paused to find out if she really loved him, as a man rather than a security blanket. She had been so despondent, so responsive to his attention—and he had let his guard down, allowed himself to be swept away by his own emotions, basking in the sweetness of her. He had read something into her eagerness that wasn't there, never was. Until it was too late. Until he was all entangled in the web she had spun around him, lusting after her, craving for more. For weeks and months and years. And then Mandy was born.

That was the beginning of the awakening, and the beginning of a never-ending rift—the constant bickering, the quarrels, the shouting matches . . . and she began to look for entertainment—and consolation—elsewhere. He had come home later and later, throwing himself into his work and making a name for himself as one of the top gynecologists in Cook County.

Through it all Brent had felt responsible for her. He had wanted her, badly, and gotten her. It was a high price to pay. Despite his demanding career and the long working hours he put in each day, he had tried to keep up with her, indulging her in her need for wild and elaborate parties, staying up later and later. "Slow down, Brent. You're burning both ends of the candle, my friend," Daryl had warned. "Not a wise behavior for a doctor, and a surgeon at that."

He had ignored Daryl, confident he could handle the strain, desperate to keep Amanda satisfied. And even when he started to make little mistakes, he refused to slow down, afraid to admit he couldn't keep up with his young restless wife, afraid to lose her entirely . . .

Instead, sixteen-year-old Yoko Hamada had died.

The radio clicked on and Barbra Streisand's vibrant voice filled the quiet room. In the big bed Amanda stirred. A soft groan escaped her and, with her eyes still closed, she fumbled to turn off the alarm. For a moment she lay very still, but the silence was deafening and she opened her eyes. The place next to her was empty. She quickly peered at the clock: seven-thirty.

With a start she sat up and looked across the room. The drapes were still drawn, but even in the dimness she saw that the boudoir was deserted. The house was silent and she frowned. What time did everybody leave? Or were they perhaps having breakfast downstairs?

A quick shower woke her up, and dashing into the closet, she chose a gray woolen skirt and a white cashmere sweater. She pulled a brush through her short curls and was about to leave the dressing area when she hesitated. A fleeting glance in the mirror made her sigh. Too pale, she groaned. A dash of color on her cheeks, a peck of pale pink lipstick. Better. Now to the kitchen.

When she got downstairs, she found only Josh and Mandy at the dinette table, eating cold cereal.

"Good morning, Mrs. Farraday." Mrs. Flynn's voice came from the kitchen. "Would you like some breakfast?"

"Just coffee, thank you. Did Dr. Farraday leave already?"

Mrs. Flynn appeared with a steaming cup and a covered bread basket. "At six-thirty, as usual," she said smiling, returning to the kitchen. "Do try the toast, or would you prefer an English muffin?"

"I'm fine, thank you, Mrs. Flynn." Amanda took a piece of toast from the basket and started to butter it. "What time did you get back here? I didn't hear you come in last night."

"Just before dawn, in time to send the doctor off with a hot cup of coffee." Mary Flynn reappeared, two box lunches in her hand and the same sunny smile on her wrinkled face. "Don't feel bad, Mrs. Farraday. I'm used to it. We've done this routine for years, at least as long as I've been with him, which was three years last month."

"I hope you had a good time?"

"Yes, thank you, very nice indeed."

Amanda swallowed the last bite of her toast and washed it down with a sip of coffee. "Good morning, you two. Sleep okay?"

Josh grunted and kept on eating. But Mandy looked up.

"Yes, thank you. And you?"

"Like a log. What time is your bus?"

"Eight o'clock, but sometimes it's late."

"Are you going to take us to the bus stop?" Josh finally looked at her.

"Would you like that?"

"Well . . ."

"Then I'll take you," she said, finishing her coffee in a hurry.

Silence reigned again. In the kitchen, Mrs. Flynn filled the dishwasher.

"Are you always so quiet on school mornings?" Amanda smiled. "I recall a livelier bunch Saturday and yesterday."

"That's when Daddy lets us help make the breakfast." Josh pushed his cereal bowl away from him.

"Don't mind him. He's a morning grouch." Mandy looked at her brother with distaste.

"Not so," he sputtered.

"You are!"

"Not true!"

"Oh, all right. Better get ready. Coats, jackets, backpacks, we can't be late." Amanda rose. "I'll be right back, Mrs. Flynn."

The housekeeper poked her head through the opening above the kitchen counter and smiled. "I'll have more coffee waiting for you, Mrs. Farraday."

A group of children were already at the bus stop, their ages ranging between five and twelve. Just as they reached them, the bus arrived. After a quick hug and a kiss, Mandy and Josh disappeared into the yellow vehicle, each securing a seat by the window. Amanda waved as the bus pulled away and they waved back.

"Great kids," a husky voice behind her said.

She turned around and came face-to-face with a tall, slender woman with dark curly hair and warm, laughing eyes. They were about the same age, she guessed, returning the smile.

"Are yours in there, too?" Amanda inquired, glancing at the disappearing bus.

"Yeah, two of them. Tara's Mandy's age, and Wesley is ten. They're not too bad, either." The woman grinned, exposing rows of beautiful white teeth and wrinkling her nose as she did so.

Something clicked in Amanda's head, and her eyes instantly lit up. "You must be Paula." She was almost breathless with relief.

Paula Manchione laughed, her whole face one ball of sunshine. "Your best friend, at your service." She grinned.

For a moment they just looked at one another; then, spontaneously, Paula threw her arms around Amanda, and they were both laughing. "It's so good to have you back, cara." Paula hiccuped, tears glimmering in her warm brown eyes. "God, how I missed you!"

"I wish I could say the same," Amanda whispered.

Her friend held her at arm's length, scrutinizing.

"I know, Brent told me." She turned Amanda around. "You haven't changed a bit. Except for the hair. I've never seen you with short hair." She grinned again. "I like it. It looks

good on you. Makes you look younger, more mischievous.
What does Brent say?"

Amanda laughed, her dimples showing. She felt light, carefree. "About the same as you just did. Except for the young
mischievous look."

"Good old Brent!" Paula laughed again. "I wonder what
Louise will say about it." She cocked her head sideways and
chuckled, her dark eyes sparkling with glee.

"Louise?"

"Dowager Farraday, the dragon lady. Brent's grandmother." She hooked her arm through Amanda's.

"Oh, never mind. You're bound to meet her, sooner or
later. I'd predict sooner, and then we'll both know." She
grinned. "I'd give my right arm to see the look on her face,
though!" They began to walk away from the bus stop. "We'd
better get back to the house, or the neighbors will begin to
wonder."

Amanda looked at her, suddenly reluctant to let go of her
newfound friendship. For the first time since leaving the hospital, she felt good. "Won't you come with me? For a cup of
coffee?" *And update me on everything?*

Paula nudged her. "Thought you'd never ask," she said,
smiling.

Walking out of the operating room, Brent removed his mask
and cap and stripped off his surgical gloves, throwing them
into the wastebasket. His green top showed dark blots where
sweat had penetrated through the cloth. He ran the tap and
scrubbed his hands, then splashed cold water on his clammy
face and sighed. It had been a busy morning and this last
surgery had been a complicated one.

He gripped the edges of the sink and leaned heavily on
them, for a moment closing his eyes. Lack of sleep during the
past two nights had finally caught up with him. He suddenly
regretted his decision to take to the chaise longue instead of
the soft, comfortable bed. A surgeon needed plenty of rest;
he could not afford another mistake.

"They said I could find you here."

He opened his eyes and saw Daryl's grinning face in the
mirror.

"You look like hell, doctor. Had some late nights?" Amusement flickered in his eyes as he watched Brent splash his face and neck a second time.

"You can say that." Brent grimaced. He grabbed a towel and dried himself off. "What are you doing here so early in the day?"

"Meeting with Fitzgerald and the brass," Daryl responded. At Brent's surprised look he quickly added, "Representing my father, of course. We're thinking of a staff exchange. This is a teaching hospital and Barrington Memorial needs practical expertise."

"And Fitzgerald agreed?" Brent could not imagine Lutheran General's chief of staff being eager to give up some of his precious team just to benefit a small, insignificant hospital on the other side of Cook County.

"Not exactly. But the hospital board is in favor of it. Don't ask me why. Me, I'm only too happy to know that they are. We'll be hearing their verdict after the quarterly board meeting next week. How about you, big guy? Want to come spend a couple of months in my neck of the woods?"

Two men in green entered, followed by a scrub nurse.

"Hi, Wills," one said. "Good work, Farraday. Glad you pulled it off, touch and go for a minute."

"Thanks, Mac." Brent nodded and gestured Daryl toward the door. They walked out together and headed for Brent's office.

"Complications?" Daryl prodded.

"Yeah." Brent massaged the back of his neck. "Now what was this about an exchange?"

Daryl grinned. He knew his friend like the back of his hand —praise embarrassed him; he was an excellent surgeon, and a damn good gynecologist, one of the best in his field, and he expected nothing less than perfection of himself when it came to his patients.

"I expect you to be the first to volunteer," he teased.

But Brent was too tired to detect the humor in his statement. "If you don't mind, I'd rather not. Nothing personal, Daryl, just inconvenient, that's all. My private practice is only three minutes from here. And to have my patients travel all across the county to be in my care, no—that would be asking a bit too much, not to mention the time I would spend on the road to get from one place to another. After all, I've got a family to consider as well, and they deserve some of my time, don't you think?"

"And what a family you have. An almost brand-new wife, too." Daryl grinned again. "I'd say that would be enough to keep me busy."

"Cut the bull, will you? I'm not in the mood."

They reached his office and a nurse hastened after Brent.

"You've had several messages, Dr. Farraday. Mrs. Farraday called, three times to be exact. She said it wasn't urgent, but you're to call her as soon as you have a spare minute." She gave him a handful of pink notes and hurried back to her station.

Brent sighed and walked into his office. Why the hell would Amanda be calling him three times? Did she not remember his routine—surgeries in the morning, rounds after lunch, then onto his private practice? No, of course not. Damn! He kept forgetting that she did not recall a thing. Even so, what was wrong with her common sense? He threw his messages on the desk and grabbed a cigarette.

"Don't worry, old boy," Daryl said, and Brent looked at him, annoyed. He had totally forgotten his brother-in-law's presence.

"What?"

"We're only talking about the senior residents." Noting the blank look on Brent's face, Daryl sighed and rolled his eyes. "The exchange, bigshot, the exchange."

"Oh yeah, right." Brent sat down and stretched his long legs on top of his desk. Then, suddenly, his eyes lit up with understanding. "You shithead, you were testing me!" He took his legs off the desk and threw a blotter at his laughing friend. Daryl ducked and laughed harder.

"We now know how selfish we are, don't we?" He kept on laughing. After a few minutes, Brent saw the bright side of the situation and began to join in. Soon they were both laughing.

Daryl got up, still grinning. "I'll let you call your sexy wife. Call me sometime."

"How about lunch?"

"No time, friend. My father expects me back at noon. Say hi to Amanda, will you?"

After he had gone, Brent thumbed through his messages. His hand stayed on the three calls from Mrs. Farraday. The phone number was not his. He stared at the number, puzzled for a moment. Just then the intercom rang.

"Dr. Farraday, it's your grandmother again." The nurse sounded anxious.

He looked at the number on the pink sheet again and recognized it. *That* Mrs. Farraday, of course! Not Amanda—Louise. God, he was tired. He should have recognized that number instantly.

"Dr. Farraday, are you there?"

"Yes, Cheryl. Please tell Mrs. Farraday that I'll call her back after lunch."

Brent leaned back in his chair and sighed. His grandmother. He should have known. He knew what she was calling about. News traveled fast and Louise was like the press, only worse. He had meant to call her on Saturday and tell her about Amanda. Yet something had held him back. Perhaps it was the knowledge that the two women had intensely disliked one another. Or perhaps it was reluctance to listen to her sharp criticism. During the past four years she had urged him time and again to divorce Amanda, and he could just imagine her reaction now that the prodigal had returned. He groaned and picked up the phone—to dial his home number.

"Good Lord!" Paula looked at her wristwatch and jumped up from her chair. It was almost noon. "How time flies when you're having fun," she said, laughing. "I must get home and make the beds and plan dinner. Not everyone is so lucky as to have a Mrs. Flynn around, you know." She smiled at the housekeeper.

"Mrs. Farraday, I have to go to the grocery store and pick up some bread. They were out of Dr. Farraday's favorite brand on Friday. Is there anything special you'd like me to bring back for you?" Mrs. Flynn asked Amanda.

"No, nothing, thank you."

"You don't mind, do you?"

"Mind?"

"I'll only be a few minutes. I'll be right back, in plenty of time to make the children their midday snack."

"No, of course. Please, just go about your usual routine."

"Hey, tell you what. Why don't you come to my home and I'll fix us some lunch?" Paula's eyes danced. "Yes, and we can talk some more. And we can meet the kids at the bus stop together."

"That would be a splendid idea. After all, this is your first day home alone, and I do feel rather guilty leaving you by yourself." The housekeeper nodded gratefully at Paula. "Oh, let me give you a key to the front door."

Minutes later they strutted off to Paula's home, two houses down, cheerfully waving after the disappearing station wagon.

In his office, Brent listened to the repeated ringing of the telephone. And frowned.

Chapter 7

HER HAND STAYED, THEN, BLINKING, SHE QUICKLY brushed a last stroke of lipstick over her lips. She stared at her face in the mirror and an odd sensation gripped her. It was the face of a stranger. The makeup around her eyes was too heavy, it made her look older; her cheeks were too red, and her lips were too dark, too . . . too sensuous. It was too daring, too bold . . . It didn't look right . . . it didn't feel right . . . it . . . it just wasn't . . . her . . .

She impetuously shoved back her chair and, after a moment's hesitation, got up and took two steps to the marble vanity sink. A last glance in the mirror, then resolutely she ran the tap and washed her face. The coolness felt good against her skin and she splashed more water on her face and neck and rubbed them until all of the oily paste had come off and her skin shone. Finally she looked at herself in the mirror, her hands touching her face again and again as if to make sure it hadn't been obliterated by all that makeup.

Staring at her pale reflection, she suddenly shivered. Apprehension resurfaced. The growing uneasiness of the past few days mounted, the nagging doubt in her blurred subconscious creeping into the big tawny eyes.

She had roamed the house for hours, searching for a spark of recognition, a trace of cognizance. She had touched everything, listened to Paula, studied each available photograph.

But nothing. No hint of familiarity, not even a remote flicker of recollection. It was as if any link to her past had been erased from her memory banks—severed, completely, irrevocably. As if she were an entirely new being, resurrected from the depths of nowhere. And if Brent and Paula had not been so sure . . .

She swallowed. Another shiver rippled across her insides and she closed her eyes. What if they were wrong after all? What if she wasn't who they said she was? What if . . .

"Amanda, are you ready?" She heard the bedroom door close and Brent's firm footsteps on the plush carpet approach the dressing area.

"Just about." She quickly grabbed a towel and dried herself, and recognizing her own pale face in the mirror, dashed back to her makeup corner. She took a deep breath, feeling much better with all that muck off her face. Quickly she applied a dash of blusher and rubbed her cheeks. A touch of shimmery moss-green on her eyelids, a couple of rapid strokes of black mascara.

"Good Lord, Amanda, what have you been doing all this time? You've been up here for over half an hour." Brent's tall figure filled the arched opening, a frown on his handsome face. Amanda almost dropped the lipstick, her heart leaping at the sight of him in the mirror.

"I'm ready," she said and brushed a last stroke of pale burnt copper lipstick on her lips.

"I'll say you are." Brent eyed her robe, open disapproval in his steel-gray eyes.

Amanda hastily took off the robe and blushed at his blatant surprise. She had chosen a simple beige cashmere dress that highlighted her shiny copper curls and accentuated her slenderness. A pair of high-heeled beige shoes completed the outfit, making her seem taller and her long legs even more shapely.

She turned to face him and remained very still, mesmerized by the odd gleam in his piercing eyes that seemed to penetrate through her like hot coal. Without taking his eyes off her, he opened a drawer. Gently he turned her around and fastened a string of pearls around her slender neck. For an endless moment their eyes met in the mirror and Amanda held her breath.

"There," he said softly, "now you're ready."

He took a step backward and Amanda began to breathe again, her heart pounding in her throat.

"Paula and Matt are downstairs, and Nicole called from the car to say that they're on their way."

The doorbell rang.

"That must be them now." Brent headed toward the door. "Oh, and Daryl had a last-minute emergency, so they'll be late."

Amanda barely heard him, again staring at her reflection in the mirror. Her earlier consternation recurred with blinding dismay. It had taken her almost twenty minutes to put on the makeup she had washed off afterward. Yet in less than a minute she had managed to redo her face. Where the hell had she learned to do that? As if she were used to doing it, by instinct, a habit . . .

"Are you coming?" Brent sounded impatient.

She shook her head to shake off her confusion and hurried to join him. Holding the door for her, Brent stepped aside to let her pass.

"By the way, you look lovely," he said, and caught her arm just as she stumbled.

"Darling, you haven't changed a bit!" Nicole Nillson trilled as she laid a cool cheek against Amanda's. A whiff of Chanel No. 5 burst around them as she handed her mink stole to Brent.

Petite and very blond, Nicole looked like a fragile miniature of her husband, who stood six feet two inches tall and was even blonder than Brent. A receding hairline accentuated the firmness of his long, square-jawed face, and his crystal-blue eyes matched his wife's. Dr. Niels Nillson took his friend's wife in his strong arms and hugged her hard.

"Damn good to have you back, Duchess," he boomed. "And don't listen to Nikki, you look better, much, much better! Slimmer, younger, and wow jiminy, you look like a million dollars with that hairdo."

"All right, Niels, cut out the bedside crap, we get the drift." Brent slapped him on the shoulder. "Come on, let's get something to drink."

"Not before I've had my chance to hug the lady." Matt Manchione held her at arm's length and looked deep into her eyes. "Just like Paula said," he murmured, then took her in his arms.

Matt was the shortest of the three men, standing only five feet eleven, two inches taller than his wife. He was broad and solidly built, and very dark. His moustache and beard were neatly trimmed and hid a pair of otherwise full lips. Why, he almost looks like a pirate, Amanda thought. A black patch over one eye and the picture would've been complete. Suddenly she shivered.

"Welcome home, Manda," Matt said.

They all walked toward the wet bar where Brent had started pouring drinks for everyone. Paula hooked her arm through Amanda's and whispered something in her ear that made them both laugh.

"Hey, you two, care to share the fun?" Nicole pouted.

"Not in mixed company," Paula said with a laugh. "Speaking of company, whatever happened to Kessler Interiors? Does anyone know?"

"Who the hell is Kessler Interiors?" Niels handed his wife a glass of dry martini.

"The decorators who did your house, darling. Thanks, Brent." Paula sipped her martini. "Or did Nikki talk them into a free lunch?"

Nicole brushed her sleek blond hair behind one ear and slowly lifted her misty ice-blue eyes. God, how she does that with such flair, Paula thought wryly. She's even perfected the gestures. Amazing how men ate it all up; can't they see it's all a pose? She almost choked on her drink as Nikki turned her head and looked her straight in the eye. She hastily raised her glass in mock salute, then quickly buried her face in her glass. She breathed easier as the object of her scrutiny turned to Matt to light her cigarette.

Paula gulped down the rest of her drink, still jolted by the woman's challenging glare. It wasn't just that cool, sophisticated pose, she suddenly realized, it was the look in those ice-blue starry eyes. With those eyes, Nikki could easily seduce half the male population of Chicago, and that look, so vulnerable, so helpless, so deceptively naïve, studied to perfection down to the faintest flutter of her dark eyelashes —it would melt even an iceberg. Although, Paula had to admit, the woman had a classic face, like a Greek goddess—in marble—flawless, perfect, and just as mythical.

"They've been bought out by some conglomerate," Nicole said.

"Don't tell me." Niels handed his empty glass to Brent. "You aren't thinking of redecorating your house again, are you, Paula darling?"

"Of course she is." Matt ignored Paula's furious look. "My wife won't be happy until she has at least one corner of the house modeled like a showcase, will you, dear?"

Paula sighed. "Only the bedroom. The rest of the house is fine, but there's something missing in our bedroom."

"Let me guess. A lover." Brent grinned.

"Oh, go ahead, laugh. Can I help it if I drool over romantic bedrooms? Keeps things warm, you know. Atmosphere helps." Paula jumped up from her chair and handed Brent her empty glass.

"Why don't I take a look at your bedroom?" Amanda offered.

A hush fell in the room. They all looked at Amanda. She had sat very quietly sipping a glass of champagne, listening to everybody, watching her friend get more and more agitated. Now suddenly the center of attention, she reddened and bit her lip. Why did she have to say that, in front of all of them? She should have waited until she could talk to Paula alone . . .

"What do you know, you'd certainly be a natural," Nikki mumbled, fumbling in her purse for another cigarette. Matt obliged her with Brent's lighter and lit a pipe for himself. "After all, bedrooms are your forte, aren't they?"

"Watch it, Nikki!" Niels shot her a glaring look, but she did not look at him, instead taunting Amanda with eyes she had narrowed to mocking slits.

But Amanda only held her breath. She sensed the uneasiness in the room and instinctively knew she was the cause of it. *What was it they were hiding? What had she done that deserved Nikki's catty remark—or was it an insinuation? Why, Nicole was supposed to be her friend, a good friend, or so Brent had said, but friends didn't behave this way . . . or did they?*

The doorbell rang. As if on cue, they all moved.

"That must be Daryl," Brent said and went for the door. Niels sat down next to his wife and whispered something to her and she winced, her eyes widening. Paula got up from her seat and slid onto the sofa next to Amanda, putting her arm reassuringly around her shoulders, and whispering

"Thank you" in her ear. Only Matt remained calm, smoking his pipe.

"Hi, gang. Sorry we're late. Karen couldn't decide what to wear. Hello, gorgeous." Daryl kissed Amanda's cheek, grinning.

"Blame it on me," Karen said, looking radiant in a red woolen dress that camouflaged her condition. "He's the one who couldn't tear himself loose from his beloved patients."

"Patient. Singular."

"How did it go?" Brent handed him a Scotch and soon the two of them became engrossed in the details of the surgery.

Amanda rose and disappeared into the kitchen. Unwrapping the plates of hors d'oeuvres, she smiled to herself. Bless Mrs. Flynn. It all looked so scrumptious, little pâté and cucumber bites, topped with chunks of pineapple, cheese, and egg slices, crackers and caviar, even delicious-looking petit fours, all homemade.

"Are you all right?" Karen's voice startled her.

"Yes, of course. Shouldn't I be?"

"Don't mind Nikki. Her bark is sharper than her bite, really."

Amanda forced a laugh, trying to hide her nervousness. "Are you always this clairvoyant, or did someone clue you in?"

"I did."

She turned to see Paula's laughing face in the arched opening.

"Here, let me help," Paula suggested. "After all, if you are to do my bedroom, I can at least assist you with the food." She inhaled the aroma of the delicacies. "Mmm, and if you ever decide to get rid of Mrs. Flynn, send her my way, will you?"

"Now, Paula, I didn't say . . ."

"I know, I know. I just like to think positive. Better chance to make my dreams come true." With a broad grin, she took a plate to the others in the living room.

"Karen?" Amanda hesitated and her sister-in-law paused in the doorway.

"Yes?"

"No, nothing."

"Spit it out, Manda." But when Amanda didn't, she came back into the kitchen. "We were friends, you and I," Karen said softly. It was her turn to hesitate, but as the moment passed, she took her sister-in-law's hand and held it, firmly. "I didn't always agree with you on everything, but we were still friends."

"Friends? Like Nicole?" Amanda threw her head back and looked at her challengingly. An amused smile crept around Karen's lips.

"You don't miss much, do you?"

"It's rather obvious, I'd say."

"Nicole is Nicole's own best friend. She can't help it. As Josh would say, she's made that way. As long as you or I can illuminate Nicole, we're her friends. You mustn't look for something more, Amanda, she's not capable of any real deep feelings, for you, me, or anyone."

"Not even her husband?"

"Not even Niels. He is her security blanket and, for as much as her shallow brain can grasp, she loves him. The truth is that she loves what he can give her—wealth, prestige, stability. The sad part is that she believes she really loves him."

Amanda looked at her curiously. "What makes you such an expert?" she asked slowly.

Karen smiled again.

"We grew up together, went to boarding school together, roomed together, need I say more?"

Amanda sighed. "It's just . . ."

"Don't let her get to you, Manda."

"I just wondered if—"

"She is your typical enfant terrible."

"—I had done something real awful to her."

"Of course you did. We all do. How else would she survive? She thrives on the dramatic, and being a martyr is simply glamorous, don't you think?"

"Oh, come on, girls. Stop talking about me." Paula put the empty plate on the counter and grabbed another. "Is this also for human consumption or what?" She sampled a bite. "Mmm . . . *delicioso.* Come on, or they'll think you two eloped or something." She looked at Amanda's solemn face. "Oh, stop it already. She's really not such a bad sort. Spoiled maybe, but quite sweet at times. And she can be a lot of fun." Paula took another bite. "And that's enough about Nikki, or she'll overhear us and start thinking she's someone important."

Laughing, they went to rejoin the group.

Brent looked up when Amanda reentered the room. His eyes met hers and Amanda held her breath sharply, feeling a sudden rush of adrenaline. It was just for a moment, then he looked away and she felt the brunt of his rejection. She turned and swallowed hard, but before she could slip away, a hand touched her shoulder.

"How about another glass of champagne?" His voice was soft, noncommittal, but not altogether unkind.

She could not know that he had observed her during the past hour, pondering on her uncharacteristic quietness—uncharacteristic because he had never known her to be content out of the limelight—waiting for the moment when she would come out of her shell and dazzle them all.

Amanda nodded, and swallowed again. How could he have crossed the room so quickly? she wondered.

Matt refilled his pipe and lit it. His dark eyes watched the group with quiet amusement, content to be the silent observer. He was used to it—long years of practice in hundreds of courtrooms all over the state; it gave him insight into people, allowed him to pick up hidden tidbits, made him into the successful lawyer he was.

Puffing on his pipe, he saw his wife talking to Daryl, her laughter ringing through the room, while Brent and Karen entertained the blond Nicole. In a corner, Niels seemed to make a play for Amanda. Periodically, the scenery changed as the couples regrouped. Yet time and again Matt's glance slid to Amanda. She seemed calm enough, a polite smile on her face, but he couldn't miss the twirling of her champagne glass, her hands clenching it in between numerous sips. He noticed Niels's efforts to keep his hands off her by keeping them in his pockets.

She had changed. Paula had said the same thing, and he had not quite believed her. But she was right, there was something missing. The wild fiery Amanda seemed to have vanished. This was a calm, sophisticated woman, no longer loose-lipped, no longer the flirtatious little vamp he had known. The years had done well by her. Not that she had lost her charm—he had only to look at Niels to see that—or her looks. Why, she was even more attractive without all that makeup, more alluring, sexier. At the same time she seemed more vulnerable somehow. A curious combination, he thought. What could have happened these past four years to have brought about these changes?

From the sofa, Karen watched her brother follow Amanda's every move, the expression in his dark eyes veiled, the smile on his lips mechanical as he appeared to be listening to Nicole's empty chatter.

Why, he still loves her, she marveled. After all these years, after all that woman has done to him. Louise was right. The little tramp had hooked her talons deep into his gut, too deep to cut them loose without leaving a scar. And even now, after all the hurt and betrayal, behind that façade of indifference, his loins were aching for her. Still.

Karen turned her head, unable to bear Brent's cloaked torment any longer, and sighed. No, she didn't feel any remorse over her lie earlier in the kitchen. Well, not a lie exactly, she told herself, just not quite the . . . ah . . . entire truth, maybe. Besides, Amanda deserved a taste of her own medicine.

Sure, they had been friends. As leopards and humans could be friends. A "friendship" that was guarded, superficial at best, as they moved around each other with a caution that had its roots in self-preservation. She, Karen, for Brent's sake, and Amanda, to shield herself from Louise's sharp claws.

Grimacing, she glanced around. Studying Matt's impassive face, and Niels's stealthy attempts to remain nonchalant, curiosity seized her. Their wives' reaction to Amanda's homecoming had been jovial, and she wondered if it was all pretense or merely a gesture of diplomacy for old time's sake? *Some happy close-knit circle we are,* she thought. *Friends. Held together by threads of hidden animosity. Lurid shadows lurking in our midst, yet each of us too insecure to break the spell.*

She recalled how Daryl had told Brent that he had checked out Amanda's natural hair color. Reluctantly, her eyes scanned the room for her husband, and found him—standing at the far side of the bar, barely visible in the dim light. Talking to Amanda.

* * *

Amanda smiled as she walked the hall toward the guest bathroom. The thick plush carpet muffled her footsteps and she reached to push the half-open door. She paused, the smile dying on her face. Soft voices drifted from behind the door.

"Are you sure she doesn't remember anything? How can you be so sure? She could be faking it, I wouldn't put it past her, the bitch." A woman's voice hissed.

"Oh, come off it, Nikki! I made a play for her, you saw it, you were there, for God's sake. She didn't so much as flinch."

Amanda froze. Why would they hide in the bathroom to talk about her? What could she have done to them to warrant such behavior? And when they were supposed to be her friends, their best friends, Brent's and hers.

"Besides, what could she possibly gain from it? To what goddamn purpose?"

She could hear Niels pace the tiled floor, and closed her eyes. She wanted to run away, but her legs wouldn't move. And part of her wanted to hear more, perhaps learn something.

"It's just like her to put on this . . . this charade. She's always had a flair for the dramatic, and—"

"Calm down, woman! Listen to yourself, you're getting paranoid for Christ's sake. Come on, let's go back inside and act rational. If she is playing with us, which I don't believe she is, at least act your part. You can do it, Nicole, here's your chance. You've always wanted to be an actress, remember?"

Amanda clasped her mouth, muffling a sob. She swiftly moved away and dashed inside the laundry room, just in time to hear the Nillsons leave the bathroom. She was trembling, and with a soft groan she leaned against the wall. God, they really hated her, those . . . those hypocrites! It was bad enough that they should pretend to be close to her, but to humiliate her like this, and in her own house—no, "humiliate" wasn't the right word, "backstabbing" would be a better description for their underhanded comments.

Her head was spinning, confused thoughts whirling around and around in a dark void. Gradually her body grew limp and exhausted; she slowly slid to the floor. And just stayed there, drained and shaking uncontrollably.

Chapter 8

IT WAS DARK. A MEAN WIND HOWLED THROUGH THE HOL-
low trees along the road. Their sharp thorny branches
loomed down, groping at her viciously as she ran past them,
frantically trying to reach the single flickering light in the
distance. Her breath came in short raspy gasps, her bare feet
were torn and bleeding from the sharp stones along the way.
The cramps in her legs worsened with each step she took.
But she kept on running, trying to stay ahead of the Thing
that pursued her. She could not see it, she only knew it was
there, in the dark, on her heels, and she sensed it was evil,
dangerous and evil. She tried to scream, but no sound
reached her lips, and she knew that if she stopped running it
would harm her.

The wind suddenly picked up; the howling intensified. She
ran faster, her arms reaching for that distant light. A horrible
sound came from behind her and she willed herself to run
even faster, a sob wrenching from her heaving chest. She felt
it closing in on her and she flung her arms as if to gain speed
from the force of the wind around her. That light . . . if only
she could get to that light . . . God, please, somebody . . .
help me . . . Her feet raked the edge of a wayward rock and
she stumbled . . . into the darkness . . . and the Thing was
right behind her . . . and she finally screamed.

* * *

"Nooo!!!" Amanda jerked up, gasping, cold sweat pearling on her forehead.

Brent flung himself from the chaise-longue and with a couple of long leaps he reached her, his chest bare, his hair tousled. The sleep barely out of his eyes, he gazed at the terrified woman in the bed and she stared back at him, unseeing. Gently, he wiped the sweat off her face with the palm of his hand.

In a daze Amanda looked about her, touching the sheets, oblivious of her half-exposed breasts or his gaze upon them. *She was in bed, it was just a dream, but it had been so real, so frighteningly real . . .*

"It's all right now," Brent soothed, trying not to look at her breasts, ivory-white in the moonlight that streamed from the bay windows into the dark room. "Go back to sleep now, it was only a dream," he murmured.

But by now she was shaking and the relief was so strong, she began to sob uncontrollably, hysterically. Despite himself, Brent sat down on the edge of the bed and took her into his arms, covering her bare shoulders with the spare blanket he picked up at the foot of the bed. He held her and comforted her, rocking her gently, until after a while, her sobs subsided and she lay limp in his strong embrace. He stroked her back to soothe her, then gently laid her down on the bed and wiped the tears from her cheeks.

"Get some rest. Close your eyes and think of nothing," he said, pulling the sheets over her. But when he got up to go back to his chaise-longue, she grabbed his hand.

"Please," she whimpered. "Don't leave me. Stay . . . a while . . ."

Brent sighed, the temptation to stay with her struggling with his better judgment. Was this one of her old tricks, he wondered? His bitterness against her returned and his face hardened visibly. Even in the darkness, Amanda saw the change. Her grip on him loosened and when he moved away, she did not stop him. Instead, she clutched the blanket and just lay there the rest of the night, wide-eyed and afraid to close her eyes. Only when the moon had gone and the first rays of the morning seeped into the room did her eyes close. And when an hour later Brent woke up and rose to dress for work, he found her sound asleep, traces of tears still on her pale cheeks.

* * *

Quietly he went downstairs, his clothes under his arm, and took a shower in the guest bathroom. He did not wake her, sensing her fatigue as he felt his. He had lain on the chaise-longue, staring at the moon for a long while, and his thoughts had run rampant.

She had been back almost two weeks now and she had never questioned his motives for not sharing the bed with her. Not once. She had accepted everything, complained about nothing. She was like a new woman, quieter than he ever remembered her, more mature, more resilient. Her tolerance and steady good-naturedness were astounding, and puzzled him. Something must have happened to change her so drastically.

For a moment he contemplated the difference. The children adored her, ecstatic to have a real live mother. She showered them with love and attention, something he had not been able to give them full time. She laughed with them, listened to their outrageous stories, read to them at bedtime, and played with them during the day. Even Kavik liked her. And Mrs. Flynn spoiled her like a mother hen. He had to admit—the new Amanda intrigued him, immensely. The only fault she had was that she was constantly late for everything.

Brent smiled. At least that was one thing that had not changed. Amanda had been late even for her own wedding. The guests had become restless and for a fleeting moment he had feared she had cold feet and decided to stand him up at the altar.

He sighed and his thoughts went back to the night before. It was the second time she had awakened him with those nightmares. He had tried to get her to talk about them, but she would not share them. He had suggested that she see a psychiatrist. Not that he had much faith in them, but perhaps he could help her express her inner fears. That something nagged her subconscious—to the point where it manifested into these nightmares—he was certain. Yet he was just as convinced that she was determined to block it out. It was fear —blind, obliterating fear. But she would not hear about it and nothing he could say would persuade her. He had even suggested hypnotism—that it might bring back her memory —but his attempts failed. She had stood her ground, adamant in her conviction that it would not do her any good and that she would remember in due time.

He was wrong, that was the second thing about her that had not changed. She could beat a mule with that stubborn streak of hers and still come out ahead—by a mile, even two. And the more you pushed her, the more stubborn she became. So he stopped pushing.

Brent lit a cigarette, and ran his hand through his hair, unruly from a restless night's sleep. The chaise longue was not the most comfortable resting place and being awakened in the middle of the night had not helped.

What did these nightmares mean? he wondered. He suddenly wished she would regain her memory. Yet the doctor in him knew that amnesia was an erratic phenomenon, unpredictable to say the least, and totally, utterly incomprehensible. Anything could trigger the return of her memory; then again, she might never remember again. And there was no known formula for either reaction.

Buttoning his shirt, he looked at himself in the mirror. As the days passed, he felt his hostility toward her lessen and at times he found himself wanting her as he had wanted her years ago, before their problems took a serious turn. Problems that had worsened the day she discovered herself pregnant with their first child. Problems that had gradually numbed his desire for her, and made him turn to other, warmer, more feeling women. He had been discreet, but he knew she had not cared one way or another anyway, living her life in complete selfishness, caring only about her own needs, her own desires, her own satisfaction. And he had known about her affairs, although for reasons of her own she had never flaunted them, not even to Paula, who was her best friend, perhaps the only one she really cared for, certainly the only woman she trusted.

He brushed his hair and straightened his tie. No, he was wrong again. The new Amanda had yet another flaw: she lacked confidence. The panther in human form had lost her sharp claws and there was no trace of the pleasure-seeking feline whose motto had been to exploit her prowess through unbridled sensuality and unscrupulous misuse of her charms. Not that he missed it; on the contrary, he liked her uncertainty—it made her seem vulnerable somehow, lending her an air of innocence that was definitely alluring.

Brent shook his head. She intrigued him all right, but he still distrusted her. She had hurt him once, badly, and he was not about to be hurt again, not by her, not by anybody. Picking up his jacket, he headed for the kitchen.

"No! Absolutely no." Amanda shook her head with such vigor, her short curls bounced around like a furious red mop. They were having after-dinner coffee later that evening.

"All I want you to do is try, just once." Brent persisted.

"I said no. Please, Brent, don't make me."

"What have you got to lose? Are you afraid that it might uncover some dark secret, is that it?"

She whirled around, her eyes flaming. "I'm not afraid of anything. I just don't see how a shrink can interpret *my* dreams. For that's all they are, dreams." She took a deep breath, clenching and unclenching her fists, trying to get control of herself. "It's a waste of time, believe me. I won't go, and that's final."

"Okay, okay. I was just trying to help. You seem really bothered by something in your subconscious."

"A psychiatrist is not going to relieve that."

"You won't know until you try."

"I said no. They'll go away in time, I just know they will. Besides, it's probably the trauma of the accident. An aftermath. After all, I nearly died in that horrible crash. Aren't I entitled to be haunted by such a narrow escape, hm? Just a little?"

Brent shook his head and gave up. He had talked to Daryl that morning, and needing to share his worries, he had spilled his guts. They had discussed Amanda's problem, argued about how to handle it, discussed it again, argued some more. Finally he had buckled down and, throwing his previous decision to the wind, followed his brother-in-law's advice and brought up the subject one more time.

Now he knew again he had wasted his time, but that was no surprise. Yet he somehow felt good about the argument. Not once, he marveled, not even in the heat of it had she yelled or screeched. She had raised her voice, but at no time had she lost her cool. And that, after the years of screaming fights, was a revelation.

"All right, you win," he said. "After all, it's your problem. I'm just trying to help you solve it."

Amanda smiled at him. "You're right, it is my problem. But thank you for the concern."

He lit a cigarette and got up to walk to the window. Outside Kavik was playing cheerfully with a ball that Josh had left in the garden.

"You know, I was thinking of moving into my den. There's a comfortable couch there, wide enough to sleep on. And I do have to work late from time to time. That way I won't disturb you if I decide to stay up past midnight."

Amanda stared at his tall, straight back for a moment, then lowered her gaze and poured herself another cup of coffee. She said nothing and merely went on sipping her coffee. Brent turned around to face her.

"It's a bit less conspicuous than sleeping in the guest bedroom, don't you agree?" he said.

She still did not say anything, but met his gaze steadfastly.

"That chaise-longue is good for a while, but after a few weeks it's become downright uncomfortable, and I do need my rest." Why did she not invite him to share her bed with him, damn it? How much more blatant could he get?

"I'll bring some blankets and a couple of pillows to your den," she said and got up. Without another look in his direction, she gathered the cups, picked up the half-empty pot of coffee, and went into the kitchen.

A sharp blast of disappointment struck him, and with an impatient shrug, he strode out of the room and disappeared into his den. He slammed the door behind him, picked up a book from the desk, and threw it against the far wall. *What did you expect, you idiot?* he thought furiously. *Did you think she would tumble into your arms after the cool treatment you've been giving her ever since her return a couple of weeks ago?*

The thud of the falling book sobered him. This was not stubbornness; this was pride. And by God, she had pride, lots of it. Suddenly, he knew that she would not be the one to make the first move.

He did not move into his den. The discomfort of the chaise-longue was somehow not important to him anymore; his need to be near her was. Yet he could not bring himself to join her in bed, not just yet. Instinctively he felt neither of them was ready for that. And wisely, Amanda did not bring up the subject, nor did she make any comment on his decision to remain in the boudoir.

Then too the nightmares stopped. And more and more she stayed up late with him, waiting for him to finish his work in the den while she read book after book in the living room. After a while, Brent would take his books and join her, and they would read together in silence, content with just each other's company.

Afterward they would go upstairs together and talk. He would tell her about his cases and the funny things that happened in the hospital, the gossip among the staff, even share some of his worries and the love he had for his patients. And Amanda would listen and subtly enter his world.

Her genuine display of interest moved him. It surprised him—in the past she had never seemed to care. Even more amazing was that she did not talk much about herself, and when he asked her about her day, she would relate the children's adventures, making them sound frivolous and upbeat.

Then, retiring separately, she would lie in the big bed and he would curl up in the chaise longue, each thinking about the other and about their proximity in the same room. And each wondering who would make that first move.

Chapter 9

THE MERCEDES SLID INTO THE GARAGE WITHOUT A hitch and at the touch of a button the electronic doors zoomed to a rapid close behind it. Amanda turned off the motor and for a moment she just sat staring ahead, her hands gripping the wheel, her eyes glassy. She had done it; she had not thought she could, but she did. She had driven a car all by herself.

It had been Paula's idea; Brent had been against it, but Paula had argued that she had to overcome her fears once and for all. Or hire a chauffeur. She owed it to her children to snap out of the trauma, Paula said, for to live in the suburbs without independent transportation was insane. After all, she was not the first woman to experience a car accident.

Amanda opened her mouth and let out a deep sigh of relief. Her hand touched the leather purse on the passenger seat, tempted to take out the driver's license she got just yesterday. But as she reached over, her glance caught the time on her wristwatch and she gasped. God, she was late. Again. Grabbing her purse and shopping bags, she swiftly jumped out of the car and hurried toward the door that led into the house.

She had missed the school bus—the third time this week—and she hated not being at the bus stop when the children got home. She knew how disappointed they were not to see her, especially Mandy, who enjoyed walking home hand in hand with her and having her guess how she had survived the day. In turn, the girl would quiz her on what she had in store for them after they had done their homework. Josh was more nonchalant, hopping around them until he would hear Kavik's impatient bark, which was his cue to take off, and by the time they had reached the house, he would be rolling in the grass in the back yard, screeching with delight as the big wagging dog grinned and jumped all over him, pretending to bite his master.

Opening the door she heard the sound of a piano and, surprised, she hastened inside, where a smiling Mrs. Flynn awaited her. Returning the smile, Amanda handed the housekeeper her parcels and after a brief exchange she advanced toward the family room. After almost three weeks, she had ceased to marvel over the woman's extraordinary ability to sense their comings and goings; she either had very sensitive ears or an uncanny way of knowing.

The sounds of Mozart's menuet became more distinct as she approached the room in the back of the house, and Amanda took off her high heels. There, almost hidden behind the huge wing of the baby grand piano that stood in the far corner of the room, sat Mandy, totally absorbed in the music and oblivious to the silent observer. The clean notes floated through the room, filling the air with romance and majestic grandeur of years gone by, and for a glorious moment, Amanda felt herself swept up in a dreamlike state of ecstasy. She forgot where she was, forgot even that the piece was played by an eight-year-old, forgot her initial amazement at the child's ability to master the notes so perfectly.

It was more than just music, it was feeling, soul, and it stirred a forgotten melancholy within her, and something strangely familiar she could not put her finger on, only that it could be something significant. When the last notes trailed away, she remained motionless, her expression still dazed.

"Hi, Mommy." Mandy's soft voice brought her back to reality. "I didn't hear you come in."

"Hello, darling." Amanda swallowed hard and smiled at her daughter. Her knees still wobbly, she stumbled toward the perplexed girl. "That was exquisite, Mandy. You're a terrific pianist, darling. I couldn't have done it any better."

Her voice was hoarse with suppressed emotion and she

bent over to kiss the girl, moved at how Mandy's green eyes lit up at her words, her impish face suddenly beautiful.

"I didn't know you played the piano. Daddy never told us," Mandy said, moving aside to allow Amanda room on the wide stool.

"I . . . I'm not sure . . ." Amanda touched the keys of the piano and began to play, and suddenly her fingers just took over and the Mozart symphony came to life. Soon she forgot all about the little girl next to her. Swept along by the happy melody her heart began to sing with the music until, to her utter disappointment, it was all over and her fingers lay still on the black and white keys. For a moment she just sat there, wrapped up in a world of her own, yet it was a world with no link to the past she so desperately sought. And it confused her. If she could remember how to play Mozart to perfection, why could she not bring forth other recollections?

The sound of applause startled her. Like Mandy, she had not heard anyone come into the room, and seeing Brent standing there, she suddenly felt ill at ease. She was like a little girl caught in the act. Until this moment she had not known she could play the piano, or that she could play it this well, and she was not ready to share the revelation with anyone, not yet. She glanced sideways at Mandy and found the girl staring at her with open admiration, her huge green eyes echoing her bewilderment.

"I see you haven't forgotten how to play, my dear," Brent drawled as he approached them. "You always were a terrific pianist. Your daughter has inherited the same passion, haven't you, Mandy?" Amanda took Mandy's hand and squeezed it. On impulse she hugged the child and Mandy flung her arms around her neck and kissed her.

"You're more than terrific, Mommy, you're superb," she cried. Amanda laughed, a little shaky, embarrassed at the abundance of praise.

"I'm glad there's something good in me to pass on," she said, smiling. Then turning to Brent, she asked, "Aren't you early? It's not eight o'clock yet, is it?"

He shook his head. "No, but we're supposed to go to Grandmother's birthday party tonight, remember?" Amanda gasped. She had forgotten all about that. "Better get yourself ready, Louise deplores latecomers," he warned.

He held back the reproach despite the irritation he felt. It was always the same; whenever she disliked doing something, Amanda would conveniently forget about it. And he knew how she hated his grandmother. But this was a special birthday, and having lost her memory of her past, how could she possibly recall her resentment toward the woman?

"I'll tell Mrs. Flynn." Amanda gave Mandy a last quick squeeze and a watery smile and scrambled to her feet.

"Don't bother," Brent said coolly. "She knows. I told her this morning." And there's nothing wrong with *her* memory, his look implied. Before she could reply, Josh burst into the room, shrieking as a barking Kavik followed closely on his heels, jumping up against the boy, his white bushy tail wagging cheerfully. Brent busied himself with the children while Amanda hurriedly made her way upstairs.

She was almost ready, putting the last touches to her makeup and pursing her lips to view the effect of the pale red lipstick, when Brent walked into the dressing room. Again, a rush of guilt swept over her and she grabbed the hairbrush and began to furiously brush her coppery curls until they were a flaming halo around her face.

"I wish—"

"Please, Brent, don't start," she quickly interrupted him, her hands high in the air as if to ward off his reprimand. For a moment he merely stared at her, then as if she had not spoken he calmly resumed.

"—she would've given this party on a Saturday night. At least some of us could enjoy the celebration until a decent hour and not rush home because tomorrow is a workday." He disappeared into the roomy closet and Amanda slowly calmed down. Her fingers expertly placated the stubborn curls, twirling and handling them until they lay subdued and perfectly in place. With a swift swoop, she lightly sprayed hairspray over them.

Brent reappeared, dressed in a white silk shirt and black trousers, a small black bow tie in his right hand. As if this were her cue, Amanda slipped into the closet, and reaching the rack of evening gowns, stood undecided, hesitant to appear too flashy or too formal. Yet she knew that she could not look like an insignificant wallflower, either. Tonight was important, to her and to Brent, but most of all to her image, her status in the Farraday family.

"We ought to be moving, Amanda." Brent sounded impatient. He straightened his bow tie and ran a comb through his wavy blond hair one last time. Then he frowned. What the hell was she doing in there? What was taking her so long? "Amanda?" he said.

"They all hate me, don't they, your family?" Amanda spoke as her eye suddenly fell on a long sequined black dress by Dior. Its simplicity appealed to her and as the tiny black paillettes caught the light, a rainbow of colors bounced off it cheerfully, giving it just enough glitter to offset its austere design. She nervously touched the gown, deliberating. Then, resolutely, she yanked it off the hanger.

When she stepped into the dressing room, Brent's look confirmed her choice. A small sigh escaped her as she viewed herself in the mirror, and her spirits soared. She looked taller and very slender as the gown wrapped around her lithe body, falling sleek and straight down to her ankles. The sleeves, slightly puffed on top, tapered to a tight fit around her arms, while the low neckline revealed a glimpse of swelling bosom, just enough to be appealing, yet not too much to appear distasteful.

"If they didn't hate you before, they will now," Brent drawled softly.

Her appearance stirred him. He had seen her only once before in that dress, and the memory was still with him. It was the night he had let passion cloud his sense of duty and it had haunted him ever since. It was the night Yoko Hamada had died. Yet, just like that night, the effect of Amanda in that fateful dress roused him, and he turned away, disgusted with himself. Stung by the sudden arousal, his bitterness against her resurfaced and his voice was gruff when he spoke again.

"Fifteen minutes. I'll see you downstairs."

Without another word he strode out of the room, leaving Amanda to gape after him, uncertain why his mood had changed. With a sigh she tried on a short string of pearls, then decided they would not go with the outfit. Finally she chose a simple gold chain with a small diamond pendant. She quickly grabbed a pair of black high-heeled suede shoes, and with one last look into the mirror, she rushed after him.

* * *

"Oh, Mommy, you look so beautiful!" Mandy whispered as she looked up from her homework when Amanda entered the kitchen. The children preferred to do their homework in the kitchen, despite their father's instruction to do it on the table in the breakfast nook.

"Wow!" Josh tried to whistle and failed miserably. Even Kavik looked up, wagging his tail and laughing.

"Thanks, guys. With such fans, who needs a party, hm?" Amanda kissed them both, wiping the lipstick off Josh's lips with a nervous laugh.

"You've got nothing to worry about, Mrs. Farraday. You're as royal as Princess Di herself, and if you ask me, you'll knock 'em dead."

"Thank you, Mrs. Flynn. I'd better go before I lose all of my nerve." She gave the woman a quick smile, warmed by her open admiration, her approval giving her a boost of confidence. "I needed that," she whispered, nudging her arm lightly.

Brent poked his head through the opening above the counter.

"Ready? It's rush hour traffic still, Manda, so we'll need more time." He held the black mink coat invitingly, his expression cloaked, and with a last hug for the children, Amanda slipped into it.

"Have a good time, Mommy," Mandy said.

"Don't worry about the children, Mrs. Farraday, trust that they're in good hands." Mrs. Flynn gave her an encouraging smile and Amanda nodded.

Mrs. Flynn's reassuring words faded as the door closed behind them and almost noiselessly the garage door opened. Helped by Brent, Amanda slid into the passenger side of the Jaguar. Taking the driver's seat, he started the motor and the car backed into the darkness, the garage door closing before them by remote control. Swiftly, the Jag vanished into the night.

Chapter 10

LOUISE TOWNSEND FARRADAY LIKED CLASS. SHE ALSO liked convenience and eloquence, and above all, style. And the Plaza Towers was all of that. As matriarch of the Farraday clan, she ruled her family with an iron fist that both controlled and protected their interests as a group and individually. She had done it successfully for years and everyone who knew her knew not to underestimate her power or to cross her in any way. The members of her family feared her; some hated her, others disliked her, few loved her for herself, but all of them respected her and knew they could always count on her. For to Louise, the Farraday blood was sacred and her family's welfare was her preserve. Tonight, to celebrate her seventy-fifth birthday, the family had come from all corners of the world to honor her benevolence and to reassure themselves of her favors by the very fact of their presence.

The elevator doors opened directly into the Farraday penthouse. The room was full of people—the women in evening dresses that looked simple but bore the mark of money, the men in dark tailor-made suits. Slow background music, the soft tinkling of champagne glasses, hushed low voices, an occasional laugh—somehow the atmosphere resembled more a night at *The Phantom of the Opera* than a joyous birthday party.

Amanda felt a wave of panic and, for a second, she thought of pressing the down button. But as if Brent sensed her hesitation, he firmly took her arm. The next instant the elevator doors closed behind them and she could hear it buzz away. This was a nightmare, she thought, trying to heed Paula's warning not to bite her lip. She was supposed to know all these people, relatives and close friends of the Farraday clan, but none of their faces was familiar. As she passed them, they became a blur, and after a few minutes even the most curious glances began to elude her. She heard her name whispered; from time to time a hand touched her and she forced a smile that did not quite reach her eyes. The atmosphere depressed her. Looking around at some of the solemn faces, she wondered if they remembered that this was supposed to be a momentous occasion.

All during the drive downtown she had been silent, wondering about the reception she would receive from people she was supposed to know intimately. Now and then Brent had tried to start a conversation, but the idle talk had only made her more nervous, and when the Jaguar reached the Chicago Loop, she was clenching and unclenching her clammy hands and grateful for the darkness in the car. Briefly, she recalled the fiasco of the other night. And those were supposedly her friends. These people had no love for her at all; how could she expect to survive the evening?

As they moved along now, her hand clamping the crook of Brent's arm, she felt the perspiration break out, yet outwardly she forced herself to appear composed and undaunted by the staring eyes and the whispers that followed them. Proceeding further into the room, the other guests automatically made way for them, except for a couple of uniformed staff who in passing offered them hors d'oeuvres and champagne, which Brent politely declined.

"Ah, Amanda." An elegant woman blocked their path, her arms outstretched. "Even after all these years, you look fabulous." Ignoring the younger woman's lack of response she hugged her, then held her at arm's length for a brief moment. "My, my, I must say you've managed to defy my son's authority during your hibernation. Don't get me wrong, my dear, I always knew you would look splendid with short hair, but then, who am I?" Lady Madeline Stanhope-Hill suddenly chuckled, and offered her cheek to Brent. "Has your grand-mother . . . ?"

"It's good to see you, Mother. Did you manage to tear Sir Giles away from the horse races or has he given you carte blanche to buy out Saks or Neiman Marcus, or both?" Brent kissed her lightly and fondly put his arm around her bare shoulders.

She was a tall woman, blond and statuesque, with traces of beauty still lingering on her smooth face. Standing next to Brent, Amanda marveled at the resemblance between mother and son. Lady Madeline feigned indignation at his insinuation, but her blue eyes shone.

"Don't be silly, my boy. Do you think your stepfather would let me out of his sight without a proper chaperon?"

"Ah! And who is it this time? One of his polo protégés?"

"Me." Slender, just as tall, although a little less statuesque, a younger version of Lady Madeline had quietly joined them.

Like her mother she wore a black evening dress by Gala-nos, her long blond hair falling in heavy waves past her bare, ivory shoulders. Amanda felt the young woman's eyes on her and her breath caught sharply at the intense hostility of the cold blue eyes. Karen, she thought wildly, where is Karen tonight? She had promised she would be here early, even if Daryl had to attend to a last-minute emergency.

"Hello, Amanda," she said. "Did you finally tire of sowing your wild oats, or is this appearance temporary?"

Brent quickly put his other arm around his wife's, a silent warning in his eyes.

"I see that living in civilized Europe has not cooled off your revolutionary spirit, Alison." They locked gazes and it seemed forever before Alison's wavered.

"Well, I see my brother has rekindled his passion, or shall we say lust, for the little woman?" she taunted.

"Beware, Princess Alison, this is the U.S., not the jungle. And in my territory you will behave like a civilized individual."

Alison's eyes flashed, and for a moment Amanda saw raw hatred so fierce she winced. Instantly Brent's arm tightened around her shoulder.

"Am I interrupting this happy family reunion?" a man's voice said.

Madeline sighed audibly with relief and laughed. She

hooked her arm into the newcomer's, but he only had eyes for Amanda. Broad-shouldered and not quite as tall as Brent, in his mid-sixties and white-haired, he breathed utter sophistication and a suaveness that would titillate many a young woman's fancy. His presence commanded immediate attention, yet his eyes were warm and kind and observant.

"You must be Amanda." He took her hand and kissed it, his sharp eyes never leaving her flushed face. He smiled at her surprise. "Come, child, Louise is wondering why it's taking you so long to reach her throne." With that he led her away, with Brent and Madeline on their heels. "By the way, I'm Jonathan Bramston, an old friend of this family." He smiled again, and patted her hand reassuringly.

In the next room, Louise Farraday stood talking to an elderly couple and their daughter, her back to the guests in the adjoining room. But at the newcomers' approach, as if she had eyes in her back, she turned and her gaze fixed on Amanda.

She was a small woman, petite, deceptively dainty, and very feminine, looking not a day older than sixty as she stood erect and perfectly still. Her regal posture emanated strength and authority and she held her head proudly above the small straight shoulders. She wore her silver-white hair parted in the middle, letting it fall in soft waves at the back of her neck where it huddled together in a loose knot, expertly held by invisible hairpins.

A handsome woman. Her heart-shaped face, almost elfin in form, still bore traces of youth and natural beauty. And at first glance, that same face with the straight aristocratic nose and the small gentle mouth seemed quite harmless. But one had only to look at her eyes, sharp and alert and very steady, to realize the quiet determination inside.

As those cool ice-blue eyes bored into hers, Amanda stiffened. A cold wave of nausea swept over her, threatening to suck the breath out of her lungs. She swallowed and willed herself not to look away, and to the curious people around her she seemed cool and undaunted.

"It's gratifying to see that your looks have improved in four years, Amanda." Louise spoke slowly, her smooth voice level.

"Happy birthday, Louise. It's good to find you well," Amanda responded. She felt the hairs on the back of her neck rise and it was with sheer willpower that she suppressed a shiver.

"Are we to assume you'll stick around for a while? At least until you've regained your memory?"

A tense silence fell in the room. Amanda remained very still, and once again it was Lady Madeline who came to her rescue.

"Come now, Mother, it's time we started serving dinner," she said. "It's past seven o'clock and I'm sure everyone is famished." Madeline was almost breathless, her face flushed at her own courage. And as if he feared Louise would brush off her daughter-in-law's suggestion, Jonathan quickly volunteered his services.

"Shall I tell the caterers, my dear? I'm sure some of your guests have begun to wonder if they would ever be fed." His short amicable laugh was disarming. "It won't do to ruin your hospitable reputation, now would it?"

After a moment, the flicker in Louise's eyes dimmed and she nodded. The room began to breathe again; chatter resumed in soft tones and the tableau dissolved, gathering around and toward the dinner table. Brent put his arm around his grandmother's shoulder and hugged her fondly.

"Happy birthday, old girl, and many, many more," he said, kissing her soft cheek and marveling at the smoothness and lack of wrinkles. He grinned. "If I didn't know any better I'd say you'd had a couple of face lifts, or that you lied about the year of your birth just to marry my grandfather."

Louise laughed, the smile extending to her blue eyes, and she looked even younger. Brent was her favorite grandson, the pride of her life, the only passion she had after her husband passed away ten years before. She held a soft spot in her heart for him and he was the only one who could actually make her laugh. His compliments and flirty quips had a miraculous effect on her; they made her feel young again, and mischievous. The only other person who could defy her and whom she allowed to tear down her defenses was Jonathan; yet even he was not able to bring out the carefree spirit she relished in Brent's presence.

"Liar." She smiled, brushing her hand lightly across his cheek. Then, serious once more, she looked him deep in the eye. "Are you glad she's back, darling?"

Brent casually turned around and, seeing Amanda's attention occupied by his mother, he smiled ruefully. "It's too soon to tell," he replied evasively, then quickly added, "But the kids are. Whatever the reason she left before, she seems to genuinely care about them, and they love having a real live mother around. We have to give her time. And you will too, won't you?" He eyed her sternly, but she only sighed.

"I won't see you unhappy, Brent, no exceptions." Her blue eyes followed Amanda pensively. "I must admit she looks good tonight. It seems she's outgrown the harlot look." Louise grimaced. "Of course, it could be an act to win herself back into our good graces, yours and mine."

Turning back to her grandson, she hooked her hand through his arm.

"You're right, let's give her time."

Arm in arm they moved toward the dinner table, where a delicious-looking buffet had been laid out.

"Well now, Amanda, what brings you back to this neck of the woods? Hm, wait. Let me guess." Alison scooped the olive out of her martini and placed it in her mouth. "I've got it. The money, right? You smelled the money." She let out a short, sharp laugh.

Amanda winced. "Wha-what . . . money?" She forced herself not to lower her eyes.

"You know, that delicious filthy green that rustles between your fingers, and that can give tarts like you an orgasm just by thinking about it." Alison sneered as she sucked on another olive. Her eyes flashed triumphantly when Amanda flinched, and seeing the pallor in the shocked woman's face, she laughed.

"So, you've lost your memory, eh, Amanda? I must say, that's a good one. Original, even coming from you." She emptied her glass and chuckled. "How odd that your subconscious still remembers Brent's inheritance. And how you simply loathe the idea of charity."

"Charity, did someone mention my favorite subject?" Lady Madeline whirled around to snatch a glass of champagne from a passing server and smiled. "Now, which charity organization has been under scrutiny here?" She took a gulp of champagne. "Hmm, there's Karen, finally," she said. And raising her glass to salute the newcomer, she heaved a deep sigh and downed it.

* * *

Following her mother-in-law's gaze, Amanda's eyes lit up. She mumbled an excuse and swiftly worked her way through the crowd.

"Good God, Karen! I've been looking all over for you."

Karen looked at Amanda's flushed face, and sensing her sister-in-law's agitation, she grinned sheepishly, feeling guilty for her late arrival.

"I can't teach that husband of mine new tricks," she said, grimacing. "I'm sorry, Manda, I should know better than to make promises I can't keep." She stopped and turned Amanda around. "Wow, you look like a million dollars, old girl. I can't wait till Alison sees you."

"She already has," Amanda retorted wryly, and made a face when Karen burst out laughing.

"Oh, she has, has she? From the look on your face I can see she was duly impressed."

Amanda shot her a reproachful look.

"Wipe that silly frown off your face, will you?" Karen rolled her eyes. "Alison is an asshole, even if she is my sister. And a pompous one at that. Totally worthless, if you ask me. Did you meet her husband? Prince Armand what's-his-face. He's worse. For what it's worth, they deserve each other." She looked around and grabbed Amanda's arm. "I don't know about you, but there's a comfortable-looking sofa in that corner that's just begging for me to plunk into."

Amanda laughed and followed the waddling Karen who, with a sigh of utter exhaustion, planted her heavy body on the deserted couch.

"How do you feel?" she asked, watching her pregnant sister-in-law's tired face with concern. "You shouldn't have come. I'm sure your grandmother would've understood."

Karen forced a faint smile, shifting her weight to a more comfortable position.

"I'm sure she would've, but I'm okay, really. Besides, this is one of the few times Daryl and I have been out together recently, and I wanted to feel normal." She sighed, stroking her big belly. "And I wouldn't miss seeing Alison claw into you. Let me know if she turns green during the course of the evening, will you?"

"Well, well, what have we here? You look absolutely stunning tonight, Manda, real foxy. If we weren't in Her Highness's domain, I would whistle." Daryl joined them, a plate in his hands. "I can hardly wait till my wife can command everybody's looks of pure envy, hatred, and lust again."

"You're a disgusting degenerate, and if you weren't the father of my child, I'd kick your ass." Karen grinned good-humoredly.

"Watch your mouth, woman. Louise would not likely approve of your choice of vocabulary, not to mention your baby's delicate ears."

"Speaking of Louise, I'd better go and say hello to her before I get too comfortable in here." Karen eyed the plate in her husband's hand with disapproval. "Aren't you ashamed of yourself? Haven't I taught you manners?"

Daryl laughed and crammed his mouth with food. "Speak for yourself, lady. I have hugged and kissed Her Highness ages ago, not like some people who sit down on couches the moment they arrive."

With a groan, Karen lifted herself up from the sofa. "Save a place for me, will you, Amanda? Be right back."

Carefully she made her way toward where she had last seen her grandmother.

Amanda leaned back against the sofa and for the first time that evening she smiled. Casually glancing around the crowded room, she finally felt herself unwind. The tensions of the hours before gradually ebbed. Soon she even dared to whisk a glass of champagne off a passing server's tray. Taking a sip, she turned to sit down, and froze. Her gaze was suspended in the grip of dark, glaring malevolence. Her breath caught in her throat at the cold hatred in the stranger's eyes—ripping, skewering her, inch by inch, burning holes through her rigid body.

Amanda swallowed. She could hear the blood sizzle in her ears. A familiar dread whipped through her stunned subconscious and instinctively her hand reached to ease the constriction in her chest. She was mindless of the glass dropping and shattering on the floor, or of the champagne spilling over her dress. A woman next to her gasped. As if in a trance, Amanda looked at the wet spot on her dress. A server rushed to hand her a towel and clean up the mess at her feet, and she mechanically dabbed at the moist fabric.

When she looked up again, she wondered what she'd been thinking of. The malicious watcher was gone.

"What happened to your dress?" Karen asked, frowning. She had returned with a plate in her hand, licking her fingers and trying to ignore Daryl's disapproving look. "I'm gone less than ten minutes and you . . . Amanda? Are you okay?"

Still dazed, Amanda slowly nodded. Helplessly, she turned to Daryl, but seeing the empty plate in his hand, she sighed—a long, trembling sigh.

"How about another glass of champagne?" he offered, oblivious to her dismay.

"You . . . did you see her . . . ?" Amanda whispered, her big eyes pleading.

"See who?" Daryl blinked, feeling guilty for having wolfed down the food; it had been his first meal since the night before and he was grateful Karen had not seen him inhale that first helping.

"That . . . that woman . . ." Amanda glanced around furtively.

"What woman?" Karen prodded.

"Never mind." Amanda shook her head. Mumbling an excuse, she left the room in search of a bathroom.

The bathroom in the hall was occupied, with a number of people waiting in line for their turn.

"There's another one in Louise's bedroom," one of the women told her, and nodding her thanks, Amanda turned and walked down the corridor.

Passing two closed doors, she paused in front of a third and, without hesitation, pushed it open. Inside, more people were waiting their turn, and with a sigh, she leaned her head against the wall and closed her eyes.

She was certain she had not imagined the woman. There had been utter malice in her glare. And venom. But more than that, there had been a deadly threat. A warning, vengeful and insidious, so fierce it had curdled her blood. But why? Who was she? What had she done to deserve such hatred?

Amanda shuddered, all of a sudden cold.

Flushing the toilet, she went to wash her hands and, looking for a towel, found none. She walked over to the louvered linen closet in the adjacent dressing room and opened it. Reaching for a guest towel, she suddenly stiffened.

How did she know where to find Louise's towels? How, too, had she known where the second bathroom was—which room to enter? Had something triggered her subconscious? Had something perhaps jarred the doors to her dormant memory banks and made her act out of habit? A rush of exhilaration gripped her and, her heart pounding, she turned.

"I can't imagine why she would come back after all these years," a surly voice said.

"I can," another replied. "She probably heard about the doxy her husband has been seeing, and you know Amanda. She never could stand being second fiddle, her ego wouldn't take that."

Amanda stopped dead in her tracks. The voices were female and from their tone she sensed they were not friendly. Her heart pounded and the towel slipped from her hands. It was happening again, she thought, and closed her eyes for a moment. Then she opened them again. Better to stop this eavesdropping; it was more than she could handle.

"So what? She's not the first tart Brent has been involved with, and if you ask me, she won't be the last, either."

"That's where you're wrong. Rumors have it he's quite serious this time. And I bet the bitch heard the same rumors. The fact that she's back in his bed confirms it."

Amanda felt sick. How could she have been so blind? No wonder Brent was not happy to see her. Now she also understood why he had refused to share her bed. Could it be the good-looking young woman he was talking to? Louise had seemed quite at ease while talking with the two of them earlier, which could only mean that she approved of her grandson's choice. It would also explain the old woman's blatant hostility toward her. Amanda weaved, her knees weak, and she leaned against the wall to keep from falling. People around her talked and giggled, but the voices in the next room were the only ones she heard.

"Do you think Brent will drop the little tramp?"

"Does he have a choice? You can count on that bitch of a wife of his to make his life miserable one way or another."

Amanda closed her eyes again. She wanted to scream at them, make them stop saying those vicious things, but before she could move they walked away, their voices fading as they left the bedroom.

"Are you all right?" A kind, elderly face peered at her with a look of concern in her friendly eyes. A second pair of eyes darted before her, viewing her with open curiosity. Slowly Amanda nodded, her hands clutching the wall behind her. The first woman muttered something to the second one and they quickly left the dressing room.

"What's going on here . . . my God, Amanda, are you all right?" Louise frowned at her ashen face. "Have you eaten anything? Good heavens, girl, come, no wonder you're faint." She grabbed Amanda's arm firmly and led her back to the living room where she seated her in a comfortable chair.

As if from nowhere Brent appeared, his expression worried. But before he could fire the same question, Louise ordered him to bring some food. Dazed, Amanda wanted to tell them that she wasn't hungry and that all she wanted was to be left alone and spared the agony of seeing Brent with that young woman who she knew was somewhere lurking in this very room, waiting for her to release her husband to her. Yet the words never left her lips and soon Brent returned with a full plate. Under Louise's watchful eyes, Amanda slowly ate, swallowing automatically, too numb to fight the two of them.

As her strength returned so did her spirit. And when she looked up and into Brent's gray penetrating eyes, she knew she could not—would not give him up. She was back in his life now and she would fight to stay there.

Chapter 11

"YOU ARE OFFERING ME MONEY TO LEAVE MY FAMILY?" Amanda's expression was incredulous, her big eyes wide with disbelief.

"Two hundred and fifty thousand, a quarter of a million dollars," Louise repeated calmly.

Amanda slowly leaned back in her chair, a feeling of dread seeping through her numb body. Louise Farraday had called her earlier that morning and invited her over for lunch at the penthouse. She had not wanted to go, but Paula had laughed at her reluctance, and when she called him at the hospital, Brent had seemed so pleased at his grandmother's friendly gesture. She looked at the old woman at the other end of the lounge table and the breath choked in her throat at the sharp, piercing look Louise gave her. Swallowing, she managed to sit up straight and clear her throat.

"If you're trying to buy me out—"

"Not trying, my dear. I am."

Smiling sweetly, Louise picked up the bottle of Chardonnay and refilled the glasses. As soon as he had served them lunch, she had waved Kam away and the butler had understood her wish for privacy. She took a sip of her wine and watched Amanda digest her blunt statement.

Observing her the other night, she had been impressed by the new Amanda. It wasn't just the absence of that dreadful heavy makeup—Louise shivered at the recollection—or even the new hairdo—and she especially approved of this hairdo—it was more. The face was the same, the eyes as mesmerizing, but the expression was softer, gentler, and there was a vulnerability about her that was both disarming and appealing. Subtle differences, a serene dignity, a more beguiling openness—the glamorous image replaced by a certain class that made her appear warmer, and yes, more attractive.

"Why?" Amanda whispered. "Why do you hate me so?"

Louise took another sip. "It has nothing to do with my feelings, or me for that matter."

"Then why? Why would you want to get rid of me?"

"It's best for everybody. You're like the plague, Amanda. You destroy everybody you touch. Perhaps you're not aware of it yourself, but the fact remains that you do. And your family is too precious to me; I won't have them suffer the misery you once put them through. Not again."

"Do they look miserable to you?"

Louise waved her jeweled hand impatiently, a frown on her brow.

"Everything's still new to you now, but it'll all come back. In time you'll regain your memory and you'll be up to your old tricks again. I won't allow that."

Amanda took a deep breath, willing herself to remain calm. The audacity of the woman! How dare she play God, savior and judge, all in one. She stared out of the broad window that overlooked the blue waters of Lake Michigan. But the serenity eluded her. She did not see the colorful boats or the spectacular view. All she knew was that her present position was being threatened, and that her opponent was relentless.

"You may try all you want, Mrs. Farraday," she said coldly, struggling to keep her composure, "but I'm here to stay. You can keep your lousy money. I'm not for sale." Her voice was but a whisper, and as she spoke, anger began building within.

Louise watched her change of mood, saw the awakening fire in Amanda's eyes that made them turn a bright green, and despite herself, her admiration grew for the woman's defiance. Reluctantly, she recalled another occasion when she had seen Amanda's anger; the circumstances had been of a different nature then, but the reaction was similar. She couldn't help wondering if this too was a bluff.

Bitterly, she remembered Amanda's greedy nature. That and the girl's selfishness. They had caused her beloved Brent heartache and misery that would put all the daytime soap operas to shame. How in the world such a bright young man could fall for this woman's tricks was beyond her. And when he could have had any female in Cook County.

"It's an awful lot of money, Amanda. Think of what you could do with it. You're young, attractive, and— Sit down!" Louise did not raise her voice, but the cutting edge made Amanda wince. Still, she remained standing, her face pale, her lips trembling.

"This meeting is over. If you'll excuse me—"

"All right, you win. Half a million. In cash."

Amanda grabbed the table to steady herself.

"You don't understand, do you? You're asking me to give up my children, to leave Brent . . ." Her eyes suddenly lit up. "That's it, isn't it? You want me to leave Brent. And in the interim, you don't give a damn if the children suffer. My God, Louise, what kind of a grandmother are you?"

For the first time that afternoon, Louise Farraday flinched. Still, she did not lose her cool.

"A very concerned one." Her voice matched Amanda's coldness. "And you're wrong; it's precisely because I do care about them that I'm asking you to disappear. Better now, before they get too attached to you again."

"No, it's you who are wrong. The children, *my* children, need me. They need a mother. Whatever I have done in the past, whatever I was, I am what I am now, and this me now cares about their welfare, their feelings, their needs. I don't remember yesterday, but I do know the present, and the present me loves them. No amount of money can drive me away from them." She was breathless, her head ached terribly, and she swayed, drained.

"You're a fool, Amanda. Better drop the theatrics or I'll start believing you." Louise folded her hands on her lap, her gaze steady, determined not to betray the emotion she felt. "Listen to yourself. All this talk about *your* children. What of Brent? What makes you think he's so happy having you around *his* children? And what about his welfare, his feelings, his needs, hm?" She felt a momentary triumph as she saw Amanda cringe and bite her lip.

"Think it over. My offer stands, at least for a little while."

"So does my answer," Amanda intoned. "It's *no*. Not now, not ever. And if I go, if I ever leave, it will be for their sake and because I love them, not because of your blood money!"

She turned and headed for the door. Then, as she stepped into the elevator, she looked back and straight into Louise's eyes. "As for Brent, you underestimate him. He's a big boy now and, I assure you, quite capable of holding his own. You ought to give him more credit."

The door closed softly behind her and Louise sank back in her chair. She felt old and tired and tears slowly trickled down her cheeks as the echo of Amanda's last words trailed across the room. Of all the people in her family, why did it have to be this one who managed to strike a chord and penetrate through to her inner fears? For it was pity she had heard in that young voice.

Inside the elevator, Amanda began to shake. No—she gritted her teeth and bit her lip hard—she mustn't cry, not here! It was horrible. That bitch. How could she! Why? Why had she done this to her? What had she done to Brent that his grandmother wanted her out of his life? That it was worth half a million dollars and a lot of pain? She groaned, blinking hard. Whose pain? She could still see Louise's cool face, the blatant determination . . . my God, she had wanted to inflict the pain, deliberately and without mercy. An involuntary sob escaped her and she put her hands against her pounding head, the harsh words still ringing in her ears.

The elevator stopped and the doors opened. Amanda stumbled out and blindly fled the building into the cool air. She did not wait for the doorman to hail a cab for her and ran up Lake Shore Drive, the tears now flowing. Impatiently, she brushed them away to clear her vision, but they kept coming and she couldn't hold back the sobs. She did not notice the curious stares around her and kept on walking, until, finally, exhausted, she sat down on a street bench and closed her eyes. The buzzing in her ears intensified. She felt like screaming, the pain in the back of her head now sharp and unbearable. Slowly opening her eyes, she got up and hailed a taxi.

The Chicago and Northwestern train station was almost deserted at that time of day. Rush hour had not yet begun. Her train would not leave for another twenty minutes. Reaching a pay phone she called Paula to meet her at the Lake Forest depot, refusing to give any details of her visit. Then she slowly headed for the train. Good thing she had listened to Paula; she was in no shape to drive a car right now. Not that the thought of driving a car had enticed her this morning—the idea alone made her queasy. She knew that sooner or later she would have to overcome her fear, but today was not the time.

She was the first to board the commuter train, and with a sigh, Amanda slumped into an empty seat. Resting her aching head, she closed her eyes. What was it that woman had said about Brent? "What about his welfare, his feelings, his needs?" Now, all alone, she did not feel so cocky anymore. All the courage had left her, and she felt drained, and suddenly scared. What kind of a dreadful person was she that people hated her so? What had she done to them? First Nicole and Niels, then Alison, and even Daryl had seemed overly cautious. And Brent.

A sharp pain pierced her at the thought of him. She still remembered that first time she had seen him in the doorway of her hospital room, tall and blond and handsome. And each time afterward his presence had made her heart lurch. Had she felt this way about him four years ago, she wondered? Then she remembered the look on his face, the cold hostile expression, the lack of joy at seeing her again.

They were having problems, he had said. What kind of problems? Why had he not so much as touched her, or was that the problem? They occupied the same bedroom, yet all this time he had not approached her. Were the gossips at the party right? Was there, perhaps, another woman? After all, she had been gone four years. But he always came home nights, early enough to spend some time with the children before their bedtime.

People began to fill the empty seats, some throwing curious glances at the sleeping young woman in the back seat. The conductor signaled and the train slowly began to move. Collecting tickets, he briefly glanced at her, then at her ticket, and made a mental note to wake her at her stop.

The train pulled out of the station heading north to Chicago's suburban areas and began to increase its speed.

Amanda briefly opened her eyes, viewed the bleak scenery through a dust-streaked window, and closed them again.

Brent, she groaned silently, oh Brent. It had only been four weeks since her return, but his presence, even the thought of him, made her warm inside. The lightest touch of his hand, the kindest word, his puzzled glances in her direction—they made her tingle. And each day she looked forward to hearing his voice on the telephone. Whatever problems they were having, she was convinced that it was not because she did not care for him.

My God! Her eyes flew open for a moment, bewildered at the revelation. *I'm in love with my own husband!* Barely a month, and she felt like a teenager with her first boyfriend. Only this suitor didn't stalk his prey with the romantic eagerness a girl dreams about. On the contrary, he'd done his utmost to keep his distance.

Amanda stirred and sighed. Her thoughts wandered to the children. They were truly a blessing. If Brent was cool and aloof, Mandy and Josh made up for his lack of friendly emotions. And she had meant what she said to Louise—she adored those youngsters.

She had attended Josh's award presentation and gone to see Mandy's ballet rehearsals, and she had felt the proud parent all over. They had introduced her to their respective teachers, who had shared their joy and enthusiasm in meeting her. It was gratifying to be wanted and she cherished every moment she shared with the children.

How could she ever have left them? There must have been an urgent reason, something terribly important, something earthshaking—although she could hardly think of anything that was so drastic she would abandon them . . . or their father . . . And like so many times before, another, more frightening thought plagued her.

Images of makeup bottles that filled her with disgust, flimsy dresses she detested, martinis she disliked—flashing through her mind with horrifying clarity . . . She closed her eyes. No! A silent scream welled from deep within her. Fear flooded her senses, clawing at the threshold of logic, and she shook her head, desperately clinging on to the dam that barred her from facing a possibility that seemed worse than the shadows surrounding her.

*   *   *

Stepping out of the train she saw Paula standing next to the little black BMW, frantically waving her long arms. A brief grin flashed across Amanda's face, exposing two mischievous dimples and momentarily erasing the fatigue lines. Thank God for Paula, she thought warmly, and quickly walked over to her excited friend.

"Jesus, I was afraid I'd miss you. That damn traffic . . ." Paula hugged her, pretending not to notice her friend's tear-stained face. "Quick, hop in. You can tell me all about it in the car."

"You really should stop parking in illegal zones, you know," Amanda said, sliding into the passenger seat.

"And miss charming those handsome young cops out of a ticket? Not on your life." Paula turned sideways and looked her friend deep in the eye. "Are you all right?"

Amanda only nodded, the lump returning to her throat.

"That bad?" Paula's husky voice was unusually soft, and it was all that Amanda could take. She suddenly burst into tears, letting herself go, not even trying to hold in the sobs that racked her shaking body.

"Oh, shit!" Forgetting about the cops, Paula reached out and cradled her, rocking gently.

"Are you going to tell Brent about this?"

They were seated in Paula's kitchen drinking hot coffee. The children were at Amanda's playing computer games under Mrs. Flynn's watchful eye, and even Wesley had let himself be persuaded to tackle Josh's newest arcade challenge. It was past four in the afternoon and the two women were all talked out.

"No, I don't think so. At least not tonight," Amanda said.

Paula did not contradict her, but her otherwise happy face was clouded. That bitch! She had always known Louise Farraday was a tough cookie, but this took the cake.

It had taken a while for Amanda to stop crying and then all she could say was: "Oh, God, it was awful!" Paula had listened to the whole sordid story, and in the end felt as angry as Amanda at Louise's insolence.

She knew of the old woman's reputation, and that everyone in the Farraday clan was intimidated by her, but this . . . this was ridiculous! And here Amanda sat, silently miserable, staring at the cup in her hands. Paula reached out and gently touched her.

"Why don't you and Brent come for dinner tonight? We'll have spaghetti and wine, and we'll talk. Or not talk," she hastily corrected herself, seeing the startled look in Amanda's big tawny eyes. "Whichever you prefer. It might be easier on you, love, having company."

Amanda did not answer her, still playing with the cup in her hands. She felt numb, the ache in her head now dulled by aspirins. The doubts that had nagged her earlier resurfaced.

"Tell me, Paula, why did I leave?" Amanda put the question bluntly.

It was Paula's turn to be startled. "I . . . I don't know . . . You just . . . disappeared. No note, no phone call, nothing, no explanation."

"Did . . . did Brent and I . . . were we having problems?"

"What kind of problems? What do you mean?"

"You know . . . problems."

Paula shifted uncomfortably in her chair.

"Cara, you and Brent were a very lively couple, always have been for as long as we have known you. Always arguing, always disagreeing, but then, you were married, and married couples do these things.

Amanda sighed. There it was again, that evasiveness, or was it caution?

"Stop sparing me, Paula," she pleaded. "Stop sparing my feelings. Damn it, help me. You're my best friend. Can't you tell me truth?"

"Darling, I don't know the truth. Only Brent can tell you that. You weren't exactly honeymooners, but who is? You should see Matt and me go at it sometimes."

"All right, then tell me about me. Am I such a bitch that my own friends and relatives hate me so?"

"You mustn't go by Nikki. She was jealous of you. You were the life of the party no matter where you went and our spoiled Nicole couldn't handle that."

"You should've seen Alison."

"Alison? Oh, Brent's sister, the princess something-or-other." Paula shrugged. "I wouldn't let her bother me, either. From what I've heard . . . Oh, hell, you weren't the most saintly person on the block, and you could be difficult sometimes, and goddamn stubborn, and people didn't always like your sharp tongue, but other than that . . ." Paula's expression softened. "I didn't always agree with you, but we had fun together and you never hurt anybody."

"Then how do you explain Louise's move?" Amanda prodded. "And Brent . . ." She bit her lip, the tears coming back.

"What about Brent? What did he say?"

Amanda shook her head. She was not quite ready to talk about Brent. But Paula persisted. The time was ripe.

"Amanda, what about Brent?"

"It . . . it's not what he says, he doesn't say anything."

"Then what?"

"It's just . . . he's acting as if . . ."

"Yes?"

"As if . . . well, he's not very happy to see me . . ."

"Cara, it must be your imagination."

"My God, Paula, I've been gone four years and he hasn't even—"

Amanda stopped, realizing she had almost allowed her friend into her bedroom.

"Hasn't what?"

"Talked about us, about why I left . . . ," she said quickly. Too quickly, Paula thought. What was it that Amanda had really wanted to say?

"Look, darling, whatever it was, it's not important anymore. You're back now and that's all that counts." She hesitated. "For what it's worth, you've changed. For the better. You've mellowed, you're calmer, more mature, softer. Not that you've lost your wit or sense of humor, but you're not as . . . as snippy anymore, or as moody."

She watched Amanda twirl the coffee cup between her slender fingers, and noting the faraway look in her eyes, she somehow doubted that her friend had heard a word she said.

"Paula . . . do you like me?"

Paula's heart lurched at the unexpected question. A flippant reply danced at the tip of her tongue, but seeing Amanda's misery she felt the temptation die.

"Of course, silly. I love you. You're my soul mate, remember?"

"No, I mean . . . really like me?"

Paula's eyes widened. "I told you . . ."

"What if I . . . I'm not . . . your friend?" Amanda

swallowed a couple of times. "What if . . . I'm not Amanda . . . ?" She bit her lower lip to restrain the trembling.

Paula's eyes widened even further. For a moment she just stared, barely noticing the tension that had taken hold of the woman across from her.

"What are you saying? Of course you're Amanda. Who else would you be?" A light suddenly dawned and a flicker of anger sparked in her dark brown eyes. "Is that what Louise told you? Is she . . . my God, that bitch! Why, of all the—"

"No, no. Louise has nothing to do with this. I just thought—"

"Well, you stop thinking this way this instant, you hear?" Paula jumped up. "Jesus, she really got to you, didn't she? Shit, girl, you listen to me, and listen good! Louise may be Brent's grandmother, but she has no right to intimidate you or take advantage of your memory loss. Why . . . poisoning and planting dirty insinuations of this kind in your mind when you . . . It's sick, I tell you, downright sick!"

Chapter 12

IT SNOWED THE DAY BEFORE THANKSGIVING. A LIGHT powdery snow, but snow nevertheless, and before long, the ground was all white. Amanda loved it. Looking out the kitchen window she felt exhilarated, and for the first time since she had come home, she realized, she was actually happy. Perhaps "content" was a better word. Somehow she felt a peace she hadn't known since that fateful day she had awakened in the hospital. Had it only been six weeks since then? It seemed like a lifetime.

The phone rang and she picked up the kitchen extension. "Sorry, did I wake you?" It was Brent. He sounded harried, but her heart sang just to hear his voice, and her spirits soared even higher.

"No, of course not. It's almost ten o'clock."

"Daryl can't make it tomorrow night. Karen had a false alarm this morning and he feels she needs to take it easy."

"Is it serious?"

"No, I don't think so. He just wants to play it safe, I guess, and Karen can hardly walk with all that weight. Besides, he feels a little guilty having his mother stay home alone."

"I'll call Karen. Thanks for telling me. Not that it makes much of a difference; Mrs. Flynn left to pick up the turkey half an hour ago."

"Good idea. Call her; it'll cheer her up." Brent paused. "By the way, I talked to Grandmother. She seemed to understand."

I bet she did. Amanda grimaced, grateful he couldn't see her. "I'm glad," she said.

"Just one second." She could hear muffled voices, then Brent's crisp instructions. "Okay, I'd better go now. I don't think I'll be late tonight," he finished. He hesitated for a moment, and Amanda waited. "If you want to we can stop by for a drink tonight."

He asked her to hold on again, and Amanda's mind raced; she had to find a solid excuse not to go. She had not seen Louise since the disastrous luncheon and she did not feel up to seeing her again this soon.

It had not been easy to convince Brent that they should spend Thanksgiving at home, just the four of them. They had argued for two days—Thanksgiving was the annual dinner gathering of the Farraday clan and he had felt disloyal for breaking the tradition—but in the end he had given in. And when Paula suggested they celebrate it together, his reluctance waned; Mandy and Josh disliked the dinners at their great-grandmother's where there were no children their age, and he knew they enjoyed the Manchione children's company. *No,* Amanda thought, *I'm not going to let that old bitch ruin my evening, I'll pretend I'm not feeling well, I—*

"Hello, hello, Amanda, are you there?" Brent's impatient voice interrupted her thoughts.

"Yes, I'm here. We'll talk about it tonight, although I'm not sure I'll have time."

"What are you talking about? Why won't you have time?"

"Well . . . I still have to bake. Oh, and I did promise the children I'd make them a surprise dessert."

"What about Mrs. Flynn? Isn't she doing all the cooking?"

"Yes, of course, but I promised to help. And . . . and Paula . . ."

"Look, I have no time to discuss this right now. I'm due in OR in less than ten minutes. When you call Karen you can let her know all the reasons why you can't go see her tonight. I'm sure she'll understand. See you at dinner."

The phone went dead and Amanda looked at the receiver, feeling foolish and relieved at the same time. Karen! And all this time she thought he meant Louise. She began to giggle. Good Lord, of course Mrs. Flynn could handle all the cooking. Paula would come after lunch and the two of them would make the surprise dessert. And Brent would shake his head tonight when she told him she had changed her mind and had time to go see Karen after all. Why not, wasn't it, after all, her prerogative as a woman? With a broad grin that showed her dimples, she picked up the phone and dialed Karen's number.

It was the best Thanksgiving dinner they'd ever had. Or so Josh proclaimed, seconded by the two girls. Even Wesley agreed. Sitting quietly beside him, Mrs. Flynn smiled, her small wrinkled face beaming. Despite her protestations, Amanda had insisted the housekeeper share their table, hosting the festivities herself while assigning the carving of the roasted turkey to Brent. Brent had looked at her with surprise: the old Amanda would have shuddered at the mere thought of mingling with the hired help.

"God, Manda, that was the juiciest piece of turkey I've tasted in years. You must give Paula the recipe sometime." Matt leaned back in his chair, stroking his stomach and grinning.

"I had nothing to do with it." Amanda laughed, and gestured to the other side of the table. "The honor goes to Mrs. Flynn, our superchef of the evening."

Matt bowed. "My compliments, dear lady. These people don't deserve you. We'll talk later, let's say, over a bottle of champagne, hm? I'm sure we can find a more suitable compensation for your exquisite talents."

They all laughed and raised their wine glasses to salute the blushing chef.

The surprise dessert was a huge success. Caramel custard flanked by rich chocolate mousse topped with the creamiest of whipped cream. Amanda glowed as they all dug in, and she grinned at Paula on hearing the audible moans of delight. Paula signaled "thumbs up" and grinned back. The children had theirs with vanilla ice cream, the adults with a dash of Drambuie, and within minutes, the dish had vanished.

"Wow, that was the bestest of all foods." Josh sighed, licking his lips.

And nobody corrected him.

* * *

It was almost midnight when the phone rang. They were sitting in front of the fireplace, laughing and talking and sipping champagne. Towering over her, Matt stroked Paula's hair, as she nestled comfortably between his legs on the floor, rubbing her cheeks against his hands now and then while talking animatedly to her friend. The children were asleep after being treated to a special extra hour of computer games; Tara happily tucked into Mandy's room, and Wesley, surprisingly without protest, in Josh's.

From the raised marble platform that surrounded the fireplace, Brent looked at Amanda. He could not remember the last time he had seen her so happy, her face radiant, the dimples in her cheeks showing every time she laughed. She looked so young, so carefree, and—an odd gleam came into his eyes—so damned vulnerable, straddled on the white fur rug with the flames casting a fiery glow on her coppery curls. He felt a long-forgotten emotion surge, a warm tingling inside, and he badly wanted to reach out and touch her. She had looked this way when they were married ten years ago. Maybe it was the absence of all that heavy makeup. Strange, but ever since her return, she seemed to have no need for that stuff.

The phone rang again and Brent rose to answer it. Within minutes he returned, a wide grin on his face, his eyes sparkling. They all looked at him, waiting.

"Don't tell me," Matt drawled. "You won a million dollars."

"Just about. That was Daryl."

Amanda jumped up, her eyes wide and shining.

"Karen had the baby! Is it a boy?"

"A girl?" Paula countered.

"Yes to both." Brent's grin widened at the flabbergasted faces.

"What?"

"Twins?"

"Daryl knew, of course," Brent nodded. "He just never bothered to tell us."

"Oh, God! No wonder she was so huge!"

"I'll be damned."

"Well now, where is the champagne? This calls for a celebration, people. We're a brand-new uncle and aunt." Brent took Amanda in his arms and kissed her. Next they all hugged each other, laughing.

"Is Karen all right?" Amanda asked. Incredible, she thought, only yesterday they had dropped by for a drink, and Karen had seemed chipper and not at all ready to go into labor.

"Yes. Exhausted, but doing fine. And Daryl complained that he did not have enough cigars." Brent popped the champagne bottle and poured.

"Amanda . . ." Paula stopped as she saw the look on her friend's flushed face. Amanda's eyes were on Brent, oblivious to anyone else in the room. There was an odd intensity in her gaze and Paula turned away, suddenly feeling like an intruder.

It was two hours later when the Manchiones left. Despite Amanda's invitation to make use of the guest bedroom, they had opted to sleep in their own home. They had to take advantage of a house without kids, Paula had said, laughing, even if it was only for the one night.

Upstairs in the bedroom, Amanda changed into her nightgown while Brent made a last house check. Slipping underneath the covers, she listened for his footsteps and she felt her heartbeat race in her chest when he came up the stairs. Instinctively, she drew the comforter around her and waited. He had actually kissed her tonight, her heart sang, really kissed her. With feeling. And warmth. She didn't even care if he wasn't conscious of it, it had felt so good. So delightfully, frightfully good.

Brent's tall figure filled the doorway, pausing to close the door behind him. Amanda held her breath. How handsome he was, his blond hair falling in thick waves around the well-formed head and over the high forehead. The straight nose and firm jaw, the fine sculpted eyebrows above deep-set piercing eyes, lent that suave look to his lean face.

Beneath the covers, she clamped her legs together to keep from trembling as those gray penetrating eyes searched her flushed face. She watched him approach the bed, the blood pounding against her temples, her throat suddenly dry. No, she willed herself, be still, get a hold of yourself. He's only on his way to the boudoir; soon he'll have passed you, and you can go to sleep. But her breath choked in her chest as he came closer still, mesmerizing her with the sensuous swing of his slim hips, making her acutely aware of his scorching gaze.

Slowly, deliberately, and never taking his eyes off her, Brent unbuttoned his shirt. Reaching the foot of the bed he discarded it, revealing a broad muscular chest covered by a soft fur of dark blond hair. The sound of a zipper opening ripped through the silence of the room, and by the time he had reached his side of the bed, the trousers had dropped from his body, baring a slim waist and a flat belly.

Amanda's bewildered eyes widened even further when he effortlessly slid beneath the covers next to her. On the verge of panic, she let out a whimper. She desperately wanted to close her eyes to blot out the giddiness and steady her head, but the next moment his hand gripped the covers that shielded her taut body and pulled them away. His mouth came down on hers and muffled the escaping moan, then with surprising gentleness, he kissed her again and again, brushing her lips sensuously, lingeringly. Amanda began to shake, racked by the heat that lashed through her body. An unbearable urge tugged at the corner of her loins and she shifted in a desperate struggle to contain herself.

She gasped as his warm hand fondled her breast, his fingers tantalizing the rosy nipple to an erection, then reaching for the other one. Her breath caught, coming in short rasps. A wave of intense feeling threatened to seize her senses, sending her spiraling. She shuddered as his tongue probed her parted lips, and her arms slid around his neck. With a fire that surprised even herself, she responded to his ardor, meeting his kisses with an almost savage hunger, the tension in her body mounting. Her mind went blank, sparks filling the void. She hardly noticed his hand gliding downward along her limbs, caressing the inside of her thighs, touching her intimate parts, heightening the gnawing need that consumed her pulsating body.

Incited by her passionate response, Brent pried himself loose from her soft lips and, with one swift move, ripped the sheer nightgown from her trembling body, baring her glistening flesh to his gaze. His own desire fully unleashed, he moved lower, his scalding kisses leaving a trail of scorching rapture on her writhing body, and as his tongue darted between her legs, Amanda began to sob.

Brent groaned, momentarily closing his eyes to bridle the fierce throbbing in his loins. He lifted himself up and covered her, rubbing his swollen desire against her, the nerves taut and palpitating, growing even fuller, and harder. And as Amanda thrashed her hungry body to his, wild and unrestrained, his ravenous need of her flared and he readied himself for the thrust.

Just then the phone rang.

Brent cursed. Reluctantly, he reached out and fumbled to take the receiver, his face contorted with unfulfilled release, the passion still raw in his dark eyes.

"What?" He suddenly tensed and tore himself away from her. He sat up, listening, a menacing frown further darkening his face.

"I'll be right there." He slammed the receiver down and jumped out of the bed.

Amanda lifted herself on one elbow, her body still throbbing, her eyes wistful.

"What is it?"

"My mother. Louise had a stroke." He grabbed his pants and dressed swiftly. "Go to sleep. I'll call you."

But Amanda was already out of bed.

"Wait, I'm coming with you." She dashed into the closet.

"No," Brent said from the doorway. "The children need you here. We can't both leave them just like this."

"Mrs. Flynn will take care of them. I'll leave her a note."

Brent turned, hesitant. He could use the company, and he still had her in his blood. Having her next to him in the car sounded awfully inviting.

"All right, but hurry. I'll wait for you downstairs." He headed for the garage to warm up the car.

Chapter 13

THE HALLS OF RUSH-PRESBYTERIAN ST. LUKE'S WERE DE-
serted. From time to time, the sound of low voices rustled at
the far end of the corridor where the night staff kept their
wakeful vigil. A couple of young nurses walked by, their footsteps muffled by the thick soles of Nike shoes, and smiled
encouragingly at her as they passed.

Amanda rubbed her arms, which were cold even in her fur
coat. She glanced at her watch. Five o'clock. In a couple of
hours Josh and Mandy would wake up and find them gone.
She should have left them a note as well, but there had been
no time. Poor Mrs. Flynn. She had given her the day off today
and she knew the woman had planned to visit her sister in
Hammond, Indiana. Amanda sighed, grateful for the housekeeper's understanding nature. She'd make it up to her at
Christmas.

As she strolled back toward the guest lounge where she
had left a distraught Lady Madeline and a surly Alison,
Amanda thought about her sister-in-law. The grim circumstances of tonight's meeting had not mellowed the haughty
princess; she did not hide her surprise at seeing Amanda
arrive with her brother. Lady Madeline had cried and hugged
her, but Alison had merely given her a cold stare and chosen
to ignore her presence. Almost immediately, Brent had left in
search of the doctor who had taken charge of Louise since

her personal physician was out of town for the holiday weekend.

She glanced at her watch again. Five after five. Almost an hour since Brent had disappeared with the head night nurse.

Entering the waiting lounge, she coughed. A cloud of smoke hung thickly inside the room and in a corner stood Alison, a cigarette in her pouting mouth, looking bored and angry. A wave of disgust filled her as she waded through the smog, and for a minute, Amanda felt like shaking Alison. Her own feelings for Louise were by no means the warmest, or the friendliest, but for Alison to be so blatantly unfeeling was completely beyond her—Louise was her own grandmother, for God's sake! And a stroke was not something Amanda wished on her or anybody. What an ending to such a pleasant evening.

Remembering Brent's lovemaking, she shivered, feeling again the tingling ecstasy of his firm body straining against hers. He had been so gentle yet so strong, and an intense longing stirred her senses anew. She suddenly felt warm, glowing with unfulfilled desire, and she sat down on the sofa next to the sleeping Madeline and closed her eyes. It had been so natural for Brent to come to her tonight and she could not help wondering if . . .

Her eyes flew open at the sound of approaching footsteps. Brent appeared in the doorway and she jerked up, waking Madeline. His face was solemn and she noticed the lines beneath his eyes. But there was an optimistic gleam in those eyes and Amanda heaved an inaudible sigh of relief.

"Brent, is she . . . ?" Lady Madeline whimpered, her hands nervously patting her disheveled hair.

Her son held out both hands, gripping his mother's in one and his wife's in the other, and shook his head.

"She was lucky. It was a mild stroke."

"How mild? What does it mean?"

"We don't know exactly yet. She's asleep now, but Dr. Monroe seems to feel that she'll be all right. Eventually. And I agree."

"What do you mean—eventually?" Alison questioned, joining them.

Brent looked at her and frowned, but the tug of his mother's hand forced his attention back to the distraught woman. "The damage is minimal, although we'll have to do some more tests. But the initial prognosis is favorable. She's paralyzed on her right side and chances are that her speech may be affected. That can be treated. With exercise and the right kind of care, she'll be as good as new in a couple of months."

"What kind of care is the right kind?" Alison's voice had a sharp edge and Amanda felt a chill crawl up her spine at the annoyance in those ice-blue eyes.

Instinctively she opened her mouth to say something, but the words died on her lips as Brent turned threateningly to his sister. The silence in the room became deafening, and after what seemed an eternity, Alison lowered her eyes and shrugged.

"Brent?" Lady Madeline gently tapped his hand.

He slowly turned his attention back to his mother and his expression softened.

"She will need someone with her all the time," he continued, "around the clock, to watch over her and make sure she's all right. We can't afford another stroke; in her weak condition it could be fatal." He looked at Alison. "That means someone will have to stay with her day and night. See to her comfort, her every need. At least for a while, or until she has regained some of her strength."

"You mean, like a nurse?" Lady Madeline asked.

"In addition to a qualified nurse," Brent continued to look at Alison, "she'll need one of us, preferably someone who cares."

Alison straightened her shoulders, her eyes flashing defensively.

"Why the hell are you looking at me? There's no way I can play nursemaid," she said. "I'm expected back in Cannes next week. We'll have a house full of guests and Armand won't stand—" She took a step backward at Brent's raised hand.

"You selfish little bitch! The only reason you show up for Louise's annual Thanksgiving dinners is to secure a place in her will. Do you think I don't know that? I don't give a damn what your precious Prince Armand won't stand for, your grandmother's welfare takes priority over His Highness's orgies right now."

"Why me? What about you, you're her grandson. What makes you so damned exempt?"

"I can't believe you actually said that." His tone was deadly and Alison winced.

For a moment they glared at each other, neither one moving. Then, sneering, Alison flung her head back.

"And what about that precious wife of yours? After all, the slut came back for the Farraday money—let her earn it," she snarled.

Brent took a step forward, his eyes spewing fire, and she instinctively backed away.

"If you were not my mother's daughter—"

"You'd what? Kill me, disown me?" Alison's contemptuous laugh rang mirthlessly. "What a fool you are, Brent! Look at you, going to bat for that cheating tramp, and with such passion. Commendable, big brother. She's really got you by the balls, doesn't she? But if you think she'd be here—"

"Please, Alison, Brent, stop it." Lady Madeline was close to tears. "I can stay with her. For a while. I'm sure Giles won't mind."

"Oh, I'm sure he'll be delighted," Alison said scornfully. "Good old Sir Giles. He'd probably pay the doctors to prolong Grandmother's condition if he could have his way." Her short laugh bounced off the bare walls and left a hollow echo trailing across the room. She lit another cigarette and blew out the smoke without so much as a glance at her bewildered mother. She almost jumped at the sound of Brent's harsh voice.

"If you can't be civil, I suggest you hold your tongue. Nobody's holding you here, so why wait until next week? Go back to your high society friends and that filth you call class," he lashed out ruthlessly. "Some class. God, you make me sick! You and that husband prince of yours deserve each other."

Amanda rose, trembling. She forced herself to remain calm, yet she hurt for Brent. It was not his anger that touched her, nor the cold look in his eyes nor the vicious attack on his sister, but the pain and the fear he tried to hide. A pain so intense, so fierce, it cut through her, and she felt helpless and small. She glanced at her mother-in-law. Lady Madeline was now openly crying, no longer bothering to wipe away the tears that streamed down her pale face, her hands clenching and unclenching in her lap.

"Darling," she said, gently putting a hand on his arm, "it's late, and we're all tired. Perhaps we should go home and rest for a while."

Brent turned to her. For a moment his vision remained unfocused, then, slowly, the tension in him eased. He took a deep breath and nodded. "Take Mother to the penthouse. I'll stay. I want to be there when Grandmother wakes up. It'll be scary enough for her to be in this condition. I don't want her to be alone."

Amanda glanced at Alison's stiff back and then at Madeline. "I'll take Lady Madeline home," she said. "Then I'll be back and you and I can go to a hotel nearby." She raised her hand to ward off his protestations. "You too need a rest. You'll be of no use to Louise if you're all wound up."

He started to say something, but she shook her head resolutely.

"That's final, Brent." Their eyes met for a moment, and a hint of a smile crept into his. Amanda helped her distraught mother-in-law to her feet and put an arm around her shoulders. "I'll see you in a bit," she promised. She forced a smile and left him, refusing to look back at Alison.

They found a Sheraton close to the hospital and checked in, ignoring the desk clerk's curious glances. Once inside the hotel room, Amanda took off her shoes and walked over to the telephone. Dialing her home number she watched Brent close the curtains and disappear into the bathroom. Mrs. Flynn answered the call and reassured her that everything was under control. She talked briefly to the children and promised to be home as soon as Louise's condition was more stable. Putting down the receiver, she suddenly felt exhausted and went to check on Brent.

She found him standing in front of the mirror, just staring. His face was taut, showing traces of fatigue. "Why don't you take a quick shower?" she suggested. "It'll help you sleep."

His bloodshot eyes met hers in the mirror and she felt like running to him and putting her arms around him to ease his pain.

"I feel so helpless. Here I am, a doctor, and there's nothing I can do to help my own grandmother."

"Of course you can, and you will. So she had a stroke. It's an illness, and we all get sick, Louise is no exception. That's why there are doctors, to help her get well again." She came closer to him and gently turned him around. "And you will do just that, Dr. Farraday, you'll see. She'll be back on her feet in no time."

"My father was a doctor. He was barely thirty-six when he died. He had cancer." Brent closed his eyes for a moment. Opening them again, he shook his head. "I remember thinking how odd that was. A doctor, who could not cure himself."

She began to unbutton his shirt, avoiding his eyes.

"Brent . . . ?" She hesitated, her heart pounding in her throat. "What was all that fuss about the money . . . ?"

"What money?" Brent frowned, acutely aware of her fingers touching his bare chest.

"Something about an inheritance . . . At least, Alison said—"

"Alison!" He tore off the open shirt and flung it to the floor. "Forget about Alison. She's a useless snob, a guttersnipe of the first degree, and the most worthless airhead ever born. Although, for once she was right—if she wasn't my flesh and blood, I probably would've strangled her. Of all the selfish, rotten creatures . . ." He whirled around, swinging his arms wildly, and losing his balance, grabbed Amanda's shoulder. For a moment they clung to one another, their bodies touching.

"Shhh . . ." She gently stroked his flushed face, her fingers cool against his hot skin. "It's okay. We won't talk about her anymore tonight." Brushing a stray lock of hair from his clammy forehead, Amanda sighed. "Now take that shower, it'll make you feel better."

She smiled and started to turn away, but Brent swiftly placed his hand on the doorway, his arm blocking her exit.

Amanda's heart leaped and she felt the blood race to her temples. No, oh God, no, she silently pleaded, not now, not this way. But she did not move, and when his hands undressed her, she did not stop him. Brent bent his head and kissed her throat. Amanda closed her eyes. Her knees felt weak. She held her breath sharply as his mouth cupped a breast, not even noticing as he shed the rest of his own clothes. With a swiftness that belied his tiredness, Brent scooped her into his arms and carried her over to the bed.

Within a week, Louise was pronounced out of danger and fit to leave the hospital. Armed with an electronic wheelchair, she went back to her penthouse accompanied by Lady Madeline and a qualified nurse. The paralysis on the right side of her body was not as critical as initially feared and tests proved that it was not irreversible.

A rigid schedule was set up for daily therapeutic exercises and Brent adjusted his routine to drive downtown and see her three evenings a week. Speech therapy was rigorous. But despite her slurred words and her semi-incapacitated condition, Louise was far from frail. There was an aura of strength around her and one had only to look into her sharp blue eyes to know she was back on track and in no way defeated. And she was determined not to be defeated, following each exercise with a relentless tenacity that was frightening, yet so typical of Louise.

The week she had come home, Jonathan returned from his annual African safari, terribly put out that he had not been alerted. He angrily rejected every excuse Brent and Lady Madeline gave him, insisting that he would have come home sooner had he known. He was at the penthouse from morning till night, daily fussing over Louise and driving Miss Wade, the nurse, crazy.

The week before Christmas, Lady Madeline announced that she was flying back to London. Sir Giles, finally noticing his wife's absence, had demanded her immediate return. Brent tried to persuade her to stay at least until after Christmas, but she stood her ground, and with his grandmother's startling progress, he really had no reason to further keep her from her husband. Besides, his mother argued, with Nurse Wade and Jonathan at Louise's beck and call around the clock, her presence was dispensable. So, four days before Christmas, Brent and Amanda took her to the airport.

It had been snowing the day before and the temperature had dropped to a mean twenty degrees below zero that night.

"Just in time," Lady Madeline said, shivering in her mink coat. "I've never liked Chicago in the winter. Even Alaska would be a better place to be in."

"Oh, come now, Mother. Have you ever been in Alaska?" Brent lit a cigarette, laughing.

"No. But it's true." She glanced at Amanda. Each time she

saw her daughter-in-law, she marveled at the change in her. And she had seen her often these past few weeks.

Amanda seemed quieter, less absorbed in herself, and genuinely caring about her family. Maybe it was good that she had gone away; the years had certainly tamed her—no, "mellowed" was the word, for the fire in her tawny green eyes was not entirely quenched. Tonight, however, she looked calm and serene, and yes, quite beautiful. Even without makeup she was striking and there was a vulnerability about her that made you want to gather her in your arms and protect her from harm.

Lady Madeline sighed. That must be the way Brent felt, she thought, feeling a sudden tenderness as her eyes traveled to her son's face. Then, seeing him look at her, she colored, realizing Amanda had spoken to her.

"I'm sorry?" she mumbled, flustered at being caught staring.

"Does Sir Giles know what flight you'll be taking?" Amanda inquired. Her eyes met Brent's briefly and she knew he was thinking the same thing. Lady Madeline's husband was not the most diligent of men where details were concerned.

"Of course he—"

"Dr. Farraday, Dr. Brent Farraday, please come to the white courtesy phone." The metallic voice over the airport intercom sounded ominous.

"Excuse me, I'll be right back."

They watched him walk over to the phone and cover his other ear to try and listen to the message.

"I'm glad you came back." Amanda, startled at her mother-in-law's touch, forced a smile.

"I don't think I had a choice," she said gently.

"Maybe not. But now that you're back . . . ?"

"I'm glad that I am, too."

"That's good enough for me." Lady Madeline patted her hand and smiled. She turned her head and saw Brent walk back to them, his face taut, his eyes dark.

"I'm sorry, Mother. We can't stay to see you off. Louise had another stroke and Jonathan fell and broke his leg on the ice. Lousy timing, all at once." He bent to kiss her. "Have a good trip, and say hello to Sir Giles for me."

But Lady Madeline got up, trembling, her face deathly pale.

"A second stroke? Oh, my God . . ."

"Don't worry. As soon as I know her condition, I'll call you."

"No, Brent, wait. I'm coming with you."

He halted and gave her an incredulous look. But Lady Madeline rushed past him to the ticket counter, and after a brief conversation with the airline agent, she joined her children.

"What about Sir Giles?" Brent frowned, still stunned at her reaction.

"I'll call him from the hospital. What are we waiting for? Let's go."

"It's definitely a setback, Brent," Dr. Kraemer said, "but she is damned lucky. It was a minor one and the damage should be minimal, if any."

Brent looked at him and breathed a sigh of intense relief. He had known Dr. Kraemer since he was a boy and trusted his judgment. Not only was he Louise's personal physician, but he was a friend of the family and one of the best doctors in downtown Chicago. And he was straightforward, never beating around the bush.

"Do you know what caused it?" Brent asked.

Dr. Kraemer shrugged. "It could be anything, or nothing. My guess is that Jonathan's fall triggered it." He patted Brent's shoulder. "I'd like to keep her for a while. Even if there's no damage, her weakened condition will slow down her progress, at least temporarily."

Deep in thought, Brent walked to the hospital lounge where his mother and Amanda were waiting. He briefly told them Dr. Kraemer's prognosis. Then he looked at Lady Madeline.

"Mother?"

"I . . . I can't stay very long. Giles was not very happy when I told him, but he understood. I'll stay until she's out of the woods."

But on Christmas Eve, Louise developed pneumonia.

Chapter 14

THEY WERE SEATED AT DINNER WHEN THE PHONE CALL came. Brent took it and when he returned to the dining table, Amanda knew the news was not good. His absentminded look grazed the children and she knew he was not going to say anything in front of them. But she felt the tension in him.

"Who was that, Brent?" Lady Madeline took a sip of her wine, a worried frown on her face.

"The hospital." His curt tone indicated the subject was off limits.

Amanda quickly intervened. "Mandy, would you ask Mrs. Flynn to bring in the dessert?"

"Sure, Mommy." Mandy slid off her chair.

"Can I go, too?" Josh pleaded, anxious not to have his sister get the better part of his favorite part of the meal. Amanda nodded and he was gone in a flash.

Brent threw her an appreciative look and wiped his mouth on the napkin.

"Louise has pneumonia."

Lady Madeline gasped, covering her mouth to suppress a cry. Brent looked at her, then at Amanda.

"I'll have to go downtown after the children have gone to bed."

"Oh, God. Every time I am about to leave . . ." Lady Madeline looked distressed. Her flight for London was scheduled to leave at nine-fifteen tonight and she had so looked forward to seeing Giles again. And the dogs, her beautiful lovely dogs, how she missed them, even more than her husband, she thought, with a touch of guilt.

Mandy and Josh returned, each balancing a tray with bowls of chocolate pudding topped with whipped cream. Josh's little tongue stuck out of his mouth, his small face red from exertion.

"What? Is it Christmas yet?" Brent feigned indignation. Mandy giggled and Josh beamed.

"We'll have an even better dessert tomorrow," he said, grinning mysteriously.

Amanda handed out the bowls.

"How would you guys like to spend the night at Paula's?" She felt a pang of uncertainty as she posed the question. What if Paula had other plans? What if they were not home? But one pair of green and one pair of blue eyes immediately sparkled at her suggestion and Josh let out a bloodcurdling scream.

"Simmer down now, first finish your dessert." She felt Brent's questioning look and signaled "later" with her eyes. "I'll call and see if she wants you two."

A moment later she returned, smiling. Paula had been very understanding, and of course she'd love to have the children. Amanda shouldn't worry about anything, she and Matt had no specific plans for the evening anyway.

"All right, you two, a quick shower and into your pajamas. We'll take some clothes along for tomorrow morning."

"I'm first." Josh raced for the stairs.

"I am." Mandy ran behind him.

"I've got to referee the battle," Amanda said, excusing herself. "We'll talk after I've taken them to Paula's."

"I really don't know what to do." Lady Madeline wrung her hands. "She's like my own mother, and I do worry about her. But I can't keep calling Giles and postponing going home. It's not fair to him, either."

"Mother, it's all right. Grandmother will be fine. She has the best of care, believe me. And she's strong; she'll get this licked in no time." Brent tried to soothe her.

"But what if she doesn't? What if her condition worsens? I'd never forgive myself."

"It won't, you'll see. Trust me. I've never lied to you, have I? And I'll call you every day until she is okay again."

"And when she gets out of the hospital? Who will look after her? Jonathan won't be there for her, at least not for a while, and God knows how long that's going to be."

"Nurse Wade is highly qualified. She'll take care of her. You couldn't ask for a more efficient person to look after her every need."

"It still doesn't feel right. Somehow I feel I've deserted her."

"Why can't she come over here?" Amanda had sat quietly on the rug in front of the fire, listening to the arguments.

The idea had come to her on her walk back from Paula's. For a minute she had thought of her bitter feelings for Louise, but she had shaken them off almost instantly. This was a sick woman, helpless and dependent on others. It was hideous to be reduced to such a condition, even Louise, with no one in her own family willing to take care of her. She looked up and saw the curious gleam in Brent's eyes.

"We have the space," Amanda took a deep breath. "She can stay in the downstairs guest room and Nurse Wade can sleep in the sewing room next to it. We can move the desk to a corner and put a bed in there, it's roomy enough." She spoke rapidly as if afraid to stop and change her mind. "And we can get Mrs. Flynn some daytime help, twice a week perhaps, so she'll have more time to devote to preparing the special menus and can help the nurse once in a while. I'll have to talk to her, of course, but I'm sure it'll be all right. And I'm here, too."

She saw her mother-in-law gape at her and she blushed. Lady Madeline recovered from her surprise and swallowed a couple of times.

"Do you know what you're saying?" she asked gently.

Amanda nodded and turned to Brent, uncomfortable at his silence. *I'm doing this for you,* she wanted to scream. *I can't just stand by and watch you suffer, worried sick over her. God knows why you love your grandmother so much, but you do, so I've got to do something.*

"Are you sure?" His voice was deep and soft and her color deepened.

"Very sure," she whispered.

He finally stirred, going to the bar and returning with a

bottle of wine. He refilled his mother's glass, then Amanda's and his own.

"We'll have time for one more before taking you to the airport, Mother." He raised his glass to salute his wife, his smiling eyes a warm caress. And she suddenly felt weak, dizzy from the emotion she saw in them.

Christmas was spent quietly. With the cloud of worry hanging over Brent, Amanda tried to keep things simple, without dampening the children's spirits. Louise's condition had not stabilized by the time they left the hospital around three that morning. But Dr. Kraemer had insisted they go home; he would call them as soon as there was some change.

Early in the morning, the children opened their presents, and they had lunch at Paula's. Then Daryl called from the hospital and Brent had gone to Chicago again. But he had come home to spend Christmas night with his family, trying to hide his concern. Amanda watched him with a heavy heart. She had told Mandy and Josh about Louise, but they did not know her well enough to share their father's anxiety. Yet they could see how distraught he was and his restlessness subdued them.

Things improved slightly at dinner. The Manchiones were there and Paula kept the atmosphere lively and light with her wit. Thank God for Paula, Amanda thought, she was one in a million, and a good friend. Even Brent smiled at some of her jokes, and by the time dessert was served, the mood around the table was happy.

Then the phone rang. Louise's fever had reached its safety limit, and Dr. Kraemer asked Brent to come to the hospital. Again Paula saved the situation.

"Why not have Josh and Mandy come to our place for the night? That's some treat, right, guys? A perfect ending to a perfect evening." She put her arm around Amanda's shoulders. "Go on, go with him, cara, and don't worry, it's an even greater treat for my brood, believe me," she whispered.

Daryl had already arrived by the time they reached Rush-Presbyterian.

"How is she?" Brent asked, ripping off his leather gloves, his face taut.

"About the same. Dr. Kraemer's with her."

Brent started to walk away, but Daryl held him back, glancing at Amanda.

"Go on." She nodded. "I'll be in the waiting room."

Brent gave her a grateful look and the two men briskly walked off. Soon their tall figures disappeared around the corner and Amanda's mood sank. Slowly she turned to go to the guest lounge. It was empty. She sat down, feeling lonely and depressed. Some Christmas. *I swear, you must be my nemesis, Louise. Even unconscious, you have managed to ruin my evening.*

She shook her head vehemently. What was the matter with her? This was no time for self-pity. If Louise was indeed her nemesis, this was the time to make things right. She would show her how wrong she had been in wanting to be rid of her. She would win her respect and her approval. She would make her see what a good mother and wife she was. She would convince her that her children loved her and she them. She would . . .

Amanda straightened her shoulders and took a deep breath. No, she wouldn't do any of these things. She would just be herself, and Louise could like or dislike her as she pleased. If she lived.

She suddenly shivered. That was the key word, wasn't it? Lived. What if she didn't make it? What if . . . Oh, Brent, she groaned, God, let her live, please. She could not bear to think of the pain in Brent's eyes. He loves her so, don't do this to him, he doesn't deserve to suffer.

She leaned back on the sofa and closed her eyes, trying to block the oncoming tears. Who was she to talk about suffering? Had she not hurt him by leaving? And staying away for four years? Why did she leave him? she wondered again. And if she hadn't had the accident, would she have returned? Or was she on her way back home that night? So many unanswered questions, so many puzzles.

Brent. She felt warm just thinking of him. He had changed as the weeks went by, softening, becoming less hostile, his expression pensive and puzzled at times as he scrutinized her. And she had caught glimpses of warmth—and yes, occasional tenderness, and surprise at some of the things she did, or didn't do. And then there was that night. The night at the Sheraton, branded in her mind forever. She stirred at the memory and hugged herself as she smiled, feeling the warmth of his passion once again.

"Amanda?"

Her eyes flew open and she jerked up at the sight of Daryl towering over her.

"I'm sorry, I didn't mean to startle you."

"Louise? Is she . . . ?"

"She's still burning up, but her condition is stable. Brent's still with her. He wants me to take you home." Daryl reached for the coat next to her on the sofa, but she shook her head.

"You go. I'll wait for him."

"Come on. You can't do anything here, for him or Louise. And you've got the kids to think of."

"No. I'm staying. Say hi to Karen for me, and the babies. I didn't get a chance to ask, how are they?"

Daryl's expression softened.

"They're fine. It's amazing, but Karen's breast-feeding them, and they're thriving."

Amanda smiled, touched by the immense love that shone out of his brown eyes. "Does she have enough? After all, two of them . . ."

"Amazing, isn't it? And from such a slender body. But yes, they're not complaining."

"Tell her as soon as Louise is out of danger, we'll drop by and see for ourselves how well she's doing. Hopefully, the twins won't have reached toddler age by then." She reached out to touch his hand and he grabbed hers.

"Come on, girl, let's go," he urged. "It won't do to have the master's wrath on our heads."

"Please, Daryl, I'd rather stay and wait for him. I'd be worried stiff alone at home anyway. Really."

"You'd better go with Daryl." Brent's voice came from the doorway. Seeing the fatigue lines in his face, Amanda rose and quickly walked over to him.

"How is she?"

"Still the same. It's going to be a long night, and I don't want to worry about you, too. So, please, Amanda. Do us all a favor and let Daryl take you home." He sounded tense, but the look he gave her was gentle and not at all devoid of warmth.

"No. I'll stay here, with you. Or you can go and be with

your grandmother and I'll wait. I can always read or take a nap, but I'll stay."

Brent started to say something, but she was adamant. "That's final, Brent."

He closed his mouth again. There was something in her that convinced him. He knew she could be stubborn and he was too fatigued to fight her. Slowly he nodded at his brother-in-law and Daryl buttoned up his coat.

"You're sure?" He tried one last time, and when she nodded, he turned to leave.

"I don't know how long—" Brent started.

"It's all right," Amanda interrupted. "Go back to Louise. I'll be fine here. It's warm and quiet and there are a stack of magazines I haven't had time to read at home." She kissed his cheek and started to walk back to the sofa. But before she could take two steps, Brent grabbed her waist and, pulling her against him, kissed her full on the lips, hard and demanding. In reflex she stiffened, then her body relaxed and she responded.

"I'll be back as soon as I can," he promised.

"Don't worry about me. Come back when she's out of danger."

He turned, but not before she had caught the tenderness in his eyes, and as the door closed behind him, she sank down on the sofa, trembling. That look. It spoke of gratitude, and of love. And she no longer felt alone. How wonderful to be in love with one's own husband, how dreadfully old-fashioned, yet how exciting and frightfully stimulating! And judging from that look, the feeling was mutual. Or so she hoped.

Chapter 15

IT WAS NOT UNTIL THE WEE HOURS OF THE MORNING that Louise's fever broke. A nurse had peeked into the waiting room and found Amanda curled up underneath her coat on the sofa, fast asleep. Knowing who she was from the night nurse, she had only smiled and tiptoed away, leaving the blinds down so the sunshine would not wake the resting woman. Brent too had looked in during the night; twice as a matter of fact, but she had looked so peaceful, he had not disturbed her and had gone back to his grandmother's room. But when he entered the lounge for the third time that morning, she opened her eyes and instantly sat up.

"The fever broke. She'll be fine now." He sank down on the sofa next to her and, pulling her close, heaved a deep sigh of relief.

For a moment he closed his eyes, drained, feeling the fatigue taking over his senses.

"Why don't we go to the Sheraton? You can rest there and we can come back here later this afternoon," Amanda said softly.

But Brent shook his head.

"I'll go and see her one more time, make sure everything's all right. Then we'll go home. You can do the driving. Okay?"

"Okay."

He kissed her forehead and got up. "I'll only be a minute."

As he disappeared she leaned back and sighed. *Thank you, God, for letting her live. Thank you for Brent.* Slowly she gathered her coat and put it on.

Louise recovered more quickly than they had expected and two weeks later Dr. Kraemer pronounced her strong enough to travel to Lake Forest. Julie Wade had moved in the day before, checking out the guest room to make sure everything was as it should be to ensure the patient's comfort. She was young, in her mid-twenties, dedicated, and very efficient. Mrs. Flynn had taken an immediate liking to her, impressed by the girl's quiet strength and charming simplicity. And Amanda had hired Amparo, the daughter of Paula's maid, who would come twice a week to help the housekeeper with the upkeep of the house.

Waiting for her arrival, Amanda made one last check on Louise's room. She had not been there when Brent told his grandmother of their decision to have her recuperate at their house and she wondered about her reaction. The one visit she had paid her had not been too encouraging. Louise had been cool and distant, and the conversation had stalled after a few minutes. Luckily, Brent had interceded, and she had just sat there, uncomfortable, waiting for the hour to end.

And now she is on her way here, Amanda thought nervously. *How will I ever survive the coming weeks?* Absentmindedly, she touched the flowers in the vase on the dresser by the wall. White roses. *I hope she likes them.*

She had purposely stayed home, letting Julie Wade accompany Brent as they took the limousine downtown. It would give Louise time to adjust to her new situation. *Who are you trying to kid?* She grimaced, pushing away a rebellious curl. *You needed this last breather yourself. Admit it. You're not particularly looking forward to the next few weeks, despite your bravado and big words.* Amanda sighed as she looked out the window. It had stopped snowing and the garden looked so clean and white covered with fresh snow.

Slowly she turned around and walked out of the room. She'd better see Mrs. Flynn about dinner tonight. Paula had once more taken the children under her wing, so Louise could have peace and quiet when she arrived. She felt a pang of guilt when she thought of Josh and Mandy; these past few weeks had been hard on them, and although they seemed to take things in stride, she still felt bad about it. Perhaps after Louise had settled in, she and Brent would have more time to spend with them. *No,* she corrected herself, *we just have to make time.*

"Why can't I go to my own home?" Louise frowned crossly at her grandson.

He sat across from her in the back of the limousine, while Julie had chosen to sit up front next to the driver. A sound-proof glass window closed off the back section, giving them privacy and a chance to talk.

"You fuss too much, Brent. Julie Wade is a capable young woman, you said so yourself. Besides, you have a marriage to rebuild, and your wife could do without the burden of an intruder right now."

Brent smiled, his eyes full of indulgence and affection as he looked at her angry face. She had lost a lot of weight, and looked almost frail, yet there was really nothing fragile about her. There was a fire and a strength in her that was mirrored in her ice-blue eyes.

"You can't pin this one on me, darling," he said. "Amanda's the one who suggested it." Her eyes widened in disbelief and he chuckled. "Mother was concerned about you. She hated to leave here, knowing you were all alone." He waved her unvoiced protestations away. "Oh, all right, but even Miss Wade needs time off once in a while, and you can't expect her to be with you around the clock, that's inhumane."

He paused, waiting for her reaction. Receiving none, he sighed. "It's also not fair to Mother. There's Giles, and he is her husband. So Amanda came up with this solution, and at the time it seemed quite a good one." He leaned over and took her hand, holding it gently between both of his. "Let's give it a try, hm? I know you and Amanda have not always seen eye to eye, but please, give her the benefit of the doubt." He hesitated for a moment. "She . . . has changed. I don't know what happened to her during those four years, but something must have, and whatever it was, it's done her good."

Louise did not move, her expression once again cool.

"Oh, come on, Grandmother, since when have you become inflexible? You've always criticized Alison for being rigid and narrow-minded, remember? Where's your sense of fairness?"

She pulled her hand from his grip and looked out the window, still not saying a word. Yet, despite her silence, Brent sensed a softening in her mood. He reached for a cigarette, then changed his mind and leaned back, his hands clasped in his lap, and as he glanced out of the window, he recognized the streets of Lake Forest.

She had not heard the limousine pull up the driveway, but the sound of a car door slamming made her jump. Her eyes met Mrs. Flynn's and, without a word, she rushed out of the kitchen and dashed toward the front door, opening it just as Brent reached for the doorbell. Her eyes went past him to the frail woman in the wheelchair and she cast her husband a questioning look. Brent nodded, a faint smile in his eyes, and taking a deep breath, Amanda went to meet her house guest.

"Welcome home, Louise," she said quietly.

The older woman looked at her for a moment. Then, after what seemed an eternity, she extended her hand and Amanda immediately took it. Flustered by the gesture, she did not see the glances Louise exchanged with her grandson, nor the smile that curled Brent's lips just before he reached out to help Julie Wade roll the wheelchair up the ramp he had specially made for this purpose.

"I've put you in the guest room downstairs and Nurse Wade in the room next to it," Amanda explained, turning to Julie with an apologetic smile. "I hope you don't mind. It is convenient for both of you and I did have it cleaned up and made as comfortable as possible for your stay."

The blond nurse smiled back. "Don't worry, Mrs. Farraday. I'm sure it's more than adequate, and I really don't need much. Thank you."

"Then let's see your room first, Louise, and you can tell me if there's anything else you want or need. Of course, you can tell me that anytime afterward also, and I'll do my best to see that you get it."

"Relax, Amanda. I won't be staying long." Louise viewed the room dispassionately, and missed the nervous twitch of Amanda's mouth at her curt remark.

Bitch! Amanda bit her lip. Amazing how she had recovered; the slur was hardly noticeable, only a lisp now and then. A pity. It would've been more peaceful if she had lost her speech, she thought wryly. A breath of relief escaped her at the sound of approaching footsteps. Brent smiled at her and put his arm around her shoulders.

"Well, Lady Farraday? Does everything meet your specifications? If the mattress isn't soft enough, we'll have Josh jump up and down on it a couple of times. That always helps."

Louise whirled the wheelchair around and faced him. Her expression was cool and her voice even cooler.

"Is there an intercom between this room and Julie's?"

Brent gave her a blank stare. "Intercom? That's it. I knew I'd forgotten something. One intercom system coming up. Tomorrow soon enough?" He looked at Amanda's bewildered face and grinned. "I know exactly the people who can install this kind of thing. Now, how about some lunch, hm? Come on, let's see what Mrs. Flynn has in store for this special occasion. Shall we?" Without waiting for a reply, he strode behind Louise's wheelchair and grabbed the handles.

"Ah." He waved Julie away. "Let me have the pleasure this afternoon. You can have her all the other times after this one."

"I'm not hungry." Louise sounded almost petulant, but her grandson paid no attention to her offhanded refusal.

"Now, Grandmother, you've taught us never to hurt kind people deliberately. I'm sure Mrs. Flynn has your welfare at heart and it would be extremely rude to deny her your delight in her efforts. Besides, Julie here—you don't mind me calling you Julie, do you? Miss Wade sounds so formal, and after all, we'll be housemates for a while." He grinned and Julie smiled back. "Anyway, Julie here looks famished. She could use some nourishment before proceeding with her demanding chores." He winked at the young nurse, and threw Amanda a disarming grin. She shook her head, rolled her eyes, and smiled back.

True to Brent's prediction, Mrs. Flynn *had* outdone herself, and despite herself, Louise enjoyed the lunch she served, even taking two helpings of the crab salad and relishing the smoked salmon fresh from the delicatessen.

* * *

As she walked toward the kitchen Amanda noticed that the French doors leading to the back patio stood ajar. Frowning, she quickly went to close them. The sound of laughter stopped her, and as she stretched her neck to peer around the corner, she saw Josh warding off a wagging Kavik. The boy was laughing gaily, obviously enjoying the game, the dog barking and jumping on him and trying to lick his face.

"Josh!" She opened the door and stepped out on the patio, the frown on her flushed face deepening. "What are you doing outside in this weather? Get in here this minute!"

The boy crawled to his feet, his posture matching the reluctant expression on his face. With Kavik still happily prancing around him, he shuffled toward his mother.

"No coat. You ought to know better!" Amanda ran her hand through his damp curls and gently pushed him inside. "What got into you? And what's Kavik doing in the backyard?"

"Grandma won't let him in the house."

"Grandma doesn't? Since when . . ." She bit her lip and took a deep breath.

"She told Amparo to put him in the garage. But he doesn't like it there, Mommy. It's cramped in there with your car parked inside. And I thought, since it's just as cold in the garage, he'd probably like the backyard better. At least he can run around and . . . and do his thing and . . ." He shrugged his shoulders and hung his head. "I'm sorry, it's all my fault."

She took him in her arms and rubbed his cold body. "Go upstairs and change into some dry clothes. I'll speak to Grandma about Kavik."

He gave her a grateful look and threw his arms around her neck.

"Now go," she urged, smiling.

Josh kissed her affectionately and, with a happy grin, ran up the stairs. At the top of the stairs he shouted, "You're the most superest mom a kid ever had!" and disappeared around the corner. Amanda shook her head and sighed. She was not looking forward to another discussion with Louise. It had been three weeks since her arrival in their home and tension was mounting by the day. She had tried to be accommodating, but the old woman had not reciprocated. And soon she had found her household routine turned upside down, her family adjusting to their houseguest's needs. As the days passed, Amanda began to wonder if she had made the right move having her in their midst.

Not that Louise demanded their attention—Julie's care tended to her every need. Every day she would take the old woman to a nearby health club to make sure she did the necessary exercises prescribed by her doctor. Julie also tended to her breakfast and lunch, as Louise had found the children's chatter at the table disturbing. Only at Brent's insistence did she partake in their dinner ritual, during which Josh and Mandy had been instructed to keep very quiet.

Slowly, Amanda strolled into the family room and sat down at the piano. Her fingers glided over the keys and Bach came to life. She pounded away, baring her soul and losing her turmoil and torment in the heavy, morose sounds.

"I'm sorry, Mrs. Farraday, I should've told you," Mrs. Flynn said.

Amanda shook her head and sat down at the kitchen table.

"What must I do, Mary? We can't go on like this. She's taking over our house, our lives, and I'm tired of these little talks with her. They don't get me anywhere anyway; they end up in arguments and it's so damn senseless."

Mary Flynn smiled and handed her a hot cup of coffee. "Keep the faith, Mrs. Farraday, she's getting better every day now. Julie tells me her condition is improving by the minute, and she's getting stronger and stronger. Soon the day will come when she's well enough to return to her own house."

"That day won't come soon enough," Amanda confessed, sipping her coffee. "Meanwhile we're all nervous wrecks. Look at me. I often feel like an intruder in my own house. It's my house, but she's running it; she's the one pulling the strings, and there's nothing I can do without hurting Brent."

She looked helplessly at the housekeeper. "It's all my fault. I should never have suggested that she stay here. Julie could've taken care of her just as well in Chicago."

"Stop blaming yourself." Mary Flynn looked at her sternly. "It was very generous of you to ask her into your home. Very generous indeed, and believe me, the good Lord will reward your thoughtful deed. Yes indeedy, He sure will."

Amanda drank her coffee in silence. The housekeeper's

words made her feel better, but she doubted their validity. She slowly rose and nodded at the smiling Mrs. Flynn.

"I think I'll go to Paula's for a while."

"You do that. Mrs. Manchione will be glad to have you."

Amanda ran upstairs to get Josh. Mandy was already at the Manchiones' playing with Tara, who was recovering from the flu. She wondered if Paula would have them for dinner tonight; she just had to get away from Louise, even if it was only for one evening.

Chapter 16

"WHAT DO YOU MEAN, AMPARO QUIT? HAS SHE GIVEN any reason?" Amanda glared at Mrs. Flynn, who only shook her head. The day had not been a good one and Amanda was not in the mood for surprises, especially not unpleasant ones.

She had woken up with a splitting headache and found a note from Brent saying that he had left for an early emergency surgery. Despite her headache, she felt guilty for not having heard the phone ring and being awake to at least pour him a cup of coffee before he started out. Then, things had gone downhill from there.

The bus had been late, and the icy wind had cut through their thick coats and nearly frozen their bones. Louise had been cranky all morning, refusing to go for her daily exercises at the hospital's gym in nearby Highland Park, and when Amanda tried to persuade her, she had snapped at her and told her to mind her own business. Then, at ten o'clock the school had called, asking Amanda to come and get Josh, who had a bloody nose caused by a fight with a second-grader. Upset about the incident, she had not appreciated the principal's condescending remarks about the boy, much less the innuendos that he was a disruptive child with a mean streak and that it would be advisable for her to pay more attention to him before it was too late.

And now this. She felt like throwing her hands up in the air, dropping everything, and walking out.

"She couldn't just quit. No explanations, nothing? Has anything happened?" She clenched her hands. Mrs. Flynn shifted uneasily; she had never before seen her employer so distraught.

"Nothing happened, not really. The only thing she said was that she had been dismissed, so she left."

"Dismissed? What do you mean, dismissed? Who dismissed her?"

"I did."

Amanda whirled around. She had not heard Louise roll up to the kitchen, and as she faced the older woman in the wheelchair, looking into the cool blue eyes, her anger flared.

"You! What right do you have to dismiss my household staff?"

"Calm down, Amanda. The girl was lazy. All she did was sing around the house and dance and prance around the rooms instead of dusting and cleaning as she was supposed to. She wasn't worth your money and I'm sure—"

"*You're* sure. Well, so am I, of this. *You* are a guest in this house. *I* am the mistress here. *I* will give the orders. And only *I* will dismiss the people I hire. Is that understood?" Amanda slammed an open hand on the kitchen table. The anger she had suppressed had built up little by little over the weeks, and it now exploded in full force.

The look Louise shot at her was deadly. Amanda felt the icy stare cut clear through her, but she did not budge.

The moment passed and Louise turned her wheelchair and wordlessly rode out of the kitchen. Mrs. Flynn let out a deep sigh and the sound stirred Amanda out of her trance.

"I'm going to Mrs. Manchione's," she said tonelessly. "Amparo's mother should know where the girl lives."

When Brent entered the house at seven-thirty that evening, he found a distressed Amanda waiting for him. Immediately alarmed, he felt all fatigue leave him. He threw furtive glances around the living room.

"What's the matter? Where are the kids?"

"At Paula's. They'll be home in a couple of minutes."

She saw relief flash in his tired eyes and felt her heart sink.

"Do I have time for a quick shower?" he asked, kissing her lightly and heading for the stairs.

"Brent?"

"I'll only be a minute, I promise."

"Brent, please. We've got to talk."

"Can't it wait, honey? I won't be long."

"No. Now." The urgency in her voice stopped him. "Before the children get home."

She told him rapidly about the incident earlier that afternoon. Brent slowly returned to the living room. For a moment he just stared at her, then heaved a deep sigh.

"I'll go talk to her."

"She's gone. She and Julie took the limousine and left."

He spun around, a blank look on his face. Amanda cringed inwardly.

"What do you mean, left? Where to?"

"I don't know, I was at Paula's, but my guess is that she went to the penthouse. Where else could she have gone?"

He strode toward the telephone on the bar and dialed Louise's number.

"Julie? Brent. Is everything all right?" He listened for a moment. "Let me talk to her, will you?" He waited again. "I see. Well, tell her I called. I'll stop by tomorrow after surgery." Julie was saying something and he vehemently shook his head. "No, no, let her be. Just make sure she eats something later. Please? Thanks, Julie, I'll see you tomorrow."

Amanda watched him replace the receiver, his expression now pensive. She did not move, waiting for him to say something. He looked up and their eyes met briefly, then he turned away and Amanda flushed as if he had slapped her face.

"She was resting. Julie thought she might be asleep." Without another word he stalked toward the stairs and, taking them two at a time, reached the upstairs landing and disappeared into the bedroom.

For a moment Amanda hesitated. But when she heard the shower running upstairs, she resolutely got up and went up the stairs.

Inside her bathroom she sat down on the cushioned bench in the bay window and leaned her head against the frosted glass. Damn it! Why did she feel so guilty? It was, after all, her right to proclaim sovereignty in her own house, wasn't it? She had tried to keep the peace, biting her tongue all these weeks, holding back for Brent's sake, but today Louise had pushed her too far. And now she was being punished for lashing back. Oddly enough, she felt no victory, only regret.

She pulled up her legs and hugged her knees, waiting for Brent to emerge from the shower, hating herself for feeling like a child awaiting a verdict.

The shower turned off and she held her breath sharply as Brent stepped out of the stall, rubbing himself dry on a clean towel. Her eyes swept his naked body, tall, lean, and masculine, and a flash of desire rushed through her. But it died as soon as he looked up and his cool eyes raked over her huddled-up figure.

Without a word, he vanished inside the walk-in closet, reappearing a minute later clad in a dark blue velvet robe. For a moment she expected him to leave the dressing area without so much as acknowledging her presence. But he walked toward the vanity, opened a drawer, and began to comb his wet hair. Finally, he replaced the brush and studied his reflection in the mirror.

"Please, Brent, say something. Anything," Amanda whispered hoarsely.

She couldn't stand it anymore. Anything was better than this silent treatment. She didn't care if he yelled at her, even hit her, as long as he communicated with her. But when his eyes met her imploring gaze she cringed at the naked pain mirrored in those dark gray cores. God, what had she done to evoke it?

"We'd better go downstairs. It's past dinnertime." He turned to get dressed, but Amanda was on her feet, and rushing to him, she grabbed a soft sleeve.

"No, don't go this way," she pleaded. "Don't shut me out, Brent, no matter what you do, don't do that to me."

"There's nothing to talk about, Manda. Let's not keep the kids waiting. If you want we can talk later."

But she would not let go of him, his unexplained pain tearing at her.

"It's not fair," she cried. "You're not being fair. You judge me without hearing my side of the story."

Brent turned, his face expressionless and closed. "What is your side of the story?"

With that she poured out the pent-up grievances, all of them, sparing nothing. And through her tears she saw him relent, slowly, gradually, until understanding dawned in his gray eyes.

"It's my house, my family. Don't I have a right to be me? I kept quiet, thinking it would blow over, but she wouldn't let up. And I can't, I won't, be treated as an outsider in my own domain." She was crying now, her body shaking convulsively. Then she felt herself drawn into his strong arms and she clung to him like a lost child, sobbing.

"Shhh, hush. I'm sorry, Manda, forgive me. Blind fool that I am. Perhaps I have noticed some of it, but I must admit, I've paid little attention to it. Like you, I thought it was just her way of getting adjusted."

"I did it all for you. And I really did try, really I did."

"Shhh, I know you did. I'm sorry."

"Still, I should not have said those awful words, at least not that way. She's a sick woman, and I should be the stronger one. I failed you."

He kissed her hair and, lifting her face, gently brushed away her tears. "No, darling, you didn't fail me. I failed you."

They looked deeply into each other's eyes, then he bent and kissed her, long and deep.

"We'd really better go downstairs, or there'll be no dinner," he murmured huskily. "Come on, I'll just be a minute." As he put on his trousers he was glad that he would see his grandmother the next day. It was high time they had a long talk.

For the first time in her life, Louise was not happy to see her favorite grandson. At first she refused to see him, but he insisted, threatening to break down her bedroom door if she would not come out. So she did, and he braced himself.

She just listened to him, not saying a word, the expression on her face cold and unwavering. And the longer he talked the more he began to understand Amanda's frustration. Why had he never before noticed how uncompromising Louise could be? Was this hard, unfeeling woman the same grandmother he loved so much? Or could it be that the stroke had changed her into this closed-minded human being?

"You really ought to give Amanda the benefit of the doubt, you know," he said. "After all, you were infringing upon her territory. And you, of all people, should understand how she felt. Admit it, Grandmother, you would not have tolerated another woman taking over your jurisdiction, now would you?"

She did not move or so much as blink an eye, and after a while, the monologue exasperated him.

"Perhaps it would be best if you did remain here. Julie seems to cope. I'll hire a relief nurse for the weekends, so she can have some time to herself." Brent turned toward the door. There was not much more to say. She refused to enter the conversation, and he had run out of patience. If she chose to be stubborn and childish, so be it.

After a moment's hesitation, he came back and kissed her cheek, then went to the elevator, nodding at Julie on his way. "Call me anytime." He kept his voice low. "Look after her for me, Julie. She's more distraught than meets the eye."

When the elevator doors closed behind him, Louise whirled her wheelchair around. She did not want Julie to see the tears that rolled down her pale cheeks. Her hands clamped the armrests with a force that strained the knuckles. Her eyes, no longer cold, mirrored the hollow anguish that stabbed her insides. She had lost him, she screamed silently. She had lost her beloved grandson.

Listening to him she had realized how wrong she was to tread on Amanda's rights. And he was right—she'd never given Amanda a fair chance; she was all too wrapped up in her own misery. God, how she hated to be dependent on other people. All her life she had had her own way; she was always the one in control, the one on top.

She had appreciated his defending Amanda; she was, after all, his wife. That she, Louise, had not apologized was due to her stubborn pride. False pride perhaps, but pride nonetheless. And a sense of saving face, holding on to her dignity if you will. But all of that was nothing. What mattered was that he, Brent, *her* grandson, whom she loved more than her own life, had ousted her from his house and home. It was a heavy blow. And for this she shed bitter tears.

In the Farraday home in Lake Forest, the somber notes of Beethoven's Fifth Symphony echoed through the family room and into the den. Brent rifled absentmindedly through the files on his desk, his eyes glancing over the printed words, his mind seeing another picture. A young woman, pouring her soul into the music, her fingers flying over the white and black keys, and he could hear her agony fill the air. As he listened, the melancholy of her lament gripped him and he leaned back in the chair, twirling the pencil in his hand, over and over.

A deep sigh escaped his parted lips and another thought took hold of him. Four years ago, Amanda would have partied her turmoil away, drinking herself into a stupor, hurling vicious words at him. Yet now, no accusations, no harsh words, not so much as a reproach had passed her lips.

Instead, the haunting piano sounds reached the chords of his emotion, churning his insides, and for the first time in his life he felt he preferred thundering rock music to the soul-searing Beethoven. Most of all he felt helpless, and it was this feeling that incited his anger—an anger that was directed toward his grandmother, and in the end, toward himself.

Chapter 17

IT WAS A GLOOMY SUNDAY MORNING, BUT THE THREE IN the cheerful kitchen did not notice it. Outside, the snow fell steadily and the dark skies showed no signs of lightening. But inside the cozy kitchen, Amanda was busy helping Mandy bake brownies for a school project, and Josh was having a ball licking off the sweet chocolate mess left in the pan. It was Mrs. Flynn's day off and she had gone to spend it with her niece.

So busy were they that at first, they did not hear the telephone ring. But after the fourth ring Amanda looked up, distracted. She brushed away a curl, smudging her forehead in the process, and reached for the receiver.

"Who is this?" She could hardly hear the voice on the other end.

"It's Julie, Mrs. Farraday. Is the doctor home?"

"Julie? What's wrong? My husband is in Minneapolis for the weekend, a medical seminar. What is it, where are you?" The noise subsided and Julie's voice became clearer.

"I'm in a phone booth down the street. When are you expecting him back?"

"Tomorrow. What is it, Julie? It's Louise, isn't it? Did something happen? Please, you can tell me." Amanda tried to keep cool, but her heart pounded at the nervous inflection of Julie's voice.

It had been a little more than a week since Brent had gone to see his grandmother. He had not talked about his visit, just said that Louise decided to stay at the penthouse for a while.

Now Julie said, "She's developed a cold, but it's her attitude that alarms me. She hasn't touched her food for three days now, and this morning she had a fever. I'm sorry, Mrs. Farraday, but I don't know what else to do or whom to turn to. I tried to call Dr. Kraemer, but he's out of town, and I somehow don't think she'd see his substitute. I'm so worried about her."

"Why don't you go back to the penthouse and make sure she's all right. I'll be there as soon as I can."

"Please, I don't want to appear rude, but you're the last person she should see right now."

"Do as I say. I'll see you soon." Amanda slammed down the receiver, stripped off her apron, and hurried to wash her hands.

Ten minutes later she was on her way, stopping briefly two doors down. Paula frowned when she saw her flustered face.

"I think I'd better go with you," she said, glancing at the still falling snow.

"No, please. The kids need you more."

"What if Louise throws you out of her apartment?"

"She won't. Don't worry. She's not in a position to demand too many things right now. And she needs me."

Paula rolled her eyes upward. "Bullshit. Who are you trying to kid, cara? It takes more than a mere cold to slay that dragon lady."

"Please, Paula. I'm freezing." Amanda stamped her booted feet impatiently. "And I really must go. Would you . . ."

"Oh, go on. I still think you're a fool, but it's your funeral. Oh, go already. I'll keep an eye on your brood, Tara is bored anyway. And drive carefully, you hear!"

But Amanda was already out of earshot, diving into her car and backing out of the driveway.

"Thank you!" she shouted, and rolled up her window.

Paula shook her head and waved until the car was out of view, then closed the front door. Stubborn little fool, she thought, calling for Tara to put on her winter coat and boots. The old Amanda would not have dreamed of going out in this dreadful weather, unless it was to a wild party. But to see

Louise, whom she considered arch-enemy number one? She sighed, amazed at how much people could change.

Driving slowly on the slick snowy roads, Amanda thought along the same lines as her friend.

God, I must've been an ogre. Except for Paula, all my supposed friends avoid me like the plague. Even Karen, although she has been quite civil to me, perhaps only for her brother's sake.

She sighed, suddenly weary and discouraged. The car skidded and she gripped the steering wheel, her heart pounding in her throat. Perhaps she should take the expressway; at least there the snowplows were hard at work, clearing the roads of the worst layers and sprinkling salt to break up the treacherous ice. She turned a corner and headed toward the Edens Expressway that led into the J. F. Kennedy and down to the Chicago Loop.

Julie let her in, but before Amanda could open her mouth the girl put a finger across her lips and gestured toward the bedroom. Taking off her gloves and coat, Amanda slowly removed her fur hat. She looked at the waiting girl again, a question in her eyes. But Julie only shook her head, a solemn expression on her face.

For a brief moment Amanda's courage sank. She felt like turning around and leaving. It was crazy to come here, she thought, feeling a touch of panic overcome her. Why not wait until Brent had returned from Minneapolis—after all, what was one day longer? She took a deep breath and walked toward the bedroom.

Louise seemed asleep when she entered, her eyes closed, her head tilted on one side of her satin pillow, facing her. Amanda looked around the room. It was spacious and airy, even on this gloomy winter day. White lace covered the large windows while rich velvet burgundy curtains had been pulled back to allow the scarce daylight inside.

The almost transparent eyelids fluttered and next the blue eyes opened, staring blankly at the apparition before her. Amanda held her breath, waiting for a curt dismissal. But the moment passed and Louise turned away from her, closing her eyes again.

"Please, Louise, don't make this any harder on me than it

already is," Amanda pleaded softly. "I came to say I'm sorry. I shouldn't have said what I did the other day. It wasn't kind of me and it certainly wasn't very hospitable." She took another deep breath and swallowed hard. "Perhaps we should start over. On a healthier premise this time. You must believe me when I tell you that you are welcome in our house. Only, please let me run it. It is, after all, my responsibility, you do see that, don't you?"

The old woman did not move, nor did she show any sign of attention.

"Let me take you back with me. Let us have a second chance to make it work. You are and always will be part of our little family, and Brent loves you very much, you have no idea how much. He worries about you. I know it, I see it in his eyes, hear it in his voice. And your great-grandchildren and I want to get to know you better, so that we can come to care for you the way he does. Is that so much to ask?" Amanda let out a weary sigh, defeat getting her down. But she went on, not quite ready to give up.

"Now I know that *you* would never stand for another person to run *your* home and *your* family matters, and had the situation been reversed, you would've told me off long before the time I spoke up. I know you would." She sighed. "Be honest, Louise, would you have respected me if I had played the wimp and handed you the scepter to rule my home?"

A chilly silence filled the room and the only sound was that of the clock ticking on the far wall above the louvered closet doors. Finally Amanda rose to leave, her face pale and taut.

Looking back at the still woman in the bed one more time, she said, "I'm not sorry I've wasted this trip, though. I wanted to clear the air between us, once and for all, and I did." She briskly walked toward the door and reached to open it.

"Amanda?" Her hand stayed, but she did not turn around, waiting. "It's I who must apologize." Louise's voice was soft, almost humble.

"You were right. You are the mistress in your home and I was wrong to meddle in your affairs. Please forgive me."

The words came out haltingly, and knowing how hard it must have been for her to say them, Amanda turned and made her way back to the bed.

"Can you forgive this old woman, my child?" Louise asked.

Instead of responding to that, Amanda happily said, "I'll have Julie pack your clothes—"

"No. It might be better to leave things as they are, at least for a while. I'm quite comfortable here, in my own surroundings. Later perhaps . . ."

But Amanda shook her head adamantly, brushing away tears of relief.

"You're coming home with me, Louise Farraday. It's time the younger generation took care of you for a while. No, I won't hear another word. Your stubborn days are over."

As she left the room to talk to Julie and order the limousine ready, she missed the warm smile Louise threw at her departing back. And tears glistened in the ice-blue eyes, their expression soft and mellow.

Chapter 18

"REALLY, MRS. MANCHIONE, YOU CAN'T EXPECT MIRA-cles. we're a reputable company, and in our expert opinion, straight curtains will do the job just fine. You'll see, your bed-room will look every bit the masterpiece we've proposed." The man looked at Paula critically, his lips puckered in com-placent superiority.

"Thank you for your time, Mr. Dunn, I'll let you know." Paula sighed as she let him out. "Smart ass. If I'd wanted straight curtains, I wouldn't need professional help, now would I?" She slammed the front door behind him and gri-maced at Amanda, rolling her eyes upward in despair.

"That was the fifth guy and my last hope. Matt was right, I'm asking too much. Perhaps I should listen to them and settle for the inevitable."

"Didn't you say that your brother is a contractor?" Amanda asked casually.

"Yeah, but he's not into interior decorating."

"Come on, let me take another look at your bedroom and you can tell me exactly what you have in mind."

Paula looked at her, surprised at her sudden interest. A sly gleam crept into her dark eyes. "I would've thought you would want me to give up," she said, grinning.

"Do you want to give up?" Amanda feigned innocence.

"Are you serious? Of course not. Come on, let me show you what I had in mind."

"I really don't see the problem. So she has slanted ceilings. So what? A pro could easily devise a way of accommodating her needs. Besides, I don't think it's really all that difficult."

Amanda sipped her glass of wine, while Brent tended to the fireplace.

"Aren't those people experts in their field?" He poked a log that had slipped off center.

"They're into curtains and wallpapering, not interior decorating. Paula has her own idea of how she wants it done, but they're only interested in the easy way," Amanda explained.

"Which is?"

"Straight curtains. No deviations, no following the slanted curves, no hard work. Imagination is expensive, but above all, it's hard work, and the more artistic you get, the less profit they'll reap."

"And you think it's possible?" Louise watched her pensively.

She had listened to Amanda and Paula for days, but this was the first time she had volunteered a comment.

"Yes, not only do I think it's possible, it's feasible. And not too hard to accomplish either, as a matter of fact." Amanda smiled a secret smile as if she knew something the others didn't.

She had studied Paula's bedroom and visualized her friend's dreams, and a wild urge had come over her to accept the challenge and make it happen. And better the odds. The rest of the afternoon she had sketched and schemed, and she had already come up with the impossible solution to Paula's dilemma. All she needed now was a good contractor with the same outlandish imagination; better yet—with the same uninhibited vision.

"Then why don't you set your ideas in motion?" Louise prodded, watching Amanda's shining eyes. She had been in Brent's house for two months now and a fond understanding had developed between the two women.

"I don't have the time." Amanda sighed. "Mandy's up for the leading role in *Cinderella,* and if she's to get the part, it'll take up all of my afternoons for the practice sessions, not to mention evenings to get her costumes ready. And then there are Josh's soccer games."

"Nonsense. Julie and I can help you with the costumes, and Amparo can take Josh to soccer practice. That should give you the time you need to start the Manchione bedroom plans, and by the time everything is ready to roll, Mandy's ballet will have taken place and you can finalize your layout."

Brent looked at his grandmother with mild approval in his twinkling gray eyes.

"Seems to me that you have things cut out for you, honey," he drawled.

He had noticed the drastic change in their relationship and basked in the warm camaraderie. He no longer dreaded coming home at night and took up his old routine of bringing files to study and analyze before surgeries.

Louise had literally tossed away her previous inhibitions and plunged into the midst of their daily life, gradually turning it back to its former flow. She no longer had breakfast and lunch in seclusion and attended the children's snack hour when they came home from school. Together with Amanda, she listened to their daily adventures and mishaps. The ban on conversation during dinnertime had also been lifted. Soon Mandy and Josh spoke of her to their friends and schoolmates in the same breath as their parents.

"Now you have a legitimate excuse not to touch the piano. You're too busy." Brent grinned at the dirty look Amanda threw him.

"I didn't know you liked my music." She scowled. "The last time I played Bach, you said it sounded morose."

"Well, not that morbid jazz, maybe, but Mozart and Haydn sound pretty alluring." The smile in his voice reached his eyes and Amanda felt herself grow warm.

God, if only he knew what power he has over me, she thought, the blood pounding against her temples. *One look like that, one smile, and each time I melt.* The memory of the night before made her skin tingle and she could yet feel the hardness of his body against hers, the touch of his slender fingers . . .

Quelling the urge to rush into his arms, she swallowed and brushed an imaginary lock of hair from her forehead. "Are you sure you want to do this? Making Mandy's ballet costumes, I mean?" She prayed Louise would not notice the hoarseness in her voice.

"I'd never noticed how transparent you are, Amanda." Louise laughed, her eyes twinkling.

Seeing Amanda's face flush, her smile broadened. How amusing, she thought, chuckling inwardly, to watch two grown people in love trying desperately to hide their visual foreplay. It had been some time since she herself had felt that way, and it was quite enlightening.

"Yes, of course I want to," she said. "You hate sewing and I love it. I used to make my own dresses, you know, and I was quite good at it. As a matter of fact, there was a time when I wanted to start my own fashion boutique and fill it with my own creations."

Brent looked up, surprised. "Why didn't you?" he asked.

"My husband died. Someone had to run his company." Her voice was gentle, without regret.

Brent lit a cigarette, suddenly feeling awkward. Somehow he had never imagined that his grandmother would have had other aspirations; she had always seemed so totally dedicated to his grandfather's legacy.

He had barely turned twelve when the old man died, but he remembered his mother lamenting the fact that his father, being a doctor, had no interest in running the Farraday business, and being an only child, there had been no one else to take over. Yet Louise had not seemed to suffer from the circumstances, and ten years after Justin Farraday's death, his company had mushroomed into a conglomerate and his widow's name was no longer invisible in the business world. Even after her retirement at the age of seventy, her input as honorary chairman of the board had substantial impact on the board's chief executives' decisions.

"You could still do it," he tried, but Louise laughed again, and he knew she had made peace with the dream.

Amanda smiled, elated. She too had a dream, and here was an opportunity that surpassed mere temptation. Her eyes met Brent's and their bold invitation made her head swim. For it was more than just passion she read in them, it was a promise.

"Oh, all right. I'll do it," she agreed.

When she glanced at Louise's smiling face, she suddenly realized that they had much more in common than met the naked eye. And from the expression in those clear blue eyes, she knew that the old woman knew it, too.

Paula was ecstatic. More than that, she was jubilant. "You're a real lifesaver, cara, an honest-to-goodness angel!" She hugged her laughing friend until Amanda gasped for air.

"Stop it . . . it was more Louise's idea. She talked me into it. Better thank her—"

"I will, later. Even so"—she kissed her again—"you're a friend's friend, my darling cara."

Amanda raised her hands to ward off further demonstrations of affection. "You silly idiot," she sputtered, "it's 'a gentleman's gentleman,' and it's the wrong expression."

"Whatever. Come on, let's call my brother."

"But you said—"

"Michael told me he has a special curtain man, who supposedly does wonders—"

"Then what the hell do you need me for?"

"—but only on direction. And if the directions come from a genius, he is said to possess the ability to move mountains." Paula dialed, and looked at the flabbergasted Amanda. "Wrong expression? Spin gold out of straw?" Her expression changed and she held the mouthpiece closer to her lips. "Michael, is that you? What happened to your receptionist? Never mind, you can tell me later. Listen, Michael, remember you once told me . . ."

Amanda wandered up the stairs and into Paula's bedroom. She stopped in the doorway, her eyes fixed on the far window that was now hung with a couple of simple curtains of an unidentified brownish gold. They were old and several cleanings had flattened the once perfect pleats. But she did not see their deteriorated condition. Only the glint of luster as the sunlight touched the outer side, highlighting the center portion to an almost shiny bronze.

She touched the fabric and shivered. A vision flashed through her mind, then another, and another. Again, she shivered. Overcome by an exhilarating sensation. *My God,* she thought, trembling, *it all feels so familiar, so . . . so natural . . . Strange, I know exactly what I should do next. But how? When . . . where?*

She shook her head. What was it that Brent had said? She

had never taken a decorating course, or seriously studied home remodeling. Still, it felt so comfortable—she felt at ease doing it. And loved it. Perhaps Brent was right; it was in her genes, pure instinct, and talent—lots and lots of natural talent. For what else could it be?

Looking around her, Amanda smiled. And she suddenly knew what colors she would use to bring out the desired effect. Paula's dream blended with her vision; she saw it all very clearly now. The picture was complete.

Chapter 19

WOODFIELD MALL AT NOON WAS A FIRST-CLASS TRIBULA-
tion. Paula groaned and grumbled trying to find a parking
spot, and finally, after twice circling the parking lot, she settled for one that was not within reasonable walking distance
of the building. Amanda grinned, hooking her arm through
her friend's, knowing just how much Paula hated the walk.

It was the week before Easter and four days to spring
break. Exhausted from running around and working on Paula's bedroom project, Amanda had decided they needed a
reprieve. When Karen called, she jumped at the chance to
break away for a day.

"Good heavens! Do you see what I see?" Paula nodded at
the people lined up in front of the Magic Pan. "We'll never
get in there. What day is this, National Housewife's Day?"

Just then they spotted Karen in the doorway, frantically
waving.

"I'm glad I got here early." Karen kissed them. "Daryl's
mother decided to cancel her dentist appointment this morning and come straight over. Jesus, I'm crazy about those kids,
but this sure is a treat. Let me tell you, if someone would've
told me that I would ever be so happy to be away from them
for a couple of hours, I'd have told them they were bonkers!"

It was Paula's turn to smile. "I'd say. I've never noticed
how much you could talk."

Karen rolled her eyes and the three of them laughed.

"Wills, party of three," the hostess called. "This way, please."

Still giggling, they followed the young woman, and for the next hour and a half, the lighthearted trio laughed and chattered.

Paula took a long, deep breath, inhaling the exotic fragrances around her with pleasure. She loved Marshall Fields; a bit beyond her budget, perhaps—or rather, Matt's budget—but a joy to visit all the same. Not that she would've admitted this to Nicole or her snobbish neighbor Vanessa Lynch. But Amanda was her best friend.

Suddenly grateful that Amanda did not remember her past, Paula smiled and reached to pocket a Halston sample. The old Amanda would've shopped at Saks or Neiman Marcus. Now she did not seem to mind stores like Fields and Carson Pirie Scott.

"What a shame Karen couldn't stay away a bit longer." She sniffed at a Gucci tester and grimaced, adding, "Gosh, I didn't know they made perfume." She nodded at the approaching salesgirl and grabbed Amanda's arm.

Paula felt mischievous, carefree. The cosmetics department was absolutely divine; just walking through it made her day.

"First she just about ran away from her babies, then after an hour she couldn't wait to get back to them. Weird specimens, those new mothers, don't you think?" She looked at Amanda with feigned innocence and they both burst out laughing.

"Hey, you know what?" Paula moved toward the next counter.

"No, but I'm sure you'll tell me."

"Let's have a demonstration done on your face."

"I beg your pardon?"

"Yeah, you know, a makeup demo. It's perfect. You don't remember how to use those makeup things in your bathroom, and why should you waste them?" She checked her wristwatch. "Let's see. One-forty. We have half an hour to spare. Come on, cara, it'll be fun, trust me." She glanced around for a makeup specialist. "Let's ask someone." Stopping at the Lancôme counter, they found a young girl, heavily made up, watching a quarreling couple nearby, her expression bored.

"Excuse me," Paula said, suppressing a giggle as the girl turned her attention in slow motion to the new customer, perturbed by the demand for service.

"Need some help?"

"If you have time." Paula kept a straight face and Amanda bit her lip trying not to laugh.

"What do you need?"

"My friend here needs professional advice, particularly with her eyes. You know, the right shades and proportions, et cetera."

The girl looked at Amanda's face, the bored expression now indignant.

"Yeah? What do I look like? A makeup artist?"

"Well, I didn't think you'd be an expert in that field myself, but perhaps you could direct us to someone who is?" Her tone was sweet, and the meaning of her words eluded the petulant girl.

"There isn't anyone like that in this store today."

"Oh? Is there someone another day?"

The girl shrugged, once again looking uninterested. "I've no idea. I only work here part-time."

"Figures," Paula mumbled.

"Pardon?"

"Thank you for your help," she said aloud and turned to follow Amanda, who had already walked away.

"Wait." She paused reluctantly at hearing the girl's voice. "Why don't you go to *Cosmetique?* They have nothing but experts there."

Paula turned. "Who?" she asked.

"It's a new store, just opened last month. Go to the wing toward Lord and Taylor, you can't miss it. It smells nice in there."

"Cosmetique. Right. Thank you." She quickly tried to find Amanda and dragged her out of the store.

The girl was right. They found the new store easily, the exotic decor of plums and mauves making it stand out and catch customers' attention as soon as they approached Lord and Taylor's. It almost looked like an extension of the luxurious store itself, standing quaint and elegant next to it. A young, clean-shaven male in a soft purple uniform greeted them as they entered.

"What can I do for you ladies?" he inquired, his voice soft and cultured, his dark eyes shining.

"Hi. We need some expert tips on facial makeup that can make you look like a million dollars without having to spend much." Paula waited for the brush-off, but the young man never flinched, his smile never wavering.

"Please take a seat," he said, gesturing.

Paula returned the smile and reached back for Amanda.

"Actually it's for my friend here." She turned around, but to her surprise found no one standing behind her. "Excuse me," she said and dashed outside, spotting Amanda's red hair in front of Lord and Taylor's left window.

"Amanda, what's the matter? What's wrong? Why did you walk out of there? I thought—"

"I changed my mind."

"What is it? Come on, I'll be there."

Amanda blushed, a sheepish look in her eyes as she tried to shake off Paula's hand. Then she relented.

"Well . . . I don't feel, you know, comfortable . . ."

"Oh, come off it. He's an expert, a pro."

Amanda shook her head.

"Oh, I get it. You'd rather have a female pro." Paula suddenly laughed, relieved. She hooked her hand through Amanda's and dragged her back in the direction of Cosmetique.

"Okay, kiddo. We'll get you a female expert, all right? Leave it to Mother Paula, I'll fix you up."

The young man appeared embarrassed when she explained the situation to him. He looked around; a young woman in a similar uniform was helping an elderly lady; another female employee was busy giving a demonstration.

"I'm truly sorry; there doesn't seem to be anyone else available at this moment," he said, glancing around once more. Then his dark eyes lit up. "Give me one minute, please. I think I can get somebody to assist you." He swiftly walked away from them.

Paula turned and winked at Amanda, her eyes dancing.

"You missed out on that one. I think he's rather cute myself."

Footsteps approached. A soft, cultured female voice spoke.

"May I help you?"

Paula whirled around and her eyes widened.

"Colleen? What the hell are you doing here?"

Colleen smiled. "I own this place. A gift from Stu. Or shall we say, a reward from his generous settlement? But what brings you into a place like this, my dear?"

Paula hesitated, then slowly stepped aside. "My friend needs expert advice," she said, her voice low.

Amanda smiled at the elegantly dressed young woman, but to her surprise, the smile on Colleen's face died as soon as she saw her.

"If this is a practical joke, Paula Manchione, I'm not amused."

Colleen's eyes had turned cold and she stood rigid, her hands clenched into fists, only her lips moving as she spoke again.

"I must ask you both to leave. This store does not cater to the likes of you."

"Please, Colleen."

"Leave. Now."

Once outside, a bewildered Amanda turned to her tongue-tied friend.

"What the hell was that all about? Why did she throw us out?" Then, seeing Paula's embarrassed face, she suddenly understood. "It's me, isn't it? She . . . who is she? What did I do to her?"

"Oh, just one of your many fans, I guess. Let's not worry about her, cara, we'll find another place, I promise." She turned to walk into Lord and Taylor's, but Amanda grabbed her by the sleeve, forcing her to stop.

"What did I do to that woman to make her so hostile toward me? Did . . . did I . . . hit on her husband?"

Paula shrugged. "Forget it, Amanda. Colleen has a vivid imagination and a flair for melodrama. Why, before her marriage she was an actress. Not a very good one, I'm told, but an actress all the same. Come, let's go home. Unless you want to try the cosmetic department here?"

She all but dragged her distressed friend out of the store and into the open air, only to realize that they were at the wrong end of the parking lot.

*   *   *

Stepping out of the shower, Amanda rubbed her wet hair on the towel draped loosely around her bare shoulders. She slowly walked to the spacious dressing area, and gazing at her naked reflection in the huge lighted mirrors, she paused. For a long moment she kept staring at herself. Then, with a heavy sigh, she turned and grabbed the white satin robe from the chair near the louvered closet doors and covered her gleaming body.

The soft cloth felt cool against her skin and she shivered. Facing the mirrors once more, she felt an urge to slam a fist into her own reflection as the events of the day resurfaced. Instead she sat down and opened the drawer to get a hairbrush. Her eye fell on the abundance of eye makeup bottles and pallets and her fingers itched to gather them all up and dump them into the wastebasket underneath the vanity.

"Why won't you tell me anything, Paula?" She had pressed her friend when they finally found the car. "Why can't you come straight out and tell me I'm a slut?"

Paula had only looked at her, her look clearly disproving her choice of words.

"Your private affairs are your business, Amanda," Paula said, grimacing. "Sorry, bad pun. Look, if you were running around with anybody, you never told me. And regardless of what anyone says, I really don't know the truth."

"But you must have some inkling, a suspicion? Why can't you tell me about them? Please, even if they are just speculations on your part."

"Look, in my book accusations are hurled only when there's proof. And since in your case there's none, I refuse to be part of dragging my best friend through the mud. You understand?" There had been pain in Paula's dark eyes, and Amanda fell silent.

She had not pressed further, knowing instinctively that Paula would not be bullied into making any statements she was not ready to give. And she had been silent the rest of the way.

The afternoon had dragged on, turning into evening. That too had crept by. She had hardly paid any attention to the children, listening automatically to their stories, listlessly picking at her dinner, until Brent, concerned, had rescued her by suggesting that she take a nice hot shower while he took the kids to bed.

Brent. The chill in her bones lessened when she thought of him. If she was what people had whispered about her, why would she have betrayed him with all those other men? It was something she could not quite understand, something so incredibly against what she felt for him . . . It did not make any sense. Unless . . .

She shook her head, her damp curls dancing wildly around her face. For some time now, she had silenced her doubts about her identity. Ever since that afternoon in the train. Ever since she had weighed the alternative, the consequence, of being someone else. And as her relationship with Brent blossomed, the doubts had faded. She had chosen to accept life as it was presented to her, for to lose Brent would be to lose her life.

Now that fear had been revived, the question staring at her in the mirror. Only this time the fear had intensified. For now she had much more to lose—too much. Not just Brent, but the children, her friendship with Paula and Karen, even Louise. And a life she liked living. God, she so desperately wanted to bury the nagging doubt, to put the question to rest, once and for all. With a deep sigh, she quietly closed the drawer.

"Amanda?"

She started at the sound of his voice. She had not heard him come into the bedroom and before she could straighten herself, his face appeared behind her in the mirror. Their eyes met and for a moment she felt all her problems fade away. Her heart thumped in her throat as she basked in the warm embrace of his dark eyes, full of concern and gentle with affection.

She rose and buried herself in his strong arms. Nestling close against him she felt Brent's instant response, and as he held her tight, Amanda closed her eyes and sighed, a long drawn-out sigh. He felt so safe, so comforting. Whatever he felt for her, this could not be hate. Somehow, nothing else mattered.

Chapter 20

"WELL, THAT JUST ABOUT DOES IT." PAULA PUSHED THE bales of heavy curtain material from her and with an air of finality closed the books of color samples that were spread all across the table. "Let's wrap it up. One more minute of these and, I swear, I'll go color-blind." She fell back on the sofa, leaned her dark head against the edge, and let out a deep sigh of relief. "Why didn't you warn me this was such a tedious venture?" she asked, throwing Amanda a reproachful look.

"I guess that's it, Jay." Ignoring her friend, Amanda smiled at the young man in jeans, who, with a sheepish look, gathered a couple of the bales together and transferred them to another table covered with more of the same.

They had packed the children off to school that morning, and driven to Skokie to visit Jay Kinski's place. He had a small warehouse, but the size was deceptive—it was loaded with samples, and whatever was on the market could be ordered, even if he did not have a sample of the material.

Amanda had chosen his services over more elaborate ones in the Merchandise Mart in the Chicago Loop, mostly because she was not registered as a professional decorator, but also because Kinski was cheaper and offered a quicker delivery of the finished product. Even more importantly, he would do all the hard work—put up the rods, hang the curtains, all according to the blueprints she had shown him. Now that she had seen his warehouse, she was happy with her choice. It was packed with material, but clean and amazingly well organized.

The man Michael recommended had declined to take the job, but instead had recommended Jay Kinski, who used to work for him before starting his own business. Amanda had liked Jay from the start. A lanky young man bordering on skinny, his moustache and beard neatly trimmed, he was rather shy, a man of few words. At her warm smile he nodded, the right corner of his bearded mouth curling up slightly.

"One month? Will that give you enough time?" Amanda rose and picked up her purse. Jay nodded again. "If you need more time, please do call me."

"I'll call you when they're done. Six weeks, no more. But I think you can have them in one month." His voice was deep and his words muffled in his throat. Amanda smiled again and held out her hand. Jay wiped his on his worn-out jeans and shook her hand, his eyes returning the smile.

"Thank you, Jay. I know I can count on you."

"Are we done?" Paula jumped to her feet. "Yes, Jay, thanks for everything. It was a real treat. Exhausting." She glanced at her watch and frowned; they had been browsing for over two hours! She quickly shook Kinski's hand and rushed back to her car.

"Don't mind her," Amanda apologized, and Jay grinned. She quickly followed her impatient friend to the waiting car.

"Come on, hop in." Paula started the motor. "After all that I think we deserve a break."

"Hold it. What do you have in mind?"

"Just sit back and relax. I don't know about you, but I'm starved and I know just the place." She threw Amanda a mysterious look and pressed on the accelerator.

At eleven-fifteen in the morning, Eden Expressway was practically deserted. Quite a treat really, and Paula could not pass up the rarity. With a mischievous grin she expertly swung the car into the fast lane and gave gas. The BMW purred with triumphant glee as it glided forward, soon imitating a jet-liner's takeoff on a cleared runway, and Paula's grin widened, her eyes two huge topaze sparklers, dancing with sheer delight and anticipation.

"Shouldn't you slow down a bit?" Amanda asked, clasping the handle above her car door, her nails digging into her right palm.

She hated fast rides, even on deserted roads and in clear weather conditions. Not that she actually remembered her near fatal accident, but even in her wildest imagination she could envision the frightful consequences. She could feel her muscles tighten and the knot in her stomach beginning to bother her.

"Paula? Please?"

A green Cadillac passed them on the right and a lecherous grin split the driver's chubby face, his bald shiny head bobbing at them. Amanda looked away, unable to watch his fleshy lips blow kisses in their direction. Then, without warning, the Cadillac pulled up and cut right in front of the BMW. Amanda gasped, her hand gripping the handle above the door in preparation for the collision. Instinctively, Paula took her foot off the gas pedal and, almost instantly, the BMW reduced speed.

"Son of a bitch." She suddenly gave gas again and the next couple of hundred feet she deliberately tailgated the Cadillac, gritting her teeth. The bald driver of the Cadillac raised a chubby hand and teasingly shook his finger at them.

"Move, you bastard." Paula pulled closer, the front bumper of the BMW almost touching the back of the Cadillac, and Amanda closed her eyes, heart pounding. "Don't worry, there's nobody in front of him." Paula fumed. "He has no business pulling in front of me." As if he had heard her, the driver of the Cadillac relented and swerved back to the right-hand lane, yet still maintaining speed as he kept on grinning at them, and waving.

"Please, Paula." Amanda was close to tears, her face deathly pale now. She felt sick and kept swallowing the rising bile.

"Oh, all right." Paula sighed, clearly disappointed.

She glanced sideways, and seeing Amanda frozen in her seat—her hands clenching the edges, eyes closed, feet rigidly extended—she frowned. For a second the car relaxed. Paula's fingers drummed the steering wheel. Sighing, she threw her friend another glance. And a sudden sensation swept over her.

An odd gleam crept into her dark eyes, and gripping the steering wheel, she hit the gas pedal. The BMW leaped forward, rapidly leaving the green Cadillac behind.

A muffled shriek escaped Amanda's ashen lips. Her eyes flew open at the spurt, terror clutching at her throat as she watched the road fly by, the cars on their right-hand side at a seeming standstill. "Pau-Paula . . . ?" Her lips formed the name, but her mouth was too dry.

She could not move. Her limbs were numb, her heartbeat so faint she could not feel it. She slumped down in her seat, and her eyes seemed to close all by themselves. Her grasp on the edge of the car seat slackened. Slowly, her body began to float along with the motion of the car.

Just as suddenly as the BMW had taken off, it slowed down and resumed near normal speed. Paula glanced in her rear-view mirror, her eyes flickering triumphantly.

"We can't let that asshole bother us again, now can we?" she murmured. She glanced at the shaken Amanda, and suddenly laughed. "Relax, cara, we're almost there. I'm sorry I scared you, but you shouldn't have attracted that sleazy goofball in the first place."

She patted her friend reassuringly and eased smoothly to the right as the first skyscrapers of Chicago came into view. As she took the third exit that led them into the Loop she smiled again. The drive had refreshed her, and the little incident along the way had heightened the pleasure. Letting out a deep sigh of satisfaction, she expertly swung the BMW up Madison Avenue.

Nick's Fishmarket was packed. The line of people waiting for a table reached the front door, blocking the entrance. A radiant smile on her face, gesturing Amanda to follow her, Paula waded through the crowd. Ignoring the stares around her, she headed straight for the reservations desk. The gray-haired maître d' looked up from his long list, and at the sight of her, his eyes lit up and he smiled.

"Mrs. Manchione, how nice to see you again," he said warmly.

"Hi, Pierre. Good crowd today."

"You noticed. A little more hectic than usual, I must say."

"How long, my friend? I'm starved." She flashed him a row of blinding white teeth, her big dark eyes pleading. Pierre studied his list, his finger casually tracing the names.

"Well, let me see. Ah, yes, you did have a reservation. For two, correct?" He glanced politely at Amanda, then turned candidly to Paula for confirmation. "One moment, please." He turned and glanced around the dining room. Catching the attention of his assistant, he signaled, holding two fingers up to the man. Instantly the other nodded and disappeared.

"We haven't seen you around for some time. Is everything well with you and Mr. Manchione?" Pierre smiled politely.

"Why, my dear Pierre, such a marvelous memory you have. But you are a dear. And a pathetic liar. Matt told me he was here last week, with a business associate." She laughed. "Are you trying to protect him? I know who the lady is, you know."

Pierre smiled, never losing a moment's composure. "There's nothing to be admired more than a solid marriage, madam. And honesty in a marriage is highly commendable."

Paula laughed harder, this time truly amused. "And since when have you become a preacher on fidelity, you old buzzard, you."

She glanced back at Amanda, her eyes dancing with glee. The man in the dining room reappeared, nodding imperceptibly at his superior.

"Ah, your table is ready." He grabbed two menus, still smiling. "Ladies, follow me, please."

Paula grinned at Amanda and trotted behind Pierre into the crowded dining room. If she was aware of the curious and somewhat hostile stares of the people they left still waiting for a table, she did not show it.

Still shaken from the wild ride, Amanda followed her cheerful friend. She felt uneasy, almost guilty for the lie and the preferential treatment. Passing the fully occupied tables, she tried not to focus on anyone in particular, or to pay close attention to the buzzing sounds around her. Still, she was acutely conscious of a woman dropping a knife on the floor, a man choking on his drink, and she quickened her pace to keep up with Paula and Pierre.

A young woman looked up and Amanda caught her startled look. The woman instantly leaned over to her friend and whispered something to her, and her friend stopped eating.

They passed the table, and despite herself, Amanda looked back, only to see both women get up and leave. Why, she could have sworn they had not quite finished their meal. She shook her head. Coincidence? Must be. Her imagination must be running wild, or was it paranoia?

"Thank you, Pierre." Smiling, Paula sat down.

"Enjoy your lunch." Pierre bowed slightly and walked away.

Amanda glanced at her surroundings. Pierre had seated them in a corner, with a strategic view of the room.

"Do you come here often?" Amanda whispered. Then, at Paula's surprised look, she opened the menu Pierre had left in front of her. "Never mind, dumb question."

A woman at the table next to them gasped, and they both turned to look at her. The woman stared at Amanda, her face matching the whiteness of the napkin she held in front of her mouth. Her male companion leaned forward and said something, and she visibly pulled herself together. She peeled her eyes off Amanda and reached for the glass of wine before her, her hand badly shaking. The man threw them a furtive glance, his eyes shifting. A forced grin in Amanda's direction contorted his taut face as he signaled the waiter for the check, his eyes bearing the same haunted expression as the woman's.

"What's going on?" Amanda whispered to Paula, anxiety written clearly all over her face.

"What are you talking about? So that woman doesn't like our looks, so what? It's a free country." Paula smiled at the approaching waitress. "A vodka martini for me. How about you, cara?"

Amanda nodded. "Make that two." Not that she liked the drink, but it was easier than ordering something else.

When the girl was out of earshot, she leaned over to Paula, a frown furrowing her forehead. "It wasn't *our* looks she didn't like, it was *mine*. She looked directly at *me*, and only at me. What the hell does this all mean, Paula, what?"

"Hey, hey, take it easy, cara. People are staring at us."

"And stop calling me cara! For once—"

"Well, well, look who we've got here." They both jumped at the drawling voice.

They had not heard him approach and Amanda gaped into a pair of dark, mocking eyes, and blinked. Towering over their table, the tall, suave stranger smiled. She flinched at the flagrant malice in his eyes. She heard Paula mumble an ugly word beneath her breath, but if the man had heard it, he chose to ignore it. Picking a peanut from the jar on the table, he stuck it in his mouth and slowly licked his fingers, never once taking his eyes off her.

"So you decided to return from the dead. Someone did tell me you had, but I thought he'd had one too many."

"Stu—"

"Hi, Paula." He never looked at her, his eyes boring into Amanda's. "What gives, Amanda? Forgotten someone? Or did you remember you forgot to fuck somebody?"

Amanda winced. It was not so much the sneer as the intense bitterness in his deep voice.

"That's enough. Get away from us, you big asshole, and take that filthy mouth with you, or I'll have you thrown out of this place." Paula hissed, her nostrils flaring, her blazing eyes ominous.

The waitress returned with two martinis.

"Are you ladies ready to order?"

"Bring me a double Scotch straight up." The stranger looked around gingerly. "And a chair."

"Scratch that. He's leaving. *Now.*" Paula glared at him and for a moment they matched wills. Then, with a shrug, he gestured at the waiting girl and turned to move away. He threw Amanda one last look and she quailed.

"You should've stayed dead, Amanda. You shouldn't have returned to your old hunting grounds. That was a mistake."

Watching his disappearing back, Paula drew a deep sigh of relief and took a quick gulp of her martini. She glanced at Amanda and frowned. Her face had lost all color, her eyes wide and bewildered and frightened.

"Shall I come back?" the waitress asked softly.

Paula nodded. "Give us another few minutes. Thank you."

"Amanda." She gently nudged her. "Are you all right?"

Slowly Amanda turned to her and without a word picked up her martini and emptied the glass.

"Please, Paula, I'm not hungry. Could we . . . could we . . ."

"Right. We'll go somewhere a little more private. Christ, this is worse than a country club." She signaled the headwaiter for the check.

"Anything wrong, Mrs. Manchione?" He looked genuinely concerned.

"No, Johnny, everything's fine. My friend here remembered she had an appointment in five minutes. We'll be back some other time, I promise."

Walking out of the restaurant, Amanda looked straight ahead. If she could, she would have run out, into the fresh outdoors, into the bright sunlight that would chase away the shadows of her dark past.

Amanda was quiet for the first ten minutes of their drive back to Lake Forest. Paula, not used to city driving, concentrated on the traffic, but once they hit the expressway, she relaxed a little and glanced gingerly at her silent passenger. After a while, she could not stand the silence any longer.

"Hey, how about a Whopper, eh? We can stop at the Burger King before we hit home. How about it, cara? Oh, sorry. I'm not to call you that. I forgot."

"Who was he, Paula?"

Paula heaved an inaudible sigh of relief. Thank God she talked. "His name is Stuart Gibbs, Colleen Gibbs's ex-husband and Matt's ex-partner. He had no business being crude to you or causing that scene in—"

"Why was he saying all those things? Did we . . . were we . . . ?"

The anxiety returned in full force and she clasped her hands together to stop the trembling. Paula sighed again, audibly this time.

"Colleen thought so. She divorced him."

Amanda turned her head sideways to hide the pain in her eyes. Staring out of the window, she did not see the cars or the buildings they passed. In her mind she saw again the two women who had left the restaurant in the middle of their meal as soon as they spotted her; the woman at the adjacent table who had gasped at the sight of her; and the bitterness in Stuart Gibbs's voice. The images were so brutally real they ripped through her with haunting force, leaving her shaken and nauseated.

God, she thought, squirming inside, *what kind of evil person was I? How could I have done so much harm and caused that much hurt to so many people? So much that they shun my presence, despise the very sight of me, wish me dead . . .*

". . . he really had her going for a while. Oh, here's our exit. Better make up your mind what you want, we're taking the drive-through. Much quicker that way. Okay with you?" Paula glanced sideways at her pensive passenger. "Amanda?"

Suddenly aware that Paula had been talking to her, Amanda forced her attention back to her friend. "A Whopper sounds fine," she said as the car swung into the drive-through lane of the Burger King.

She was not hungry, but it was after all her fault that they had not yet eaten.

"How about going to the park, hm? It'll be more peaceful than home and it'll give us a chance to catch our breath."

"Yes, thank you." Amanda threw her a grateful smile. Good old Paula. It was nice of her to say "us" and "our," and she did feel reluctant to face the kids at this moment.

The park was quiet, deserted but for a couple of chattering birds and, at the far side, two women watching three toddlers at play.

They ate their lunch in silence. Chewing her hamburger automatically, Amanda was aware of her friend's worried glances, but stubbornly kept her peace. Part of her desperately screamed to get answers to the many questions that could shed a light on her past. Yet another part shied just as desperately away from learning more for fear of what she might discover—the kind of person she did not want to, was not ready to accept as being her, the Amanda who had left the scene four years ago.

Or was that perhaps the very reason why she had left? Not a marital dispute, perhaps not even problems with Brent, but a realization of the person she had become—a despicable ogre, disgusting even to herself? It certainly would make sense. A lot a sense.

"Cara?" Paula prodded softly. "Want to talk about it?"

Amanda sighed, hesitated, then slowly shook her head. "Let's go home. The kids will be wondering where we are," she mumbled, getting up. Paula touched her arm, gently, and when she spoke her voice was warm and husky, full of fiber, brimming with emotion.

"Don't let Stu Gibbs get to you, Amanda. He's a chronic skirt-chaser, an incurable womanizer. Always was, still is. And he likes to live life in the fast lane. Colleen knew it, everyone did. If she picked on you, it was just because you happened to be there at the right time. She could've named anybody, really."

Amanda looked at her and Paula felt a knot in her stomach. Sudden tears brimmed and she turned her head. God, she hated herself. Some friend she was. Those eyes, and that stricken look—like a lost doe—enormous with hurt and pain. How could she tell her that some of the ugly rumors were based on sordid fact? How could she bear the agony in those doelike eyes if Amanda were to discover that her past appetite had been targeted at the inaccessible? Or that she had basked in being Cook County's number one cock-teaser, irresistible to man and beast?

Paula sighed. The knot in her stomach tightened. She turned around and silently watched Amanda's forlorn figure leaning against a tree a couple of yards away, staring across the lake and beyond the pale blue horizons. Paula sighed again. If only she could erase the bleak despair, chase away the haunting shadows that seemed to creep up wherever Amanda went. Perhaps, if she were to go away for a while . . .

She suddenly sucked in her breath. Why, that's it! Spring break. She'd forgotten all about it. Matt's partner had made his house on Maui available to them for that period. God, one whole week . . . just enough for Amanda to catch her breath . . .

Grabbing her handbag, she got up. For a moment she hesitated, recognizing Amanda's need for solitude. Then, resolutely, she approached the tree and touched Amanda's arm.

"Come. It's time to go home now," she said.

"Matt? How would you feel about the Farradays joining us in Hawaii?"

"What do you mean? I thought Amanda was working on our bedroom."

"She is. But I feel guilty about skipping town for a week and leaving her to slave away all by herself."

"She might welcome the peace."

"Matt!"

"You know I don't mind," he said. "Sure. The house is big enough."

Paula smiled, throwing her husband a kiss.

"Thank you, darling. I'll call Amanda right now. That'll give her two days to get things ready." She darted toward the telephone.

"Brent might not be able to get away," Matt said.

"God, I love you. Such an optimist." Grinning, Paula dialed Amanda's number.

Chapter 21

MANEUVERING THE AVIS RENTAL OUT OF MAUI'S KAHULUI airport area and into the steady flow of traffic, Brent suddenly remembered that he had not called the number Matt had given him. Then, listening to Josh's excited chatter and Mandy's happy giggles in the back seat, he pushed his worry aside and reached for Amanda's hand.

It had taken some fast talking to get others to cover for him. And the art of persuasion did not come naturally for him. But he had managed somehow. His friends knew of his past problems with Amanda, and her recent return convinced most of them that he needed some time with her, time away from the daily routine. So he had found willing bodies.

He turned in the direction of Wailea and smiled, sharing the children's awe at nature's hand when they passed the road shaded by windblown trees that formed an arched path. Like a bridal arch, Mandy said. So romantic, Amanda sighed. While Josh mumbled "Awesome," gaping at the wonder from the back window. Too soon the scenery changed and they sped along a two-lane highway flanked by tall, lanky sugarcanes ripe for the harvesting.

When the burgundy Cutlass Sierra turned onto the wide Piilani highway, Brent relaxed. Then, with a mischievous grin, he pressed his foot down on the gas pedal, and enjoyed the rare ultrasmooth ride. The car flew across the road, passing an odd car here and there, and he felt a sense of triumph, of power, an exhilaration not shared by a terrified Amanda.

"Daddy! You're doing ninety," Mandy shrieked, and Josh scurried forward to peek at the speedometer.

"Yeah! Yippee!" he cheered, his blue eyes dancing.

"All right. The fun is over. It won't do to start our vacation with a speeding ticket." Amanda nudged Brent's hand and he slowed down, still grinning.

"Oh, Dad!" Josh sounded crushed and threw himself back on the back seat. "Party pooper," he muttered, glaring at his mother.

"Fantastic instinct," his father praised as he spotted the police car drive up from a side ramp and slide behind them up the highway. "Better give your mother a kiss, my boy. That cop does not look overly friendly. Good thing he wasn't around a few minutes ago."

Josh jerked back up, half expecting an empty bluff. Then, seeing the black and white on their tail, he sank back in the soft seat, his little face no longer sullen. After a while the police car pulled up and, apparently satisfied with Brent's driving speed, passed the Cutlass. Two exits later it turned to head back toward Kihei. Amanda glanced at the back seat and grinned at Mandy's sigh of relief.

"Let's just hope that Matt's picked up the key to the house," Brent muttered as he passed the rock that had "Wailea" engraved in it and swerved onto Alanui Way. Amanda clasped her free hand in front of her mouth, her eyes wide with alarm.

"Weren't you supposed to . . . ?"

"Yeah, yeah, I forgot. No big deal, we can still go to the real estate office and pick up those keys, but first let's see if our efficient counselor hasn't beaten us to it. Knowing Matt, he's probably already started the barbecue, and I wouldn't be surprised if—" He suddenly braked and the children in the back seat shrieked.

"What the h—" Amanda gasped. Her startled eyes caught sight of the lanky boy frantically waving his long arms to get their attention. From nowhere a little blond girl appeared and, pushing the boy aside, dashed toward the Cutlass.

"Wes! It's Wes!" Josh cheered, jumping up and down, pulling at the car door handle, which remained locked.

"Tara!" Mandy screeched, just as excited as her brother.

"God! He could've gotten himself killed," Brent fumed, still a bit shaken, glaring at the grinning youngster.

He deactivated the children's lockproof button and they instantly bolted out of the car, almost stumbling over their own feet in the process.

"What did I tell you?" Brent grinned at the flabbergasted Amanda. "I knew he wouldn't let us down."

The front door opened and a beaming Paula appeared in the doorway. "Hi, guys! What took you so long?"

The house was beautiful. Set amid idyllic surroundings, it resembled a storybook version of a quaint European hideout. Partially hidden behind bushels of colorful flowers and flourishing bougainvillea of all colors, it overlooked the rolling greens of the Wailea golf course and still caught a glimpse of the wide, cool blue Pacific ocean beyond the luxurious Stouffers hotel across the street.

Inside it was spacious and sparsely, yet tastefully, furnished, and Amanda felt breathless just looking around. It was amazingly cool with only ceiling fans to combat the outside heat. And while Brent and Matt carried in the suitcases, she stepped out on the tiled balcony that bordered the entire bungalow. It was wide, and each room had access to it.

"Amanda, where are you?"

She quickly went back into the house where Paula, now in a bathing suit, grinned at her from inside the kitchen.

"Here, have a beer, cara. Get your bikini on, girl, it's too hot to stay dressed. Come on, stay a while."

Accepting the bottle of beer, Amanda sank into a deep, comfortable chair and let out a contented sigh. "This is the life, Paula. This is how the angels in heaven feel. I must thank you for inviting us," she purred.

Paula laughed. She was pleased that things had worked out so well, for until two days ago, Brent had not been able to get any of his colleagues to cover for him. And watching Amanda's serene face right now, she knew she had done the right thing.

"My, my, look at this kaffeeklatsch." Brent walked into the room, feigning annoyance. "While we men are slaving away, the ladies sit back boozing it up." He looked at the bottle of beer in Amanda's hand. "Are you going to drink that or just stare at it?"

Amanda stuck her tongue out at him and took a quick sip.

"Oh, here." Paula offered him a bottle. "There's plenty more where that came from."

"I really should unpack and get our bathing suits." Amanda rose.

"Excellent idea. They really have some swimming pool in the backyard." Brent heaved himself onto a bar stool. "Boy, this is the life, I tell you. Could it be that I've died and went to heaven?"

Amanda paused in the doorway and looked at Paula, and seeing Paula's startled expression, she suddenly burst out laughing.

The children were shrieking. Laughing just as hard, Amanda dove into the pool, instantly followed by her pursuers. Tara and Mandy ran along the edge and, keeping up with her, cheered her on.

"Come on, cara, swim. Go, girl, go! Don't let those sharks get you."

Paula swung her slender arms frantically, gesturing, beckoning, slapping her long legs in between fits of laughter. Amanda swam for her life, but the boys were faster, more agile, and soon they caught up with her. Wes grabbed one of her legs, and as he finally reached her sideways, Josh triumphantly hugged her waist, pulling her under.

Laughing at the frolicking swimmers, Brent handed Matt another bottle of Heineken beer and turned to say something to his daughter. As he did so, he noticed the approaching figure of a man from the side of the house. His face fell.

"Oh, shit." He had said it under his breath, yet Matt heard it, and peering around his friend, he too grunted.

"How the hell did he get here? Who told him?"

"I did," Matt admitted reluctantly. "Sorry, buddy. The man hasn't taken a vacation for years. How was I supposed to know . . ."

He rose and forced a friendly smile. "Hi, Niels. Fancy seeing you here."

Niels Nillson smiled broadly, his eyes following Amanda, who had hoisted herself out of the water and, dripping, accepted a towel from a helpful Paula. His look assessed her slim figure, caressing the curvaceous lines, the swelling atop the one-piece bathing suit, and his smile widened.

"Hi, guys. I'm not crashing the fun, am I?" He put on his most innocent face and pretended not to see Brent's grimace.

"No, of course not," Brent mumbled sarcastically.

"No, of course not," Matt said out loud, ignoring his friend's displeasure. "Come join us. Want a beer?"

"Don't mind if I do."

Matt handed him a cold Heineken.

"Hey, Niels. Where did you come from?" Paula shouted. "Where are Nikki and Cole?"

"They're coming. Nikki went shopping with her sister and Cole—"

"Here I am." The boy ran toward the pool and, without waiting for an invitation, unceremoniously jumped into the water.

"Easy, kid." His father grinned, still watching Amanda rub her hair dry on the towel, and catching her weary glance, he looked away in the direction of the men. "How about that, eh guys? My first vacation in years. When Matt told me about this place I thought, what the hell, why not? All work and no play makes any man a dull good-for-nothing, so here I am." He grinned at Brent and, ignoring the latter's dark scowl, slapped him good-humoredly on the back. "Here, I even brought steaks for all of us. Damn expensive on this island, but what the hell—you're worth it."

Matt smiled, but made no move to accept the peace offering. Niels put up his arms and sighed.

"Okay, okay. I know when I'm not wanted."

"I'll take that." Paula darted forward and took the package off his hands. She threw her husband a dark look and went inside the house.

Soon no one remembered the hostility that had greeted the newcomer. He outdid himself chasing the children in and out of the pool, and they were having the time of their lives trying to beat an adult.

"Hey, is there more beer in this place?" Niels yelled at Paula.

Despite their previous reluctance, and after a couple more Heinekens, they all enjoyed the steaks. More beer went around, and the mood became rowdy and festive. Nikki called to say that she and her sister were heading for Lahaina and would see them tomorrow. Toward eight o'clock in the evening Matt and Brent went to Kihei to get more beer.

Amanda opened the refrigerator door and peered inside, looking for the pack of wine coolers she had seen Paula stash in there earlier that afternoon. Fumbling through the food, she finally spotted the bottles hidden behind the stacks of Coca-Cola cans, and picking one she straightened up and turned. A hairy arm blocked her exit and she gasped. Towering over her, his blue eyes flickering dangerously, his face unsmiling, stood Niels. His hair still damp from the swim, he just stood there, barring her, his chest bare, his scanty suit bulging.

"Did . . . did you want . . . something . . . ?" Her throat tightened, but she forced herself to remain calm, keeping her expression aloof.

"You know what I want." His hand touched her breast and she shrank back.

"Step aside, Niels, or—"

"Or what, darling? You'll scream?"

She tried to push him away but it was like butting against steel.

"Don't be a fool," she hissed. "What do you think they'll say when I tell them—"

"Tell them what, pussy-face? That you tried to seduce me? They know your reputation." He moved closer, a menacing smile curling the corner of his mouth.

Amanda backed up, and bumping against the refrigerator door, she winced at the coldness that stung her bare back. Her heart skipped a beat, stricken by a sudden fear. The intensity of his gaze pierced her shivering body and she swallowed, her hand clenching the rim of the open refrigerator door.

"What's the matter, kitten? You used to like being cornered like this, remember?" He moved closer, his face contorted with lust. "Oh, come on. Fight for your freedom. What happened to the little wildcat who'd stop at nothing to get her kicks out of pain? Like this . . ." His hand grabbed her breast and Amanda flinched at the pain.

"You're drunk!" she hissed, but before she could turn her

head away from him, his mouth had covered hers, devouring, savagely, hungrily.

Amanda moaned, struggling to pry herself loose from his iron grip, but his unleashed desire made him invincible. The stench of his sour breath revolted her and the rising bile lodged in her throat, making her gag. Instinctively her fingers raked his bare back, digging viciously into his flesh.

If Niels felt the pain, he did not show it. Instead, he ravaged and plundered her mouth, thrusting his tongue inside, while pressing his rigid torso against her. Amanda tensed. She could feel his throbbing hardness pulsating against her stomach, straining and stabbing through her thin bathing suit. With the strength of a cornered jungle cat, she tore her head sideways and bit his lip, fierce and deadly.

With a grunt of pain he released her, staring at her with disbelief, and slowly touched his mouth. Then, seeing the blood on his fingers, he let out a snarl of anger.

"Get out of my way, Niels." The words were wrenched out of her dry throat and she bit her lip to retain her self-control. Her knees were shaking, but she willed herself to stay erect, keeping her expression cool and her eyes scornful.

"Why, you little bitch!" he growled, licking the blood off his lips. "Go ahead, scream. Let them all come and see for themselves what you're up to. It's your word against mine, and who would believe your version, hm? The words of a slut."

Her hand lashed out, but he was quicker. With one swift move and holding her hand in a firm grip, his other hand grabbed her breast once more and Amanda flinched at the pain that seared through her. His head came down and she shifted her head sideways and closed her eyes, expecting the touch of his distasteful lips on her skin.

"Let her go, Nillson. NOW!"

Niels jumped at the sound of the deadly voice.

"Unless you wish to explain the scars on your face, I suggest you leave this house immediately." Brent's taut jaws were clenched, as were his fists at the side of his hips, his dark eyes spitting fury and contempt at his wife's accoster.

"Hey, look Brent, I—"

"Get out of my sight. And don't show your face to me again, not here, not ever." His voice was soft and low, but the menacing tone unmistakable. Without another word Niels took off.

Amanda sighed and slumped to the floor. Brent rushed forward and instantly moved her away from the refrigerator, closing the door with his right foot.

"It's all right, honey. He's gone and I'm here now." He took her trembling body into his arms to warm her, gently rocking her.

"He . . . he was going to . . . to hurt . . . me . . . ," she said, sobbing.

"Shhh, hush baby, hush now. He won't try again, trust me. I'll make sure of that, I promise."

She looked up, her eyes wide in her tearstained face. "You . . . you believe me?"

Brent frowned, puzzled. "What? That he tried to rape you? Of course I believe you."

"He . . . he said—"

"I know what he said. I heard it all."

Amanda froze.

"You what?" she whispered. "All this time you stood there and let him scare the crap out of me?"

Brent bent his head, his fingers raking through his hair.

"You . . . you . . . bastard! How dare you pretend you're any better than he is? Don't touch me." She scrambled away from him, feeling betrayed and soiled somehow.

"Hey, wait a minute. I had to make sure, don't you see that?"

"All I see is a fool who evidently enjoys watching his wife being mauled by another man." Her eyes spat disgust.

"Look, how was I to know if this wasn't one of your old games? The last time I interfered, I made an ass of myself, remember?"

"No, I don't remember, you oaf. Damn you! Get the hell out of my sight—" She shrieked as Brent grabbed her ankle and pulled her across the floor toward him. "Let go of me. Your touch makes my skin crawl—" Her words were muffled as his mouth came down hard on hers and she struggled to get loose, pounding her fists on his chest. Then, slowly, gradually, her resistance weakened, and against her will she began to respond to his kisses, still sobbing, yet savoring the feel of his lips against hers. His hand stroked the curve of his hip and down the smooth bare skin of her thigh. Finally, even the sobbing stopped.

"We'd better stop this, or the children will see an R-rated

show before their time," Brent muttered, his voice husky, his lips nibbling behind her ears.

"Hey, you two!" They scrambled apart and sheepishly faced a grinning Paula. "In case you forgot, there are such things as bedrooms, you know, even in this house." She threw a towel at them and left the room, snickering.

Amanda and Brent looked at each other and simultaneously burst into a fit of laughter. Then, sobering up, Brent wrapped the towel around her shoulders and, rising, pulled her to her feet. "On second thought, let's go for a swim and cool off. At least until after the kids are asleep."

Arm in arm they went outside. Paula grinned at their approach and Matt just watched them. Neither of them asked about Niels's abrupt disappearance.

Chapter 22

SHE WAS DROWNING. THE WATER EMBRACED HER LIKE A whirlpool, merciless, vicious, pulling her, sucking her into its core. She flung her arms wildly, kicking her feet hard, desperately reaching for the surface, to lift her head out of the current, and failing miserably. Then, for a brief moment her head leaped above the woolly water and she frantically gasped for air. At that very moment her terrified eyes caught sight of the man standing at the edge of the pool, watching her struggle with unmasked triumph, his cold eyes full of hate.

She gulped once more and swallowed more water than air, then she went under again. Kicking harder she once again came up to the surface and her fear intensified. The man jumped into the pool and she flung her arms with such force she could feel her muscles torn by the effort, but she hardly paid attention to the piercing pain as she tried to swim away from the new danger.

She opened her mouth, yet the scream gurgled in her throat, overpowered by the wave of water that threatened to subdue her senses. As she went under another time she felt a strong male hand push her down, keeping her head under water until she felt her lungs explode. With a last surge of energy she kicked at her assailant, aiming between his hairy legs, and his hold slackened. Struggling with the strength of the damned, she managed to elude his arm and reached the surface just long enough to gather a breath of air before a strong arm ensnared her, pulling her down, and down, and down . . .

". . . wake up, Manda . . . wake up . . ."

The voice echoed through her subconscious and she jerked up to a sitting position, still gasping for air. Her eyes flew around the room, wild and full of horror; sweat pearled on her forehead, her face deadly pale.

"It's all right, it was just a dream." Brent's voice was soft and gentle, and slowly her fear subsided.

Yet the horror remained with her, and as he wiped off the sweat and gently pulled her into his arms, her body began to shake uncontrollably. The sound of her chattering teeth was a sound as ominous as the horror that was still in her wide eyes. Wordlessly he just held her, rocking her to soothe her fears, his hands gently stroking her wet hair. He closed his eyes for a moment, suffering with her, yet feeling helpless.

It had been a while since she had had these nightmares and she had never wanted to share them with him. He only knew that they were real to her, haunting her. Deep down he instinctively sensed that she did not even know herself what brought them on, only that she was hounded by some unknown villain. Perhaps it was something, yes definitely, something in her past; something that had happened to her that she could not recall.

Finally the trembling stopped and she lay very still against him, clinging to him and unwilling to let go.

"Do you want to tell me about it?" Brent forced her from his embrace, looking her deep in the eye. This time she did not look away.

"It was him," she whispered. "It was Niels. He tried to kill me. I was drowning and he tried to finish me off . . ."

Brent heaved a long sigh. "Darling, he only tried to make you, remember? You probably just relived the experience of this afternoon, love. It's quite normal, you know. It was, after all, frightening to you."

But Amanda shook her head, vehemently and with conviction. "No, Brent, please. He tried to kill me. He really hates me, you know, he really does. He didn't try to make me this afternoon, he was venting his hatred."

She was almost hysterical and he gave up disputing her despite his firm belief it was pure paranoia. But he also realized that she believed what she felt. He was no psychiatrist and he made a mental note to talk to her further when she was calm and more rational. He felt Amanda stir in his arms and he tightened his protective embrace.

"Make love to me, Brent," she murmured, turning her head sideways. Looking into her misty eyes, he bent to kiss her, and she responded hungrily.

Brent shifted, and tearing his lips from hers, he looked at her once more, hesitant to take advantage of her mood. There was something so utterly vulnerable about her, so hopelessly lost, hurting, and her pain stirred him. He tasted the salt on her lips and when her soft breasts brushed against his hand he obliged, his already aroused body ready to chase away her shadows. Gently he straddled her, and as his desire flared, his kisses deepened and he abandoned himself to her passionate surrender.

"That was Nikki on the phone," Paula came out of the house and handed Matt a plate of hamburger patties and wiped her hands on the towel around her neck. "She wants us to join her and Cole in Hana tomorrow night."

"Why Hana?" Matt squinted as a waft of smoke billowed from the barbecue at the unabashed invasion of the juicy meat.

"Her sister had rented a cabin there, but it seems Penelope was called back to the mainland this morning. Her father-in-law suffered a serious heart attack last night. So now Nikki is all by her lonesome self over there, and you know Nicole—"

"Lonesome? What happened to Cole, and Niels?"

"Oh, Cole is with her, but Niels left last night for an emergency board meeting at the hospital. Oh, come on, guys, it'll be fun. I've always wanted to see the illustrious sunrise in Hana. This is a chance in a million. Do you know how long it takes to get a reservation for a cabin there?" Paula was almost jumping, her big brown eyes sparkling with excitement.

Turning the hamburgers, Brent glanced at Amanda, noting the reluctance behind her silence, and grinned.

"Sounds like a great opportunity to me," he drawled. "Why don't the two of you go? We'll just stick around here with the kids."

"Go? Go where, Daddy?" Mandy demanded. They had not heard her leave the pool and her clear voice startled them.

"Oh, come on, Brent, it's just for one night, for Christ's sake." Paula pretended to pout, her eyes signaling an urgent plea to Matt.

"Go where, Daddy?" Mandy persisted, tugging at her father's sleeve.

"It would be an experience," Matt tried cautiously. "Not to mention an education for the kids."

"Daddeeee . . ."

Brent glanced at Amanda, remembering her nightmare, but before he could say something, Paula gasped.

"I've just got the most wonderful idea." Her eyes, bright and shining, were dancing. "We'll go, Matt and I, and we'll take the kids. Yes, all four of them. And you two can have a whole day and a whole night all to yourselves. Now, how's that, hm?" She laughed and swiftly hugged the flabbergasted Mandy. "We'll go to Hana, darling, and get up very early in the morning and see the glorious Hana sunrise. Won't that be fun?"

Mandy turned to Brent, her eyes wide with confusion.

"Will we, Daddy?"

"Oh, of course you will. Go tell the others. We'll leave first thing tomorrow morning." Paula patted her and giggled.

"Dinner is almost ready," Brent called after his disappearing daughter and, looking at Paula, shook his head.

"Amanda?" Paula cocked her head, a wide grin on her face.

Amanda sighed. Slowly she moved to get the buns from the table. A whole day and night just with Brent. Bless Paula for her innovative ideas.

"Are you sure? Four of them? Nikki—"

"Screw Nikki. She'll only be too happy to have company, and Cole will love it. It'll be a little cramped, but then, it's only for one night."

Just then, an Indian war cry echoed through the night and four wet, hungry little savages, led by Josh, invaded the territory and plundered the grill. Wolfing down the food, they loudly shared Paula's enthusiasm at the prospect of exploring the other, more rugged side of the island.

* * *

Brent touched her hand and she started. A sheepish smile flew across her face, and she squeezed his hand lightly.

"Penny for your thoughts," he said, smiling. "Or is it a dollar these days?"

Amanda shook her head and, still smiling, sighed.

"Feeling guilty? Wish you'd gone along?"

"A little."

He had taken her out for a sumptuous prime rib dinner in Kihei, but she had scarcely touched the food. Even the cozy, romantic atmosphere of the restaurant had not quite succeeded in shaking off her gloomy mood. Still, when Paula and the children had waved good-bye this morning, Amanda had seemed calm, almost relieved.

"If I didn't know any better—" He bit his tongue, realizing he had almost voiced his inner thoughts; thoughts he had forcibly quelled during the past few weeks, each time a little more forcefully, desperately wanting to dismiss them.

"Yes?" Amanda tugged at his hand. "If you didn't know any better, what . . . ?"

He shook his head and smiled.

"What, Brent? Tell me."

"I think we should go." He waved at their waiter.

"No, please, tell me."

He looked at her. How lovely she looked in the dim lighting, the red hibiscus behind her ear accentuating the coppery flames of her hair. And those eyes, huge with childlike curiosity, teasing, pleading, touching him deep inside.

"Sometimes," he said, slowly, "just sometimes, it's like . . . I'm looking at a totally . . ."—his mind chose the words cautiously—"a totally different . . . person."

Amanda stiffened, and he instantly tightened his grip on her hand, furious at himself, regretting his impulsiveness.

"And I'm glad, very glad." He stumbled over the words in his haste to reassure her. "It's worth the four years of agony . . ." Not to mention guilt and self-reproach and anger, but he did not say that. "All I'm saying is, please don't change, Amanda. Be as you are now, from here on in, and always."

She blinked at his pleading eyes and swallowing, lowered hers. Her heart was pounding; his doubts echoed her own. So he had noticed the changes. Or was it the difference? Why was he so sure she was the prodigal wife who had disappeared four years ago? What if she wasn't Amanda? What if she was just someone who happened to look exactly like her? What if . . .

The waiter came with the check and Brent gently released her hand. A trembling sigh escaped her and she shivered. Perhaps they should talk about it. Tonight seemed a good time.

"Amanda? Shall we go?"

She looked into his dark eyes, and her heart skipped a beat at the intensity of his gaze. For what she saw was more than just love—it was longing, a deep, unrequited longing for one he had wanted for so long. Quivering inside, she stilled her fears, and silenced the nagging little voice in the back of her mind.

Brent parked the car off the small deserted road and wordlessly pulled her into his arms. His lips brushed hers, gently at first, languorously, sampling, tasting. But her response was far from passive, her lips meeting his with ardent intensity that soon broke his game of caution. And unleashed the gnawing hunger within him.

A bleating horn hurled them back to reality. Dazed and breathless, they clung to each other, and as the group of laughing teenagers dispersed into the darkness, their tense bodies relaxed.

"Come on." Brent opened the car door. "Let's take a stroll along the beach. Take off your shoes. The sand is warm here."

With arms around each other, they headed down the sandy strip. A full moon smiled down at them, indulgently, and they smiled back, feeling young and carefree.

The house in Wailea was dark when they got back. Wading through the bougainvillea, they entered from the side—hand in hand, two lovers, whispering and giggling mischievously. Gleaming in the rays of the moon, the patio appeared enchanted, and as they passed the illuminated swimming pool, Amanda halted and held her breath.

Lit by underwater lights, the blue water clear and even, the pool reflected the illustrious mosaic art on the bottom. For the first time they could actually see the design—two frolicking dolphins, their forms lithe and majestic, their beauty pure and touching.

"It's phenomenal," she whispered. "How odd that I haven't noticed it before."

Brent put his arm around her shoulders and, burying his face in her hair, inhaled deeply.

"Grand," he mumbled. And as he looked down at the gigantic mammals, his eyes brightened. "How about joining them, hm? They seem to be having fun. So, how about it?"

Amanda looked at him, her eyes wide. Then, without warning she swiftly undid her dress, and seeing Brent stare at her naked figure, she laughed. "Come on, last one in gets to fetch the towels."

Jumping into the water, she splashed her stunned partner, and with strong strokes swam to the other side of the pool.

"Why, you little . . ." Brent scrambled out of his clothes and dove after her.

Reaching her in no time, he grabbed her bare bottom and she shrieked and flung her wet arms around his neck. She kissed his nose, then, on impulse, bit his lip. Brent growled and playfully sunk his teeth into the side of her neck. Throwing her head back, Amanda laughed and pulled his face between her firm, voluptuous breasts.

The moon smiled as it watched the sensuous loveplay heighten in intensity. Its silvery light illuminated the scintillating expression that crossed Amanda's face as her lover's hands stroked her body and caressed her intimate parts. Her lips parted, her breath coming in short, heavy rasps, and shuddering with ecstasy, she moaned. Writhing, she eagerly met his touch, her senses reeling, her burning flesh sizzling against the cool, rippling water.

Brent moved, shifting his body to brush against hers, and as if the slight interruption awakened her, Amanda pried herself from his grasp and suddenly dove underwater. A gasp escaped him as her fingers touched him, and touched him again, and again. His hands clung to the edge of the pool, holding on, his rigid body shuddering as her tongue nibbled, enticed, teased.

When she finally came up for air, he grabbed her, and took her. Their breath mingled in a heated race for the finish line, riding together, fast and hard, spiraling, peaking . . .

* * *

Lying on the cool, tiled edge of the deserted pool, Amanda smiled and looked up into his pensive eyes. As she traced the firm jawline with one finger, her sated expression melted even more.

"Don't look at me that way," Brent whispered hoarsely, his hands gently fondling her firm, rounded breasts, relishing the velvet feel under his slender fingers.

"What way?" she mumbled.

"Not unless you mean it . . ."

Smiling, she pulled him down and kissed him, and his body instantly awoke again.

"God, Brent Farraday," she murmured. "How I do love you."

Chapter 23

"WELL, DARLING, CONGRATULATIONS." BRENT, SMILING, put his arm around Amanda's waist and hugged her affectionately.

"Isn't she just terrific?" Paula beamed, her eyes sparkling as she watched her friend's flushed face.

Amanda laughed, her tawny eyes dancing. She felt warm all over, and not just from the compliments that were flying across the room. The pressure of Brent's arm around her body topped the nice words and she nestled against him, wishing for the moment to last forever.

That afternoon the finishing touches had been laid to the Manchione master bedroom, and unable to contain her excitement, Paula had invited all her friends and neighbors for cocktails and hors d'oeuvres to celebrate its completion. Never before had the Manchione home been so crowded, bustling and humming like a good old-fashioned bazaar.

"Amazing," Nikki mumbled, reluctantly admiring Amanda's artistic creation. "I could've sworn it was impossible. Are you sure you didn't hire a contractor to knock out parts of the walls? It looks so much spacier somehow."

"'Spacious,' darling, the word is 'spacious,'" Niels corrected and, ignoring his wife's vicious look, threw a broad smile in Amanda's direction. "And I thought you were a genius when you created your house, but this"—he waved at the illustrious transformation before them—"this is art, genuine unbridled art. My hat's off to you, Amanda, if I can find one."

He had apologized, to both of them, said it was the booze, and Nicole had backed him up. Niels was a poor drinker and an even lousier drunk, she had said. The last time he had had one too many, he had gotten into a fight and the cops had almost arrested him. And remembering, Brent relented, though reluctantly. For his sake, Amanda too had accepted the apology.

"Well, Vanessa, how does it feel to have an artist for a neighbor? That ought to boost the property value around here, don't you think?" Paula grinned at her snobbish neighbor, ignoring Matt's warning headshake and feeling great. Triumphant. For a change she was the one with the upper hand, and she'd be damned if she wouldn't milk the moment.

But Vanessa Harper-Lynch did not reply, her silence more effective than any praise she could have offered. Her cool expression seemed unusually ruffled. And behind her fashionable back Paula grinned at Amanda as their ostentatious neighbor glanced around the room as if in a trance.

The oohs and aahs went on for a while, and soon Amanda began to feel uncomfortable answering the incessant flow of questions and politely turning down requests for various remodeling jobs that had suddenly surfaced.

"Look at that vaulted ceiling. Amazing how she managed to utilize the curves to highlight those heights."

"I've never seen drapes done that way. Did you ever dream it was possible, darling?"

"It definitely is artistic, no question about it. And those mirror strips on that wall behind the bed, ingenious."

"And those inlaid marble tiles woven in between; I've never seen anything like it. It's better than ordinary wallpaper, that's for sure."

"Tell me, darling, are you sure you dreamed this all up?" The speaker turned to Amanda, blatant curiosity in her eyes. "How did you do it?"

How indeed, Amanda mused. *I wish I knew myself.* It had all come to her spontaneously, automatically almost. She had let herself be guided by her instinct, and to her own surprise, she had known what moves to make. When flashes had come to her, she had paused to linger at the twitch of familiarity of those golden moments. The sensation had been frightfully real, as if . . . as if she'd experienced it before . . . as if a door to her subconscious had been opened . . . But as soon as she had consciously pondered it, the door had closed again and the hope for a glimpse into her memory had jammed shut once more.

Yes, how indeed, Amanda thought. Where did she get the ideas, the eye for such design, or the knack for such intricate detail? More than raw talent, it required skill and experience. She had neither. At least, not according to Brent. Yet . . . then how . . . ?

The chatter continued, even after they had all returned downstairs where the champagne flowed and the petits fours found welcome takers. At the stroke of midnight, after the last of the guests had said their good-byes, Brent took Amanda in his arms and kissed her.

"Time to turn into a pumpkin, princess," he said. "Good thing tomorrow is Sunday, or I would keel over a patient's body and be all smeared with blood."

"Ugh, do you have to be so graphic?" Paula wrinkled her nose. "There are some laymen in this room, you know."

"Speak for yourself, darling." Smilingly Matt put his arm around Amanda's shoulder. "The doctor is right. It's been grand, and we all had a good time, but now it's time to call it a night." He gently kissed her. "I haven't had a chance to express my sincere gratitude to you, Artist Farraday, or my admiration for your wonderful talent. You're an absolute marvel—thank you."

"Oh, stop it." Amanda blushed again. "I loved doing it."

"Cara, Matt is right. You're incredible, absolutely fantastico. Thanks for making my dream come true, and more." Paula put her arms around Amanda and kissed her cheeks, again and again. Then suddenly laughed.

"God, guys, did you see Vanessa? I'd never thought it possible, but she walked around with glassy eyes—you know, like she just had an orgasm." Paula laughed harder. "I somehow can't imagine—"

"Come on, Paula, let them go." Matt pulled her away from Amanda.

"Good night, darling." Amanda kissed her.

After the usual amenities Brent pulled Amanda outside,

and waving at their friends, they walked away, arm in arm, into the cool night, and in the direction of their own home.

The house was dimly lit when they entered, the silence overwhelming after the rowdy evening. Amanda patiently waited while Brent locked the front door behind them and then handed him her jacket. For a moment he looked deep into her wistful eyes, a warm smile around his well-formed lips. He took a step forward and their bodies almost touched. Slowly he bent down to kiss her.

"Well, how did it go?"

They jumped away from each other, their hearts pounding wildly.

"Good God, Grandmother! What are you doing up at this hour?"

Brent scowled at the quiet figure in the wheelchair, her face in the shadows of the bar light in the adjacent room.

"I'm sorry, I didn't mean to interrupt a love scene."

Amanda quickly approached her and, taking her hands, knelt before her.

"You're an incurable nosy broad, Louise," she said, smiling, "but if you must know, it was a huge success. They loved it, and I got a million job offers that would keep me busy from now till I'm two hundred and ten."

Louise sighed, a contented smile forming around her thin lips.

"And you? Are you satisfied with the finished product?"

Amanda nodded, her eyes warm and soft. "Yes, darling. It turned out even better than I had dreamed. And Paula is so happy, you should've seen her face. All evening long she walked around like—"

"Like she'd won the lottery, a million dollars' worth." Brent walked over to the bar at the other side of the room. "Now that we're up, can I interest you girls in a nightcap?"

"Congratulations, my dear. I hope Brent is as proud of you as I am." Louise bent over and kissed Amanda on the forehead, her hands clasping the younger woman's.

Brent returned with three small snifters of cognac and handed each of them one.

"Here's to my wife, the artist." He raised his glass to her. He reached into his inside pocket and something rustled at his touch. Frowning, he produced an envelope, then, with a grimace, put it back in his pocket.

"What is it, Brent?" Amanda rose from her kneeling position, her instincts alerted by the expression on his face.

"Nothing important." He reached inside his other pocket and found the pack of cigarettes he had been fumbling for.

"Brent?"

"Nothing that can't wait till the morning, darling. Don't look so worried, it's nothing, trust me." He lit a cigarette and inhaled deeply.

"It is morning, so tell me." Amanda looked at him stubbornly.

Louise turned her wheelchair. "I'll see you two later."

"No, stay. Please. It's really nothing, I tell you. Just an invitation to the annual medical symposium in Vienna next month."

Amanda heaved a deep sigh of relief. "Is that all?"

"You almost look disappointed. I told you it was nothing."

"When next month?"

"Oh, in the second week of May."

"That's two weeks from now. How long will you be gone?"

"One, two weeks."

"Well, what is it, one or two weeks?"

"The symposium itself lasts for one week, but then there's an extension held for those in the gynecology field."

"And you'd like to attend that one as well," Louise said calmly.

"Well, yes. If it's possible."

Amanda sank down on the sofa and sipped her cognac.

"Of course you must go. It's important that you keep up on things. One week, two weeks, what's the difference? We'll survive somehow." She threw him a watery smile, forcing herself to look at him steadily.

"Nonsense." Louise waved impatiently. "What kind of rot is this—survive, my foot. You'll go with him, of course. Vienna is lovely this time of year. As a matter of fact, stay another week after that and have a real vacation. You deserve it, both of you."

They both stared at her, Amanda's startled eyes enormous, Brent's eyes filled with surprise.

"That's impossible," he drawled. "Very kind of you, Grandmother, but we can't leave you here alone for that long."

"And the children. We can't both be gone and leave them to themselves for that long, either." Amanda sighed. For a moment it had sounded so wonderful, two, three weeks alone with Brent . . .

"Then take them with you. I'm well enough now, and I was thinking of going back to my penthouse in a week or two anyway." Louise waved Brent's unspoken protestations aside. "Yes, yes, it's time I got back on my own. I'm not an invalid, you know, and Julie will be there to help me. And of course, Jonathan. So take Mandy and Josh with you." Her eyes suddenly lit up. "I've got a better idea. Take them to London. Madeline would love having them for two weeks. Then, after the symposium, the four of you could tour Europe for a week, even two. They'll love Europe, believe me."

She looked at them with a triumphant smile, her eyes bright and shining. For a moment Amanda felt a pang of guilt —was it the idea of them going to Europe that delighted the old woman, or was it perhaps the thought of going back to her own home? Despite the fact that they got along now, and that Louise seemed happy here, it must be hard not being in her own surroundings. After all, she had been independent for so long.

"It all sounds so wonderful," she said, sighing.

"Good, then it's settled." Louise beamed.

But Amanda shook her head. "No, I'm afraid not. They're both in school, remember? And Josh maybe, but Mandy is in third grade, and—"

"Rubbish." Louise sounded almost angry. "Mandy is a bright child. Have a talk with her teacher and take along the schoolwork that she would do if she were here. Simple. It's done all the time, my dear."

Amanda looked at Brent, her eyes full of hope, questioning.

"You think of everything, don't you, Grams? Next you'd be telling me to take a second honeymoon before taking the kids on a tour through Europe."

"Well, there's a thought." Louise's eyes twinkled.

"Never mind." Brent lit another cigarette and walked to the bar to refill his glass. "We'll talk about it later."

Louise glanced at Amanda. "Well, child?"

But before she could answer, Brent returned. "I said we'll talk about this later, after we've all had some sleep."

Amanda rose. "Come on, I'll take you to your room, Louise. Brent is right, it's been a long day and an even longer night." But when they were in Louise's bedroom, she kissed the older woman fondly. "It's a splendid idea, Louise. Thank you." She helped her into the bed and tucked her underneath the blanket.

Outside the room again, Amanda paused for a moment to gather her thoughts, then slowly made her way back to the living room where she knew Brent would be waiting for her. Could it be possible? A whole two, maybe three weeks alone with Brent? Would he take her along? He had seemed hesitant, even reluctant, or was that just her imagination?

She shook her head and paused at the threshold. She was tired. The excitement of the evening had worn her out. Even so, she could not shake off the anticipation, and suddenly she wished that Brent had shown more enthusiasm.

Taking a deep breath, she reentered the living room.

Chapter 24

"THAT'S FANTASTIC! HOW EXCITING FOR YOU. OH, CARA, I wish I could go with you. My God, Europe in May, the best time of year to go there, you'll love it! And you thought Brent did not care about you." Paula paused to catch her breath and Amanda chuckled, her friend's excitement fueling her own exhilaration.

"It wasn't Brent's idea, darling." She almost hated to burst Paula's bubble. "It was Louise's." She held the receiver away from her ear at her friend's surprised exclamation, and grinned, her eyes sparkling.

She had awakened that Sunday morning to find Brent staring at her and she had smiled at him, a lazy, sleepy smile. He had not smiled back, his eyes remaining pensive and serious. Instead he had gently touched her face and caressed her cheek. And inevitably, they had made love. Slowly, unhurried, their passion sweet, their union a sigh of contentment. And he had invited—yes, invited—her to accompany him to Vienna.

"I'll be damned." Paula laughed in her ear. "I never would've thought the old buzzard to be that creative. What brought on that brainstorm?"

Still grinning, Amanda told her. "Don't be so hard on Louise. Remember, it was she who talked me into doing your bedroom."

"Oh, yeah. I guess there's hope for the dragon lady. Do you think she's seen the light?"

They both burst out laughing. Paula went on raving, then continued to give her hundreds of tips on Europe.

"Whoa, whoa, slow down. We're only going for three weeks, and two of those are mostly business. But we'll talk about it later when I have a chance to jot down everything you just said, okay? And tomorrow I'll go to the library and brush up on Austria and Switzerland. Oh, and England, of course."

"Well, I've never been to Austria, but I can tell you about Switzerland and England. Did you check if your passports are valid? Better do that, it might take a couple of days to have them renewed. Oh, got to go, kiddo, Matt's home. Bet ya he hasn't eaten yet. Talk to you tomorrow. I'll go with you to the library, call me."

Amanda hung up, smiling. Right, passports. Good thing Paula had reminded her of that, or she would not have thought of them. She ran up the stairs, taking two steps at a time, feeling young and carefree.

"Brent?"

She found him standing in front of the mirror with only a scanty towel wrapped around his waist, shaving. Another early surgery tomorrow, she thought. When Brent did his shaving at night she knew he was scheduled for what he called an awakening surgery, for which he had to leave home shortly before dawn.

She hated these awakening surgeries. They mostly meant complicated cases. Brent took all his surgeries seriously, but these were even more special to him and they drained him emotionally for days afterward, especially when the success was marginal and the patient's condition unconfirmed for months to come.

"Sorry, where do you keep our passports?"

He stopped shaving and gave her a blank look. "Try the upper drawer of my dresser." He calmly resumed shaving the lower part of his chin, his thoughts drifting back to the impending surgery.

Amanda rummaged through the right drawer and, finding nothing, opened the left one. She found them, neatly packed in a black plastic folder. With a relieved smile she reached for it, and as she eagerly pulled out the passports, something dropped on the thick carpet. She briefly glanced at it, then devoted her attention to the navy blue booklets in her hand.

The children's faces were much younger and she almost giggled at Josh's baby face. Then, as she studied Brent's solemn expression, a smile formed on her lips, and with a curious sensation she opened the last one and stared at her own face.

It looked older somehow, and she recognized the long hair from the pictures around the house. But there was an arrogance in her expression that puzzled her. Could something have happened during the past four years that had subdued her spirit? Then, attributing it to the flawed quality of passport pictures, she shrugged and quickly checked each expiration date.

Satisfied that they would not expire until next spring, she put them back in the folder, placed it inside the drawer and closed it. Just then her eye fell on the object on the floor.

It was a long manila envelope, the kind used to store or mail documents in, and as she picked it up, two sleek paper jackets slipped out of it. At a glance they resembled airplane ticket jackets and a sudden rush of color brightened her face and her tawny eyes sparkled gold. Why, that sneaky wonderful scoundrel! He must have anticipated her reaction and planned the charade, and she had fallen for his trick. She hesitated for a moment, but her curiosity got the upper hand and she opened the colorful paper jackets, and gasped.

Inside were two tickets to Puccini's *Madame Butterfly*. A flyer with pictures of the cast accompanied the tickets. Her head whirled and she bit her lip not to shout out the excitement and the joy that threatened to take hold of her.

"Find them?" Brent's voice made her jump. With the tickets still in her hand she laughed.

"Oh, Brent, what a wonderful surprise! I'm sorry, I didn't mean to find them, but I'm glad I did. I love it, I simply love it."

In her happiness and excitement she barely noticed Brent's astonished look as she waved the newfound treasure at him. "How did you guess? How did you know I adore Puccini?"

Before he could recuperate she rushed to him and flung her arms around his neck. Spontaneously she kissed him full and warm on the mouth and hugged him so wildly he almost lost his balance. He put his strong arms around her supple body, burying his face in the nape of her neck and inhaling the soft scent of her hair.

"Are you sure you like it?" he mumbled, his mouth nuzzling her earlobe. "You don't have to pretend. If you'd rather go to a rock concert or a disco party—"

Amanda pulled back and looked him straight in the face, her tawny eyes dancing. "Do I act like I'm pretending?" She held his face between her hands. "I don't even like rock concerts, and disco parties don't particularly interest me. But this, this is gold."

She sobered for a moment, her dancing eyes widening. "Oh, no! I spoiled the surprise, didn't I? I'm so sorry, me and my meddling curiosity."

For the second time that evening Brent gave her a blank look.

"It's my birthday present, isn't it? You darling. I love it anyway, even if it is a bit early."

Next she was in his strong arms and he too laughed, kissing her again and again, until they were both out of breath. And suddenly their kisses deepened. The towel around his waist fell to the floor and he stood naked, his muscled body still gleaming from the hot shower. He inched toward her, an odd, intense look in his dark eyes. Amanda stepped back, her head spinning, her blood rushing even more rapidly through her charged-up body. And as she fell backward on the soft bed, she sighed, shivering with anticipation, her arms welcoming his strong body to her embrace.

Amanda read the note and her gaze went to her daughter's sullen face. The girl had come home from her ballet lesson without the usual enthusiasm and for a minute Amanda suspected that she had been crying. She gently knelt before her and took the elfin face in her hands.

"What happened, sweetheart? Tell me everything. I promise I won't scold you."

"Nothing happened, I swear. She just said to give you the note." Mandy avoided her mother's eyes and shuffled her feet.

"Then why do you look so stricken?"

"I don't. Why don't you believe me?" Now the tears brimmed.

Amanda sighed and got up. She knew how stubborn the girl could be. Both the kids had that from her, she thought wryly. Oh, well, she would know soon enough. Mandy's ballet teacher had requested her audience on Friday afternoon. She took a closer look at the note. It was from the prima ballerina herself.

She had never met the woman. The time she had attended Mandy's first performance, the ballet dancer had been in the hospital recovering from bronchitis and her assistant had accepted the compliments on her behalf. And most of the time Brent had taken his daughter to practice sessions, which were held right next door to the racquet club where he worked out on Wednesday afternoons.

Amanda glanced at the calendar on the wall. Friday was the day after tomorrow.

Chapter 25

THE PARKING LOT BEHIND THE YOUTH ARTS CENTER AU-
ditorium was practically empty. Stepping out of her car,
Amanda took a deep breath and straightened her skirt.

As she climbed the steps of the building, her thoughts went
to the purpose of her visit. Why would that woman want to
see her, she wondered? Unlike Josh, Mandy had never been
in trouble before, not in school, or anywhere. Yet something
must have happened, or she would not have been summoned. The note had been brief, requesting her presence
and signed simply "Yvette Rousseau."

Pausing in front of the tinted glass doors marked "Rousseau School of Royal Ballet," Amanda frowned. She had
never heard of the woman, but Mandy insisted that she had
once been a great prima ballerina with the New York Royal
Ballet, and that she had danced with such leading dancers as
Nureyev and Baryshnikov.

After a moment's hesitation she stepped inside, and was
taken aback by the enormous space that stretched before
her. Perhaps it was just the illusion projected by the wall-to-
wall mirrors and the mirrored ceiling, she mused, but after a
few minutes she realized that the room was indeed spacious.
Impressive, she thought.

"Mrs. Farraday?"

She turned at the sound of a soft voice. Dressed in black

leotards that clung tightly to her limbs, Yvette Rousseau looked more like a sensuous model than a ballet teacher. Her walk was smooth, her movements lithe and pantherlike, and as she came nearer Amanda noticed how sinewy her body was. Why, she is young, she thought with surprise, noting the smooth skin, accentuated by blond hair worn brushed back and in a pigtail.

Amanda stood very still. She did not know what she had expected, but this woman certainly did not look like she was in her mid-thirties. Her skin was flawless, her face naked of makeup except for her eyes. The eyes of a cat, Amanda thought, a jungle cat, cool and dangerous. She suddenly felt uneasy.

"Thank you for coming at such short notice," Yvette said, in a cultured, slightly nasal voice. Her thin lips lilted into a curve that resembled a smile, yet her eyes remained cold and aloof.

She could've been beautiful, Amanda thought wryly, if only she would put some warmth in her expression. But then, the lack of warmth in Grace Kelly and Catherine Deneuve never deterred the flock of men drooling after them. And the blonde before her had a better figure by far.

"Is there a problem with Mandy, Miss Rousseau? I take it that's why you summoned me here." She tried to keep the tremor out of her voice, clasping her purse for support.

Mandy's ballet teacher nodded, gesturing Amanda to a chair.

"Your daughter is a fine dancer, Mrs. Farraday. She has the right instincts, the feeling, the flair, and the talent, above all, lots of talent—"

Amanda frowned, puzzled. "Then what . . . ?"

"—but she lacks the fire, that all-consuming flame that makes a great ballet dancer . . ."

"I don't see—"

"In other words, Mrs. Farraday, Mandy hasn't got what it takes."

Still puzzled, Amanda now remained silent, waiting. Yvette's shoulders sagged a little and her expression softened as if she realized the effect of her harsh words on the parent.

"It doesn't have to be, you know. I'm not saying she's hopeless. She did, at one time, show promise . . ."

"What *are* you saying, Miss Rousseau?" Amanda's voice was soft and the deadly undertone eluded the teacher.

"What I am saying, Mrs. Farraday, is that your daughter danced much better before. There was much more fire, much more drive in her movements, far more commitment."

"Before? Before what?"

Yvette Rousseau stared at her, a blank expression on her delicate face. "I'm sorry?"

"You said, Mandy danced better before," Amanda repeated patiently. "Before what?"

"Oh. Before . . ." She looked away, shifting in her chair. "Yes?"

"Before you . . . ah . . . well . . . showed up, came back home." She took a deep breath, and when Amanda remained silent, she burst into a rapid flood of explanations. "She was doing great, her movements were superb, perfect, so aesthetic. My best student, so full of expression, of life, so full of promise . . . and she could have become a star if it hadn't been for . . . I mean—"

She broke off and an awkward silence hung in the huge room.

"What *do* you mean, Miss Rousseau?" The fury in Amanda's voice was now quite plain and Yvette blushed.

"Well, she . . . ah . . . it's just that . . . ah . . . ," she stammered. "It's just that she never had to compete . . . she's always had all the attention . . . For all these years . . . she's been in the limelight constantly and—"

"Wait, hold it." Amanda's eyes went wide with confusion. "What does all this have to do with me?" My God, she thought, the woman is rambling. Limelight? Competition, what competition?

"My dear, it has everything to do with you. Mandy's no longer the center of attention, she now has to share her spot with a woman who, till a few months ago, was nothing but a figment of her imagination, a treasured memory if you will, a face on the mantelpiece. Since you showed up she's no longer her father's prime concern . . ." She paused, catching her breath and waiting for the impact of her tirade to hit Amanda with full force.

Father? Amanda stared. All this time while she'd thought Yvette's rambling didn't make sense, the woman had been talking about Brent . . . his attention, his focus, his love

. . . *My God, what is she saying? That I should've remained in obscurity, a mere shadow of a memory on the living room mantelpiece? That I made my own daughter's life miserable by turning up alive? That it'll be my fault if Mandy fails to become a success in ballet? That I should've . . .*

". . . Mrs. Farraday . . . Amanda . . ."

She suddenly realized that Yvette was talking to her again. "Are you all right?"

Amanda just stared at her, not replying.

"I'm sorry to be so blunt, but your daughter's future is at stake here, and I care very deeply for her. She's a marvelous child, and she does possess the right ingredients, that rare quality that makes or breaks a good dancer. It would be a pity to destroy such talent, and I really would hate to see that happen." Yvette sighed, moving her head dramatically. "All I'm saying—"

"Yes, what *are* you saying, Miss Rousseau?" Amanda looked at her coldly. "Are you suggesting that I disappear from my daughter's life so she can have a brilliant future as a ballet dancer? Or that she's better off not having a mother in her young life so that she can monopolize her father's devotion?"

"Well . . . ah . . ."

"Aren't you forgetting something? Mandy has a brother who equally deserves, and gets—thank God—his father's attention. Or would you rather he'd vanish from her life as well?"

Yvette blushed at the sharp rebuke, and her eyes flickered in defiance.

"Dr. Farraday is a most intelligent man and a terrific father. I have no reason to think otherwise. I'm sure he knows exactly how to handle his affection for both his children."

"You seem to know my husband pretty well," Amanda commented dryly. "Do you make it your business to analyze the parents of each of your students in the same thorough manner?"

Yvette's gray eyes flared visibly.

"Only the ones that count. Mandy's welfare is vital to me and her happiness is not a mere fleeting interest. Brent—" Yvette's face turned crimson and she bit her lip. She drew a deep breath and, once more in control of her emotions, calmly resumed, her expression detached once more. "Dr.

Farraday knows how much I care about his daughter and he appreciates that."

She reached out, but Amanda quickly withdrew her arm as if the woman's touch scorched her and Yvette's face darkened at the obvious rejection. "Look, I know this is hard for you, but you weren't around the last two, three years. Mandy is a highly sensitive girl who needs a creative outlet and lots of encouragement. You couldn't possibly know how to approach her or give her what she really needs most."

Amanda felt a chill creep up the back of her neck.

"And you do?" She did not attempt to hide her anger.

Yvette shrugged her shoulders, lowering her eyes to veil her triumph.

"If you'd spent as much time as I have with her, you would've also," she murmured.

Amanda rose and sauntered to the wooden bar that ran along a mirrored wall.

"Tell me, Miss Rousseau, what makes you think my daughter"—she emphasized the word—"wants to make ballet her life ambition? After all, she's only eight years old. And if you're as interested in her creative life as you say you are, you would know that she plays the piano flawlessly, and I'm not talking jazz."

Yvette too rose, a look of indignation in her eyes.

"Yes, I'm fully aware of that. As a matter of fact, Brent and I have been taking her along to concerts and operas—" She suddenly bit her tongue and, noting the frozen look on Amanda's face, realized her error. Quickly she added, "To further her education, of course. And her artistic growth. How else could we nurture her needy soul . . . ?"

But the harm was done.

"How else indeed?" Amanda sneered, her eyes frosty.

She walked toward the door and exited, carefully.

The envelope flew across the cluttered desk and jabbed the back of his hand. Startled, Brent stared at the two opera tickets that had slid out and looked up.

"You can stuff those up your cheating ass, Farraday! And don't ever, *ever,* pull that crap on me again!" Amanda hissed, her taut face white, contorted with rage.

For a moment Brent held his breath, perplexed at her unusual choice of words. Towering over him, her shoulders erect, her eyes shooting daggers, she reminded him of a modern-day Nemesis. If she was not so agitated, he would have smiled.

"What are you talking about? Last week you were ecstatic to get those tickets. And what . . . crap . . . are you referring to?" Brent frowned, trying to sound concerned.

"Stop the charade, doctor. You never meant for me to have those tickets, or for that matter find them. That's why you hid them in your drawer." She started to walk away. "What a fool I was. Did you and that Rousseau woman snicker at my ignorance? To think that you kept them from me to surprise me . . ."

Her bitterness stung him and he jumped up from his chair.

"Wait!" He ran around the desk and sofa and blocked her exit.

"Don't . . . touch me," she snarled, holding both arms out of his reach.

"Okay, all right. I did buy them for Yvette, but not for the reason you think I . . . Look, I didn't think you'd be interested. You never showed an interest in opera before. Oh, come on, Amanda, can't we discuss this rationally . . . ?"

"You do admit, then, that you and that Rousseau woman—"

Amanda swallowed. She hated the word "affair"; it sounded cheap and dirty and despite her hurt she did not feel that Brent's dignity deserved to be soiled. It was, after all, she who had deserted him. To expect him to remain celibate and faithful to her memory for all these years was absurd, abnormal. Yet . . . it was not the physical aspect she worried about—what if his feelings for the woman . . . ?

For the second time that afternoon, her thoughts flashed back to the night of Louise's birthday party. "Another woman," the gossiper had said. "Rumors have it he's serious about her . . ."

She narrowed her eyes. What if "the other woman" was . . . ? That night she had barely caught a glimpse of the woman in red. Could she have been Yvette?

"We did . . . ah . . . go out a couple of times," Brent was saying. "And as for those tickets . . . I did buy them for her, months ago. But then you came back, and I forgot all about them. I swear, I . . ."

"Liar! Traitor!" she spat, her fury rekindled by his treason.

"It's bad enough to take me for a fool, don't you humiliate me by brewing more nonsense and expecting me to swallow—"

"Please, Manda, it's the honest-to-God truth. Believe me!"

But his pleading eyes incensed her even further, and the misery she had tried to conquer all afternoon was now unleashed with deadly force.

"You double-faced son of a bitch!" she lashed out. "If you'd come to me and told me that you were sleeping with another woman, I would've accepted it. I might not have liked it, but I would've understood. But to underhandedly, deviously lie like this—" She choked and gasped for air.

"But I didn't! I mean—"

"Spare me. Go to her. You have my blessing." She sidestepped him, but he was faster.

"Now, you listen to me, you little spitfire!" He grabbed her wrists and shook her.

"Let go of me. Get out of my way!" Close to tears, Amanda fought to wrench her arms from his iron grip.

"I don't need anyone's blessing, least of all yours. If I'd wanted to bed another woman, I'd damn well do it! With or without your permission, lady. After four years away, you're the last person to demand fidelity on my part." He pushed her away from him and the force flung her down on the leather sofa.

Rubbing her sore wrists, Amanda glared at him. Yet she made no move to get up.

"That little tramp," she said, sobbing, her eyes still blazing. "She's lusting after you. She actually had the nerve to . . . to—" She bit her lip and wildly shook her head, sending her fiery curls flying around her face.

As he stared down at her—curled up on the couch, a heap of infinite misery—Brent's anger abated, and he took a deep breath.

"What brought all this on?" He frowned, calm once more. "When did you talk to her?"

Slowly, haltingly, Amanda related the meeting, and listening, his frown deepened.

How ironic, he thought. Only days before Amanda had turned up from nowhere, he had decided to terminate his relationship with Yvette. The opera tickets had been intended as a farewell present. She had been good company, but no candidate for a lasting relationship on his part. Ambitious, self-centered, unconditionally dedicated to her craft and her dancing, Yvette could not accept the fact that there was a life outside ballet. And he could not accept a life within such stringent confines. As things were, he had begun to feel the strain, and it had smothered him.

He cautiously sank down on the sofa and began to explain. Gradually the embers in Amanda's eyes were doused, and when she finally rose, she was calm. Yet he sensed that her faith in him had been shattered. Looking up into her misty eyes, something in him snapped. Giving in to impulse, he grabbed her arm and slammed her back down on the leather couch.

The sensation of tumbling threw her, and her eyes flew open. Her startled gasp died between his lips as they covered hers, ravishing and consuming them. His mood captured her, sweeping her up in the whirlwind of his heat, her blood soaring, even before his hands reached downward and stripped her. Her body squirmed as he burrowed his hand in the thicket between her thighs, arching against his rubbing palm, quivering feverishly at the frenzied probing of his fingers.

She never heard him unzip his pants. Nor his heavy breathing as he took possession of her. Riding her hard, he forced her to soar with him. Their bodies shook. In the heat of their passion they rolled off the couch and across the floor, bumping against objects in their way, not feeling any pain but that which they each sought to exorcise.

Amanda flung her arms wide, gasping. With one last fierceful thrust, he exploded. His body toppled on top of hers, and burying his face in her neck, he shuddered.

For a long time they remained very still, their arms around one another, their sweat mingling. Then, finally, Brent rose. His eyes met hers, and a pang of remorse coursed through him at the sight of her bruised mouth. Still, he made no move to touch her. She diverted her gaze and helplessly he watched her walk away.

Chapter 26

THE DRIVE THROUGH TRAFALGAR SQUARE WAS AN EXPE-
rience enjoyed not just by Mandy and Josh. Amanda enjoyed
it so much that she rolled down the taxi's dirty window, ignoring the drizzling rain that sprinkled her glowing face and
seeped inside the cab. She hardly heard Josh's shouts of joy
as he spotted the double-decker buses, nor Mandy's excited
shriek when they passed a rare nineteenth-century carriage
complete with horse and coachman. Earlier they had crossed
Piccadilly Circus—at Brent's request—but the traffic had
been too jammed for them to fully appreciate it.

In the front seat, Brent smiled at the hilarity in back. It
amused him to see Amanda lose herself this way, her face
transfixed by the scenery, totally, completely absorbed in a
world of her own. He had never seen her like this, and her
mesmerized state evoked a warmth in him he had not felt
since the day he had first seen her, blowing kisses at a cheer-
ing audience.

The taxi turned a corner and the scenery changed. Gradually they entered a more sedate neighborhood, Mayfair's res-
idential section, and Amanda's expression relaxed visibly.
She leaned back into the seat as they passed the London
town houses.

How strange, Amanda thought, *I feel quite at home here.
It's like I've been here before. Déjà vu?* She glanced at Brent

and smiled. Of course, he must have taken her to Europe many times. This was where his mother lived. She turned to the window again and stared at the rows of houses.

They all looked so lovely, cozy with those colorful flowers in their window boxes and the lacy sheers in the windows. Rather early for those flowers to bloom, but then she recalled that England did not suffer the dreadful cold winters that plagued Chicago, and she smiled again, at peace with the world.

Not that she actually remembered being here. Yet it strangely felt a bit like coming home, and the feeling was a comfort to her. Why, she wondered, had she not felt this way when she stepped into the house in Lake Forest? That was, after all, her own home and one she was supposed to have masterminded.

The taxi turned and stopped in front of an elegant town house with an abundance of white and yellow rosebushes surrounding the entrance gate. As they stepped out, the front door opened and a jubilant Lady Madeline rushed to greet them. Followed by a pack of loudly barking hounds.

"Come in, come in," she urged. Lady Madeline seemed different somehow, more carefree and quite European. If it had not been for the American accent, she could have passed for one of the many British matriarchs they had seen puttering in their dainty front yards.

"Just put those bags in the front hall, my good man," she told the driver, and led them all inside the house.

During afternoon tea they were joined by Sir Giles, who had been away till then. Playing golf with friends. Doctor's orders, Lady Madeline had explained with a smile. She had not added that the doctor also advised him to stay away from strenuous gatherings, and that the game had been her suggestion. He was not used to chattering little children and she thought that by the afternoon Josh and Mandy would have simmered down a bit, enough to spare him any undue anxiety.

But for once she was wrong. Sir Giles had taken immediately to the youngsters and soon they were bosom buddies, laughing at each other's stories. He had seen them only once years ago, the only time he had traveled to America, shortly before the arthritis bouts had set in. They were very little then, and neither of them remembered him much. Like any other children, they adored their new grandfather.

"Children, would you like some more scones?" Madeline looked fondly at the three heads, whispering and giggling away in conspiratorial fashion.

They were sitting in the back garden surrounded by more rosebushes, sipping tea and eating scones. It was a perfect spring day, still a bit chilly, but devoid of any wind.

"No, thank you." Mandy declined politely and even Josh shook his curly head.

"How extraordinary, don't you like them? They were freshly baked this morning."

"I like brownies better," Josh said.

"Josh!" Amanda pretended to be appalled, but her eyes twinkled, and as she met Sir Giles's eyes she saw that he too was amused.

"Better order some cakes tomorrow, dear. Their American taste is not ready for our delicious scones yet." He chuckled and tousled the boy's curls.

Lady Madeline feigned a sigh and rolled her eyes. "I can tell who's going to spoil them this coming fortnight." She looked at her daughter-in-law and they both burst out laughing.

"How long will you remain in London, Brent?"

"Three days. It's awfully kind of you and Mother to take these brats under your wing. Believe me, it's a load off my mind." Brent smiled at him fondly and took out a cigarette. "We'll take them off your hands as soon as the symposium is ended."

"No hurry, my boy. These old bones need some stimulation now and then, and what better way than to keep up with the tribulations of youth, eh?" He grinned at Mandy, then nodded at Josh. "We'll have a good time together, won't we?"

"Thank you, sir."

Sir Giles rose. "Come, I have something to show you, children."

They walked away, hand in hand, chatting and giggling like old friends. Once they were out of earshot, Lady Madeline sighed and began to discuss her husband's health with her son. As she listened, Amanda's thoughts drifted away. A bird now and then broke the dreamy tranquility, to be answered by another. Far away the distant sound of an occasional car could be heard.

She leaned her head back and gazed at the clear, light blue sky. For the first time in months she felt at peace with the world. For the first time since she had awakened in the hospital, she felt no anxiety.

Right after dinner Josh dropped the bomb. It was so unexpected it took all of them by surprise. All but Grandfather Giles, of course, who seemed to be in on the plan.

"No! Absolutely not." Amanda was the first to recover.

"But, why not? Grandpa said—"

"No. It's far too dangerous. I won't allow it."

"Oh, come now, Amanda. Every child dreams about horseback riding. I bet you did yourself when you were a chit of a girl." Sir Giles came to Josh's rescue and received a grateful smile. Amanda took a deep breath, her expression stubborn, but after more discussion gracefully gave in to the majority view that Josh should have a chance to ride. Still, she could not shake off her feelings of uneasiness.

The next afternoon Sir Giles accompanied a jubilant Josh to the McWilliam's Stables just outside of London. A less rowdy Mandy followed holding her father's hand, her face as radiant as her brother's and anticipation shining brightly in her wide green eyes. Amanda had chosen to remain with Lady Madeline, who had reveled at the prospect of having someone to shop with.

Lady Madeline was an avid shopper and the best stores in London welcomed her with pleasure, bending backward to see to her every whim. For they knew that to keep their best customers happy would be to ensure a continual flow of profit, and of all their revered clientele, she was one of the least demanding. But if fashion was a hobby, jewelry was an obsession, and not a month went by without her acquiring at least one little trinket. An investment, as she put it. During the twelve years of marriage, that investment had flourished to a sizable collection.

The young woman at Cartier smiled as they walked in, quickly replacing some pieces in the display counter and locking it. "Good afternoon, Lady Stanhope, what can we show you today?" Then she looked at Amanda and her smile widened.

Amanda winced; the smile was friendly enough, yet in some way it was disconcerting—it held a familiarity that made her uneasy somehow, as if the woman knew her. She shook off her apprehension. If this was one of Lady Madeline's hangouts, it would only stand to reason that she would've accompanied her here from time to time.

"Not for me, this time, Grace. Let's see." Lady Madeline scrutinized the items inside the glass counters, and finally lingered at the bracelet tray. "If my memory serves me correctly, you fancy bracelets more than rings, don't you, my dear?" Receiving no response, she turned her questioning eyes to Amanda.

"Me?" Amanda's eyes widened. "Oh, no, not me. We're here to get something for you."

"Nonsense. I always buy something for me. Today we'll get something for you. After all, you need a souvenir to remember this trip by, and what better token than a simple gold bracelet? Or not so simple if that suits you better." She suddenly gasped. "Oh! Come and look, Amanda. Could we see that one, Grace? No, no, the one second to the right."

It was an exquisite piece—little sculptured gold hearts linked together by tiny rings. When she moved it, the light caught it and the effect was a subtle glitter that was both breathtaking and alluring.

"Put it on," Lady Madeline urged, and despite herself, Amanda obliged. "Do you like it?" Her eyes shone. She looked so happy, Amanda could not bring herself to deny her, and she nodded.

"Well, it's settled then. We'll take this one, Grace. Oh, and make the receipt out in her name, she'll need it for U.S. Customs. The bill goes to my husband, of course."

Grace Proctor smiled and locked the drawer. "Do you wish to wear it now, Mrs. Farley?"

Amanda stared at her, confused, then shook her head.

"No, please put it in a box. I'd like to show it to my husband first."

She watched Lady Madeline browse around, and inevitably her mother-in-law found a necklace of the finest quality for her granddaughter: little gold balls with tiny little hearts in between. Her protests fell on deaf ears, and with a sigh, she accepted the two boxes from a smiling Grace. She glanced at the receipts and shuddered at the amounts.

"Excuse me, you spelled my name wrong," she said, handing them back to the salesgirl. "The name is Farraday, not Farley."

Grace seemed puzzled. "I'm so sorry, I could've sworn . . ." She shook her head and mumbled something under her breath. Shortly she gave Amanda two corrected receipts and apologized once more.

"Lady Mad—"

"Say no more." Lady Madeline raised her hands. "You're not going to deprive an old lady of her pleasures, are you, my dear?"

"You're not playing fair, you know."

"Maybe not. But then, who is?" She smiled and pulled Amanda's hand through her arm. "Besides, Sir Giles will love the idea that I have spent his money on another woman for once. How many men live to exult in that knowledge?"

They both laughed and set off in the direction of Harrods.

Jake McWilliams had an extensive stable of horses, one more beautiful than the other, and all of them bred from the finest stock with quality and strength in mind. His steady clientele counted on the best of care and those not-so-steady customers came recommended, and by qualified references only.

Looking at the ones that had not been taken riding in the field, Amanda could not help but admire the man's efforts—they were by far the best-looking pack she had ever dreamed existed. She could just imagine Josh's excitement and visualized him choosing the tallest one in the pack.

A slow smile softened the worried expression on her face; Brent was an experienced rider his mother had told her, and she knew he would keep his word and make sure his son rode a horse compatible with his level. A white stallion snorted as she went by his stable and she reached out to pat him.

"I wouldn't do that if I were you," a man's crisp voice said.

Amanda retracted her hand in reflex and whirled around. With his back turned to her, he calmly finished saddling a tall Arabian, then turned around to face her. "I'm sorry I startled you, but—" His hand stayed in midair, the incredulous look in his bold eyes almost insulting.

She felt the blood rush to her temples at the blatant familiarity in his gaze, and instinctively clasped her hand to her throat. In a daze, she noticed how impeccably dressed he was, a picture of the perfect British equestrian, complete with tall leather riding boots, a gray tail coat, and the hat to go along. Only the whip was missing. She suddenly felt over-dressed, out of place in the long woolen skirt and turtleneck sweater.

"Well, well. Bored with the Mediterranean so soon, mi-lady?" He spoke with a distinct British accent, but she could not help wondering if the lilt in his tone was a deliberate affectation of some sort, as though to conceal a more ob-scure origin. An ugly grin distorted his arrogant features. "Or have we decided to hunt for British aristocracy this time? That, my dear, is of course not a very wise move, for as everyone knows, most English blue bloods are penniless." He laughed at her astonished face, and the mocking gleam in his eyes deepened. "But then, you have a nose for money, don't you, my dear? It wouldn't surprise me one bit if you had already sniffed out the very one who isn't condemned to pauperism."

Amanda swallowed hard. What on earth was he talking about? Why would he talk to her this way? What had she done to deserve his blatant contempt?

"I . . . I don't believe we've met . . ." Her words drowned in his thundering laughter.

"Splendid, my dear. Absolutely stupendous, indeed!" He patted the Arabian and moved toward the entrance. As he reached her, Amanda took a step backward and he grinned at her reaction.

"Does your precious lover know you're here? Ah"—he raised his hand—"let me guess. You'll tell him after you've caught bait."

With a swift move, he extracted a small whip from behind the saddle and reached out to stroke her face with it. Amanda shrank away from his reach and he laughed again.

"Who's the victim this time, *ma chérie?* Or is that none of my business?"

Her mind reeled. There it was again—the insinuation of a darker past and a reputation as hideous as it was loose. She opened her mouth, about to ask him a question, when the sound of a galloping horse coming to an abrupt halt outside the stables interrupted her.

"Amanda? Are you in here?" Her heart leaped at the sound

of Brent's concerned voice. But before she could answer him, he strode inside, and seeing the stranger with her, he stopped.

"I see," the man muttered softly. He glanced at Amanda and smiled, his eyes mocking her. "It *is* none of my business." Tapping his hat with the whip, he led his horse out of the stables.

He waited politely for Brent to let him pass and, for a moment, the two men matched wills. Amanda held her breath, watching her husband's next move, his posture as ominous as the dark scowl on his face. The moment seemed suspended in time.

Then, slowly, Brent stepped aside and she heaved a sigh of relief as the impudent stranger tapped his hat a second time and disappeared. A moment later they heard him gallop away.

"Who the hell was that?" Brent demanded.

Amanda shook her head, her knees now shaking. She threw her head back, gasping for air.

"Did he hurt you?"

"N-no. I . . . I've never seen him before." She began to cry. Alarmed, Brent took her into his arms and held her until the sobbing subsided.

"Did he do something to you?"

She shook her head again.

"Then what? Why are you crying?"

"I—I'm so . . . glad you came . . . when you did. He . . . he said some weird . . . things. I was so . . . scared . . ."

"What are you doing here anyway? Jake came to tell me that you were here. Why aren't you shopping with Mother?"

"We were through and I was worried about the kids." She suddenly looked up, her eyes wide. "The kids, where . . . ?"

"They're okay. Jake and Sir Giles are with them." He brushed her tears away and kissed her. "Come on, let's go join them."

He heaved her into the saddle in front of him and spurred his stallion back into the meadows. Amanda nestled her head against his wiry chest and sighed. She felt safe again. That awful man. He must have mistaken her for someone else, but whoever it was, his babblings were not flattering in any way.

Perhaps Brent was right; perhaps it was time she saw a psychiatrist.

She closed her eyes. As before, the thought alone made her shudder. God, why this insane fear? Wasn't it better to know the truth than live in this void? But what if the truth proved to be more horrible than she bargained for?

What was it that psychiatrist had said in that television interview last month? Amnesia was not a disease—it was a state of mind, a mental condition. Until the victim ceased renouncing that condition, the chances of clearing the thick fog was minimal. And she wasn't sure she was quite ready.

Her heart gave a sudden lurch. What if that man hadn't mistaken her for another? What if it was really she whom he had recognized?

Chapter 27

HEATHROW WAS LIKE ANY OTHER BIG AIRPORT, BUZZING with people, running children, and bright fluorescent lights. Hollow metallic voices echoed over the intercom system, announcing the arrival and departure of flights in several languages, and on occasion, paging a wanted passenger. Men and women in business suits trotted briskly, the late ones running to catch a flight, dodging the many vacationers who walked at a more leisurely pace, chatting and laughing. Among them, small groups of uniformed airline personnel carried cabin suitcases on their way to their designated flights, keeping their glances indifferent as they passed the crowds of prospective passengers they might have to serve at a later hour. Through it all, the mood was light and the air filled with anticipation.

Reaching the gate from which their flight to Vienna was to depart, Brent handed Amanda his briefcase and gestured to the row of vacant seats at the far side of the waiting area. "Wait there for me. I'll go and get us our boarding passes." He disappeared into the crowd to take his place in the long line in front of the ticket counter.

Slowly Amanda proceeded toward the far wall, then, spotting a drinking fountain across the corridor, decided to make a detour. She tried to shake the empty feeling that had set in as soon as they left the house in Mayfair, but her mind would not let go. Perhaps it was a mistake to leave Mandy and Josh with Lady Madeline.

Not that her mother-in-law had been displeased with the prospect of spoiling her grandchildren for an entire two weeks, and even Sir Giles had gruntingly admitted that he looked forward to the distraction the youngsters would provide. But Mandy and Josh had voiced intense disappointment at not being allowed to join their parents for their trip to Austria.

Straightening up from the water fountain, Amanda sighed. Mandy's huge green eyes loomed before her, sad and dejected as she had waved listlessly after them. And Josh. Josh had cried, clinging hysterically to her skirt when she had kissed him good-bye. The anticipation of being alone with Brent for a solid two weeks had rapidly dimmed. She no longer felt the joy, only the guilt. Amanda strolled toward the vacant seats, barely paying attention to the bustling traffic. A man bumped into her, almost knocking her off her feet in the process.

"I'm so sorry." He grabbed her arm. to steady her. "I didn't—" His eyes widened in happy surprise. "Amanda? Good God, fancy seeing you here! Are you by yourself?" His accent was distinctly British and he was impeccably dressed, a suave businessman in his mid-thirties. She automatically shook her head. He glanced at his watch and gasped. "Look, I'd love to stay and chat, but I'm late for my plane. I'll be in touch, all right?" He kissed her cheek and before she could recover, he had dashed away and vanished in the crowd.

As if in a trance, she got to the far wall and sat down. God, not again! Who was that man? He obviously knew her, but how and when? Amanda found she was shaking.

"What was that all about?" She started at the sound of Brent's voice. A dark frown clouded his brow and she knew he had seen it all.

"I . . . I don't know. I've never seen him before." At least not that she remembered. But she felt uneasy, the unspoken question heavy between them. "Brent? Have I . . . ever been here . . . in London, I mean?"

"Once, a long time ago, at my mother's wedding. Just before Mandy was born." Puzzled himself, he studied her face, but she shook her head, her mind a total blank. Reluctant to let the incident go, he forced himself to reassure her. "Forget it, Amanda," he said. "It's in the past and long gone. This is now and us. You do remember me, don't you?"

She looked up at him and a warm smile broke the tension in her face. He bent down to kiss her alluring dimples.

"Ladies and gentlemen, we are announcing boarding of Austrian Airlines flight 452 nonstop to Vienna . . ." the voice over the intercom boomed.

"Come on, let's think only of our second honeymoon." Brent pulled her up and, taking his briefcase, put his free arm around her waist. Together they headed toward the boarding crowd.

"No, no, Madeline, don't be sorry. I'll be on the first flight out tomorrow morning. Please, just try to keep his fever down. Pardon?" Amanda listened for a moment. "Yes, aspirin is fine. Just make sure it's children's aspirin. Can you get some?" She listened again. "Good. I'll see you soon. Give my love to Mandy and kiss the little guy for me, will you?"

Slowly she replaced the receiver. They had been in Vienna two days now and tonight was the symposium's opening night, to be initiated by an elaborate black-tie dinner. Brent had been elected one of the main speakers of the evening and he had gone down earlier to check on the audio system. Amanda had rushed to get ready and was just about to join him downstairs when the phone had rung, and a distraught Lady Madeline had come on the line.

Instantly alarmed, Amanda had barely grasped the unintelligible prattle between the loud sobs and it took a few minutes before she finally understood that Josh was sick. The boy had developed an ugly dry cough last night and this morning he had come down with a fever that had steadily risen and caused his grandmother to pick up the telephone.

Amanda reached for the phone again and, glancing at a directory, dialed Austrian Airlines.

"I'm sorry, madam, but all of our morning flights to London are sold out in both first and economy classes. We have an extra section at ten, but that too is booked up. The first availability would be around four in the afternoon. Would you like me to reserve a seat for you on that one?"

"It's really quite important that I get there as early as possible." Amanda did not hide her dismay. "Could you put me on your waiting list for the first one out?"

"Yes, of course. That would be the one at eight o'clock. May I have your name, please?"

Amanda told her, listening to the clicking of the computer on the other side of the line. "Confirm the four o'clock flight for me as well, just in case the morning one does not open up."

More clicking.

"Would you like me to check if British Airways has a morning flight available?"

"Can you do that?" Why hadn't she thought of that? Amanda reproached herself.

More clicking.

"No, I'm sorry, Mrs. Farraday, their earliest flight is around one o'clock in the afternoon, and that's all booked up as well. One moment, please. Perhaps KLM Dutch Airlines has a connection service via Amsterdam." More clicking. "I'm truly sorry. It's the weekend, you see. Many European travelers like to go on a shopping spree to London then."

Oh, God! Tomorrow was Saturday. How could she have forgotten that? But Brent wouldn't miss her, the symposium's program was in full swing as of tonight, weekdays and weekends alike.

"Mrs. Farraday? Is there anything else I can do for you?" The courteous voice pulled her attention back to the dilemma at hand.

"Could you wait-list me for the ten o'clock flight, as well? Either class will do."

"I've put you on the first class waiting list for both the eight and the ten A.M. flights. That should give you priority. And I've noted in your record that you would accept economy as well."

"Thank you. You've been most helpful."

Amanda put down the receiver, her expression pensive. Should she, perhaps, leave tonight? She had not checked that possibility. But she brushed the idea aside. It would not be fair to Brent. This was his night; it was important to him, and she owed it to him to be there to share it with him. Josh was her son, her baby, but Brent was her husband, and he, after all, came first. Besides, it was probably just an ordinary cold, and there were excellent doctors in London.

* * *

Waiting for the elevator, Amanda felt the guilt return in full force. A worried frown clouded her face and dispelled the serene expression of just half an hour ago. Should she tell Brent, she wondered? After all, Josh was his son, too. But as quickly as the idea had sprung to mind, she dispelled it; she would wait until after he had delivered his speech, perhaps even after dinner. No use having him worry, not when there was nothing they could do about it anyway.

Amanda sighed, her thoughts on Brent. And last night. Her expression brightened, the memory of the night before coming back to her in vivid color. They had gone to the Opera House and afterward he had ordered a late light supper in their room, complete with candles, Dom Pérignon champagne, and red long-stemmed roses. They had gazed deeply into each other's eyes, and made love with fire and passion.

The elevator doors opened and she stepped inside. A broad-shouldered man in a well-fitting black tuxedo smiled at her and she politely smiled back.

"Well, well, Amanda, it's so good to see you again." She turned ashen. It was happening again. She looked at him without recognition, trying to suppress her bewilderment as he grabbed her hands with a friendly familiarity. "You look even more beautiful than the last time I saw you. Life must treat you well, or is it my good friend Brent?" His voice was deep and warm and his light blue eyes shone. She forced herself to smile at his compliment.

"Ah, but of course. Forgive me, the memory loss, ja? Your husband told me about the accident, very unfortunate I must say. I'm Werner Gebhardt, an old friend of Brent's, and yours too of course."

"I . . . I'm sorry . . ." Her knees went weak with sudden relief.

"No, no, my dear, don't be. It is I who must apologize for being so tactless and causing you embarrassment. May I make it up by offering you my arm and leading you to your distinguished spouse?"

He held out his arm and this time Amanda genuinely smiled. She liked this big man with the heavy German accent and the boyish grin on his open face. It made him look younger, compensating for the thinning hairline and the whitish-blond hair. It was thus that Brent saw them approach, arm in arm, smiling like old friends.

"Thanks for seeing to my lady's needs, old boy," he said, shaking Werner's hand warmly.

"No, my friend, not her needs, merely her safety. A beautiful young woman like her should not be allowed to wander alone in a dangerous hotel like this." Werner grinned.

Brent turned to Amanda, his eyes mirroring Werner's admiration. *She does look exceptionally beautiful tonight,* he thought.

His appreciative glance caressed her trim figure, sensuously outlined by Dior's latest creation, a simple black satin evening dress that embraced her full, firm breasts, revealing but a glimpse of swelling in a shy touch of décolleté, and flowing around her slender hips down to the trim ankles. Above the halter that collared her gracious neck, the flaming copper of her cropped curls accentuated the fairness of her bare shoulders, and as he stood close to her, the exotic fragrance of her light perfume tantalized him.

"Can I buy you a drink, Mrs. Farraday?"

Amanda blushed at the sound of his husky voice, sensing his arousal and catching her own sensation at the brush of his hand on her bare arm. Suddenly she knew that she would not tell him about Josh and her promise to Lady Madeline to fly to London the next morning. At least not until they were alone again, back in the privacy of their hotel room.

The ballroom was crowded. Men in black tuxedos and black ties that made even the most obscure look distinguished, most of them accompanied by women in evening wear, talked and laughed while accepting the long-stemmed glasses filled with sparkling champagne served by efficient-looking waiters in black and white uniforms. Many a head turned to cast admiring glances at her and Amanda forced herself to act indifferent, smiling whenever Brent introduced her to his colleagues. But she could not help but heave a sigh of relief when the emcee announced that dinner was about to be served.

To her delight, she discovered that Werner Gebhardt had been assigned to their table along with a couple from Norway and another lone gynecologist from Holland. It was during the soup course that she found out Werner was a widower and not German, but Swiss, and the conversation led to winter sports and an invitation to visit him in Geneva.

The dinner was superb. Hot turtle soup, veal scallops excellently prepared in cognac and whipped cream, served with fluffy mashed potatoes and tender asparagus, topped by flaming crêpes suzette and strong dark Viennese coffee. Then the speeches began.

Brent was the second speaker and Amanda listened to his strong voice, her heart swelling with pride as she watched him stand on the podium, tall and self-assured, the aristocratic features of his handsome face emanating an authority that was felt throughout the room. Once in a while, glancing around, she found a captive audience hanging on his words, and a smile stole about her mouth. Her eyes met Werner's and they both smiled.

At the end of his speech, thunderous applause shook the room accompanied by some male voices shouting praises at the speaker. Brent quickly left the podium, shaking hands with many on his way back to the table where Amanda awaited him with a radiant smile. There was a look of such overflowing love in her huge sparkling eyes that it caught his breath and he had to sit down to steady himself before he leaned over to kiss her.

A light kiss. But as he straightened himself her eyes were practically glowing, and he impulsively leaned over once more and kissed her again, more expressively this time. Neither one of them heard the chuckle that escaped Werner. The room had evaporated in a misty cloud and they were only aware of each other.

Vaguely, as if from a far distance, a female voice penetrated their world, shattering the illusion of the moment.

"Hello, Brent," the voice repeated, and as their lips parted they looked up at the tall, voluptuous blonde, her blue eyes mocking, her sensuous mouth pouting, and her hand resting on Brent's shoulder. Resting with a familiarity that did not escape Amanda.

Chapter 28

AMANDA STARED. HER FACE WAS STILL FLUSHED, HER body still tingling from Brent's passionate kiss. Her eyes went from the blonde to her husband and she tumbled back to earth with such suddenness that it left her dizzy. A slim young man walked up to them and put his arm around the blonde, a possessive gesture that left no room for the imagination.

"Hello, Farraday," he drawled. "I see the leopard doesn't change his spots. I only wish my wife would be as perceptive."

At this snide remark, the blonde tried to shake off his arm, but he tightened his grip and pulled her close to him. His dark eyes went to Amanda, evaluating her boldly, smirking as he noticed her involuntary shiver.

Against her will, Amanda found herself fascinated by this stranger. There was something volatile about him, something bestial yet dangerous at the same time. At first glance he seemed young, but she sensed a worldliness about him that belied his youthful look.

"Well, now, who is this sexy little redhead you've picked up tonight? I must say, I do commend your taste, old boy."

Amanda felt Brent tense up, his gray eyes flashing dangerously at the crude remark. Her heart leaped as she watched his jaw clench and for a moment she thought he would lunge at the stranger.

"Ah, Bianca, it's been a while since I've seen you." Werner's jovial voice cut in. The blonde instantly smiled at him, visibly relieved by the intrusion.

"Two, three years, isn't it? You haven't changed a bit, Werner. Still looking for the perfect mate, are you?" she inquired.

"The beautiful ones are always taken, I'm afraid."

A man waved from across the room and Brent rose.

"I'm afraid duty calls," he said stiffly, reaching out for Amanda. "As Werner said, it's good to see you looking so well, Bianca. Married life seems to agree with you, even if it is with someone as ill-deserving as your husband."

"The secret is love and attention to the beautiful lady, Farraday. Things that scum like me seem to understand better than ambitious bastards like yourself."

Fearing a confrontation, Amanda quickly put her hand on Brent's sleeve. But Brent ignored him and briefly nodded to Bianca.

"We'll see each other again, I'm sure."

"Will you stay for the entire week?" Bianca smiled at him.

"And the gynecologists' workshop after that," he said, nodding.

"Good, I'll be around. At least for this week."

Brent took Amanda's elbow and led her away.

"By the way, Farraday, that was quite a powerful speech you gave. If only there wasn't so much hot air in it—" His wife's deadly look silenced him and he shrugged, sitting down on the chair that Brent had vacated.

Without so much as a second glance at the table, Brent moved through the crowd and in the direction of the man who had waved at him earlier, steering Amanda in front of him.

The rest of the evening passed uneventfully. Brent introduced Amanda to his friends and colleagues, more faces and unpronounceable names for her to remember. And soon the bitter taste of the ugly scene at their table was pushed into a back corner of her mind, only to reemerge when they finally reached their hotel room shortly after midnight.

Exhausted, Amanda made straight for the bathroom, and looking at her bedraggled face in the mirror, she suddenly recalled the tall blonde. A feeling of dismay came over her and she shivered.

It was her own fault; she had left him alone for four long years. How could she expect any virile man in his prime to remain faithful to a memory? And who knows what a memory she had left in him? From the attitude of that crude creature who claimed to be Bianca's husband, it must have been pretty serious. For what woman would have degraded herself by marrying that . . . that uncouth parody of a man unless it was done on the rebound? An act of desperation because she could not have the man she really wanted. Amanda had seen the look that passed between them—even a child of two could have seen . . .

Brent's face loomed up behind her and he smiled at her in the mirror. His arms went around her waist and he buried his head in her neck, nuzzling an earlobe. She struggled loose, her heart pounding in her throat at his touch, and stepped away from him. She saw the look of surprise in his eyes, but meeting her accusing stare in the mirror, Brent heaved a deep sigh.

"All right. So I dated the girl for a while." He took off his tie and put it on the counter, not taking his eyes off her. "You were gone. You left me, remember? Can you tell me that you—"

"Dated? Is that what you call it, dated?"

"We had a fling, that's all. Nothing serious. Short and sweet."

"She's in love with you."

"What is it you want from me? An apology? What about the men you slept with, even when we were married?" He angrily unbuttoned his shirt. "Oh, you didn't think I knew about that, did you?"

She turned her back on him, but he grabbed her arm and whirled her around. "Where do you think you're going?"

"I'm tired. This evening is over." Amanda looked at him coldly.

"Look, Manda, I was lonely, and she happened to be there. It was over in less than six months. Believe me, if I had felt anything for her, you wouldn't be standing here with me tonight." He took her hand, but she snatched it away and took a step backward. "Besides, it was you who had insinuated for years what a good lay she was, so I decided to try her out." Brent grimaced at the shocked look in her enormous eyes. "Sorry, sick joke."

"Me? I suggested that you . . . ?"

"Look, Bianca was my assistant at Skokie Valley Hospital. She wasn't sure whether to become an obstetrician or a gynecologist or both, so I took her under my wing and taught her the ropes. Later she opted for obstetrics, but we worked well together, and I offered her a partnership in my private practice. It didn't last very long. When we broke up, she left town."

"And this all happened while I was gone?" She looked at him incredulously. All that in a span of four years?

"Yes. She joined me two years after you'd left, and left me less than a year later."

"And that . . . that man?"

"Alan? He was her boyfriend before she jilted him—"

"For you?"

He shrugged and took off his shirt. "If you want to put it that way."

The truth suddenly dawned. She understood now why Alan hated Brent so much. Bianca must have told him the truth about her feelings and he had married her despite it, probably hoping she would get over Brent.

"She *wanted* to marry you." It was a flat statement and again Brent shrugged.

"I didn't want to marry her. Apart from the fact that I wasn't free to do so." A tired frown wrinkled his brow. "Why are we still discussing this? Come on, Manda, it's late, we've been up since six this morning, and I don't find the subject stimulating enough to pursue further."

At that impatient note, Amanda turned away and disappeared into the bathroom. She quickly undressed, exchanging the black evening dress for a black negligee that Brent had bought for her just before their trip. Her feeling of dismay had subsided and she once again felt secure in her hold over him, although not certain of his love.

She looked at her image in the mirror and thought of "the other men" she was supposed to have slept with. She shuddered—why, the idea alone was repulsive. Was there, perhaps, a reason behind it—something that had driven her to do it? A momentary urge to ask Brent rushed over her.

Amanda cringed at the thought of confronting him. *No,* she

thought, *not tonight, I don't have the strength or the courage to go into those details. One of these days I'll ask Paula again, and one way or another, she will tell me. The truth, all of it.*

When she reemerged from the bathroom, she found Brent on the telephone, talking to one of the symposium's committee members, and she quietly slipped into the bed. She heard the click of the receiver, and turning on her side she closed her eyes, feigning sleep. The lights went off and the bed moved as Brent slid next to her underneath the cool covers. His arm went around her waist and found the outline of her breast. She did not move, even though her heartbeat accelerated at his intimate touch.

"Amanda? Are you asleep?" His voice was soft and husky. "I'm sorry I snapped at you earlier. You were right, perhaps I was feeling guilty at seeing Bianca again. But not for her sake, for yours. I should never have given in to the temptation, it was a mistake." He nuzzled the softness of her neck, inhaling the gentle fragrance of her hair.

Amanda shivered involuntarily, unable to deny his intimate caresses. She did not resist when he gently turned her over to face him. His mouth found her quivering lips, covering them hungrily, greedily, until she moved her head sideways to catch her breath.

"You know something?" Brent mumbled, his voice now thick. "I never did get over you. Even when we were having problems, I kept on hoping . . . waiting for you to come to your senses . . ." His lips brushed hers again. "Hoping for that sweet you I married . . ."

Amanda swallowed, her body now trembling. "Were we ever really happy?" she whispered hoarsely.

"You were so sweet, so vulnerable."

"What happened to us, Brent? To me? What made me change?"

"You grew up. But I kept on praying for you to settle down at one point."

"Was I really that bad?" A sob escaped her and the tears suddenly broke loose. The events of the evening, the fatigue, his gentle words, they had all become too much for her.

"Hush, hush, now," he soothed, kissing her tears away. "You are back now and sweeter than ever before. No more tears tonight, my darling, not while I have you in my arms . . ." He kissed her again and again, her eyes, her nose, her lips, until she clung to him with the desperation of a lost child.

His hands explored her trembling body, stroking and touching every sensitive inch, every intimate curve, and she felt her blood race to her temples. The sensation mounted and she wildly flung her bare legs around his hard torso, her feverish body wanting him, craving for the hardness of him to enter her. A deep groan escaped her throat at his sharp penetration, and a deeper, more exhilarating sensation took over.

Then, vaguely as if from a distance, a sound floated through the darkness. Amanda's eyes flew open as she felt Brent stiffen inside of her. She dug her nails deep into his taut buttocks, urging him to go on, but the ringing persisted, and his thrusts wavered. Brent swore, fumbling in the dark for the phone.

"What?" He quickly shifted the receiver from his left ear to his right. Amanda winced as he left her body, shielding her eyes as the room was bathed in the soft light Brent had switched on.

"Did you call the airlines?" He looked at her incredulously.

Josh! My God, she had forgotten all about him. Amanda snatched the receiver from him. It was Austrian Airlines. She had been cleared from the waiting list and could leave on the eight o'clock flight to London.

"Why didn't you tell me? I'm coming with you."

"No, Brent, listen to me. It's probably nothing. Children do get colds, you know. He'll probably have recovered by the time I get there."

"Then why not call Mother tomorrow and find out before you waste a trip?"

"I . . . I'd like to go, and see for myself. Please, Brent?"

"You could've told me."

"I wanted to, but first there was your speech, and it was so important to you—"

"Nothing is more important to me than my son."

"I know. I'm sorry. I wanted to do the right thing."

"Why didn't you tell me after the speech? Oh, never mind." He suddenly sighed. "All right, go and come back as soon as you can." He looked at her. "You are coming back, aren't you?"

Amanda nodded, tears stinging her eyelids. Only a moment ago they were so intimate, and now they were fighting again. As if he read her thoughts Brent softened and gathered her back into his arms.

"Promise me you'll be back. I need you, Amanda, I need you here with me."

He kissed her trembling lips and gently brushed her tears away. Gradually she stopped crying, and when she looked at him, the odd gleam in his eyes all but took her breath away. She did not move when he reached out and slowly pulled her negligee over her head, baring her firm breasts, still swollen with desire. He bent down and she gasped at the feel of his warm breath on her taut skin. He parted her legs and sank deep and full within her. Amanda wept silent tears of joy.

Chapter 29

FOUR DAYS LATER AMANDA RETURNED TO VIENNA, JUST
in time for the gala evening that was to mark the end of the
general symposium. And what an evening it was! Despite her
fatigue, Amanda felt herself swept up by the gaiety, the lighthearted atmosphere. Louise would've loved this, she
thought, noting the grandeur, the all-out festive decor, admiring the lavish style. Not to mention the sumptuous dinner,
and the handsomely dressed couples.

"You look very royal tonight, Frau Farraday." Werner
bowed. "May I have the honor of this dance?"

She laughed and turned to Brent, who rose and grinned.
"Next one, old boy, this one is reserved for Herr Farraday."
Laughing at the rejected suitor, they waltzed away.

The evening passed quickly. Werner had joined them at
their table, while Bianca and her husband had chosen to stay
at the other side of the room. Another couple from Holland
had taken the remaining seats and within minutes Amanda
had found common ground with the woman, comparing
notes and exchanging anecdotes about their children.

But the wine had taken its toll and just after midnight,
Brent noticed the dark lines under Amanda's eyes.

"Going so soon?" Werner feigned indignation. "Ah, you
young people, haven't you learned how to stay up late in
America?"

"I'm so sorry, it must've been the trip." Amanda stifled a yawn.

"Oh, go on, you two. You don't fool me. You want to make up for the loss, eh? Four nights' worth."

They all laughed and Amanda blushed.

"Well, have fun. Are you still game for tomorrow night, *Herr Doktor?*"

"Wouldn't miss it for the world." Brent grinned and slapped his friend on the shoulder.

"Tomorrow night?" Amanda asked.

"It's a surprise," Brent said quickly. "You're coming too, aren't you, Cees?"

It was Cees's wife's turn to gape. But like Brent, Cees Verbeek only grinned, a mysterious glimmer in his eyes as he nodded.

"Like you said, wouldn't miss it for the world."

With Werner's laughter echoing across the crowded room, Amanda let herself be led into the hallway and then the elevators. She was too tired to pursue her initial curiosity, too eager to shed the straining corset and crawl into a soft, comfortable bed.

"Where are we going? What is this 'surprise' you're talking about?" Amanda asked the next night as the taxi stopped at the corner of a dark alley. But Brent only grinned and paid the driver.

"Come on, we've got a ways to walk."

Taking her hand he led her into the alley, and Amanda almost stumbled over a loose cobblestone. Passing door after closed door, her curiosity heightened. They were little cafés of some sort, she noted, all closed for the night. She was suddenly hungry.

She had slept in that morning, and in the afternoon, Brent had treated her to a massage at the hotel. It was so relaxing that she had taken a nap afterward. A long nap, too long really, for when at six o'clock they had gone for dinner, she had been too tired to eat. But now, three hours later, she wished she had forced herself.

Brent stopped in front of an unmarked door and opened it. It was dark inside, but instantly the hum of voices and laughter reached them, and opening another door, Amanda found herself in a crowded room. She squinted her eyes, trying to adjust to the dimly lit interior and after a few seconds she could see the people silhouetted against the light from the platform in the middle. Smoke spiraled up inside the beams of light, and the tinkling sound of glasses mingled with the laughter all around her.

A man waved at them and Brent waved back. Taking her arm, he led the way to a table close to the raised platform.

"I thought you two got lost," Werner said, holding out a chair for her and waiting for Amanda to sit down before seating himself next to her.

"Hello, Mies." She smiled and leaned across the table to Cees's wife. "What is this place?"

"I don't really know," Mies Verbeek said, laughing. "Looks like a playhouse of some kind. I'm sure this"—she pointed at the platform—"is not here just for show. A show, maybe. I guess we'll just have to wait and see. Cees won't tell me."

A waiter brought the drinks the men had ordered. Suddenly the lights dimmed. For a moment they were wrapped in complete darkness and the buzzing across the room died. A suspenseful silence fell. In the hush the platform slowly brightened.

Amanda gasped. The audience gasped with her. Slowly the music crescendoed, haunting notes swelled, rising, sweeping . . . And in the middle of the platform a huddled cape stirred.

A velvet cape, of rich deep burgundy. It rose upward, stretching out, slowly, moving higher and higher, until, tall and formless, it stood. Erect, still formless. With one sweep the cape slid to the wooden floor, draping a pair of female ankles.

Amanda gasped a second time, and the room let out a long, heavy sigh. They all stared at the woman on the platform. A woman right out of Scheherazade's *Arabian Nights'* harem, scantily clad in sheer veils. Slowly the music crescendoed.

Her body began to move with the rhythm. The sound of tiny bells around her ankles, her waist, her wrists, tinkled across the room. Dancing across the round platform, her feet barely touched the wooden floor. She moved faster and faster as the beat became a rapid whirl. Until, suddenly, it died. The dancer stopped. For a minute she seemed suspended. Then, with one sweep she tossed a veil and the lights around her died. Instantly they were replaced by a red spotlight, silhouetting the dancer's body through the sheerness still wrapped around her limbs.

The dancer moved. Her silhouetted body sensuously visible through the transparent veils. It was a well-formed body, slender and lithe, seemingly bare of any other garments. The light changed to a deep purple, following the smooth movements, clinging to the coiling form. The body whirled, curving effortlessly, rhythmically, with the beat of the music. As the light changed once more to a misty yellow, the veil came off and the crowd sucked in their breath.

In the eerie light she stood. Naked. Or so it seemed. Clad only in flesh-colored strips of sheer cloth. Sheer and transparent, for when the light changed to a dark green, the curves of her swollen breasts showed almost grotesque—two pomegranates, firm and ripe for the plucking. Taut, dark nipples straining. An even sheerer veil clung to her hips, the navel below the tiny waist exposed.

The drums began to roll, slowly. The dancer stirred, moving as slowly as the beat. Moving her hips, whirling her body sensuously, seductively, in circular motion, around and around and around. And her whole body began to move, rhythmically with the roll of the drums, bending backward, her hips circling, the swollen mounds heaving in their restraints, ready to pop. And again the music stopped.

Still bent back in a horizontal position, her hands reached down, touching the inner sides of her thighs, sliding upward and meeting in a clasp atop her flat abdomen below her navel, yet barely touching the skin. Slowly, her hips moved again, and her belly billowed up and down, the pelvic area thrusting upward, again and again.

The audience held its breath, as the long sinewy legs spread out. Parallel to the wooden platform, she began to move again, her waist circling, the bare belly rippling in sensuous motion. With a sudden move her arms flew back, followed by her head, her hair flowing down and reaching the floor. And as the room began to breathe again, she moved her bare shoulders, and with one thrust the veil around her hips slid to the floor, leaving but a tiny sheer strip to cover her intimate parts.

The gasp around the room was more than audible. The audience roared, bellowing for the rest of her to be bared.

The music swelled. The sinewy legs bent, and the suspended body lowered, until, effortlessly, she lay flat on the wooden floor. Then, without warning she bolted upward, the disarray of thick black hair billowing across the heaving bosom. The beat crescendoed. Her body moved. Her hips gyrating in furious tempo, thrusting, circling, faster and faster, in wild, unleashed abandon.

And she turned around, exposing a pair of firm, naked buttocks, and again the room screeched. And whistled. Turning around once more, she raised her arms, her hands brushing up the hair to cover her face as her body gyrated, thrusting and twirling, taunting, inviting. Faceless, the bouncing breasts appeared almost ominous in contrast to the tiny waist and the flat, breathing belly.

With one sudden note the music stopped. The dancer released her hair and turned. And the room exploded.

Amanda glanced at Brent, her cheeks flushed. But before she could catch his attention, a wild shriek racked the room, and when she quickly turned her head, her eyes widened.

Bursting onto the scene were four young males, barechested and clad in tight, shiny leotards that clung to their slim hips, showing off an impressive bulge beneath the flat bellies. Whirling around on the platform, now bathed in bright light, their feet barely touching the floor, they swirled around the girl, their sinewy limbs supple yet strong, their movements a symphony of sensuous harmony. The girl rushed from one end to the other, as if trying to escape, but each time a male pursuer blocked her exit. Until finally, one of them caught her.

Standing behind her, the young man grabbed her under the arms, pinning her shoulders with his forearms, pulling them backward. Her full bosom protruded, brazenly taunting, heaving, the erect nipples visibly straining against the sheer cloth. Her head bent back at a slight angle, her lips parted.

Two of the male dancers kneeled before her, one embracing her right leg, the other holding her left. And so she stood, pinioned between the three men, helpless and spread-eagled. Gentle fingers began stroking and caressing the inside of her thighs, and slowly she moved her hips. The tiny bells around her waist jingled and chimed. The faster she moved, the clearer the sound.

Then the last of the four men jumped into the act, pirouetting and gyrating with an almost savage fervor, his body visibly tensing. Stalking the female captive with the ferocious approach of a panther. Moving in closer and closer, his body readying itself for the kill.

Trumpets blared. Bolting the audience to their seats. In whirled a cloud of female dancers, wrapped in sheer harem veils, their lithe, slender figures transparent through the cloth. Like the male dancers, they swept across the floor, the sheer veils flying around them as they hurled themselves at the men. Breaking the circle and claiming the captors their own. Pairing, they danced around the freed girl, who, grateful at the rescue, pirouetted among the whirlwind of dancers. And slinked into a heap on the floor, her long bare arms folded over her head, bent to bow toward the breathless spectators.

Amanda heaved a deep sigh of relief. Catching Brent's eye, she managed to throw him a quivering smile. But before she could say something, a naked arm reached past her and grabbed Werner, dragging him from his seat and toward the raised platform. His protests were drowned out in the roar of the audience as he stumbled up the steps and all but fell at the dancer's feet.

Amid loud cheers and excited applause, the music began to play again. The dancer moved, her hands gesturing for her embarrassed partner to dance with her. Werner looked back as if for help, but found only encouragement to do as he was bidden. A sheepish grin crossed his flustered face. Then, shrugging, he took off his jacket and began to move.

The crowd went wild. The belly dancer moved and leaned backward, and Werner bent forward as if to accommodate her. A sly smile spread across the woman's face as she took his hands and placed them on her writhing hips. Thrusting her pelvis upward, savagely, again and again, she leaned backward even more, so that Werner, his hands still gripping her hips, had to lean forward. With each ferocious thrust she brushed herself against him.

The frenzied audience all but tore down the place. As if inspired by the crowd, Werner boldly braced the dancer's bare buttocks and began to move with the rhythm of the music. Pulling her upward against him, he rubbed her pelvic area against his loins, his eyes glazed. The girl began to move her bare shoulders, her eyes looking deep into his, watching his reaction as her breasts jingled before his flushed face. The audience screeched.

"Pull it off!" a man's voice yelled in German. "Yank that damn thing off!"

The crowd roared, screaming their demands. After a moment's hesitation, Werner took the bait. Reaching for the valley between her breasts, his fingers groped the sheer strip, and with one swift, forceful tug, the skimpy strap snapped and the swollen mounds burst to their freedom.

As the crazed jeers around her erupted, Amanda turned away, her cheeks crimson, tiny beads of perspiration pearling on her forehead. The blood had surged to her temples at Werner's bold maneuver, and her heart thumping in her throat, she swallowed. Leaning across the table, Brent held out his hand to her.

A little after two o'clock in the morning they stumbled back to their hotel room, Brent still laughing about Werner's dance ritual and chiding Amanda for her embarrassment.

"He was only having fun," he said, grinning.

"I could see that!" she retorted, feigning indignation.

"Of course, she could've picked me." He burst out laughing when she spun around with deadly fury in her eyes. "Some women just don't have taste."

Amanda kicked off her shoes and disappeared into the bathroom. But before she could slam the door in his face, he grabbed her and pulled her to him.

"Come here, woman," he growled.

She tried to struggle loose and held her face away from him. With one swift move, Brent pulled her to him and kissed her.

"Ummm . . ." Amanda wrenched her lips free. "That . . . that . . . show . . . made you . . . ah—"

"Horny? You betcha." He sampled her lips, hungrily, tasting, savoring them. "But it isn't just the show . . . ," he mumbled against her throat, withdrawing, "it's the feel of you."

His hands slid inside her dress and cupped a firm breast. "And this . . ."

Kissing her again, he thrust his tongue deep inside her parted mouth. And his other hand slid underneath her skirt and touched her. "And this . . ."

Amanda shivered, her flesh tingling at his intimate touch. Feverishly her fingers reached to unbutton his shirt.

"I missed you so," he mumbled, nibbling on her earlobe, her neck, her pliable lips.

"And I you." She suddenly did not care if his arousal was a result of the show they had seen, all she wanted now was for him to love her.

Her dress fell to the floor, next to his trousers. Their lips never parting, their remaining garments quickly joining the heap. She clung to him as he scooped her naked body into his strong arms and carried her to the bed.

His mouth covered a swollen breast, enticing the nipple to erection. First one, then the other. Kissing the valley between them, he scorched her flesh where he touched and stroked and nibbled. Amanda closed her eyes. A moan escaped her lips, her body burning for the feel of his steel muscles. The tightness in her body building, she wildly arched her hips to meet his rock-hard strength.

As he reached the inside of her thighs, she eagerly parted her legs to receive him, wanting him as much as he wanted her.

And the telephone rang.

Chapter 30

"DAMN, THIS IS BECOMING A BAD HABIT!" BRENT SAID AN-
grily, holding back a stronger word as he reached for the
phone.

"Hello."

His eyes lit up with surprise.

"Paula? Good God, don't you know what time it is, girl?"

He frowned for a moment, then grinned.

"Oh, all right. You tell her yourself." He handed the receiver to Amanda.

"Paula? What's wrong?"

She listened for a moment, acutely aware of Brent's watchful eyes.

"What?" She suddenly sat up in the bed, her eyes wide
with surprise and pleasure. "Say that again. Where are you?"

"I'm in Salzburg, you nitwit. Am I disturbing something?
Brent didn't sound too pleased."

"Well, what do you expect? It's after midnight, you twerp!"

"I'm in Salzburg. We're in Salzburg. Yes, Matt and I. Can
you believe this? He had to come here for a special assign-
ment. We just arrived half an hour ago, and I couldn't sleep
from all the excitement."

"Christ, it's wonderful! Are you planning to come to Vienna?"

"Of course we are, why do you think I've called you?"

"When?"

"Soon, in a few days probably."

"Oh, Paula, that's fantastic. We'll tour the town together, have coffee in a sidewalk café and stuff ourselves with those sinful little cakes you like so much."

"You know how to tempt me, don't you?" Paula laughed. "But how does that sit with your lord and master? Don't you have to accompany him to all those wonderful luncheons and dinners?"

Amanda glanced at Brent and seeing his impatient frown, laughed.

"My lord and master wouldn't mind that one bit, and even if he did"—she giggled when Brent reached to take a taunting breast in his mouth and she playfully pushed him away— "it's good for me to miss out on those wonderful luncheons as you put it."

"Such a nice guy! God, did you have to bring up those scrumptious tortes I've read about? Yummy, I can taste them already."

Amanda laughed again, nodding her understanding at Brent's gestures to cut the conversation short.

"Slow down, it's the middle of the night, you pig. So when will you be here?"

"I'll call you. After tomorrow night we'll have a better idea."

"What did you do with your brood?"

"You'll never believe this, but Nikki volunteered to take them under her wing for the next two weeks. Said it'd be good for Cole's environmental education."

"But what about school?"

"What about it? She's over sixteen, drives, and has her own car. They won't even miss us."

"All the way from Northbrook?"

"Sounds like you disapprove."

"Oh, of course not. I'm delirious you could get away. God, I still can't believe it. Two weeks, you said? Can't you make it three? Brent and I plan to go to Switzerland the week after the symposium, but you know that."

"We'll see. A lot depends on Matt's progress here. Anyway, I'd better sign off. Talk to you tomorrow. Kiss your lover for me."

Slowly Amanda handed the receiver back to Brent, a pensive frown clouding her face.

"What is it, what did she say?" Brent replaced the telephone on the nightstand, alarmed by her expression. But Amanda only shook her head, deep in thought. When she finally raised her eyes to meet his, it was Brent's turn to frown, yet he said nothing, waiting for her to break the silence.

"It's not like Paula to leave her children in the middle of a school term," she mused softly. "It's almost like . . ."

"Like what?"

"Like they're also on a second honeymoon of sorts."

"What's wrong with that? We're doing it. Well . . . sort of . . ."

Amanda shook her head again. "Have you noticed . . . ?"

"What? That she and Matt are going through rough times? Don't all married couples, one time or another? Come on, Manda, where were we?" He drew her into his arms and nuzzled her neck. "You are hallucinating, darling. If you must fantasize, let me at least help you . . ."

His lips trailed hot kisses along the pulsating vein in her slender throat and down between her naked breasts, and Amanda closed her eyes, a soft moan escaping her parted lips. Her worries about Paula rapidly evaporated in the heat of the surging desire that ripped through every part of her body, heightening with each stroke of the exploring hands, and soon she lost herself in the sensations of the moment.

Lying very still, her head on his wiry chest, Amanda listened to Brent's steady heartbeat, feeling satiated and complete. She loved the aftermath of their unions almost as much as she enjoyed their lovemaking itself. There was a feeling within her that was tranquil and serene, and she wondered if Brent felt the same way.

Had she always felt this way? Had it always been this good? Each time she felt a little closer to him, each time it was better than before, each time she grew to love him more. But if it was this way before, why then had she cut herself loose from him? Why wouldn't he tell her why she had left him? Was there anything else perhaps, something he refused to disclose, something he didn't want her to remember . . . ? Sometimes it seemed as if he closed the door, just like Paula did. She stirred and instantly his arms gripped tight around her.

"Brent?"

"Hm."

"Has Paula ever done this before? Left her children for weeks?"

He did not answer immediately.

"Has she?"

"No. I don't really remember that she has. But then, I never did pay much attention to her comings and goings."

Amanda raised herself on her elbows and looked at him. Brent slowly opened his eyes.

"How then did I know . . . ?"

"Know what?"

"That she's never done this before?" Suddenly excited, she sat up. "I remembered, don't you see? I remembered!" Brent reached out to fondle her bouncing breasts, but she ignored his touch, too wrapped up in her own discovery. "I remembered," she kept on repeating, delighting in the revelation.

"My darling Amanda, come here. Don't remember too much, it might spoil our second honeymoon." He drew her back into his arms, his hands caressing her bare back.

"What do you mean?"

"I want you to remain the way you are now. I love you this way. Why not put the past behind you and live from this point on? Let's bury the old Amanda. Just be as you are now, forever." He kissed her gently. "Trust me. You really don't want to remember the past."

She pushed him away, almost angrily.

"How can you say such dreadful things? You don't know what it's like to live without a past, a memory."

"But I've told you everything worth knowing. Isn't that enough?"

"What is worth knowing to you, you mean. I'd like to know for myself, is that so much to ask? Can't you understand that?"

Brent sighed. "I guess you're right. I'd probably feel the same. All right, what else comes to your mind?"

Amanda strained to remember, wildly searching for some remote spark that would trigger a familiar recollection. But after a few minutes her spirits sank; her mind remained blank, devoid of any sensation other than the ones she knew of now.

"Come on, don't try so hard. It'll all come back to you when you least expect it. And even if it doesn't, it's okay. Life's not so bad as it is right now, is it?"

With a sob of despair, Amanda buried her head in his arms, and he immediately embraced her, holding her close, until she relaxed. He reached for the light and switched it off. In the sanctuary of the darkness Amanda felt the tension inside her ebb away. She closed her eyes and sighed. Brent was right; life wasn't so bad the way it was.

"No, for the hundredth time, no! How many times do I have to repeat it, what do I have to do to convince you that there's nothing wrong between Matt and me? Nothing, you understand, absolutely nada. We're happy together; now stop badgering me, will you?" Paula sighed dramatically, shaking her dark curls in exasperation at Amanda's insistence. "What makes you think we were having problems, anyway?"

"You've never left your children like this, and for so long." Amanda still looked not quite convinced.

Paula had arrived that morning, four days after her midnight phone call, and without Matt. The investigation of the case he was working on had taken a bit longer than expected, and bored, she had decided to join Amanda alone in Vienna. And here they were, sipping coffee at an outdoor café, while Brent focused on the latest surgical innovations in the gynecology field.

"When are you leaving for Switzerland?" Paula sipped her coffee.

"There's been a slight change in plans," Amanda said. "We're going to the Tyrol instead. Werner, Brent's friend, offered us his winter cabin in the Tyrolean Alps, a couple of miles outside of Innsbruck, and we've decided to take him up on it." She smiled and stretched her arms.

"Friday is the symposium's last day. Then there's a farewell dinner that evening, and off we go. We'll meet Mandy and Josh at the airport in Innsbruck and rent a car."

"Does your invitation still stand?"

"For you and Matt to come along? Of course. Are you game? Brent wants to go skiing up on the glaciers of Stubaital."

"Sounds like fun. I haven't skied for years, but I guess it's just like biking."

"Can I do it? Ski, I mean?"

Paula laughed. "You're no champion, but you're all right. Not like dancing or anything, you know."

"The kids are all excited about it. Josh even talked me into buying him some ski boots." Amanda laughed at the recollection of the store clerk's bewildered face when she had asked her for winter clothing.

"How are things between you and Brent these days?"

"Couldn't be better. Why?"

"Oh, he didn't sound too happy when I called that night. Were you quarreling or something?"

Amanda burst out laughing. "Far from it." She giggled, and Paula grinned.

"Gee, I'm sorry if I interrupted something serious."

Amanda sipped her coffee again, hesitant to voice the question that had been nagging at her.

"Paula? Did you ever leave Tara and Wes for this long?" She held her breath, her heart pounding.

"Not since my mother died. Why?"

"Your mother?"

"Yes. She used to look after Wes when Matt and I would go for a long weekend somewhere by ourselves. But she died a year after Tara was born."

"I was right," Amanda whispered.

"About what?"

"I thought . . . I remembered . . . something."

"Remembered?"

"It's nothing."

"Remembered what, cara? That my mother died?"

"No, that you never took long trips without your kids. But then I could not recall anything else."

"But, Manda, that's fantastic! Your memory is coming back. What does Brent say about it, did you tell him?"

"He doesn't say it, but I don't think he's taking it too seriously." Amanda sighed, suddenly uncertain. Perhaps Brent was right, she should stop trying so hard. She looked at her friend, and her uncertainty made way for concern.

"There is something else, isn't there?" she prodded softly.

Paula jumped up, laughing nervously.

"What the hell are you talking about?"

"You and Matt . . . go ahead, tell me it's none of my business."

"You're right, it's none of your business."

Amanda turned her head, trying to hide the hurt in her eyes.

"Oh, cara, I'm sorry," Paula conceded, hesitant. "All right, you win. You're right, of course. There is something wrong between us." Paula sat down again. "It's been going on for some time, ever since . . . ever since the baby died."

"I'm sorry about the baby. Brent told me."

"Yeah? Did Brent also tell you how it died? It was stillborn. I went into labor at six months. It never had a chance . . ."

"Please, Paula, you can't blame yourself."

"Me? Blame me? No, Manda, it was Matt. He had VD, but I didn't know it. At six months I became severely ill and my baby never survived its premature birth. It . . . there was no time for a cesarean, my body was aborting spontaneously, and . . . and the baby—my baby—got infected, and it wasn't strong enough to fight it."

Her voice trailed away and she turned her head, biting her lip to keep it from trembling. Amanda touched her hand, gently, the bitterness in Paula's voice cutting her deeply.

"Then it was better that way, wasn't it?"

"Yeah." Paula fumbled in her purse, impatiently brushing the tears from her cheeks. "That was more than a year ago, almost two. We haven't had sexual relations since. This . . . this trip is supposed to bring us back together . . ." She took a deep breath, her lower lip trembling visibly.

"But?"

"But I'm scared. Funny, isn't it? A grown married woman, scared of having sex with her own husband?" She let out a sharp, short laugh; the sound was harsh and without merriment. "I guess I'm not quite ready to let go of him, but to . . . to make love with him . . . I can't forget that tiny bundle . . . she was so beautiful, so peaceful as if asleep. Only I knew she wasn't . . . just . . . asleep." Her voice broke and she began to cry.

Amanda quickly went over to her and hugged her.

"You must learn to forgive him, Paula. It's important that you forgive him. You can't forget, but you love him, don't you? And your love must find that forgiveness, or you'll destroy both of you. He's a man, Paula, remember that, he's only a man—a human being with faults like you and me. I'm sure he's regretted his mistake. Probably kicked himself over and over again. Must you keep punishing him so?" She kissed Paula's head. "And you? Must you punish yourself for the rest of your life?"

Gradually Paula stopped crying. Her body stopped shaking and she lay still in Amanda's embrace.

"It's so hard," she whispered.

"Of course, it is. But you can do it, I'm certain of it. You're so full of love, you've got so much to give. Don't hold back now. And Matt is a nice man, just not perfect. But then, who is?"

Paula straightened up and turned her head, her eyes brimming again. How easy it all sounds, she thought bitterly. And how ironic to hear it all from Amanda. Matt. A nice man, just not perfect. How many times had she lain awake thinking the same thing—saying to herself that it was *her* fault he strayed? Matt. Of course, she loved him—she *knew* she loved him. Why else would she hang on to him, put up with his infidelities?

Her lip trembled and she bit it to hold back the tears. God, if only she didn't love him so much, if only she could stop caring. Damn him! Damn him for making her life miserable. Damn him for making her want him so. Even now, despite everything. She slowly turned to the silent Amanda, and sighed.

"Thanks, friend." She forced herself to smile through her tears. "You're right. It's time to let old wounds heal."

The receptionist at the American Embassy looked up from her typewriter and smiled politely.

"I'm here to see a Mr. Babcock," Paula said.

"I'm sorry, but Mr. Babcock is gone for the weekend. Did you have an appointment?"

Paula frowned, trying to suppress her irritation.

"No, but I called a couple of days ago and was told to see him. I've lost my passport, and I need a new one to get back into the States."

"I'm sure Mr. Greer can help you." Undaunted, the woman picked up the telephone and pressed the intercom button. "Mr. Greer?" She glanced at Paula's perturbed face. "No, that's okay. There's a lady here who's lost her passport. Can you get someone to help her?" Replacing the receiver, her smile returned. "Someone will be with you in a minute."

Less than a minute later, a tall, bearded man appeared. "Can I help you, ladies? I'm sorry—" His eyes bulged, almost out of their sockets, as he stared.

Amanda stiffened. His gaze was directed at her, not Paula. Instinctively, she took a step backward.

"Why, Jeremy! Jeremy Frost! What are you doing here?" Paula exclaimed, her surprise matching Jeremy's.

Reluctantly he took his eyes off the stunned Amanda. "Paula, it's so good to see you," he said, taking her hands in his, throwing one more furtive glance in Amanda's direction. The look of surprise was now unmistakably hostile. "What can I do for you?"

"I didn't know you'd left the States," Paula crooned.

"Two years ago."

"Is Meghan with you?"

"Meghan left me. It's to be expected, I guess. After all I've put her through." Again that hostile look directed at the silent Amanda. "But Scott is with me now."

"I'm sorry about Meghan. How's Scott?"

"He's very well, thank you. Doing great, as a matter of fact. There's so much more he can learn here than back home." He looked almost sad. "Besides, he needed to get away from . . . the commotion . . ." He glanced at the receptionist. "Why don't you step into my office? I'll get you fixed in no time."

"I'll . . . I'll wait outside," Amanda quickly interjected, and without waiting for Paula's approval, fled the stifling arena.

"Who was that? Why did he look at me like that?" Amanda demanded.

"Who, Jeremy? You mustn't mind him, he was just being emotional. After all, he hadn't seen either of us in years."

"Don't patronize me, Paula. What have I done to him?" Amanda's tawny eyes flashed green, and her voice was edgy.

They were walking across the park, heading back toward the Inter-Continental Wien. Within an hour, Paula had joined her outside the embassy, a brand-new passport in hand.

"It's really nothing, cara. It all happened a long time ago. Let's forget about it, okay?"

"No. I want to know. If I'm to piece my life back together, I'd better find out what kind of a wicked past I've lived."

Paula sighed. She knew how stubborn Amanda could be, and one look at the dogged expression in her flashing eyes told her this was one of those times.

"Why don't we stop by that cozy café and have a cup of coffee, hm?" she said.

It was a nice day, sunny and mild. The little sidewalk café was deserted at that hour and they found a strategic corner half in the shade.

"After Josh was born, you went through a terrible after-birth depression," Paula began. "The Frosts were your neighbors, and Meghan tried to help you as best she could. But it was really her husband who got you out of it and back to normal, you might say. When Meghan found out, she swore revenge, and one day she bought a gun. Jeremy tried to reason with her, and during that fight, the gun went off. It hit their four-year-old son in the spine."

Paula paused to take a sip of her coffee. Amanda's face had lost all color, horror in her stricken eyes. "Wha-what happened . . . then . . . ?" she whispered hoarsely.

Paula sighed, still unable to look at her friend's face. "Well . . . Scott was paralyzed from the waist down, and Meghan wound up in a mental institution. Jeremy sold his house and moved away. This is the first time I've seen him in years."

Amanda shivered. How could she . . . ? No wonder that man had looked as if he'd seen a ghost. No wonder he hated her so.

"Did . . . Brent . . . ?"

Paula nodded. "He did. But his reaction was . . . different. He blamed Jeremy as much as he blamed you. As for Meghan, he strangely showed no sympathy. It was guilt that flipped her over the edge, he said. After all, it was she who bought the gun that maimed little Scott." She shrugged her shoulders. "That's probably why she's now given custody of the boy to Jeremy, so Brent could've been right."

"But why? If she'd wanted revenge, why shoot her husb—" Amanda stopped, sudden understanding in her eyes. "She'd bought it for me, wasn't it? It was me she intended to kill."

She stared across the park, fighting off the sick feeling churning her insides, threatening to overcome her. Like so many times before, she hated herself, hated her sordid past. A chill ran down her back and she shuddered.

"Oh, shit! Do you see what time it is?" Paula jumped up and waved at the waiter. "Come on, Amanda, we've got two minutes to make it back to the hotel, or Brent'll kill me." Then, seeing the raw misery on Amanda's face, she winced. "Sorry, bad choice of words."

She quickly paid the check, and grabbing Amanda's arm, rushed her out onto the street.

Chapter 31

THE DOOR OF THE CABIN CREAKED OPEN, BUT AS SHE stepped inside, Amanda's eyes widened in surprise. It was clean and light and cozy. A large leather sofa, looking comfortable and inviting, flanked by two deep leather chairs, blended right in with the dark oak floor and the wood-paneled walls. Tall wooden beams supported a high vaulted ceiling while smaller ones framed the numerous bay windows around the room. A huge open fireplace covered the entire far side and heaps of chopped wood lay neatly stacked in a corner nearby.

"Not bad," Paula commented, over her shoulder.

"Not bad at all," Amanda agreed, glancing at the wooden table in an alcove surrounded by wooden benches built along the walls that enclosed it. An abundance of light streamed from outside through a huge bay window, making the corner seem airy and warm.

She watched Paula walk into the kitchen and smiled at her friend's exclamations of joy at what she found there.

"God, cara, come look. You won't believe this, but there's a real old-fashioned stove in here. I've never seen anything like it. I thought those things went out of style at the turn of the century. And, oh, a real earth oven! We've landed in the witch's domain!"

"What witch?" Mandy wanted to know. Hearing her question, Josh tumbled after his sister, echoing, "Who's a witch?"

"Look guys, this was the oven where the witch of Hansel and Gretel baked the other little children."

"Paula!" Amanda warned, but it was too late. Mandy and Josh flew into the kitchen, screeching with glee at Paula's discovery.

"What's going on here?" Brent demanded, lugging two suitcases and a traveling bag inside. Amanda quickly moved to help him.

"Oh, Paula thinks we've landed in a witches' coven," she said, laughing.

Brent raised an eyebrow, his eyes widening. "A what?"

"Never mind. Let's find the bedrooms to put these in. How many did Werner say there were?"

"Two. But there's a loft here somewhere." He looked around and his eyes lit up. "There's a staircase hidden behind that extension next to the fireplace. Bet ya it leads to that loft."

"I found the bedrooms," Amanda called out from beyond the narrow hallway past the kitchen.

"Hey, will somebody get these bags from me?" Matt growled, puffing beneath the heavy burden in his arms.

"Oh, darling, let me." Paula rushed to relieve him and together they filled the kitchen counter with bags of food supplies.

"There's more in the car. Come, Josh, let's you and I get them."

"Good lord, how long will we be staying here? There's enough food to feed an orphanage for a month." Paula handed Mandy a couple of packages. "Here, darling, put these in the refrigerator, will you? Thank God, this place is not completely medieval."

Mandy giggled and opened the refrigerator.

"Okay, that should be all of it." Matt put the last of the bags on the counter and gave his wife a friendly slap on her butt.

"Ouch, you moron! Here, do something." Paula threw him a loaf of bread. "Slice, please. And not too thick, Matt. We have to taste some of the meat, too."

Brent and Amanda returned to the kitchen and Josh immediately cornered his father, while Mandy showed her mother the witch's oven.

"Do you think we can bake our food in there?" Her green eyes danced with anticipation. "Can we bake some cookies, Mommy? Can we, please?"

Amanda grimaced, throwing Paula a dirty look. "We'll see." She looked around and relief showed in her face when she spotted a regular twentieth-century gas oven next to the refrigerator. "I don't know how to use that one, but we can give it a try."

"Come on, Josh, let's check out your sleeping quarters, boy. Remember that loft you saw in Nikki's summer house?" Brent asked, putting his arm around his son's shoulders. Josh wriggled himself loose, his eyes sparkling.

"A loft? Am I going to sleep in a real loft?"

"Yep. You and Mandy. But you must promise not to fight and no quarreling either, or you'll be down here on the couch."

"Oh, Dad, why can't I sleep there alone?"

"Well, for one thing, because it's big enough for two, and for another, because I have a sneaking suspicion your sister would also like to experience sleeping in a loft."

"But girls are such a bore. She'll probably grind her teeth and keep me up all night."

Brent halted. "First your word, young man, or we'll forget the loft right here and now." He looked at Josh sternly and the boy relented, although reluctantly.

"Oh, okay. I promise."

But as they proceeded toward the half-hidden stairs, he mumbled under his breath. "It's not fair. I always end up holding the short end of the stick."

He did not see his father's stealthy smile. And a moment later his Indian war cry rang through the cabin, bringing Mandy scrambling up the stairs.

The next morning dawned bright and sunny. The air was crisp and clean and after breakfast they decided to walk down and explore the village.

Toward lunchtime they were all exhausted and, armed with packages, they finally stumbled inside *Die Grotte*, the only inn and eating place in town. To their surprise it was cozy and quite attractively decorated.

Waiting to be seated, Matt pointed at a sign by the cash register and Brent chuckled.

"What's so funny?" Paula demanded. Following her husband's gesture, she read the sign and began to laugh.

"Hey, care to share the fun?" Amanda looked at the sign that said American Express Accepted Here and frowned. "What's the big deal?" She felt cheated and did not hide her disappointment.

"No, silly, look below that," Paula pointed.

Below the first sign was another: *"If you think our staff is bad, you should see our manager."* Amanda's face split into a broad grin. Then, looking up, she came face to face with a friendly waitress.

"Welcome to our home," she said, smiling. "Karl will have your table ready very soon, ja?"

She was young and pretty, and dressed in a bright Tyrolean costume and customary dirndl.

"I am Johanna." She smiled again and glanced in Karl's direction, and when he nodded she turned back to her guests. "Come with me, please."

They ordered wienerschnitzel and sauerbraten, which were delicious. The brisk walk in the fresh air had stimulated their appetites. Even Mandy and Josh finished their plates in record time. Johanna came back to clear the table and brought hot coffee and scrumptious apple strudel and strawberry tortes.

"Compliments of the chef," she said.

"God, I like this place." Paula grinned and reached for a torte.

Brent laughed. "Especially those compliments of the chef," he teased.

It was after two when they finally took their leave. As he paid the check Brent asked Johanna for the nearest ski lift to the glaciers and in her best English she tried to give him directions, using her hands to point out the shortest route. Her eyes lit up when he handed her the tip and she blushed.

As the end of their vacation drew near, reluctance to leave mounted. Life was so simple here, so carefree, removed from all the worldly temptations that threatened to have them lose sight of the real value of happiness.

And at night, when the children were asleep, the adults began to wonder if they would ever recapture the peace and the contentment they had found in this simple lifestyle.

* * *

The slopes were magnificent. Tempting white snow, glistening in the morning sun, stretching out with deceptive smoothness. It was their last day in the Tyrolean Alps; tomorrow they would all fly back to the States. Not that any of them looked forward to it, but both Matt and Brent had to go back to their respective duties. Already the medical exchange in Vienna had tried to put a couple of telegrams through to Brent; mostly cries for help from the hospital.

At the bottom of the slope, the distant figures of four skiers could be seen zigzagging toward the ski-lift station. Amanda's heart lurched as she witnessed a smaller one tumble down in the snow, then quickly scramble back to his feet and get back on track.

"Such a fast learner, that Josh of yours," Paula commented, nudging her. "How about you, mother? Ready?"

Amanda threw her a dirty look and made a face. She had decided she did not care for this sport. What made Josh's adrenaline flow scared the wits out of her, and she hated the sensation of falling and sliding downward without control.

"Come on, darling," Brent had said that first day he had fastened the skis under her feet. "You were such a marvelous skier. You can do it again, trust me. It's like riding a bike, once you know how you'll never forget it."

But she had not caught on, falling and slipping each time, and sprawling on her back more than she was on her feet. The slopes were smooth and the ground unpleasantly hard. After a few days, the men had joined Mandy and Josh, who had proven to be excellent students, leaving her more and more under Paula's wing. But even Paula's patient coaching could not take the edge off her fear, although she did improve a little as time went by.

"Okay, off you go, kiddo. Easy does it. Just remember to hold your skis in a straight parallel, and you'll do fine. Ready?" She held Amanda's arm. "Remember, I'm right behind you."

"It's a good thing I left my shawl with Johanna in the café." Amanda stalled, her heart pounding as she looked down the steep white slope. "Remind me to pick it up on our way back to the chalet."

"Don't worry, I will. Ready? Here we go . . ." Paula suddenly staggered and grabbed her unsuspecting friend's arm. With a scream, Amanda hurtled down the slope.

The cold air whizzed in her face and she could hardly see through the cloud of snow her skis made along the way. Her lungs burst, and down she flew. The urge to close her eyes and put her fate in providence's hands was strong and growing stronger by the minute. Desperately trying to heed Paula's teachings, she bent her knees, on and off, zigzagging, following the path. To her horror she rapidly gained speed and, before long, had lost complete control.

She could hear Paula's voice behind her, the words lost in the wind that blasted her face and around her muffed ears. She slid downward, faster and faster. The landscape became one white blur and she panicked. She crashed down on the hard white ground, spinning on her back, skis high up in the air.

Slowly, she sat up, supporting her body with both hands planted in the snow. Her fingers touched her legs, gingerly, expecting numbness.

"Are you all right?" a deep male voice asked in English.

Amanda jolted at the touch of his gloved hand on her arm, and as she turned her head he instantly loosened his firm grip. He searched her face and his deep blue eyes widened in surprise.

"Good God, Amanda! It's you."

She looked up into his face—young, handsome, and with an arresting smile that was both charming and infinitely sensuous.

"I thought . . . you said you didn't want to come with me here." He sounded hurt, the accusation raw in his eyes. He spoke with an attractive lilt. Definitely not German or Swiss, she thought, trying to clear her buzzing head.

"Please . . . ," she whispered, bewildered.

"You could've just told me. This . . . this is infinitely worse."

Oh, God, not again! Not another one, please! Why, she must have been awfully busy these past four years . . . She swallowed. "Told you . . . what?" she whispered.

"That I was just a one-night stand." His voice was bitter. "A quick tumble. But I thought—"

"Amanda! Are you okay?" Paula slid abruptly to a halt next to them.

"Sven! What's taking you so long?" A woman's voice yelled from down below.

The young man peered at his caller and glanced at Amanda's stricken face. He clearly wanted to say something more, and she wished he would, but Paula's presence held him back.

"Are you sure you're all right?"

"Thanks, but I'll take it from here," Paula answered for her, and with a nod he got up. One last, hesitant look in Amanda's direction, and off he went, down the slope to rejoin his female companion.

"I'm okay," Amanda grumbled. She resolutely took off her skis and sighed. "That does it. That was the last tumble for me."

"Who on earth was that?" Paula watched the young man put his arm around the waiting girl, and say something that made her look back at them.

Amanda shook her head. "I've never seen him before," she said flatly.

But her mind whirled, questions and speculations spinning at alarming speed. Suddenly, she felt her head split with such force she had to close her eyes. She rose to her feet, then grabbed her friend's arm and slowly slid back to the ground. For a moment she just sat there, unable to move.

The cold from the snow penetrated through her ski suit, but she did not feel it. Nor did she feel the sharp pain in her right leg where her left ski had tried to poke a hole through during the fall. Only the dull ache in her pounding head.

For from the depths of her subconscious, a disconcerting thought had pushed to the foreground—she remembered what had hurled her to an almost untimely death . . . A hand had grabbed her—grabbed . . . or . . . pushed . . . ? A hand—Paula's hand.

A chilling sensation gripped her throat. For an insane moment she felt herself sucked into a whirlpool of horror and disbelief. The buzzing in her head intensified. The hammering in her ears drowned out the hollow echo of the wind. She looked up and her heart lurched as she stared into Paula's concerned eyes.

And a different kind of fear emerged.

Chapter 32

THE GRAVEL CRACKLED UNDER HER FEET AS AMANDA strolled up the steep hill. The morning air smelled pure and crisp, the dew heavy on the wildflowers alongside the winding path. Taking a deep breath, she looked at the tall pine trees that formed a natural hedge on the far side of the narrow road. There was something idyllic in the rustic surroundings that was both arresting and soothing, and she felt herself irrevocably drawn to the edge of the forest beyond the hill adjacent to the cabin.

Reaching the top of the hill, she sighed. The path that had led her there ended, and for a moment she stared at the far horizon. Then, slowly, she walked toward the edge and sat on a smooth gray rock, looking down on the sleeping village below. Pulling up the collar of her coat, she inhaled the air, relishing the fresh outdoor scent of the dawning day.

It had been ages since she had watched a sunrise, not since Louise had her stroke. She had been waiting for Brent then, pacing the floor of the visitors' lounge in the hospital, and the sight of the rising sun had had a calming effect on her. She dreamily gazed down below, and gradually the serenity of the slumbering village swept over her.

She had not slept much the night before, the incident with the stranger heavy on her mind, and afraid of another nightmare, she had risen early and slipped out of the chalet. She needed the fresh air, the cold, the open outdoors to clear her mind and rid herself of the nagging doubts that had once again taken hold of her. So many questions and never a satisfactory answer, only more disrupting events.

A light came on, and soon another. Her eyes wandered across the awakening village and to the horizon where a hint of daylight began to spread. In the trees above her birds began to announce the birth of a brand-new day.

"Oh, there you are." Paula's husky voice rang through the air.

Her big brown eyes, still full of sleep, looked at the early riser reproachfully, and stifling a yawn, she waddled toward the empty rock next to Amanda's.

"What on earth possessed you to get up and roam around at this ungodly hour?"

Amanda watched her friend rub the sleep out of her eyes, and an involuntary flicker of amusement crept into her own. The tension surrounding her fall had evaporated, chased away by Brent's reassuring argument that it must have been her imagination playing tricks on her. And resting in his passionate arms, she knew he was right.

Of course it had been just her imagination. Paula was her friend—what possible reason could she have to harm her? She had obviously lost her balance, so what would be more natural than grabbing someone? That must've been it, she decided, a reflex. What else could it have been?

"Call of the wild. How about you?" She hooked her arm into her friend's and squeezed her affectionately.

"Right. Next you'll tell me that you responded to an Indian love call," Paula grumbled, but she relented at Amanda's warm gesture.

"It's so peaceful out here, isn't it?" Amanda said. "Listen to those early birds, smell the morning air, it's all so soothing, so reassuring. No worries, no doubts. Just life, simple and pure."

Paula glanced at her sideways and frowned.

"Spit it out, cara. What's eating you?"

Amanda looked away, silent for a moment. She was determined now to push for an answer to the question that had haunted her throughout many a sleepless night. When she had stared into the darkness and suffered the void in her memory banks.

But if before she could ignore the insinuations, she could no longer shrug away the strangers—the men who came up to her and implied intimacy. Three in such a short time seemed quite a record—how many more were there, she wondered? What did she do, sample the European male population in four years' time? And before that? She shuddered. Suddenly she remembered Jeremy.

"I was having multiple affairs, wasn't I Paula?" Amanda swallowed, and took a deep breath. "I mean . . . I was . . . promiscuous . . ."

When her friend did not respond, she turned to face her and, ignoring Paula's astonished look, repeated the question.

"You're my best friend. Please tell me the truth. I need to know the truth."

"What a funny question." Paula shifted uneasily, lowering her eyes, but Amanda shook her slightly.

"Look at me, Paula. I know you care about me, I know you don't want to hurt me in any way, but if you really do love me, you must stop shielding me from myself."

"I'm not—"

"Yes, you are. And I love you for it. But the game is over. I need to know. You must understand that. The past is no longer a sanctuary if it starts haunting a person. You know me better than anyone else I know. Better than even Brent." She put her arm around her friend's shoulders and hugged her lightly. "It's time you helped me put some of the ghosts to rest. Please, Paula, darling." She took a deep breath. "Was I sleeping around?"

Paula swallowed hard. "Yes," she whispered, wincing at the pain that flashed across Amanda's face. "I mean . . ."

"Thank you." Amanda nodded, her heart suddenly pounding. "It's all right, I can take it." She swallowed hard, her throat feeling dry. "With whom, Paula? All these men who have claimed to know me in the past few weeks? *Please.* You must tell me, I want to know, I *need* to know," she pressed, her voice hoarse with emotion.

"I . . . you never really did say. I mean, you never actually came out and told me that you were. I merely assumed." Paula swallowed again.

"What do you mean?" Amanda whispered.

"Well, you never did say that you , . . you merely insinuated, and you acted . . . well, you didn't exactly hide the fact that you didn't think your marriage to Brent was . . . ah . . . enough. And then there were the men. They openly lusted after you, and you encouraged their chase. And, of course, the rumors . . ."

"Who were they, Paula? The men, who were the men?"

Paula sighed, her uneasiness growing to embarrassment.

"Paula? Their names."

"I . . . I can't say for sure . . ."

"Was Niels one of them?"

Paula nodded uncomfortably, lowering her eyes and swallowing.

"Who else?" A name suddenly flashed through Amanda's memory.

"Tyrone. Who's Tyrone?"

Paula looked at her, startled.

"I don't know a Tyrone." Then her eyes lit up. "You mean Travis?"

"That's it. Travis. Who's he?"

"He was a professional tennis player, and Alison's boyfriend before you caught his attention. Brent . . . well, we all thought you'd run away with him to Europe. He played the tournaments there and you disappeared around the same time he left the country."

So that's why Alison hated her, Amanda thought, that's why Nikki and all her other friends hated her.

"Did . . . did Brent . . . know . . . of all these . . . lovers?"

"I don't really know. I guess he did. Like I said, you made no secret about your conquests. I must admit, you could charm a snake if you wanted to, and I suppose you wanted to."

Amanda stared at the horizon. The sun had meanwhile risen and the sky was clear, the day bright and full of promise. But she hardly noticed any of it, her heart heavy with regret, shame and confusion.

Why had she needed all these men? Why had she felt a need to go bed-hopping? The thought alone was repulsive— being touched by anyone but Brent turned her off . . . What was more—she could not possibly imagine herself wanting anyone else. So, then why . . . ? It didn't make sense . . .

"That man, yesterday afternoon . . . ," Paula said cautiously.

Amanda shook her head. "I don't know. I don't remember." She turned away, her eyes brimming. "Oh, Paula, I must have been such a horror . . ."

"Cara, please." Paula pulled her into her arms, holding her as the sobs racked through her body. "Hush, now, baby. It's all in the past. You've atoned, you're different now."

Gradually Amanda stopped crying, pulled herself loose and straightened her shoulders. Seeing the pain reflected in her bloodshot eyes, Paula cringed and she instinctively held out her hand.

"Why, Paula? If I was such a bitch, why did you remain my friend? Were you not afraid I would go for Matt, too? Or was he immune to my charms?"

"Please, cara, don't talk like that. I didn't always approve of your actions, but we grew up together, and I loved you. As for Matt"—she smiled wryly—"you always went for the blond ones, and he was too lazy to dye his hair."

For a moment they just sat staring at the horizon, the silence between them soothing.

"Was I always like . . . that?"

Paula got up and began to pace.

"When we were little girls, you never wanted to play with me, always going for the boys. Even then. One day, one of the bigger boys tried to rough me up, so to speak, and I was terrified. You came and saved me. You yelled at the bully and got him away from me. Ever since that time we were best friends." She threw her head back and laughed. "Oh, you would still favor the company of boys, but you always made time for me, too. I felt flattered that you had chosen me for your only female buddy."

She laughed again and her laughter was contagious. A small smile formed on Amanda's lips as she watched her friend.

"Tell me more. Were we schoolmates, you and I?"

"That, and neighbors, and soul mates." Paula suddenly grinned. "You vowed to protect me. So, one afternoon—we were about ten at the time—you decided to cut our wrists, and we mingled our blood. Said you'd seen it done in the movies. A holy pact. Made us soul mates, forever. I always thought it was blood sisters, but you convinced me otherwise." She grimaced, then laughed. "God, I still remember the pain. But you were so serious about the whole thing, and it seemed so important to you. If you'd wanted to cut off my whole hand that time, I probably would've let you."

Paula paused. For a moment she seemed lost in thought, her mind rerunning the days of yesteryear. Then, shaking her head, she took a deep breath and smiled again.

"Tell me more . . . about myself . . . ?" Amanda pressed. Brent had vaguely mentioned her parents' tragic death, and she had met her uncle Jed. Briefly. But neither had been too keen on reminiscing. "Did I have any brothers or sisters?" She knew it was an odd question, but Paula only shrugged.

"I don't remember seeing any," she said. "We never played at your place, always in the park or at my house. I have two older brothers, you know, and you liked their company."

"And?"

"And when we were teenagers, the boys just swarmed around you. I'll never forget that first dance we went to. They were practically standing in line to have you dance with them, and you took charge, making half of the line dance with me first and exchanging partners that way. I had a ball."

"You didn't resent it?"

"What? Resent not being a wallflower? Are you kidding? I was an ugly duckling. Good thing you don't remember, kiddo. I was formless and lanky, no boobs to speak of, no elegance of any kind. Not like you at all. But none of those boys dared to show even the slightest reluctance to dance with me, you made sure of that. And I loved you for it." She grinned. "I was wearing glasses then. 'Four-Eyes,' they called me behind my back. Sometimes the brazen ones called me that right in my face. Although, never twice. You wouldn't speak to them until they'd apologized. Pity you don't recall that part."

She threw her hat up in the air and caught it gracefully.

"I was so proud of you when you won the Miss Teenage Chicago beauty contest. I was even prouder when you introduced me as your best friend to everyone. And then came Brent."

"Yes? Go on."

"Well, he was head over heels in love with you the first time he laid eyes on you. Anyone could see that. Your parents reveled in the situation. He was a prominent resident physician even then, you know, and very handsome. And the way he pursued you . . . it was so romantic. For the first time I felt jealous of you."

She took Amanda's hand in hers.

"It drove you away from me. Well, sort of. You were swept up in his world, and he in yours, and I lost you. Or so I thought. But after about a year of your marriage, you came to me one day and . . . well, we were friends again."

"What happened? Why did I . . . was the marriage in trouble?"

"I don't know. You didn't exactly complain about it. I just had that feeling that . . . well, that Brent was not the Prince Charming you had dreamed he would be . . ."

"And I began seeking other pleasures."

"Well, no. At least, not at first. Later perhaps. Then, of course, Mandy was born, and later on Joshua."

Paula paused, playing with Amanda's fingers.

"I think it was Brent's idea, about the babies, I mean. I don't think you actually wanted them. As a matter of fact, it was shortly after Mandy's birth that you developed an insatiable craving for parties. You always did love dancing, and you were a fantastic dancer. I've never seen anyone who could dance like you. It's in your blood, cara, it still is. The music, I mean, the rhythm."

"Are you saying I did not care about my babies?"

"Well, I . . . you weren't exactly the motherly type. Not like you are with them now. You simply dote on them now, but back then, you felt they were a burden. I guess . . . well, you were young, and beautiful, and immensely desirable . . . so what can you expect? I understood it, sort of."

"But Brent didn't?"

"Perhaps he had hoped that the kids would settle you down."

Suddenly Amanda did not want to know any more about her past.

"And Matt? When did you meet Matt?"

Paula's eyes lit up, her face glowing.

"I guess I must thank you again. You know, for not having time for me when Brent was wooing you. I was so miserable I accepted a blind date, double-dating with my brother. Matt was his roommate at college, and terribly shy. We hit it right off, and by the time you remembered me, we were married.

For the first time in my life I found myself on equal footing with you. It felt good."

"And no matter what I did, you stood by me, remained my friend."

"I loved you, cara, and when you love someone, you take her as she is, good or bad. Anyway, you were not completely bad, just lost, that's all."

"Lost?"

"You didn't know what you wanted. All your life you got everything, and you took it all for granted. Even a doting husband like Brent."

"You never stopped caring, not even when you . . . did Nikki tell you or did you figure things out by yourself?"

"Both. I suspected something, then Nikki did confide in me." She sighed. "Don't worry about Nikki. She's not so clean herself. Yes." She grinned at Amanda's astonished look. "She strayed, too. Only Niels doesn't know about it. I do. She told me. Oh, not to brag, just out of bitterness. It slipped out, so to speak. But I caught the slip. So, you see, she's got nothing to complain about, cara. And if you ask me, you knew about it too, and took advantage of that knowledge."

"Still, she was a friend."

"No. You're wrong. Nikki pretended to be a friend, but she never was one. Not really. She's extremely ambitious, and being friends with you would make points for her husband. It worked. Brent took Niels under his wing and made him what he is today."

They were silent once more. Then Amanda fumbled for Paula's hand, and finding it, clasped it tight. A lark flew past them and circled way above their heads. In the valley down below a couple of small children played, running in the snow and throwing snowballs at one another.

"Amanda, Paula, where are you?"

Brent's voice echoed through the air, and they both started.

"My God, they're up. Come on, we're late for breakfast."

Jumping up, Paula resolutely heaved Amanda along with her. She looked at her friend, a gentle smile belying her stern expression.

"It's over, you hear? It's a brand-new day, a brand-new life. You've been given this second chance. Use it. Make something out of your life with Brent." She hugged her lightly, then searched her face again. "You will, won't you?"

Slowly Amanda returned her smile and nodded.

"I will. I have, and I will. I love him, you know. Brent, I mean. Whatever happened before, I will not lose him again. I know that now."

"Amanda, Paula." Brent's voice sounded worried.

"Coming," Paula called back.

"What on earth . . . ? Where the hell have you two been?" Then seeing Amanda's swollen eyes, he frowned and put his arms around her. "Anything wrong?"

She smiled at him and shook her head.

"Not anymore," she whispered and nestled against his firm chest while Paula hurried back inside the cabin.

The delicious aroma of bacon filled the small cabin and Brent sniffed demonstratively. Amanda laughed. Her spirits revived, she had volunteered to make breakfast, but Paula had ousted her from the tiny kitchen. So, instead, she had quickly packed the last of their suitcases and done her last-minute check of the cabin.

"Paula?" Matt poked his head around the front door. "Did you take the car-rental contract out of the glove compartment?"

"It's on top of your briefcase, darling. You told me to leave it out there," Paula said, expertly flipping the eggs.

"Out where?"

"Oh, Matt, can't it wait?"

Amanda jumped up. "I'll get it."

"Thanks, cara. On the dresser, in our room."

She found it almost immediately. Impetuously snatching the envelope off the brown leather briefcase, her hand accidentally caught Paula's handbag and swiped it to the floor.

"Damn!" She frowned, glancing down at the scattered mess. "So much for efficiency." And kneeling down, she quickly gathered the pieces back into the purse. Lipstick, a pack of gum, a nail file, tissues, a pen, a small address book—Jesus, such garbage—keys, another pen, more chewing gum, passports, three of them, a credit card wallet, a piece of paper—

Amanda frowned. *Three* passports? Taking them out again, she quickly flipped through the pages. And stiffened. The feeling of dread returned. Two of the passports were in Paula's name; one issued in Chicago a year ago, the other stamped in Vienna, bearing last week's date.

For a moment she remained very still. Why did Paula lie about losing her passport? Was she going crazy? What was the meaning of this charade? Then, slowly, she glanced at Matt's passport and, on a hunch, flipped through it. It had an entry into Amsterdam, four days before entering Austria. She nervously flipped through Paula's—the Chicago one—and sighed. No sign of an entry into the Netherlands. And the date of arrival in Salzburg—two days after Matt's . . .

Another lie. But why? Why had Paula not wanted her to know that she had followed Matt? Why had she wanted them to think that they had traveled together?

Amanda stared at the wall, seeing nothing. Wondering, again, about the hand—Paula's hand—that had grabbed her on the slopes. Was it, after all, not a figment of her imagination? Had Paula, perhaps, indeed meant to push her?

Chapter 33

THE DAY THEY RETURNED FROM EUROPE, NICOLE CALLED Amanda to tell her that Niels had bought her a new house. Or so she put it. Actually, the house was quite old, and Nikki did not like anything old. She did, however, like the way Amanda had redone Paula's bedroom, and she had heard rumors that Vanessa Lynch wanted to have her family room enlarged and remodeled this summer. So before that pretentious snob could charter her services, would Amanda come and look at her new house next week?

"But Nikki, why me? I'm not a professional decorator, and—"

"That's just it! I don't want to deal with those overbearing people, who only talk down to you and treat you like a piece of shit. All the while I'm footing the bill and making them rich." She sighed dramatically. "Please, Amanda, you're my friend, and I know you won't snub me, or take me for a ride. Of course, I'll pay you for your services, but I trust you. Most of all, I simply adore your vision."

"Friend" and "vision," Amanda thought wryly, what a flair for words she has. A frown furrowed her brow. What was behind all this? Despite outward appearances, they had not been the best of friends since her homecoming, and after Niels's abominable assault on Maui, their relationship had sunk close to subzero.

"Nicole," she said, "I've just come home and I still feel a bit of jet lag. Can't this wait a couple of days?"

"Oh, of course, darling. I'm sorry, it's damn thoughtless of me. But I did want to be the first to ask you, you see."

Then, when the next day Vanessa called, and a couple of days later a friend of Paula's she had never even met, Amanda understood Nikki's urgency. By the end of the week, Louise invited her for lunch.

"Why not start your own business?" Louise, who was feeling much better, handed her a piece of crisp fluffy cracker buttered with homemade orange marmalade.

About to bite into it, Amanda paused and stared at her.

"I don't see why it wouldn't be a success. You have the talent, and the fruits of your labor are proof themselves—your home, Paula's bedroom, Brent's den, to name a few," Louise argued.

She'd done Brent's den, too? That was news to her; he'd never mentioned it. Neither had he shed any light on the mystery that shrouded her unexplained skill in remodeling and interior design. It wasn't so much the vision—it was her knowledge of the technical aspect that puzzled her. Somehow she knew exactly what to look for, whom to turn to for what, and what was or wasn't feasible. But how?

Natural instinct, Brent called it, talent, inborn creativity. No matter where she had looked, there were no traces of books on the subject, no signs of study material anywhere in the house—and she had looked. Even Mrs. Flynn had become intrigued and helped her in her futile search. Oh, a magazine or an article here and there—but nothing specific that could offer a plausible answer.

How about college—what had she studied then? But Brent insisted that she had majored in literature, and besides, she'd barely finished two years of it. Then what? Even if she was a raw talent—a wunderkind—it seemed odd that she wouldn't have kept any books, or pictures—any kind of material on home decorating. Unless . . .

She shook her head vehemently, shutting out the doubts she had so desperately tried to lay to rest. What did it really matter? A little mystery in one's life had yet to harm anyone. The alternative was far worse, and at this point in her life she was not about to give up Brent.

"It's nice of you to say that, but I think it would be a big mistake." she said. "Besides, the children need me at home. Already I've been away too long. I owe it to them and Brent —and to myself—to be there for them, at home where I belong."

"Poppycock. They need a mother, yes, and Brent needs a full-time wife, but that does not preclude your dabbling in a just cause on the side."

"Just cause? Who are we kidding? This is nothing more than a hobby, and you know it." She took a sip of her coffee, lowering her eyes to hide a pleased smile.

But Louise's sharp eyes had caught that smile. "Hobby, interest, call it what you will. I see it more as creative juices, talent—a gift from the gods. Who are you to deny mankind that gift?"

"Nice try, Louise." Amanda laughed.

To receive praise from Louise Farraday was rare, and it made her feel good. For the first time in months she felt like a real person. Not just Brent's wife or the mother who had deserted her babies, or even the prodigal Amanda who had left her family without saying good-bye, but a woman who was her own person, an individual who had something to offer the world.

"I wouldn't know how to begin," she mused. "I don't have the right connections, no names of reliable subcontractors, no inside knowledge of who to contact, none of that."

"Nonsense. You managed to finish Paula's bedroom with no trouble at all. Use the same sources, talk to them. They'll refer you to others you need along the way. You'll see."

Amanda sighed. Trust Louise to have an answer for everything.

"What's the catch, Louise? Why are you so anxious to have me busy myself with something as trivial as my creative juices?"

"My dear child, anyone knows that a bored housewife is a danger to herself. And to her family," she said wryly.

So that's it, Amanda thought. *She's afraid I might run away again. I should've known. This encouragement is a means for self-preservation rather than a way of looking out for my interest. Still, Louise may have a point. Perhaps that had been one of my past problems.*

"Okay, you win. I'll take a look at Nikki's house." She saw

Louise's eyes light up and hastened to add, "But only a look, mind you. No strings attached." She gathered her purse and rose.

"As for starting my own business—I don't think so. I like being a full-time mother and a wife. If I am to do some . . . dabbling, it's to be just that. A passing-the-time sort of thing, nothing more."

Brent appeared pleased. He had always admired her eye for detail. Louise was right, he said, she had vision, and one that captivated the soul of any room she touched, giving it an atmosphere that was at the same time unique and breathtaking.

She had to admit that it surprised her to get his support. Not that she had expected anything in particular, one way or the other, but his favorable response had been so spontaneous, that for a moment she wondered if it could have been prompted by his grandmother. Louise had a way of getting through to people; then again, she remembered how strong Brent was and she knew that no decision he made would be other than the one he wanted to make himself.

"But what about the children? And you? There will be times when I will need more time than just those few hours in the morning, and I still have to think of their needs."

She knew her sputtering was nothing more than empty noise, but she wanted to hear him say it; she had to be sure he was not just obliging her. After all, she was not certain herself that this was not a whim on her part, one that would blow over as soon as her interest had died down.

"Why not have Amparo come work for you full-time? She knows how to sew, she could help you make Mandy's ballet costumes. And if need be, Mrs. Flynn could drive Josh to soccer practice, while Amparo gives her a hand in all her other chores."

"I don't know if the girl is still available," she said. When Louise had gone back to Chicago, she had terminated Amparo's services, and she could not imagine that the girl would not be employed elsewhere. After all, it had been over a month now.

"Talk to Maria tomorrow. As for me, I'd rather have a happy wife than a dissatisfied mope."

Amanda's eyes widened with indignation. She opened her

mouth to say something, then seeing the twinkle in his eyes, grabbed a pillow off the sofa and swung it at him. Brent laughed, ducked, and with a swift move pulled her into his arms.

"Just remember who's still the boss in this family," he warned, kissing the tip of her nose.

Amanda sighed and pretended to pout. "And what if Niels makes another pass at me?"

She instantly realized her mistake. Brent's eyes darkened and she felt his body tense up. In her excitement she had neglected to tell him what had prompted the whole idea.

"Niels? What's that son of a bitch got to do with all this?" Brent scowled, his eyes flashing dangerously.

Amanda scrambled to a more dignified position. Then, scraping her courage together, slowly, cautiously, she told him.

"Of course, if you don't think it's a good idea . . ." Amanda waited.

"I won't use the word 'forbid,'" Brent said, his face a thundercloud, "but I would not do it if I were you. I don't trust them. It's probably a ploy to discredit you."

"A trap, you mean?" She laughed at him. "Oh, Brent, don't be silly. What could they do? Display my talents and declare it fraudulent?"

"I wouldn't put it past them. Especially Nikki. She's wicked, that one. They're dying to see you ruined, one way or another."

"Ridiculous. With their money? They may be vicious, but certainly not at the cost of their own finances. Besides, Louise says this is my chance to create a masterpiece—and I promise you, this masterpiece does not come cheap."

"I still don't trust them."

"Maybe they feel guilty and want to make good."

"Guilty? Nicole Nillson?" Brent sneered. "Fat chance, milady. That little bitch was born without a conscience, believe me."

"My darling paranoid lord and master, how I do adore thee. Why, you're even more transparent than I am," Amanda said, laughing.

But Brent remained tense, definitely not amused. "I'll break every damn bone in his miserable body," he said slowly.

She quickly pulled his head down and kissed him. "I'll stay out of his reach, I promise," she soothed. "My, my, such a frown," she teased, her heart pounding, uneasy under his piercing glare.

He suddenly grabbed her hair and his mouth came down on hers, hard, devouring her angrily, hungrily, almost savagely, until she moaned and gasped for air.

Chapter 34

THE HOUSE THE NILLSONS HAD BOUGHT ON THE OUT-skirts of Winnetka was quaint, and quite unlike any of the surrounding ones in the neighborhood. From the outside it resembled an English cottage, complete with rosebushes and green creepers climbing up the once red brick, a far cry from the impressive mansions on either side of the house. Yet it curiously seemed to blend in well, almost as if the cul-de-sac needed a breather to tone down the solemnness of its environment.

Inside, however, the house was amazingly spacious, and surprised, Amanda felt her excitement building as she wandered from room to room, sizing up possibilities and visualizing changes. By the time she had reached the upstairs she knew she was lost.

Yes, oh yes, her heart sang. She could see it all, in living color. A showcase, Nikki had said. And a showcase it shall be, she thought dreamily, her eyes gleaming as images flashed through her mind and concepts rapidly began to take form.

Producing a sketchbook, she made her pencil fly across the paper. She filled page after blank page with lines and curves and circles, jotting down notes and ideas and potentials. Nikki had given her carte blanche and she fully intended to take her up on it, especially since Nikki had insisted that the job be finished by Thanksgiving.

Looking up from her rough drafts, Amanda smiled. It's a cinch, she nodded, pleased. All it needed were minor changes—a wall knocked out downstairs, another in the main bedroom—the basics were all there. With luck she would have this place on display by Halloween. Quickly moving through each room, she noted every detail, drawing and sketching feverishly. Her pencil projected the images in her head, and as her dreams came to life, her nagging doubts died, and she no longer questioned her ability to create a masterpiece.

The sleek Ferrari sports coupe raced through the curvy Winnetka streets and onto the expressway.

"Where are we going?" Amanda frowned, suddenly apprehensive and wishing she had not let Nicole talk her into tagging along on some obscure excursion. Why hadn't she listened to Paula and taken her own Mercedes to the Nillsons' place? "I thought you said it wasn't far."

"It isn't. We're almost there."

Amanda bit her lip. She should have insisted on going home. Soon the kids would be out of school and she liked to be there to greet them and listen to their daily tales. Already too often lately she had not been present when they came home, and she knew from their expressions that they had been disappointed.

Covertly she glanced at Nicole, who only smiled mysteriously as she rapidly maneuvered the red Ferrari along the expressway.

Damn. She should have thought of an excuse, but she had been anxious to regain Nicole's friendship—why, she now wondered?—and it had seemed innocent enough; a luncheon, a step in the right direction and a small price to pay.

The Ferrari swung off to exit the expressway and the frown returned to Amanda's face.

"Cicero?"

Amanda read the sign, amazed they were this far from home. Nicole smiled again, still not breaking her silence. The car swerved smoothly along the inside streets and suddenly back to the main section of the town. But before Amanda could ask any questions, they turned a corner and Nicole expertly drove up a narrow alley. She parked in a crowded parking lot behind a row of rundown town houses.

Nicole smiled at her oddly and finally spoke.

"This is where you took me years ago, only a few weeks before you disappeared on us, although I have since graduated to more sophisticated joints in more respectable neighborhoods. But once in a while it's fun to return to our roots—less pretense, less veneer, which leaves more room for just plain down-to-earth pleasure, don't you think?" The gleam in her cold blue eyes had intensified, and totally puzzled, Amanda felt her initial uneasiness return with strong currents.

"What are you talking about?" It was barely a whisper, and Nicole's eyes narrowed.

"Come," she ordered, stepping out of the car and waiting for Amanda to do the same.

They entered one of the town houses through a back door, and to Amanda's surprise, they had to walk down a long narrow hallway before reaching another door. It was closed. A surveillance camera looked down on them ominously, but Nicole seemed undisturbed as she rang the doorbell. A metallic voice answered.

"Yes?"

"Ticketron admission, please," Nicole replied, undaunted.

"What show?"

"Marie Antoinette."

"Your preference?"

"Private seats, row 83 section 6 Briar Rose." Nicole turned her head and looked straight into the overhead camera.

"One moment, please."

Amanda's confusion grew as she witnessed the entire transaction. Ticketron? Why would she come all this way . . . My God! She suddenly shuddered. It was a code—Nikki was talking in code. Jesus, what kind of a joint was this that the security was so tight?

A buzzer sounded and Nicole quickly grabbed the door handle and opened the door. Amanda hesitated, but before she could protest Nicole had pulled her arm and the door closed behind them with a decisive click. Instinctively, she knew they were locked inside.

"Christ, Nikki, what—"

"Don't talk," Nikki hissed, pulling her along.

Another hallway. At the end, another door. A small opening slid sideways and an invisible creature on the other side scrutinized them.

"Two tickets, please," Nicole announced flatly.

"Come back on initiation night," the invisible creature snapped, and the little opening closed instantly.

"Wait!" Nicole pounded on it. "She's a customer. I don't know her personal password, but she was the one who brought me here years ago." Nikki strained her memory. "Rumpelstiltskin, that's it, check your records for Rumpelstiltskin." She seemed agitated, waiting for a reaction, but none came.

The silence on the other side of the door was deafening and Amanda started to move away, but Nicole grabbed her by the sleeve, motioning her to remain quiet. Suddenly the door opened and Nicole heaved a sigh of relief, smiling nervously at her companion. Her spirits sinking, Amanda slowly followed her inside.

The room was dark and smoky. Her eyes began to tear within minutes and she felt an overwhelming urge to stop breathing. She could hear sounds buzzing all around her, muffled sounds, a faint tinkling of ice in a glass, a hoarse chuckle, a man's voice mumbling unintelligible nothings. At the far end a light broke the darkness, not bright, but enough to throw shimmers into the gray area.

She blinked a couple of times, trying to get a glimpse of the place. Through the thick smoke a peculiar odor tickled her nostrils and she wriggled her nose. It was a sweet, pungent smell mingled with sweat that threatened to choke the breath out of her, and Amanda coughed. She made a face and was grateful that the darkness hid her expression. Gradually her eyes got used to the dimness and she could vaguely see the shadows of people, couples hanging on to each other, necking, kissing.

How odd, she thought, the place did not look like an ordinary bar; it was too dark for that. She looked around and saw Nikki talking to the man behind the bar counter, probably the bartender. He nodded shortly and she came back to Amanda.

"Come on," she directed and headed for the light at the far end, periodically turning to make sure Amanda was following.

"What is this place?" Amanda kept her voice low, instinctively knowing not to disturb the engrossed couples.

Nikki did not reply; instead she took Amanda's arm and led her along a dim hallway, passing a number of closed doors before finally stopped in front of a larger door. She knocked softly; it sounded like a code and Amanda opened her mouth, but before she could speak, the door opened, just slightly. A face peered at them. Nikki mumbled something and they were given access. What she saw next caught her breath and Amanda took a step backward, but the door had closed behind them.

In the middle of the dimly lit room a young woman moved on a raised platform, stark naked, her body glistening in sweat and oil. A purple spotlight cast an eerie shine on her moving body as she played with herself, her face in a trance, her eyes closed, her moves sensuous, suggestive. All around her, men and women squirmed together in the heated act of lovemaking, some naked, others sufficiently exposed.

Amanda gasped for air, desperately wanting to get away. Just as she was about to scream, Nikki dragged her onward, across the room and into an adjoining one. Amanda blinked, the sudden brightness taking her by surprise. But not for long.

A huge bed stood in the middle of this room, and on it a naked woman lay surrounded by more naked men and women. She was strapped, loosely, by the wrists and ankles to the four bedposts, her glistening body writhing suggestively, invitingly, her breathing heavy, guttural groans escaping her parted mouth, seemingly oblivious to the stroking hands that touched the most intimate parts of her body. Like the dancing girl in the next room, she was in a trance, her eyes closed, while the others around her took delight in her sensual moves.

Amanda felt her stomach churn, and a wave of nausea surged, reaching her throat. She took a step backward and bumped against a massive form. Something covered her mouth, her nose. Her eyes widened in horror. Her hands groped at the thing to free herself, clawing at the arm that strangled her neck. An awful pungent odor penetrated her nostrils, and slowly she slumped into darkness.

* * *

Hushed sounds jarred her conscious mind, vague rustling noises, intermingled with raspy breathing. Her senses still sluggish, she stirred. Trying to open her eyes, her eyelids refused to cooperate, feeling like lead. Her body felt cold. Shivering, she moved her arms, but something held them from her.

Amanda tensed. She forced her eyes to open. Blurred images weaved in front of her. Then, slowly the images focused, and her heartbeat jolted.

She yanked her arms. She felt a sharp pain and she turned her head to one side. Her wrists were tied by a rope hanging from the wall behind her. When she tried her feet, they too were shackled by the ankles to the floor. A horrified gasp escaped her—she was standing spread-eagled, not a stitch of clothing on her trembling body.

Terror chased away the sluggishness and her head jerked up to cry for help. Just then she spotted the two couples in opposite corners of the room. And the scream lodged in her throat.

They too were naked, both in an upright position, making love in ways she had not thought existed. Their bodies moved in slow motion, writhing, their breathing heavy. Even in the dim light, she could see their bodies glistening.

A soft click startled her, and as if from nowhere, two men kneeled before her, their naked bodies tanned and gleaming. One of them rose and began to suckle her breasts, his hands caressing her taut abdomen. She opened her mouth to cry out, but her throat was dry and all she could muster was a moan. A second pair of hands began to stroke the inside of her thighs, a tongue darting between her legs, flicking at her intimate parts. Her heart jumped, sudden fear numbing her senses. Her breath came out in trembling rasps; her eyes bulged.

What is happening? What are they trying to do to me? Jesus, someone, please, help me. The sensation was frighteningly familiar, horrifyingly real. *This can't be happening to me. Not for real. It's a nightmare. I'll wake up and find this all gone. Oh, God, please, not again* . . . She closed her eyes. Her body tensed to its limits. With a last trembling sigh, she blissfully sank into oblivion.

Chapter 35

SHE DID NOT KNOW HOW OR WHEN SHE HAD MADE IT out of the room or even out of the place altogether. When she came to again, she was outside and fully dressed. As the fresh outside air hit her hot face, Amanda gasped for breath, and facing the graffiti on the red brick wall, she gave way to the rising bile in her throat and threw up. Her knees were wobbly. She was soaked with perspiration and she could feel moisture trickling along her hosiery and down her legs. Her head spun; she was dizzy and her ears were buzzing.

"Are you okay?" Nikki's soft voice behind her was flat.

She was still nauseated and she spat against the wall again and again, coughing and choking, clasping her chest. Her throat burned, and with her eyes closed, she leaned her head against the wall, trying to steady herself.

"Are you okay?" Nikki repeated.

Amanda did not turn around. Slowly, her hands clenched to fists, and cold fury took over.

"Why? Why did you bring me here?" She coughed, heaving.

What was it Paula had said? Nikki had only one friend: Nikki. Everyone else served only one purpose—to please her whims. She straightened and slowly turned.

"Why, Nikki?"

Nikki shrugged, lowering her eyes to hide malice. "I

thought you might like to see the old stomping ground. After all, you and I had a lot of fun there once." She turned away. "Oh, it's been a while since I've been back there myself, years as a matter of fact. It was not much fun after you left. You were the life of the party, my dear. Without you, it just wasn't the same." She raised her eyelids with deliberate coyness and at the sight of the blatant horror in Amanda's widened eyes, she smiled with grim satisfaction, then quickly turned her head to hide it.

But Amanda did not notice it. Her breath choked and her stare became glassy.

"I . . . you said . . . I . . . have been . . . in . . . there . . . ?"

"Darling, yes. Pity you don't remember. As a matter of fact it was you who introduced me to this place." Nikki glanced at the pale face, not in the least bothered by Amanda's devastated expression. "Are you sure you don't remember?"

Amanda shook her head slowly. She felt sick; worse, she felt unclean—and betrayed. "Take me out of here, please," she whispered.

Nikki instantly headed for the parking lot without once looking to see if Amanda was following. Once inside the car she fumbled for the keys and hesitated. Glancing at Amanda's pale face, she reached for her handbag and held up a videotape.

"This will help you remember. It's all on here, what you did in there." Her look filled with deadly venom.

Amanda shuddered, disgust and disbelief in her stricken eyes. The nightmare was real after all.

"Just remember, if you ever so much as think of using those pictures you took of Niels and me years ago"—she raised the tape—"this will go to Brent. And the press." She turned the engine, and the Ferrari screeched out of the parking lot.

Amanda closed her eyes, but the visions of naked bodies loomed and she opened them again, forcing herself to focus on the traffic. The sun was bright and she fumbled in her purse for her sunglasses. Next to her Nikki kept on talking, but she did not hear the words. As her body rocked with the motion of the car, she suddenly knew what it must have felt like to have been raped.

* * *

"Orgy? I thought the cops raided that filthy joint a few years back. Are you sure?" Paula poured her another cup of coffee, frowning.

Amanda waved an imaginary cobweb from her eyes and nodded. She did not question her friend's familiarity with the place she had described, nor did she notice the odd gleam in Paula's eyes when she told her of her experience.

She had waited three days; three days of hoping that the ugliness would go away, three days of torment. She did not tell Brent, aware of his questioning glances at her morose mood. Three days of misery, during which she had warded off his amorous overtures, gently, feigning female disorder. She had felt guilty about the lie, but not guilty enough to give in. The thought of being made love to simply made her skin crawl. Worse yet, she could not bear to be touched, cringing when he did and forcing herself not to push him away.

But the nausea had not faded and as time passed she had become uneasy until, finally, she had broken down and shared her anguish with her friend. For despite her recent distrust of her, Paula was still the only one she felt she could turn to. And Paula had listened, without judgment or reproach.

"The bitch," Paula mumbled under her breath.

She looked at Amanda, and something in her stirred. There were dark circles under her friend's eyes, making them look even bigger, the haunted look in them lending the small face a fragile vulnerability—a hurt child, lost and frightened.

The bitch, Paula thought again, pursing her lips. Not that it surprised her—nothing Nikki did would surprise her, not since that fateful day last summer.

It had been a hot and humid day. They had all gone to the lake, the children had gone swimming and the adults had sought refuge from the blazing heat and remained underneath the shady trees. Afterward they had all gone to the Nillsons for a barbecue dinner. Except for Matt, who had gone to his office to pick up an important file.

She had not felt well. The death of a six-month fetus two months before had hit her hard and it had drained her, physically and mentally. When Brent was called away on an emergency, she had asked him to take her home and drop her off on his way, grateful to Niels who had offered to take the children home later.

But her peaceful retreat had not lasted long; an anonymous phone call had her take the BMW and drive to Wilmette. The voice had been muffled and it was more curiosity than concern that had prompted her to act on its message. There she had found Matt making love to Penelope Cord in the gazebo behind her house, just as the caller had implied.

It had been the beginning of the rift between her and Matt, a rift that had lasted for more than a year. Only later had she thought about the anonymous caller. Penelope was Nicole's sister, married to the pompous Senator Taylor Cord, fifteen years her senior and hardly ever at home. The sisters were not on friendly terms; Nicole was envious of Penelope's stature in society and Penelope lusted after her sister's cavorting husband. Who else could have tipped her off? Who else would, knowing full well that it would rock her marriage?

"She lied," Paula said aloud. Amanda looked at her listlessly. "What?"

"That miserable little bitch lied," Paula repeated. "You didn't introduce her to that filthy place; you saw her there. She went on her own accord."

Amanda looked up, puzzled. "What?"

Paula got up from her chair and began to pace the floor, wringing her hands, her otherwise sparkling eyes clouded.

"That place caters to a special clientele, you know—kinky stuff and all that. For a price they accommodate your wildest fantasies. You name it, they have it." She took a deep breath and looked at Amanda. "The Nillsons were there that day you decided to give it a try. With a man, a prominent businessman of some sort, involved in a ménage-à-trois. Well, the man died of a massive heart attack, and the police closed the place down."

Amanda gaped at Paula. She suddenly felt sick. *What the hell was I doing in a place like that?*

"How . . ."—she swallowed hard—"how do you know all this?"

"You told me," Paula made a face. "For some unearthly reason you decided to have pictures taken of them in action. Don't ask me how, for supposedly that place is run with the strictest discretion." She paused for a moment. "I saw those pictures, they were pretty awful. Sordid."

Amanda shook her head, her lips trembling. "But why? What reason could I possibly . . . ?"

"You never told me exactly why. For fun, you said. Of course, Nikki never believed that. She thought you were out to ruin her, and Niels."

"And . . . and you believed . . . me?"

"I had no reason not to. Whatever you did, cara, you never lied to me. And I must say, you did have a kinky streak in you at times."

"So Nikki thought I'd set it all up."

"Nikki's a sly, conniving little bitch. An empty-headed, spoiled-rotten brat. Selfish through and through. She lies and cheats for the sake of self-preservation and self-indulgence. It's a way of life with her. And she has Niels wound around her pretty little finger. She snaps and he jumps."

Paula walked to the bar and opened the cabinet.

"I need a drink. How about you?"

Amanda shook her head. "Too early." She sipped her cold coffee absentmindedly, staring blankly across the room.

Paula closed the cabinet again. "You're right, damn it. One of these days I'll turn into a lush, but today isn't it." She walked back to the table and sat down, watching her pensive friend.

"What are you thinking, Amanda?"

"Hm? Oh, nothing, everything." She looked around. "Is there more coffee?"

"I'll make some."

Paula disappeared into the kitchen. When she came back with a new pot of coffee Amanda had still not moved.

"Cara? Are you okay?" she asked.

She winced at raw despair in her friend's eyes when she finally looked at her.

"Does Brent know all this?" Amanda twirled the cup in her hands.

For a moment Paula remained silent, then sat down slowly. "You know, I don't know. I honestly don't know. He's never said anything." She reached out and touched Amanda's hand, holding it firmly in her own. "Please, cara, don't torture yourself so. It's long gone. The past is dead. There's only now."

"Is it?" Amanda rose and moved like a sleepwalker to the window. "Perhaps that's the reason why I went away. Perhaps he found out and sent me away," she said tonelessly.

When Paula did not answer, she turned around, her expression blank once more.

"That's why Niels tried to rape me on Maui. Not because he lusted after me, but out of revenge. He wanted to hurt me, and he wanted Brent to witness it."

Paula bent her head, her long nails tapping the table furiously.

"What was I doing there, Paula?" It was not a question, yet at the same time she needed to know. "What was I doing in a place like that?" She looked at Paula without seeing her.

"Why, Paula? Why?" Pain flashed in her tawny eyes. "Why did Nikki take me back there today? Why did she want to hurt me? What could she possibly gain from it?"

Paula shrugged.

"Who knows? No telling what goes on in that empty head of hers. Nikki does what Nikki feels like doing, and perhaps she felt like being rotten that day. Or perhaps she just felt like a diversion from her boring life. It's futile to try and figure out the whys. I know it's easier said than done, but do try not to dwell too much on it. It . . . well, dismiss it as a prank of some sort. Because that's all it was, trust me, nothing more, nothing less."

But Amanda did not hear her.

"Perhaps she tried to bring back my memory. Yes." Her eyes suddenly lit up. "That's it. She tried to help—"

"Bullshit!" Paula jumped up from her chair, her eyes spitting fury. "Don't you for a moment try to upgrade her motives. It wasn't for you! If anything it was revenge. That bitch is incapable of self-sacrifice, least of all to help somebody else. No, Amanda, a thousand times no! Nikki thinks only of Nikki. You or I have no room in that selfish brainless head of hers, believe me." She gasped for breath and sat down again. "If you ask me, she was simply bored. You just happened to come along for the ride."

Amanda said nothing. Slowly she drank her cold coffee and avoided Paula's eyes. *I've got to talk to Brent, I have to ask him if he knew. But what if he didn't? It might strain our relationship, and it's going so well now. Do I dare take the risk of losing him, again? Perhaps for good this time?*

She emptied her cup. How else was she ever to find out? She'd only be deluding herself. Running away from the truth never solved anyone's problem before. And clearing the air could possibly bring them closer together, to a better understanding, perhaps even friendship? Well, maybe that's pushing it.

Amanda sighed, oblivious to Paula's concerned stare. *I'll ask him tonight. I just have to know. Even if it means putting my life on the line; it'll still be worth it. Or is it?*

She suddenly jerked. The tape! God, she had forgotten all about the videotape. But of course. That was why Nikki had taken her there. It had all been part of a plan. A deliberate, premeditated plan. The tape in exchange for the pictures she supposedly took. Insurance against her silence.

She drew a deep breath and put down her empty cup. "You know what?" she said to Paula, forcing a watery smile. "I think I'll take that drink now."

It was one-fifteen in the afternoon. Less than twenty-four hours before the arrival of the note.

Chapter 36

THE NOTE WAS UNSIGNED, TYPED ON A BLANK PIECE OF ordinary paper with an IBM Selectric. The message, though brief, was devastating. For a moment Amanda just stared at the words, reading the succinct sentences a second time, and a third, her mind refusing to grasp their meaning.

> IF YOUR MARRIAGE IS SO HAPPY WHY DOES YOUR HUSBAND FREQUENT A BROTHEL? OR DID YOU THINK HE LIKES TEA SO MUCH HE MUST HAVE IT ONCE A MONTH? WHAT'S SO SPECIAL ABOUT THE FOURTH OF JULY AT THE TEAHOUSE OF THE RISING SUN? COULD IT BE THAT THE KIND OF FIREWORKS THEY CREATE THERE ARE TOO ADDICTIVE FOR HIM TO PASS UP?

She turned the paper over and over, but there were no other marks that could tell her any more than that it was an anonymous note.

The sender was obviously educated—no spelling mistakes, no grammatical errors. It could be a prank, or a practical joke. The letter had come in the mail, looking like an ordinary letter, addressed to her, and of course, with no return address.

Her first impulse was to call Brent and confront him. Instead she wandered around the living room, picking up imaginary and not so imaginary pieces of dirt and collecting them in her empty hand to finally throw them in the hidden wastebasket by the bar. What would he say? Would he laugh it off or, worse, get angry, perturbed that she should bother him in between surgeries?

And what if it was a prank? She would look foolish; it was childish to display jealousy on the basis of a mere anonymous note.

Last night, after they had put the children to bed, they had walked hand in hand down the stairs and she had braced herself, waiting for the right moment to tell him about her escapade with Nikki. As was usual, Brent had poured her a glass of wine, and when he lit a cigarette, she had cleared her throat, her heart pounding, ready to start the ordeal. Just then the doorbell had rung, and the rest of the evening they had entertained Daryl and Karen, who had decided to stop by on their way home from a wake in Waukegan.

She had felt strangely relieved, grateful for the extension, and convinced it had to be so. She would ask Brent in the morning, she promised herself. But when she woke up that morning, Brent had already gone, leaving her a note at the breakfast table that he had forgotten to tell her he had a surgery at six. Amanda looked at the note in her hand. And now this.

Inside Brent's den, she feverishly thumbed through the Yellow Pages. Her finger raced along the columns in the restaurant section and suddenly paused. There it was: *"Teahouse of the Rising Sun*—authentic Japanese sushi place offering genuine Japanese cuisine in an exotic teahouse atmosphere." It looked innocent enough and quite legal, no hint of anything more bizarre. But then, prostitution was illegal, so how could she expect them to blatantly advertise such underhanded activity?

She read the note again. The Fourth of July, Independence Day. It was only a week away, less—five days. She leaned back in the chair and stared at the oak-paneled walls of the room. Slowly a plan began to form in her mind.

* * *

The Fourth of July arrived with hot, humid weather and Amanda was glad the day was finally there. The last five days had dragged along and she had been both preoccupied and quiet. When Brent or the children asked if she was okay, she lied, telling them she wasn't feeling well. Today, America's Independence Day, they had enjoyed an early outdoor barbecue dinner at the Manchiones'. Then as the afternoon turned to dusk, they had all gone to the Lake Forest Park to watch the fireworks. Afterward they'd gone to Farrell's for dessert.

It had been a wonderful happy day. The children loved it and by the time they went to bed, Amanda felt both relieved and guilty. She had been tense all day, but Brent had acted normal and cheerful the whole time.

She had watched him like a hawk, yet he had shown no signs of restlessness or made any uncharacteristic moves of any kind. If anything, he had seemed more congenial toward her, treating her with more gentleness and affection because she wasn't feeling well or so he believed, hugging her protectively from time to time and stealing a kiss or two during the barbecue. The children too had been most mindful of her condition. Only Paula had thrown concerned glances in her direction, staying close to her during the fireworks display at the park, yet asking no questions.

Now, kissing the children good night, she felt her tension ebb. It was evening and Brent was still home. With a smile she descended the stairs to join him in the family room, expecting him to await her with a glass of wine. Her glass was on the bar, filled with cool white wine, but there was no sign of Brent.

The sound of soft footsteps made her turn, and her heart stopped.

"Darling, don't wait up for me, I could be a little late." He had put on his navy blue blazer over the tan corduroy trousers he had worn all day.

"Where are you going?" she whispered.

"To the hospital. Sorry, no rest for the wicked and doctors." He grinned and kissed her. "Go to bed, get some rest, okay?" He patted her affectionately on the butt. "Nice ass," he said and walked away.

For a moment she just stood there, numb. Her mind whirled. It was true after all. Just as she had started to relax, the ominous meaning of the anonymous note blasted back at her. At the sound of the Jaguar driving away, Amanda snapped into motion, and putting down the glass of wine, she rushed to Mrs. Flynn's quarters.

She found an empty parking space a block away from the restaurant. Earlier that week she had driven into Evanston and found the *Teahouse of the Rising Sun*. It had been quite easy, really. She had called them up and asked for directions, and she had memorized the drive.

In front of the restaurant, Amanda hesitated, suddenly uncertain of what she was about to do. Then, taking a long deep breath, she opened the door and entered. The place was dimly lit, but even in the semidarkness she could see the shoji screens partitioning blocks of space inside the area. Immediately she was greeted by a bowing Japanese woman in a kimono, her hair done up in old-fashioned geisha style.

"Good evening, madam. Are you meeting someone here?"

Amanda shifted, feeling foolish. What was she supposed to say now? Apparently women did not come here unescorted and the smiling geisha in front of her waited for her answer.

"Er . . . yes. I . . . I'm here for a . . . ah . . ."

"Oh, I see. You are here for the Benson party, neh?" The woman bowed again and gestured for her to follow. "This way, please."

Amanda blushed in the dimness. She started to follow the hostess when suddenly the woman halted, causing her to almost bump into her.

"Oh, I'm so sorry." The woman pointed down at her feet. For a moment Amanda looked puzzled. What was wrong with her feet?

"You're supposed to take off your shoes," a deep male voice behind her said and she jumped. Brent's face was impassive.

"This is a Japanese house. It's customary to remove one's shoes before entering." He waited for her to reach down to remove her shoes.

"It's all right, she's with me." He smiled at the waiting hostess, who bowed again. He took her elbow and led her past the shoji-screened private dining areas and to the end of the hallway. "I could've saved you a trip if you'd told me you wanted to come along."

Before she could reply, he opened a door and pushed her inside a bright room.

Amanda froze. A group of Japanese all bowed to her, and after a brief hesitation, she returned the bow.

"Welcome to our humble home," an old Japanese man in a kimono said to her, bowing again.

"May I introduce my wife, Amanda. Darling, these are my friends, Tadeo Hamada, owner of the teahouse, his wife, his daughter Michiko, his son Kenji, and Hiroshi Sakamura, a friend." Brent turned and his expression softened. "And this is Lisako."

The little girl held up a fuzzy pink bear almost half her size and shyly buried her head in Mrs. Hamada's kimono. Amanda's heart skipped a beat. The child was about five, she guessed, but it was the face that held her fascination. Unlike the rest of her family, her eyes were large and round, more deep-set—the eyes of a Eurasian child. Her hair was thick and the curls definitely natural, its color a sandy-colored brown. Her little nose was slightly upturned and her features sharper than the usual flat Asian.

"Hello, Lisako," she whispered, hoarse with apprehension.

"Today is Lisako's birthday," Brent said, pulling the shy little girl away from Mrs. Hamada's protective embrace and into his arms. "Can you tell Amanda how old you are, Cricket?" He lovingly stroked the child's curls.

"Five," Lisako murmured, clinging to Brent. It was evident that they were great friends and that the friendship was accepted by the Hamada family.

"How did you find me? How did you know where I was?"

They had left the Hamada family to finish their celebration of Lisako's fifth birthday in private and, upon Brent's insistence, driven away in his car. Hiroshi had volunteered to get the Mercedes back to Lake Forest, together with Kenji, and without hesitation Brent had handed him Amanda's car keys.

To her surprise Brent had not driven directly home, but had swung off the expressway just outside of Highland Park and stopped at a place called The Barn.

"We've got to talk," he had said and as they entered the cozy bar, still buzzing with cheerful laughter even at the hour of midnight, Amanda realized that he was not a stranger here.

"Hi, Doc. The usual?" The bartender greeted them with a broad smile, glancing impassively at her.

"And a bourbon Seven-Up for my wife here. Amanda, this is Joey."

"Welcome to The Barn, Mrs. Farraday."

Brent looked around. "Full house tonight, Joey. Do you mind if we take the table in the far corner?"

"You go right ahead, Doc. I'll bring your drinks in a jiffy."

Here they were, sipping the drinks and looking at each other.

"If you'd told me, I would've saved you the trouble and taken you with me." Brent looked at her, one hand supporting his head, a glowing cigarette between his fingers.

Amanda twirled her glass around with both hands, her eyes lowered.

"You lied to me. Why?" She now looked him straight in the eye, trying to keep her gaze cool, yet feeling the tension of earlier that evening come back to her.

"I was afraid you might not understand."

"Understand what? Try me. What are these people to you, Brent?"

"It's a long story."

"I have time."

He shook his head, drawing deep on the cigarette.

"The little girl . . ." Amanda paused, unable to voice the accusation.

"She's not mine." Brent sighed, then suddenly made up his mind. "Okay. All right." He took a deep breath. "Five years ago, I was on duty at Skokie Valley Hospital. That particular evening you decided to go to a wild party at the Nillsons' that I originally had declined to attend, but the night before you and I had had an awful fight and I changed my mind at the last minute. Maybe I had wanted to make things up to you or maybe I was just plain bored. There were no surgeries scheduled because of the holiday and no casualties had come into the emergency all evening." He took a sip of his Scotch. "Anyway, I left the hospital in the hands of the senior resident and joined you. I drank too much. And just after midnight a young girl was brought in, hemorrhaging heavily."

He paused and swallowed hard. When he spoke again his

voice was harsh, and he talked rapidly, as if wanting to shed the words.

"She was barely sixteen and in a bad way. The senior resident could not stop her bleeding, and when they finally got hold of me, she was almost gone. By the time I got to Skokie Valley, she was dead . . ." His voice trailed off, his eyes staring past her, reliving the agony, and when he looked at her again, they were dull.

"I barely saved the baby she was carrying." He took a deep breath and lit another cigarette.

Even in the dim light Amanda noticed that his face was contorted and he looked years older.

"The young girl's name was Yoko Hamada." Brent gulped the rest of his Scotch and put down his glass with a sharp clunk.

"And the baby's name is Lisako," Amanda said softly. She gently touched his hand. "I'm so sorry. If it hadn't been for me—"

"It was my own fault," Brent interrupted her sharply. "I'm a doctor, I should've known better. It was most irresponsible on my part, unforgivable from a doctor's point of view." He elaborately extinguished the half-smoked cigarette, then quickly lit another.

"You see, I *left* my post, and I had no business leaving my post, not when there are lives at stake. If I hadn't been so drunk, I could've rushed back to the hospital, and the Hamada girl would still have been alive today."

Amanda gently squeezed his hand, the expression in her eyes tender. "You don't know that," she said softly. "If she was bleeding so profusely, she might've been too far gone for anyone to save her."

But Brent stubbornly shook his head, his jawline twitching.

"She died only minutes before I arrived."

He picked up the empty glass and watched it twirl in his hands.

"As it was, it took me over an hour to sober up, at least enough so I could drive. That hour cost Yoko her life. And that makes me responsible for her death."

He waved at Joey for a refill.

"Since then I've played godfather to Lisako. It's the least I could do."

They were silent for a moment. Joey brought the Scotch and replaced the full ashtray with a fresh one.

"If only I had known," Amanda whispered, brushing away the tears. Then, remembering the note, she fumbled in her purse. "This is how I knew where to find you tonight."

Brent frowned when he read the anonymous note. "Who the hell—" He suddenly looked at her. "Hiroshi. It must've been Hiroshi."

"Who?" Amanda's eyes went wide with disbelief. "But why?"

"He's a very jealous young man and terribly in love with Michiko. A couple of months ago, he proposed marriage to her, but she turned him down, saying that she loved another man." Brent suddenly laughed. "He must have thought she meant me."

"Is she?"

"Is she what? In love with me?" He laughed harder, genuine amusement now gleaming in his eyes. "Shit, I'm old enough to be her father. Well, almost. No, darling, there is nobody else, but she couldn't think of another good reason to say no to him."

"How about the truth? That she doesn't love him, for instance?"

Brent smiled and grabbed her hand.

"You don't understand," he said gently. "Hiroshi is a bright young man with an excellent future ahead of him. Did I tell you that both he and Kenji are medical students? And he, for one, is a straight-A student at that, breezing through Northwestern Medical School on well-earned scholarships. To top it all off, his family is well-to-do, bordering on wealthy. How can any Japanese maiden turn someone like him down?" He smiled again. "That, my dear, would make him lose face, and Michiko knows better than to do that and upset both her and his parents."

"And to choose another above him is not making him lose face?" Amanda shook her head, unable to understand Japanese logic.

"That's different. This is the twentieth century and even the Japanese culture accepts the mystery of love and its inexplicable preferences."

Amanda sighed, shaking her head again, but not arguing

the point any longer. Brent seemed so certain and so convinced, and she was too tired to pursue the subject.

Brent lit another cigarette.

"By the way, The Rising Sun is not a brothel. Far from it. Hiroshi must've exerted his imagination just to lure you there."

Amanda grimaced. "It worked."

"It's an authentic Japanese restaurant, complete with a sushi bar and waitresses dressed up as old-fashioned geishas. Hamada says it enhances the atmosphere. And that too works." Brent grinned, his eyes sparkling mischievously. "Sorry, no call girls, no hanky-panky, not even a Japanese massage parlor stashed away in the back. All on the up-and-up. And respectable."

"I feel like such a fool," Amanda whispered.

"The food is quite good, really. I'll take you there sometime."

He looked her deep in the eye and sighed.

"You still don't trust me, do you, Amanda? Have I given you any cause to deserve your continued doubt?"

She blushed, grateful for the darkness, and pressed her lips together.

"I'm sorry," she whispered.

Suddenly she remembered the incident with Nicole, and stiffened.

"What's the matter?" Brent frowned, alarmed.

Amanda hesitated. Tonight seemed to be perfect for revelations. She looked at Brent and saw the tired lines under his eyes, the weary expression, and she shook her head.

"It was nothing," she avoided his gaze. "A ghost walked over my grave."

Brent extinguished his cigarette and did not press.

"Would you like another highball?" he asked.

Amanda shook her head again and sighed.

"I want to go home now," she said.

Chapter 37

"HUGH FITZGERALD HAD A HEART ATTACK LAST NIGHT."

Amanda's outstretched hand stayed in midair, the plate of roast beef tilting dangerously, and he quickly took it from her. She stared at him with anticipation, waiting for more, a question in her eyes.

Brent continued to cut the meat, and calmly began serving them both. He had deliberately kept his tone casual, yet he knew that he had not fooled her.

Dr. Fitzgerald was Lutheran General's chief of staff, a man of integrity and enormous all-around talent. His subordinates worshiped him, jumped at his slightest command, nurses and orderlies alike, and he commanded the respect of his medical staff, even those who disagreed with his methods. The man was barely fifty-six.

"How is he?" Amanda asked, handing him the potatoes.

"He'll be fine. Strong as a horse, thank God. But he's been told to take it easy, at least for a while."

"And?" She took a small bite and laid down her knife.

"I've been asked to fill in for him. Temporarily, of course."

Brent refilled her wine glass and smiled again. It was an honor, to say the least, and he had been flattered when Dr. Bennett, chairman of the hospital board, approached him—him, of all people; he was not even a full-time staff member. "How temporarily?"

He threw her an amused glance.

"Until Fitzgerald is strong enough to come back full-time."

"Which is when?"

"Who knows? It could be a month, two months, even three."

"What happens then?"

"It's hard to say. I could—"

The telephone rang. Amanda frowned and raised her hand as if to silence it.

"Go on, Brent, you could what?"

"We should discuss this later. There's really not much else. All we can do is wait and time will tell."

The ringing persisted, and with a sigh, Amanda rose. Just then the doorbell rang.

"I'll get that." Brent wiped his mouth on the napkin and went to the front door.

When he returned to the kitchen, Amanda had just hung up the phone, a warm smile in her tawny eyes.

"That was Josh. He wanted to say good night, and have me give you a big kiss. Like so . . ." She reached up and brushed his lips.

"You call that a kiss? Come here, let me show you." He whirled her into his arms and gave her a passionate demonstration. "How about Mandy?" he murmured, his lips barely leaving hers.

"Mandy, too . . . ," she whispered.

When he finally took his lips off hers, they were both trembling, their bodies clinging to one another. Still breathless, their lips met a third time.

Brent touched the roast beef on his plate and wriggled his nose in disgust.

"I'm not hungry anymore. You?" he asked, reaching for the wine.

She slowly shook her head, the embers of his kiss still smoldering in her eyes.

"Why don't we clean up this mess and move to cozier pastures?" Without waiting for a reply, Brent began to clear the table. "It was nice of Louise to take the children for the weekend," he said.

"Josh was ecstatic. Jonathan took them sailing and Louise

treated them to the movies. She bought Mandy a new dress." Amanda opened the dishwasher for him.

Brent glanced at the kitchen clock, and grinned. "Wow! Nine o'clock, that is a treat."

They both laughed. In Louise's book, children belonged in bed by eight.

"Who was that at the door?" Amanda wiped the table and threw the damp towel into the empty sink.

"Door? Oh, just somebody soliciting magazines." He reached for her and, with one forceful swing, heaved her on top of the kitchen table, his hands slowly traveling underneath her dress, and up her thighs.

Amanda ran her hands through his hair, marveling at the softness, the luster of finely spun pale gold. Millions of women would kill to possess this color, she thought, so even, so naturally blond, hair of the sun god. She smiled and pressed her lips on it.

Suddenly she remembered Hugh Fitzgerald.

"You really want this, don't you?" she murmured.

"This? Oh, baby, yes, yes . . ." Brent nuzzled her throat and she laughed.

"No, silly, the position."

"Ummm . . . great position . . . so inviting. Best offer I've had in days." Deliberately misinterpreting her question, he reached up and pulled her head down, tracing her full, sensuous lips.

Amanda shivered, her blood racing. Her fingers dug into his hair, and parting her lips, she responded with fiery abandon.

With one swift move Brent pushed her skirt up and smoothly slid the sheer lace bikini down her legs. Amanda gasped, her eyes widening in surprise. His fingers touched the bare flesh between her thighs, and she gasped again. His kiss deepened, his tongue probed. His hands expertly unbuttoned her blouse, cupping her voluptuous breasts, fondling, stroking them until they were swollen and taut.

Feverish, Amanda fumbled at his shirt, her blood pounding against her temples. The gnawing in her loins intensified, and moaning, she reached down for his zipper. Brent shuddered at her touch, desire raging in his dark eyes. Her hands stroked and fondled and kneaded, with tantalizing rhythm, and his body tensed. Every nerve was acutely aware of her probing fingers teasing, tormenting, torturing.

With a savage growl he wrenched himself from her grasp and dove between her legs, his tongue lashing back, repaying the torment. Amanda clutched his hair, her breath rasping, her senses reeling. She threw her head back, her grasp tightening. She thrashed wildly against him, sobbing for release.

Brent grabbed her bare buttocks, and squeezed them, hard. His tongue probed her tremulous desire, sending her spiraling to delirious heights and onto the very edge. With a scream, her body erupted and she shuddered against his perspiring face.

Standing between her legs, Brent watched Amanda open her eyes. How beautiful she looks, he mused, how desirable. He narrowed his eyes. God, nothing turned him on more than a woman with the residue of passion still in her eyes. There was something positively erotic about that.

The throbbing in his groin became unbearable, and with the agility of a leopard, he jumped on the table. Pushing her down gently, he stretched out alongside of her, his mouth ravishing her lips, his hands fondling her breasts. Traveling downward, he stroked her flat belly, and downward still. Cupping the furry mound, rubbing his palm seductively, his fingers strummed her intimately.

Her passion fanned ablaze once more, Amanda moved her hips, arching against his enticing hand with frenzied fervor.

Brent groaned. The heat in his body now raging to limits, he quickly straddled her. Thrusting inside of her. And with each forceful stroke, his muscles tensed, until the swollen hardness within her reached its peak. With almost inhuman control he held himself back, closing his eyes, waiting for the frantic fire underneath him to burst.

Amanda flung her arms violently, throwing her head back, her legs pushing her body upward. Grabbing the edge of the table, she arched her body, again and again. Her blood soared, her flesh burned, and she closed her eyes as fireworks sparked all around her. With a deep guttural growl, Brent exploded, and toppled down on her, shuddering as he filled her.

* * *

Brent poured her a glass of chablis and took a Scotch himself. Accepting the wine, Amanda smiled at him. It was cozy, just the two of them, a rare treat, the first in weeks. Why, she did not even miss the children, she thought, feeling a momentary pang of guilt.

They had moved into the living room, clad merely in satin robes.

"You really want this, don't you?" She repeated the question he had chosen not to answer earlier, leaning her head back on the sofa's edge.

"Chief of staff? I do, and I don't," Brent said. He lit a cigarette and took a sip of his Scotch. "It's a lot of responsibility, and it'll take up a lot of my free time, if not most of it. On the other hand, it's a good experience, not to mention a hell of an opportunity." He emptied his glass and walked back to the bar.

"What are you saying? What about that trauma center you dreamed about? And what about . . . ?" She suddenly stopped. "Unless . . . Oh, I see . . ."

Brent threw her a quick look. Sharp girl, he thought, not much escapes her. He lit another cigarette.

Driving home the night he had told her about Yoko Hamada, he had confided in her his innermost secret, known only to Louise and the Willses. For years he had dreamed about opening up a trauma center. For years he had gathered data that was needed to operate one effectively. Then, when the Hamada girl had died, he had sworn that one day, he would build one in her name. One day, when he had accumulated enough collateral. It might not be soon, but he was working on it.

"It would be interesting, and it'll only be for a little while," he said, smiling. "Fitzgerald is a strong man. He'll be back on the job in no time and things will get back to normal."

"You don't really believe that, do you?"

"I'm a doctor, and a doctor believes in anything, including the impossible." He sat down next to her and pulled her onto his lap.

"Relax, honey. I promise I won't overdo it. Just think of it as a learning experience. Okay?" He kissed her.

"Are you sure?"

"Absolutely. Trust me."

She said nothing more. She knew he had made up his

mind, and it was, after all, his career—his dream. Who was she to undermine that?

"You know, I could use some dessert," he said huskily, his hand slipping inside her robe.

"You can't still be hungry," Amanda murmured.

Nibbling his earlobes, she writhed. And mischievously bit his right ear.

"Why, you . . ." Brent threw her on the sofa and, with one tug, loosened her robe.

His hands began to caress her, his lips scorching her bare flesh wherever they touched, and a quivering sigh escaped her. Ravishing her bare breasts, his hands trailed across her trembling curves, and as her body responded, Amanda shivered.

"Jesus, I never thought I'd ever say this again, least of all to you," he mumbled huskily. "But I love you, Amanda Farraday, and I'm damn glad you're back."

Her eyes grew moist, and as renewed desire flared, she suddenly knew that whatever her past misdoings, they were dead now. Dead and buried.

It was the last evening they were to have together. During the next weeks she saw very little of Brent. He was either at the hospital or at his private practice in Glenview. Before long, Amanda began to feel lonely. She became restless, and bored. Finally, in desperation, she turned to the Nillson project.

When the last of her drawings was finished, she waged an internal battle with herself. Could she set aside her bitterness against Nicole and call her? After much soul-searching, she decided to give it a try.

"I'm so glad you phoned, Amanda. I really should have apologized to you for what I did, but I must admit, I didn't have the guts," Nikki said smoothly. "I don't know what came over me. I was bored, I guess. Can you forgive me?"

At the other side of the line Amanda grimaced, not believing one word, least of all Nikki's hypocritical remorse. "Forget it, Nikki. What's a little hoax between friends, hm?" She doubted Nicole would catch her sarcasm, but it made her feel better. "Now about your house, I've finished the plans."

"That's wonderful, darling. When can you start?"

"Not so fast. I'll have to hire an architect to make the blueprints first. Meanwhile, I'll draw up the final decorating sketches for your approval."

"Yes, yes. When?"

"Another week or so."

"Oh, Amanda, I'm so excited. I can't wait to tell Niels. Do let me know when you can start, darling."

"I'll call you in a couple of weeks."

As she put down the receiver, Amanda sighed. For a moment she wondered if Nicole would have called her if she had not made the first move. Then she shrugged. Who cares? She did make the call and the job was still hers. Not that she doubted for a minute that it wouldn't be, but it was better to make sure.

She suddenly frowned. Perhaps she should have asked for the tape. As advance payment for her work, so to speak. In the wrong hands, that videotape could have nasty repercussions. But why worry? It seemed highly unlikely that Nicole would risk a scandal for the sake of pure entertainment. Or would she?

"I don't think so," Paula agreed when they saw each other. "Nikki may be a selfish brat, but she's far from stupid. A scandal would ruin her husband as well, and I don't think the bitch has that in mind. After all, Niels is her bread and butter, and if nothing else, she is vain. Niels's position at Skokie Valley feeds her vanity."

"I hope we're right."

"Besides, that videotape is supposed to be strictly insurance, remember? You must still have those photographs somewhere, and unless Nikki has those, your video is safe." She glanced at Amanda's worried frown. "Good move, cara. God, I admire your guts. I don't know if I would've done what you did."

"Nonsense. Of course you would've. Besides, I did it mostly for me. I really enjoy doing her house. It's a real gem, you ought to see it." But Paula's words did her good and Amanda laughed.

"You finish it and I will. I promise." Paula grinned and on impulse hugged her. "You're the best," she said warmly.

Six weeks later she called Nicole to tell her the blueprints and final sketches were done. Nikki was ecstatic and for once her enthusiasm seemed genuine. Despite her previous misgivings, Amanda found herself looking forward to getting started on the Nillson home.

That same evening Brent came home early. Dr. Hugh Fitzgerald had been pronounced fit enough to come back to work; he would resume his responsibilities the day after Labor Day.

And the next day, Louise called.

Chapter 38

LABOR DAY WEEKEND WAS A SPECIAL WEEKEND FOR THE Farradays. But this Labor Day, in particular, held a significance that stretched beyond the family circle.

It marked the fiftieth anniversary of Farraday Enterprises, a milestone greeted with joy and pride by its employees. In celebration, the company had invited everyone to share the triumph and reap the rewards of half a century's worth of success. As well as listen to Louise Farraday's speech, which she delivered promptly after lunch and just before the first round of games.

Rushing back inside the Farraday Building afterward, Louise waved away the two security guards, and turned to her escort.

"Happy?" Jeffrey Bramston pulled her arm through his, smiling at her affectionately.

Like his father, he was tall and distinguished-looking, although not quite as broad-shouldered, and a bit more solemn. And like Jonathan, he harbored a deep fondness for Louise.

"Yes. Justin would've approved of our decision." She beamed, her smile dazzling her young companion.

"He would've been so proud of you. As we all are," he said, patting her hand.

When his father retired, five years ago, he had taken over

Jonathan's position as chief corporate lawyer of the Farraday conglomerate, sharing his father's dedication toward his responsibilities. And toward Louise. When shortly thereafter, the Farraday family attorney died, he had gladly taken on the added responsibility. Over the years, Louise had come to depend on his counsel, and with each meeting, his respect for her sound judgment grew.

"Thanks for my new office," Jeffrey said, smiling. "It's quite impressive, and very nice."

They paused in front of austere-looking double doors, and Louise sighed.

"Now for the hard part." She grimaced.

"It'll be okay," Jeffrey said. He waited a moment. "Ready?"

Louise straightened her shoulders and took a deep breath. Then, with a smile, she nodded. Resolutely, Jeffrey opened the door.

They were all there, Louise noted with satisfaction as she entered the room. The entire Farraday clan, her brood, complete with the surly Alison and her illustrious prince of undisclosed royal standing. *How very fortunate for her that I personally witnessed her birth,* Louise mused, *or I would never have believed she had Farraday blood.* So different from Brent and Karen.

"Thank you all for coming on such short notice," Louise said, smiling.

Why, they're all on edge, she thought, surprised. This is a joyous occasion. There was no reason for anxiety. Still, the silence in the room was palpable—a curious mixture of apprehension and speculation. And, yes, a tinge of suppressed hostility.

"It's getting late, so we'll skip the preliminaries, and get right to the point, shall we?" She nodded to Bramston. "Jeffrey?"

Jeffrey Bramston cleared his throat and opened the file on the desk before him.

"I too thank you for coming on such short notice. As you all know, today marks the fiftieth anniversary of Farraday Enterprises. Twenty-five years ago, just before he passed on, Justin Farraday drew up a will. Those of you who were present during the reading of that will, will recall that there was a codicil attached to it, involving a special trust fund to benefit the Farraday offspring, or Justin Farraday's grandchildren to be exact." He cleared his throat again. "This afternoon, we will disclose the provisions and current status of that trust fund."

He put on a pair of glasses and turned a few pages. " 'In that all of my grandchildren are legally married and living with their spouses at the time of disclosure of this trust fund, I, Justin Farraday, being of sound mind and free will, bequeath them each equal shares of this trust fund, to be retained in their names and theirs alone, and in the case of their early demise, their legal offspring and their names alone.' "

Pausing, Jeffrey Bramston took off his glasses and placed them on the desk.

"The capital of this trust fund was set at $30 million."

A gasp echoed across the room. They all began to talk at once. But the young lawyer raised his hand, and the chatter subsided.

"Mrs. Farraday had been named to police the execution of these stipulations. Since it seems all of you three grandchildren of Justin Farraday have met his conditions, you are now legal inheritors of this fund. Now—" The chatter suddenly resumed, and again he raised his hand. "Now, Mrs. Farraday also had the power of attorney to either leave the initial capital of the trust untouched, or use her judgment to invest it. Mrs. Farraday opted for the latter. Thus, as of twelve hundred hours this day, and with the expert aid of professional investment brokers Messieurs Bernstein and Lanier, this fund has now accumulated the healthy sum of one hundred forty-three million dollars. Congratulations to you all."

This time there was no holding back the excitement that permeated the room. They all started talking at the same time, rushing to thank Louise, hugging, laughing, and crying all at once. Even Lady Madeline forgot her composure and smothered her mother-in-law in an embrace.

"You knew all about this inheritance, didn't you?" Amanda asked.

They had spent the rest of the afternoon at the celebration, but after an elaborate dinner at the Ritz-Carlton, they had excused themselves and gone home early. Now, half undressed and in the privacy of their bedroom, they could feel exhaustion set in.

Brent nodded. "Mother told me a long time ago."

He did not tell her that Louise had reminded him of it time and again, and for the past three years, urged him to divorce his prodigal wife and marry a more suitable woman or he would lose it all. For what Jeffrey Bramston had not mentioned, Louise had dangled before him—in not meeting Justin's conditions, his share would have gone to charity. And with it, half of each share of his siblings.

"One hundred forty-three million dollars—a lot of money . . . ," she said, sighing.

"One-third, my dear, just one-third," Brent corrected her.

"That's still a lot of money," Amanda persisted. "What are you going to do with it?"

He reached for her and pulled her onto his lap.

"First of all, I'm going to forget about it for a while. Then, I'm going to ravish you." He nuzzled her neck and she laughed. "Then I'm going to take you on a long weekend somewhere. Just the two of us. How does that sound, hm?" He opened her blouse and suckled a taunting breast.

"A long weekend, just you and me?" She put her bare arms around his neck and buried her face in his hair. "Where? When?"

"Ummm . . . delicious . . ." He ran his tongue over an erect nipple and, deliberately slow, began to trace the sensuous curves of her body. "How about The Abbeys in Lake Geneva? We spent our honeymoon there, you know."

"Sounds wonderful," she mumbled, becoming aroused by his intimate touch.

"Are you this accommodating because you lust after me, or is it my money you're after, lady?" He gently bit her lower lip.

Amanda stiffened. Her head flung upward, her eyes wide.

"The money! That's what she meant, this money."

"What? Who are you talking about?" Brent frowned.

"Alison. She kept referring to my coming back for your money, remember? And it going to charity. This is what she meant."

Brent sighed, annoyed at hearing his sister's name. "Can we continue our carnal business now?" he asked.

"I don't understand. Why, she should've been glad to see me back, or she would've lost half of her share to charity."

Brent gaped. "How do you know all this . . . ?"

"Why, Louise told me."

"Now you believe me, when I tell you she's an airhead? A total nitwit, a waste. Now, where were we?" Brent fondled a breast and nibbled at her throat.

Amanda flung herself against him and they toppled across the bed, laughing. Soon, Alison was forgotten, and their bodies began to meld, and in the heat of their throbbing passion, the millions of dollars blended into the shadows. And they lost themselves in the urgency of their need for one another.

A curdling scream woke them up. Amanda bolted up in bed, her eyes wide with fright, not bothering to cover her naked breasts.

"What the hell was that?" Brent lifted his head from the pillow, his eyes still heavy with sleep.

A second scream pierced the shadows, and Amanda jumped out of bed. Snatching a robe from the chair, she stumbled down the hallway. Pausing in front of the children's rooms, she hesitated. Then, reaching for Josh's door handle, the sound of heartbreaking sobs from the room next door stopped her.

"Mandy? Darling, what is it?" Amanda hurried to the bed, leaving the door ajar to let the corridor light seep inside, and pulled away the blanket.

Curled up into a ball, Mandy's trembling body shook uncontrollably, both her fists clenched against her mouth. Her eyes were closed and she was crying.

"Mandy, sweetheart, wake up." She gently shook the girl's shivering arms, then, as the sobbing continued, a little harder. "Sweetie, it's me, Mommy. Wake up, darling, open your eyes."

Mandy's eyes finally opened, and seeing her mother, she flew up and flung her arms around Amanda's neck, almost strangling her in the process.

"Oh, Mommy, Mommy, you're here. You're still here, you didn't go away," she said, sobbing.

"Shhh, hush. It's all right. Yes, of course I'm here. It was only a dream."

"It . . . was terrible. You . . . you went away again, and

. . . you left Josh and me and Daddy . . . You were going in a plane, far, far away. With . . . a man . . . he looked a little like Daddy, but it wasn't him. Oh, it . . . it was so awful . . ." She began to cry again.

"Shhh . . . it's over now. You see, it wasn't true, I haven't left, and I never will. I'll never ever leave you and Josh again." Amanda held her tight, stroking and kissing her hair. "Okay?"

"What's going on?" Brent towered in the doorway, his hair still tousled. "Munchkin . . . ?"

Cradling the shaken child, Amanda shook her head, her eyes flashing a silent warning. Brent frowned and opened his mouth to speak, but she quickly put a finger across her lips to silence him.

"Daddy? What was that noise?" Rubbing the sleep from his eyes, Josh wandered into the room.

"It's okay, buddy, just Mandy having a bad dream." Brent scooped the boy into his arms and carried him back into his own room.

Gradually the trembling stopped and Mandy lifted her tearful face, her eyes pleading.

"Promise you'll never leave us again?" Her lower lip began to tremble again.

"I promise." Amanda kissed her eyes, the tip of her nose, and gently brushed the tears away.

"I love you, Mommy. I'll die if you leave us again."

"Shhh, no you won't. But then, I won't leave you. And I love you too, very, very much."

After a while Mandy lay down again and Amanda tucked her in, smiling at her and kissing her again.

"Go to sleep, now. Here"—she beckoned Brent, who, after having tucked Josh in, had returned—"give Daddy a big hug, too."

"I love you too, Daddy," Mandy whispered.

"That's my munchkin." Brent mussed her hair and kissed her.

"No more nightmares, okay?"

"What was that all about?" Brent asked.

Stepping back into the bed, Amanda crawled into his arms and told him. When she fell silent, he tightened his embrace and quietly rocked her, glad that she could not see the worried frown on his face.

"About that long weekend . . ." Amanda lifted her head.

"We'll wait a week or two." He kissed her, gently.

Amanda sighed, the feeling of guilt she had felt when Mandy had poured her heart out returning. Didn't Brent say that the child had psychic powers?

"She'll be all right. In a couple of weeks, the whole thing will have been forgotten. Trust me." Brent buried his face in her hair.

He's right, of course, Amanda thought. The girl had probably picked up on signs of their impending trip. And after all, it was just for a long weekend. A bad dream, that's all it was. Or was it? She sighed again, nestling deeper into Brent's comforting arms. But she could not seem to shake off the guilt, and it made her uneasy.

"Good-bye, guys, have a good time. And remember, don't drive Paula and Matt nuts, especially not Paula." Amanda grinned as her friend stuck her tongue out at her. "It's Daddy's birthday next month and I need her help for the costume party."

Amanda waved at them, then closed the door and leaned against it for a moment. She would miss the kids, but the thought of a long weekend alone with Brent in Lake Geneva brought a smile to her face, and with a sigh she picked up the jacket Mandy had left and swung up the stairs, wondering why Brent was taking so long on that phone call.

She was halfway up the staircase when the doorbell rang, and she stopped.

"I'll get it," Brent called, having hung up the phone. "You go and get started or we'll still be here tomorrow morning."

Amanda watched him go to open it, smiling, expecting either or both of the children to dash in, having forgotten something. She bent to pick up two more of Josh's little toys and glanced downward.

In front of the open door stood Brent, wordlessly staring into the falling darkness outside. The hushed silence alarmed her and she leaned across the railing.

"Who is it, darling?" she called out, wondering why he had not moved or said anything to the caller outside. Perhaps it was one of Josh's pranks, ringing the doorbell then disappearing.

She was just about to go downstairs again, when she heard a woman's voice. A deep, melodious, sensuous voice.

"Hello, Brent. Aren't you going to ask me in?"

A shadow loosened itself from the darkness and entered the hallway. She momentarily paused in front of the silent Brent, and Amanda froze. In the dim hallway light his face turned ashen and the horror in his eyes sent a chill spiraling up her spine. The woman reached out and touched his cheek with one gloved finger, playfully, teasingly.

"Aren't you even going to kiss me hello?" she mocked.

Instinctively Brent backed away and she laughed, a deep throaty laugh. With one swift gesture, she removed the streaked white fur hat and waves of flaming red hair fell past her shoulders and down her back. As she moved, the light caught the fiery sparks in the billowing blaze, and suddenly the placid hallway came to life.

How odd, Amanda mused, it was barely the end of September and she was wearing a long sable coat. What would she do when it got to be fifty below zero? Amanda stirred and noticed that her right leg had fallen asleep. At the movement, she lost her balance and grabbed the railing, dropping Josh's toys on the marble floor below. The sound made the stranger whirl around. She took in the little crashed cars and looked up.

Amanda gasped, her eyes widening to gigantic proportions. Her hands clutched the railing. In the dim light, the woman's face appeared almost bloodless, but the features were unmistakably familiar. She was staring at her own reflection.

Chapter 39

THE TWO WOMEN STARED AT ONE ANOTHER IN STUNNED silence, neither of them moving. Only the ticking of a faraway clock filtered into the room. As seconds passed and grew into minutes, the tension in the atmosphere became unbearable. Then the stranger laughed, softly at first, then louder and louder. At the sound Brent suddenly stirred into action. He swiftly closed the front door and strode toward the laughing woman, grabbing her roughly by the arm.

As suddenly as the laughter had started, it stopped. She viciously jerked her arm loose and glared at him. Then, with a contemptuous smile, she brushed past him and, with an air of familiarity and confidence, stepped down into the living room.

Brent glanced up at Amanda and pain flashed across his face at the look of disbelief in her big tawny eyes.

He ran up the stairs two at a time, but when he reached her, she shied away from him and stepped down with one hand on the railing to keep her balance. All the while she kept her gaze fixed on the woman, her movements almost trancelike and sedate. Brent followed her into the living room where the stranger had made herself comfortable on the sofa, and waited.

"Who are you?" Amanda whispered hoarsely.

"I could ask you the same thing." The woman frowned,

then laughed again. "Well, well, I never dreamed that you cared this much for me, darling." She threw Brent a challenging look. "You truly outdid yourself. Where did you find her? Or has science come this far and she is a clone?"

Brent's eyes flashed dangerously. Anger possessed him and it took iron self-control not to fling himself at the visitor and choke the life out of those taunting eyes.

Despite his confusion, he had rapidly grasped the situation. He instantly recognized the intruder. There was no mistaking the mannerisms, the haughty gestures, the flaunting impudence. And notwithstanding the tumbling questions that shook his sanity, one look at Amanda's stricken face prompted him to lash out.

"What the hell are you doing here?" he demanded. His gray eyes were dark and menacing, and the woman flinched at the blazing fury.

"What kind of a question is that? I've come home, of course."

"You're mad, absolutely insane. I could call the police—" Brent said.

"Oh, do that, by all means. Get that imposter out of here."

"I don't know who you are, or what your game is, but—" It was a bluff, of course, but he had to protect Amanda.

"Cut the bull, Brent. You know in your heart that I'm your wife. I'm the real Amanda Farraday. Now get rid of your harlot. You no longer need her." She turned to the pale Amanda. "It's amazing, she looks just like me. I must say, you flatter me, darling, to go to such lengths to find the perfect replacement."

She rose and languorously took off her coat and leather gloves as Amanda watched her. In a daze she noticed the long red nails, and she shuddered. They look like blood, she thought. *Why, she really doesn't look like me at all.* From up close she noticed the heavy makeup and the hard lines around the woman's mouth and eyes.

Makeup. Her mind flew to those hundreds of little bottles and compacts in her vanity drawers. Her eyes fervently scanned the stranger's clothes; there were hundreds like the dress she wore in the wardrobe upstairs—same style, same flair. She suddenly felt weak.

"But the fun is over and the real me is now back. So tell your little tart to go and—"

A gasp whirled her around. Wide-eyed, her hands clasped in front of her mouth, Mrs. Flynn gaped at her mistress's double.

"Who the he—Ah, but of course, you must be the house-keeper." She looked at Brent.

"What does a woman have to do to get a decent drink around here?"

"I must insist that you leave. Now." Brent stepped forward and held up her sable coat.

"You're asking the wrong woman. This is my house, I'm staying."

"You can't prove that—"

She raised her eyebrows.

"Oh, can't I?" She looked around. "This room, this house, I designed it, it's my creation. I even carved my initials into the brick next to the fireplace to mark it mine." She did not miss the jolt that went through Amanda, and smiled triumphantly. So the little hussy didn't know that, did she?

Amanda stood very still, her ears buzzing, her senses numb. *This can't be happening,* she thought, bewildered, *this is one of my horrible nightmares. I'll wake up and find her gone. She's nothing but a mirage, a figment of my imagination, something I've always feared deep down.* But as she listened to the other woman's vicious chatter, she knew it was not a dream.

The chatter droned on and on and the world started spinning around her. As if from a distance she saw Brent's concerned eyes watching her, the clenched jaw, the twitching muscle in his neck. Then the room dimmed and she quietly escaped into oblivion.

When she came to she was in her own bed. The first thing she saw was Brent sitting at the edge, watching her. The soft light from the lamp on her nightstand shone on his blond head and she could see the strands of silver.

How odd, she mused, that she had never noticed them before. His eyes were almost blue and the strange intensity of his gaze made her feel warm and safe. She reached out to touch his cheek and he instantly caught her hand and held it firmly. Then with a start she remembered, and her eyes widened in horror.

"Is she . . . has she gone?" She barely recognized her

own voice, hoarse and filled with terror. Brent shook his head, the pain in his eyes returning with full force.

He had carried her unconscious body into their bedroom, and as he sat there watching her with heavy heart, he thought about the past year. They had shared so much, so many precious moments, the love he had thought they lost. She had been a changed woman and he had cherished the change and attributed her warmth to the hardships she had encountered during the years she had been gone from him. The increased ardor in her lovemaking, the genuine feeling he had found lacking in her before, the wistful passion in her huge tawny eyes at his intimate touch—a response he had, for years, only dreamed about. Now he understood.

The moment he had opened the door and seen the other Amanda, he had known the truth. It all fit. She had not changed; the woman he had come to love all over again was another woman, a totally different person. The same face, the same body, but with a completely different personality. And he loved her. "She's downstairs. Mrs. Flynn made her comfortable in the guest room." He kissed her hand gingerly, his eyes never leaving her frightened face.

"I love you. No matter what happens, always remember that I love you." He felt a sudden need to say it.

"I love you, too." Her eyes brimmed and she swallowed hard. "What's happening, Brent? Is . . . is she . . . am I . . . ?"

"I don't know." He did, but he couldn't bring himself to admit it to her, not now. "I'm sorry about Lake Geneva. I'll call and cancel our reservations. Perhaps we can go there after all this is over."

But he knew that this was the beginning of the end, and looking in her eyes he saw that she knew it, too. He did not have all the answers—how it could have happened, a switch in a million so incredible it made his head spin—or who she really was. Nor did he care, at least not at this moment. All he knew was that no matter what the cost, he did not want to lose her.

He took her in his arms, desperately wanting to ease the pain, the fear. Yet he felt the same pain, the same fear, and he remained silent, just holding her as she clung to him, her body shaking.

"Oh, God," she whispered, her voice trembling. "I wish I could remember who I really am. I should've pursued it, but it didn't seem to matter before."

"Amanda—"

She quickly put her hand over his mouth, her tawny eyes wide and stricken. Brent gently kissed the palm of her hand and shook his head.

"It doesn't matter. To me you'll always be my Amanda, the woman I love, the woman with whom I'm happy." She was right, he thought sadly, it had never mattered before—it still didn't, not to him. He had waited so long for her, wanted her for all these years.

"You must've loved her once, you said so yourself."

"Stop it. You're torturing yourself needlessly. Tomorrow we'll think of something, a plan to get rid of her. For now, I want you to rest and get some sleep."

She touched his face, and he caught her hand and kissed it. He held it against his chest as he reached for the telephone and dialed The Abbeys.

How strange life can be, Amanda thought, waiting for Brent to return. He had gone downstairs to talk to Mrs. Flynn and give her instructions to have Amparo bring a light supper upstairs for them. Brent. *My* Brent, she thought warmly. How awful this must be for him, too. Imagine what a shock it must have been to open the door and see that intruder . . .

Intruder. That's what she is. Even if she proves to be the real Amanda and I'm the fake. What Brent and I have built together during the past year, that's real, too. Not even she can take that away from us.

Amanda sighed. *If she's the real Amanda, then who am I? Where do I begin to find out who and what I was before I got here?* All this time she had met so many people, and never anyone who had shown the slightest sign of suspicion, or implied she was someone else. Yet, from the very moment she had seen the intruder's face, she had known. It all made sense now: the makeup, the clothes, Brent's reaction.

She suddenly remembered the times she had wondered if she was not somebody else—that she was not Amanda. And how, as time went by, she had shaken off the nagging doubts, wanting to hold on to Brent's love. Now it was all over. The doubts had manifested themselves. And she was to lose him after all.

When Brent returned she was staring at the ceiling, her face ashen and her eyes bottomless pools of agony.

Seeing her anguish, Brent's insides churned. Something in him broke; cold rage surged. For a moment he wanted to rush downstairs and confront the woman who had shattered their happiness. Perhaps he could strangle her. Nobody would be the wiser. After all, her double lay here in his bed, and he could always tell Mrs. Flynn that the intruder had left. Then they could go on with their lives.

"Brent?" She reached out for him, her eyes wide and pleading.

It was just past midnight. Amparo had brought their dinner, but neither of them had eaten much. They had talked and talked, until there was nothing more to talk about. Nothing of importance anyway.

"Make love to me, make her go away?"

The night dissolved in their union. They clung to each other, hanging on to the feel of each other's body, hungry for each other's touch, and for a time, a very brief time, they lost themselves in each other.

The dinner at the country club had been outstanding. They needed a break from the uncomfortable situation at the house and the evening had provided just that. They had gone to The Barn afterward and enjoyed a private couple of hours there. When they returned home, Amanda felt almost care-free.

"Why don't I get us a nightcap, hm?" Brent held her close and kissed her with lingering tenderness. "You go ahead and make yourself comfortable, and before you can count to ten, I'll be there."

She laughed and ran upstairs. The light in their bedroom was on and she smiled. Good old Mrs. Flynn. She really is worth her weight in gold. Amanda walked to the bathroom and stopped in the middle of the archway. Seated in front of the vanity was the intruder, examining the makeup in her drawers.

"What are you doing here?" she whispered.

The stranger looked at her astonished double in the mirror.

"I suppose I'm impressed that you haven't abused my makeup."

"You're invading my privacy," Amanda said.

"Yeah? So what? You acted out mine."

"Hey, honey, why don't we—" Brent stopped in the archway behind her. "What the hell is going on here?"

He frowned at the flimsy negligee the intruder had swiped out of the wardrobe in the closet, revealing most of her swelling breasts and exposing her body through the thin chiffon.

"What does it look like? I'm getting ready for bed."

"Not in this bedroom, you aren't."

"It's *my* bedroom, and I'm going to sleep here tonight."

"Wrong, lady. *Was* your bedroom. You left it years ago."

"I have a right to be here. Me, not her."

"Wrong again. You gave up that right five years ago. Now get out, or I'll throw you out." His eyes flashed dangerously and Amanda held her breath, her heart pounding. Still the intruder did not move.

"Don't you have the facts confused, darling? I'm still your wife, whether or not you like it, and *I* don't like your mistress wearing my things, or sleeping in my bed."

"I don't give a damn what you like or dislike. Get out this instant!"

She shot a malevolent look in Amanda's direction, and catching it, Brent snarled. "I will have whomever I please sleep with me in my bedroom. Out! *Now!*"

She threw her head back and sent her blazing hair flying. At the doorway she turned and sneered.

"You always were a sucker for sluts," she said.

"That's probably why I married you," he snapped and slammed the door in her face.

He turned around, his jaws twitching, murder in his dark eyes. Then, seeing Amanda's shaken expression, he swiftly strode to where she stood and took her trembling body into his arms. He held her close, burying his face in her hair.

Deathly pale, Amanda closed her eyes, trying to block out the scene she had just witnessed. The words echoed through her mind. It was finally out in the open. He had said it. She felt the numbness set in. Part of her wanted to push him away, the other part screamed for his love. She began to shiver, her knees going weak, and a sob tore from her insides. She knew that her real nightmare had just begun. If that was the real Amanda, then who was she?

Chapter 40

"GOD, PAULA, I'VE GONE OVER IT, AGAIN AND AGAIN. Nothing, absolutely nothing." She buried her head in her hands, pulling at the cropped coppery curls.

"You mustn't give up. It's only been one day, there'll be more. We'll go back tomorrow and the day after and the day after, until we find something, a clue, someone who knows you." Paula reached out and touched her friend's arm, her dark eyes concerned.

They had gone to Barrington Hills that morning and scoured the hotels, motels, restaurants, anywhere people would gather, anywhere someone might remember Amanda. But there had not been anyone and finally, exhausted and frustrated, they had come back to Lake Forest.

For the past week Amanda had been staying at the Manchiones' to relieve the tension in the Farraday household. And every day that week Brent, Mandy, and Josh had come and stayed for as long as they could, just to be with the woman they believed belonged in their family. The children begged her to come home, not understanding why their mother had left them with a strange woman. How could *that* woman be their mother if the only mother they knew and loved was two doors down the street?

The exact likeness confused them and they were puzzled by the entire situation. Each night Josh cried when Brent took them home again. He became obstinate and difficult to handle. But it was Mandy who worried them the most. The girl withdrew into a shell of silence and she grew listless and apathetic. Her schoolwork suffered drastically. The once lively green eyes were now dull and expressionless, and even the daily visits to the Manchiones could not perk her up.

"I can't stay here much longer. It's too hard on Brent and the kids, and the strain is too much for all of us. It's not fair to you and your family, either," Amanda said.

"Please, Amanda—"

"Don't call me that! It is *not* my name."

"But you don't know that." Paula sighed. They'd been over this a hundred times, and each time Amanda would get more vehement.

"The fact that I am here and she is there, in my home, proves—"

"Proves nothing. You are here because you chose to leave your home. It was your choice, nothing else."

"I couldn't bear to watch them suffer. All because of me."

"You've got it wrong. Because of that woman."

Amanda got up, brushing away a curl. "I must leave," she murmured tonelessly. "I must go away."

"Oh, cara, stop that nonsense. Where would you go?"

"I don't know. Anywhere. Just so long as it is away from here."

"And what? Leave Brent to the likes of that—that—And what about your children?"

"They're not mine, they're hers! Don't you see—"

"No, I don't see. And neither do you. Damn it, Manda . . ." Paula threw her hands up in the air. "Oh, all right, whoever you are, can't you see what you're doing? Those kids love you, you're the only mother they know. How can you abandon them?"

Amanda sat down, tears rolling down her face. "I can't go on like this," she cried. "It hurts too much to see them. And each day, each time, it gets harder and harder." Her voice broke and she bit her lip. "Oh, God, Paula . . . who am I? I don't even know my name . . ."

Paula rushed to her and took her into her arms, sobbing as heartbreakingly as the woman she was holding. Finally, she straightened up and staggered into the bathroom, returning shortly with a box of tissues. She put it next to Amanda. "It's not fair," she sniffed. "I should go and have a hard talk with that bitch."

Amanda looked up, her swollen eyes red and moist. "How can you talk about her like that?" she said hoarsely. "She is your friend, remember?"

"Was, cara, was. *You* are my friend now. I don't associate with low, scheming bitches." Paula's voice was firm.

Yet she kept her face turned from Amanda, so her friend could not see her expression. Better a white lie than to compound the bitterness, she thought and closed her eyes for a second, cringing inwardly. Why, after all these years, did that bitch have to return? And why, of all times, now? What was she up to, what hideous reason could she possibly have?

"Paula? Please, you don't have to choose between us. She was your friend before you knew me." Amanda's voice was soft and gentle and Paula's eyes brimmed. "Just help me get out of town. Believe me, it'll make it easier on all of us."

At that Paula whirled around, impatiently brushing her tears away.

"Running away is a coward's way of eluding problems," she snapped. "Didn't anyone tell you that no problem has ever been solved in that manner?" Then, at the raw pain in Amanda's eyes, she softened. "And Brent? What about Brent? He loves you, you know. He'll never forgive me if I let you disappear from his life."

"I must. Please, Paula, try to understand. I know he will."

For a moment Paula remained silent, studying her feet as they traced circles across the linoleum floor. Suddenly, she jumped up and strode toward the kitchen window. She stared outside, chewing the inside of her cheek, pursing her lips. Then, taking a deep breath, she turned to face Amanda.

"Cara . . . ," she said softly. "Cara, there's something I must tell you . . ."

Brent tapped the pencil against his desk, his eyes following the swing of the pendulum on the wall. Ten after seven. His last patient left over half an hour ago. He leaned back in his chair and closed his eyes. God, he was tired. Tired of the bullshit at home, tired of his screwed-up life.

A pair of huge wistful eyes loomed in the shadows of his mind. Never before had he felt so helpless, and he hated it.

There had to be a way to restore his family's harmony. He had to find that way. Soon. Before it was too late.

He opened his eyes and stared into space. Why had that bitch come back? What was the real reason behind it? It couldn't have been boredom. Why, there were more than enough fools in this sick world to entertain her sordid needs. Neither could it have been the money; he had never told her about his impending inheritance. Could it have been that she found out about her look-alike? He narrowed his eyes. Highly unlikely, her surprise at seeing her double that first time had been too genuine. But then, what? And why now?

He sighed, his expression suddenly hardening. He had to find a solution to this dilemma. Every time he saw Amanda— *his* Amanda—he knew he had to do something to get rid of that snake, and fast, if not sooner. She was on the verge of breaking. They both were.

A sudden fear gripped his throat. Last night the bitch had crashed Paula's home, and finding Amanda there, had hurled vicious accusations at her. He could still recall the hatred in her eyes. A dangerous panther, ready for the kill. God, no! He would kill before tolerating any harm to the woman he loved. His fingers tensed and snapped the pencil in two.

Rage surged to his temples. With a growl he reached for the telephone and dialed Louise's number.

Amanda stared at her friend, her mind numb. She was still trying to digest Paula's confession. The roller-coaster car ride to downtown Chicago, the "chance" meetings with Stuart Gibbs and Jeremy Frost, even the accident in Austria. All designed to scare the living daylights out of her. Revenge. To punish her. All because Paula thought Matt had had an affair with the real Amanda.

She felt no anger, no bitterness, just weariness.

"Cara, please . . . say something . . . ," Paula pleaded. "For what it's worth, I feel like a heel. An absolute asshole." She heaved a deep breath. "I've come to really like you, you know. Even when I tried to hate you, you were always so . . . kind . . . And now that I know—" She brushed away the tears, impatiently, almost angrily. "God, how can I make it all up to you? I love you, cara. You're one of a kind. And a good friend. A real friend. Not like that rotten two-faced bitch I thought you were . . . Amanda, I mean . . ."

She paced the floor, wringing her hands, her face contorted with remorse.

"If only I knew how to make things right. You don't deserve all this shit. I wish—"

There was a moment's silence and the room grew very still. And as her words echoed through the silence, Paula suddenly jerked up, her face brightening.

"I've got it! Holy shit, why didn't I think of it before?"

And while Amanda's listless eyes widened momentarily, she rushed into the alcove and yanked the phone off the hook.

"Karen? Hi, it's me, Paula. You got a minute?"

In a daze Amanda listened to her friend as she talked rapidly to Brent's sister. It was all part of a bad dream, a never-ending nightmare that seemed to hurl her from bad to worse. And all this time, she had no idea who she was or where she had come from.

She had read that amnesia victims usually regained their memory, but nothing had triggered even a semblance of recognition in her—not a spark, nothing. The shadows of her mind remained a huge void, a blank blur, and now, after a year of living the life of another, she felt despair creeping in, threatening to suck her inside the black whirlpool of nothingness that was her past, and all that was left of her present life . . .

"Well, that's settled." Paula replaced the receiver with a click and smiled broadly. "After dinner I'll take you to Karen's. She's really looking forward to having you with them, cara. Said the twins are giving her a hard time and she needs a grown-up around her. I should've thought of it before. After all, they live in Barrington Hills, right smack where the action is, or where you want to be right now. And Daryl can take you places. You know, the country club or something. Perhaps you'll meet someone who'll recognize you."

"I'll only be bothering them."

"Bothering them? Bullshit. They care about you, as much, if not more than I and Matt do. Look, you didn't want to stay at Louise's and you don't want to stay here. Why not give it one last chance, hm?" She shook her gently. "Come on, cara, cheer up. Shake that gloomy face, girl! Something's bound to break, mark my words, something always does."

Young voices from outside reached their ears and Paula

quickly rose. She walked toward the hallway, then, as she reached it, turned back to Amanda.

"Shape up, Manda. They've had a rough day at school. They don't need a sour face to greet them at home." She shook her head and started to head for the front door.

"Paula? Why did you lie about your arrival date in Austria?"

Paula whirled around in astonishment.

"You told me you and Matt arrived together in Salzburg. But you didn't. You arrived a couple of days after Matt. Why the lie?" Not that it really mattered anymore, Amanda thought, but it did bother her. "I also know that Matt had been in Holland before he went to Salzburg."

Slowly Paula retraced her steps, not saying a word.

Amanda sighed. "Look, forget it. It's not important—"

"No!" Paula interrupted. "No, I don't want to forget it. It's . . . I . . . Matt and I . . ."

"You didn't trust him. You thought he'd gone to Europe to meet with me. With Amanda. And you were jealous." Amanda smiled wanly.

Paula blinked. Pressing her lips together, she nodded, and lowered her eyes. When she looked up again, her eyes were moist.

"Can you ever forgive me . . . ?" Paula whispered.

The voices outside became louder. A deep sigh escaped them both, simultaneously. Amanda's expression softened. The smile she flashed her friend once more warm and reaching. But before Paula could rush to her and hug her, the doorbell chimed.

Karen was ecstatic with Amanda's stay. She even talked her mother-in-law into baby-sitting the twins in the afternoons and drove Amanda around to see if they could find somebody who could point her toward the truth. Twice Daryl had taken her to bars and the local country club. Yet all their efforts brought zero results, and after a week in Barrington Hills, Amanda gave up searching.

Nevertheless she remained at the Willses'. Brent had not been happy about her decision to move to Barrington Hills, but in the end he had agreed that it would be easier on the children. And it was better than to have her disappear to some place where they could not see or talk to her at all.

Twice every day he called her and they talked. About their daily encounters, about the children, about nothing much. Just talk. Just to hear each other's voice.

Her hand lashed out and slapped the boy across the face. Josh uttered a cry. In the corner a stunned Mrs. Flynn held her hand in front of her mouth and bit her lip. *Her* Mrs. Farraday would *never* hit the boy, no matter what the circumstances. This one had no tolerance for the children whatsoever, and no interest in their needs. That much she had made clear during the past three weeks. She glanced at Mandy. The girl showed no emotion and continued to calmly nibble at her food.

"Don't ever raise your hand to my children." Brent's tall figure towered menacingly in the kitchen archway and Josh immediately left his chair and ran toward his father.

Mrs. Flynn heaved a sigh of relief. She had not noticed his approach, but she had noticed that lately he would appear from nowhere just in time to shield the children from their mother's moods.

"You're right. They're *your* children. Mine would behave like normal human beings, not impudent little brats." Her eyes flashed and she got up from the table.

"Where are you off to at this hour?" Brent asked.

She threw him a contemptuous look. "What do you care? I don't ask you any questions, do I?"

"Amanda, this is Saturday. You came back to get to know the children, remember? At least, that's what you said. And weekends are the perfect time to spend with them."

"Well, maybe another time. I have an appointment today." She smiled wickedly. "An old friend, who has invited me on his yacht. I tried to talk him into bringing you along, but you're such a stuffed shirt, and you might get bored. Unless you've developed a taste for good old-fashioned fun, with lots of champagne and delicious desserts afterward?"

Brent scowled, and walking over to the empty seat next to Mandy, sat down, nodding his thanks to Mrs. Flynn as she poured him a cup of hot coffee. Desserts, my foot, he thought, still fuming over the abuse he had witnessed. He could just imagine the kind she liked.

"No, thanks. Enjoy yourself. Just make sure you're sober and dressed when you get back here. In case you've forgotten, this is the home of a decent family, and we do act accordingly."

She made a face and walked out. Brent took Mandy's hand into his and waited for her to look up.

"How about visiting Aunt Karen and the twins, hm?"

Her green eyes instantly lit up, and Josh threw his arms around his neck.

"Easy, easy. If you strangle me, you'll lose a driver, and I don't think Mrs. Flynn would like to sacrifice her weekend for a funeral," he said winking at the housekeeper. He received a grateful smile.

They quickly finished their breakfast, and at the garage door, Mrs. Flynn held back Brent's arm and handed him a box.

"Chocolate chip brownies I baked yesterday. Please give her my regards," she said softly. Brent nodded and squeezed her hand. They were his Amanda's favorite cookies.

Chapter 41

"IT'S TERRIBLE, ABSOLUTELY HORRIBLE! I DON'T KNOW IF I can take much more of this . . ." Karen sobbed.

"Come now, honey, let's not lose heart." Daryl put his arm around her. "You heard what Brent said the other night. He'll get a divorce in no time, you'll see."

It was Halloween night and Amanda had gone to Paula's to escort Josh and Mandy around the neighborhood after dark. She had spent more and more time at the Manchiones after the violent incident two weekends ago. Josh had given her the blow-by-blow details and she had been upset for days. But like Brent, she worried especially about Mandy, who seemed only to come to life when she was in her mother's arms. The mother she knew and loved and trusted. The only mother she acknowledged.

The girl never spoke of the "other" as Josh called her. She lost weight and her color had disappeared. And the "other" Amanda had neither the time nor the interest to see what was happening to the youngsters, taking up her own pleasures where she had left off years before. Nobody seemed to be able to do anything about that.

"She looks like a ghost. She's miserable, and I'm miserable for her. I wish Brent would see that." Karen blew her nose angrily.

"Don't you think he does? I spoke to him just yesterday,

and he said he had a plan. So let's give him a chance, shall we?" Daryl took her into his arms and kissed her. "Don't you trust your own brother?"

"I don't trust *her!* She's the same selfish bitch she always was, and worse. I don't know where she's been all this time, or why she came back, but she's up to no good, Daryl, none whatsoever!"

"Come on, we'd better be going or my mother will put a hex on the twins."

Karen went to get her coat. How ironic, she thought, she had never liked Amanda, nor trusted her. But for Brent's sake, she had been civil toward her, even amicable at times. Then, when the look-alike showed up, she had, thinking it was Amanda, kept up appearances, all the while reserving judgment on the "change" in the woman.

Yet, as time went by, she had come to genuinely like this "new" Amanda. Gradually her feelings for the woman had deepened and real friendship between them had blossomed. Now that the real Amanda was back, her loyalties had taken a different turn. The dislike for her sister-in-law resurfaced with full force; she resented the bitch for making her new friend miserable. What was more, she was making Brent miserable, and that was a criminal act in Karen's book.

"Divorce? So you can marry that slut?" Amanda scoffed, her eyes glaring.

"Watch your mouth, woman, or I will shut it for you," Brent snapped, his dark eyes flashing with near hatred, and she winced.

She had seen him angry before, but never this fierce. Her heart lurched; he was a stranger to her, menacing and dangerous, and she was convinced that, given the chance, he could hurt her. She took a deep breath, the stubborn streak in her emerging; she could not let him see her fear of him; that would mean defeat, and "defeat" was not a word she would allow in her vocabulary.

"Why, Brent, she really has you hooked, hasn't she? Those tricks in bed will do it anytime."

"You ought to know, you do it often enough." Brent turned to the bar and poured himself a Scotch.

She'd done it again. Five years, and she still managed to

get under his skin. He downed the Scotch, furious with himself.

"What is it you want, Amanda?" He tried to keep his voice calm. "Why, after all these years, have you come back?"

"How about a drink for me?" she responded.

He looked at her impassively, then turned around and poured her a gin and tonic. For a moment he just stared at the glass, recalling how her double detested this concoction. Slowly he picked it up and handed it to her.

"You haven't forgotten," she crowed, throwing him a triumphant look. "So, you want a divorce. What's it worth to you?"

Taken aback, he raised an eyebrow and stared at her.

"Everything."

"Everything?"

"You name it, you got it." He lit a cigarette, wondering what game she was playing.

"I tell you what. I'll make you a deal. You let me back into your bedroom and give me back my status as mistress of this household, let's say for six months, and we'll talk."

Amanda cocked her head, gauging his reaction. Shit, what was she saying—*six* months? She'd die in this boring craphole. One month, two maybe, but six . . . ? Still . . .

She narrowed her eyes, wondering if he would call her bluff. How she had loathed his conventional lovemaking, but the thought of him smitten over a look-alike irked her. She was determined to make him suffer for it.

The corner of her painted mouth curled up in contempt. A clone, that's all she was. But Brent had dared to choose *her* above the original, and for that they had to be punished.

"I've missed you, darling," she cooed. "All these years, there hasn't been a man quite like you."

"I'll bet." Brent sneered.

A cold fury swept over him, threatening to take control of his senses. If this was her way to wriggle her worthless self back into his good graces she had the wrong man.

"We'll talk *now,"* he snarled, clenching his fists.

"Okay, three months. But that's it, take it or leave it."

Amanda gulped down her drink, her newly acquired fear of him reemerging in full force. She jumped up from the sofa and walked over to the bar, trying to shake the feeling.

"You can sleep in the upstairs bedroom while we finalize

the divorce." He spoke slowly, as though thinking over each word he said. He no longer hid his distrust and his contemptuous look sent shivers down the back of her neck.

"With you?"

You wouldn't catch me dead in the same bed with you, he thought. "I'll take the guest room," he said evenly.

Amanda emptied her second glass and threw her head back.

"No. No dice, darling. We do it my way or not at all."

Brent glared at her for one tense moment, then put down his glass and strode out of the room. Next, the door to the garage slammed behind him and the garage door opened.

"I failed. I guess I played my cards wrong."

She put her arms around his neck and kissed him. Brent looked at her, his expression reflecting the dejection and despair in his voice. With a long, drawn-out sigh, he buried his head in her neck.

"Isn't there another way?" Paula looked at her husband for help, but Matt only shook his head.

"I'll have to look into it," he said. "It's not my bag, really. Perhaps I could ask one of my colleagues, someone who's more familiar with these matters."

"The nerve!" Paula exploded, her face flushed. "I can't believe she'd actually pull that crap."

Brent lifted his head and sighed again. "If only I knew what she's up to. Why has she suddenly returned here? Why now, after all these years?"

He had driven around for a while, then, remembering that *his* Amanda was staying for the night at Paula's, he had turned the car around and gone to the Manchiones'. Just being near her had comforted him, and made him want to strangle the bitch in his house all the more.

"Perhaps I should talk to her?" Paula sounded hesitant.

She had spoken to her old friend just once since her return, but they had been strangers; too many years had passed to pick up the pieces in that one short meeting, too much had happened to set them apart. They both knew that the presence of Paula's new friend had made all the difference, and the gap seemed irreparable.

"Don't bother, she doesn't trust you any more than she

trusts me." Brent shook his head and lit a cigarette. Suddenly his face brightened.

"But perhaps I know just the person who can get through to her."

He got up and walked to the telephone to dial Louise.

Louise looked at the woman across from her. The face was older and her sharp eyes detected lines around her eyes and mouth. The expression in her tawny eyes too seemed harder than five years ago and so did the sound of her laughter.

"We were worried about you, Amanda. Why did you disappear without leaving a note of some sort?"

Amanda looked at her contemptuously.

"Cut the crap, Louise. Why did you summon me here?"

"Summon? Is that how you feel?"

"It's Brent, isn't it? I should've known. Anytime he can't handle a situation, our precious little boy runs to Grandma for help."

Louise leaned back in her chair, her expression inscrutable. She was surprised that Amanda had actually come. After all, they had never been the best of friends, and at the time of her disappearance, Amanda had loathed her. Curiosity, Louise thought wryly, had always been one of her weaknesses, and the opportunity to flaunt her power over Brent to the one enemy she was dying to crush.

"Sign the divorce papers, Amanda, and I'll show you my eternal gratitude."

Amanda threw her head back and laughed. "You too, Louise? That little cunt really got to all of you, even the tough Farraday Godmother."

"What do you stand to gain by lingering on?" Louise wondered aloud, ignoring her snide remarks. "You don't give a damn about Brent or your children, so why not go back to your Italian Count and enjoy a life of glamour and luxury in the Mediterranean?" Louise noted with satisfaction that she had hit a nerve, as Amanda narrowed feral eyes and glared at her.

"Now, why doesn't that surprise me? You and your puny spies! Life would be boring for you if you couldn't find somebody's dirt to dig up, wouldn't it?" The hatred in her eyes was alarming, but Louise did not so much as blink, returning her gaze with calm indifference.

"You're right. They are *my* children, and they need their mother. So I'm back."

"They need *a* mother, a real mother. Which they have in the woman they think is their own mother. And she cares about them like you never could, never would. You just don't have it in you, and if you were to stay, soon you'd be arrested for child abuse," Louise spat out.

"I always knew you were thriving on gossip. Is there anything else you'd like to predict?" Amanda asked.

"A quarter of a million dollars. Deposited in the bank of your choice as soon as you've put your signature on Brent's divorce papers."

Amanda's eyes widened. "Generous, aren't you? You must be desperate, or was this your precious grandson's idea?" She laughed hoarsely. "Where did you find that little tart anyway? I read somewhere that everyone has a double in this world, but I must admit, the likeness is phenomenal. All this time, you really thought she was me. How insulting, really. That little wimp, me?" She laughed again.

"Just think, my dear, what you could do with all that money." Louise remained undaunted.

Amanda rose, her expression haughty. "You can stuff it up your sophisticated ass. I told Brent I'd give it some thought, but only on my terms." She started to walk away, then stopped and slowly pivoted. "Of course, that contribution could help sway me to have a discussion a little sooner. Double your offer, old bitch, and that asshole grandson of yours can start his negotiations by Thanksgiving."

With a sneer, she swung the long woolen scarf around her neck and walked toward the elevator.

"Double, Louise. Let me know if she's worth that much to you."

She stepped into the elevator and waved mockingly.

"No, I won't have it. I won't allow you two to go through with that . . . that despicable deal. It's downright bribery, and it makes me feel cheap and soiled . . ." She was close to tears and Brent pulled her head down to kiss her.

"My silly little darling, how delicious you are," he drawled. "Don't ever, ever change." He kissed her again, but she tore her lips from his, her eyes so solemn they looked like jade.

"I'm serious. Half a million dollars, indeed! I feel like a piece of meat being bought at an overpriced auction."

"More like a priceless gem, really." His eyes twinkled at her indignation. "Besides, you're worth far more than that, angel face. But if it makes you feel any better, it's our freedom that's at stake here. Not just you, or me, but our future together, ours and that of our kids. Satisfied now?"

They were spending the night at the Ritz, compliments of the hotel manager, whose premature baby Brent had delivered a week ago after a strenuous labor that had almost cost the mother her life.

"I can't believe Louise would resort to such measures—" She suddenly stopped, remembering that horrid afternoon Louise had tried to pay *her* off, and with a sigh, she laid her head on his wiry chest.

"Would you rather we went to Mexico like Matt suggested? It would be one option, but this way it's definitely legal. Money isn't everything, you know. Trust me, darling, this is by far the best recourse."

She sighed. She knew he had made up his mind and he was right—a Mexican divorce could be contested in some states.

"It's insane," she mumbled.

Brent chuckled and lifted her head with one finger. "So is your effect on me," he said softly. Tenderly, he rolled her over and slid on top of her.

Chapter 42

"I'M WARNING YOU, AMANDA! YOU PULL YOUR OLD tricks on me and I'll see you rot in hell."

Amanda ignored him, seemingly concentrating on getting the colors right as she expertly maneuvered a dainty brush around her eyes.

"What is it, darling? Got a stiff caught in your pants?" She lowered her eyes to hide her smug satisfaction at the anger she had ignited. "What's the problem, anyway? You've been banging her all this time, with or without me around, so why—" She shrank away as Brent approached her, his eyes dark and menacing.

"You'd better learn to curb your vile tongue or I'll slit your worthless throat," he hissed, losing control. His breath came heavily and he willed himself to keep his fists at his sides.

Amanda slowly straightened up, her eyes still watching him in the mirror. Brent took a deep breath and, unclenching his fists, took a step backward. She continued to put the finishing touches on her makeup, all the while wary of his every move.

As he watched her in the mirror, Brent's lips curled in disgust at the sight of her painted face, and another, fresher version of the same features came to mind. How he ever could have mistaken her look-alike for this crude creature was beyond him; they were such opposites in almost every way—he should have trusted his initial instincts when the other Amanda had first reentered—or so he thought—his life.

Perhaps Paula was right and his judgment had been clouded by his intense desire to have her back, an Amanda he thought he loved, a woman who—he knew now—only existed in his mind. As the days passed and that woman came to life, he had selfishly ignored his own suspicions and after a while had been only too eager to accept her as his wife, his Amanda. Now that she was gone, he—

"Breeent!" Amanda's shrill voice hurled him back to reality. "Shit, where were you? Thinking about your hussy, no doubt." Then, seeing his threatening frown, she quickly grabbed her shoes and headed for the door. "Let's go, huh, I don't want to miss the best part of the party."

Some party, he thought wryly. He hated her kind of parties, and for the millionth time since she had left his house, he wished the other Amanda was back and they were going to the opera or a Mozart concert instead. Yes, he admitted, he should have known then; a person's taste did not change *that* drastically, and *his* Amanda genuinely shared his love for classical music. Neither of them had missed the thrill of these dreadful noisy affairs. Slowly he went downstairs, his mind searching for a plausible excuse to leave Ted's party early.

One more party, he thought, just one more party. And what was one more party if it would buy him his freedom?

Theodore Maxwell, known to his friends as Ted or Teddy, knew how to throw a party. At forty-two he owned six private clubs around the state and Dragon's Den was just one of them. His parties were famous—or infamous, depending on your point of view—for their glamour and versatility. They even attracted celebrities, and best of all, the most ambitious personalities of the Land West of Oz.

He was very generous and among his hobbies was his collection of rare talent, or what Teddy Maxwell considered to be rare talent, which often coincided with the taste of the in crowd and more often than not was the in thing. Someone invariably got discovered by some big talent scout from the wicked west. So to be invited to a Maxwell party was like winning the lottery, and depending on the need, the winning ticket could be the jackpot. At least to the likes of the glitter-hungry Amanda Farraday.

As the doors opened for her, Amanda smiled her most beguiling smile, her big eyes glistening with anticipation. She was in her element, her adrenaline pumping at top speed as she took in the bright lights and turned-on faces in the crowded room. The loud music was sweet to her ear, the boisterous laughter the ultimate stimulant to her soaring spirits, and she laughed. She felt right at home here, she was back, finally back, and she loved it.

She darted forward in search of the host, and soon was swallowed up by the laughing, drinking, snorting crowd. Slowly Brent made his way to a quieter corner and lit a cigarette. It was going to be a long night, and he only hoped he could last a couple of hours, at least until Amanda was drunk enough to be taken home.

He could, of course, concoct a phony excuse of being called away on an emergency at the hospital, but he knew Amanda wouldn't fall for it, and he did not want to antagonize her further. First he needed her to agree to give him a divorce, and perhaps, later, when she was good and high, he might persuade her to see things his way.

The blaring music bothered him and he moved to another room. But it was not any better. A sickening sweet odor hung in the air, mingled with the smell of sweat. He noticed a bunch of creatures huddled together along the wall, and as he passed, one of them looked up and offered him a cigarette butt.

"Want some, old man?"

Brent shook his head and made his way into a third room. My God, he thought, let's hope the cops don't raid this place tonight. That's all he needed. He could just see the headlines —WELL-KNOWN SURGEON ATTENDS POT PARTY. It would do wonders for his career.

A couple of women whizzed by and he frowned at their scantily clad figures and multicolored hairpieces. Jesus, he felt like an alien among interplanetary specimens in a *Star Trek* movie. He turned around, expecting some green-skinned creatures to waltz by any minute, and he suddenly grinned. Perhaps he could amuse himself after all.

He did not see Amanda all night long, neither did he look

for her. Quite content to sip champagne and nibble on caviar and exotic hors d'oeuvres, he managed to stay out of the limelight, making light conversation and getting unintelligible replies. From time to time he glanced at his watch, and each time a smile livened up his bored expression. At eleven o'clock he finally spotted Amanda and moved in her direction.

As he got closer, he noticed the glazed expression in her wide eyes, the unnatural pitch of her laughter, and he felt his skin crawl. A wave of intense disgust swept over him. How much longer, he wondered? She was worse than he remembered. How could he ever have believed he loved this creature?

She was leaning against Teddy Maxwell's bare chest, her breasts about to pop out of her low-cut dress, and Brent stiffened despite himself. He tried to brace against the feeling of humiliation, telling himself that soon he would not have to put up with his wife's revolting behavior. Then, just as he reached her, Teddy's hand slid up her long dress and openly fondled her buttock.

"Come on, Amanda, we're leaving," he said coldly. He grabbed her arm, but she hissed and shook off his grip, never even turning her head. As if he were invisible, Maxwell continued to play with her, his hand roaming freely from her rump to her front, and with an excited giggle, she parted her legs invitingly. Brent swore.

"Come on, Amanda," he threatened, shaking her roughly, but this time she pushed him away with a force that made him stagger, and Teddy Maxwell looked up, a hint of annoyance in his glassy eyes.

"Fuck off, man." His nasal voice was cracked and he spoke in a disinterested fashion. "Can't you see the lady is enjoying herself?"

Before Brent's bewildered eyes, Teddy gave Amanda's dress one powerful tug and the skirt ripped away clean, exposing her bare buttocks. With a swift move equal to the first one, Maxwell plunged three fingers of his right hand inside of her and she gasped. Then, shamelessly, she thrust the lower part of her body forward and began to writhe against his hand.

Brent felt a wave of nausea, but before he could recover, Teddy's left hand had reached around Amanda's torso and its middle finger disappeared between her naked buttocks. Amanda's eyes flew open in surprise and a deep guttural groan wrenched from her. Then she laughed, a shrill, eerie sound of triumph; a sound that offended her husband's ears but seemed to stimulate everyone else around her. A bleached blonde wriggled herself between Maxwell's straddled legs and with feverish sobs began to fumble at his front, her hands shaking furiously as she tugged at the stubborn zipper.

Brent averted his eyes from the scene before him and swallowed hard. It reminded him of a ritual he had once seen on cable television rather than a human orgy of sorts, and either way, he had seen enough. More than enough. Angrily he whirled around and waded to the front door.

He slammed the door of the Jaguar, turned on the motor, and backed up with such speed he barely missed the car behind him. The Jag screeched out of the parking lot, swerving dangerously as he raced up the street and ran a red light, hardly paying attention to the furious honking of a motorist crossing the intersection.

"Bitch!" He stepped on the gas and the Jaguar leaped forward.

What a fool he was, a demented idiot, a class-A asshole. He should've kicked her ass out the minute she set foot back in his house. Or at least forced the issue and demanded his freedom. Or taken a stand, charged her for abandoning her babies, anything that would set him free. He had told himself he did not care what she did or with whom, yet what he had witnessed tonight was more than he had bargained for.

He gripped the steering wheel until the whites of his knuckles showed, and he gritted his teeth. *How dare she humiliate him this way?* He was sure she had done this on purpose. And in front of all those people.

He could still see their smirking faces, the mocking eyes, the contempt. They never even paid the slightest attention to Amanda's play for Maxwell, at least not until he had staged the action. No, their curiosity had been for *his* reaction—the poor son of a bitch who got suckered into witnessing his wife's sexual voracity. And they had enjoyed watching *him.*

He swung the Jag onto the Edens Expressway without bothering to slow down, cutting in front of a truck who vi-

ciously switched on his bright lights. Brent narrowed his
eyes, temporarily blinded, and almost hit the station wagon
in front of him. After a few minutes the truck dimmed his
brights and he took a deep breath, then changed lanes.
Calmer now, he slowed down to the normal speed of the
Chicago night traffic and gradually his mind began to clear.

Amanda, I must see Amanda, he thought, and he was not
thinking of the slut he had just left behind at the party. He
glanced at the clock on the dashboard: eleven-thirty. Perhaps
he ought to call her; Paula and Matt were late bed-goers, but
they might be alarmed if he just dropped by at this hour. Oh,
the hell with it. He did not feel like making a pit stop, and by
the time he found a phone booth . . . Besides, a phone call
would be just as alarming at this time of night.

But when he finally swung up their driveway, the house
was dark and for a moment he hesitated. He was completely
calm now. Still angry, but once again in control. The drive
had done him good, as it always did when he was upset. And
the Jag was an exceptional therapeutic asset—its adaptability
to his moods, its flexibility for speed, its agility—all helped
get him back on track.

He quietly opened the car. Far away a dog barked. It
sounded almost like Kavik, yet it came from too far a distance to be him. Gently closing the car door, he moved toward the front entrance. His need to see *his* Amanda
resurfaced in full force; he needed to see her face, hear her
gentle voice, just to make sure the resemblance went no further than appearances. Just to erase the revolting scene of
less than an hour before.

Good thing he remembered that she was staying at the
Manchiones' for the weekend. Daryl and Karen had gone to a
wedding in Wisconsin and taken the twins with them, but in
his befuddled state of mind it was truly a wonder that he
recalled all of this, or was it because his mind was constantly
with her, no matter where she was?

But as his hand touched the doorbell he could not make
himself press it. Jesus, it was uncivilized to barge into someone's home in the middle of the night, even if they were his
best friends. Or even if he wanted to talk to his own wife. He
withdrew his hand and stuck it in his pocket as if to make

sure he would not be tempted to touch the bell, and slowly walked back to his car.

Wife. That's who she was, *his* Amanda, *his* wife. No other. The other one was a nightmare who only resembled his true wife, and one day, soon, he would wake up and the nightmare would be over. Then there would be tomorrow, a new day with *his* Amanda, his wife. Pausing, he gazed back at the dark house and stood very still. Perhaps they would understand his need to see her tonight. After all, they were his, their, best friends. And they had lived through this nightmare together. And . . .

Abruptly he turned around and strode toward the car. Tomorrow. Tomorrow he would find the best divorce lawyer in Chicago and rid himself of that trash once and for all. Why, there must be a way; it was done all the time. He should have thought of it before. Yes, why had he not thought of it before? With a frown, he reached to open the car door, and froze.

A small figure came walking slowly up the driveway, shoulders slouched, hands buried in her coat pockets, head bent so deep in thought she did not notice the parked car or the man awaiting her approach.

"Amanda?" She jumped and gasped at the sound of his hoarse whisper. "God, Manda, what the hell are you doing out here at this ungodly hour?"

Her heart still pounding with fright at the unsuspected apparition, she swallowed hard. "Brent?"

"Who else?" he exclaimed. "Did you expect the milkman at this hour?"

A sob wrenched from deep within her throat, relief flowing through her. She had just come from his house, spending the evening talking to Mrs. Flynn.

Restless and depressed, she had called on the kind housekeeper and had found a sympathetic ear, and as the hours passed so had her distressed mood. She had known about the party and had not expected him back so soon. And certainly not in the Manchione driveway.

She inched backward as Brent reached her. *No,* she thought frantically, *he can't touch me. I can't let him touch me. I can't let him tear down my defenses. Not now, not tonight. Not after it took me a whole evening to build up my strength.* And as if he sensed her apprehension, Brent halted, his hand arrested halfway in midair, and remained very still, waiting for her next move.

Eternity passed as they stared at each other's shadow, their expressions hidden by the dimness of a faraway street-light failing to cast enough illumination to their surroundings. Even so he noticed her move her head toward the Jaguar and sensed more than he saw that she tried to peer inside the darkness of the car.

"I left her at the party," he said softly, and at the defensive lift of her chin he knew her shields were still up. "I came to see you."

Why? she screamed inwardly, still not comprehending the full impact of his statement. *Liar! You went out with her to-night. All this time you had told me you were going to divorce her for me, then you turned around and went out with her to a party.*

"It's near midnight," she whispered.

"We've got to talk. It's not working out the way I had planned, but I think I've come up with another solution. Why don't we go back home—"

Home? Amanda cringed at the word. She wanted to lash out bitterly, but the words never formulated.

"—and discuss my new strategy? Please, Manda, I need your input as much as I need to have you near me tonight." Brent held out his hand. She did not take it. Her voice was almost harsh when she spoke.

"Tonight? What happened tonight?"

"Everything. I'll tell you all about it at home. Please?"

She turned her head, forgetting that the darkness could not reveal the bitterness in her eyes.

"You went out with her tonight. Why, Brent, why? After all you said . . ." The pain in her voice cut deep into him, and he raised his hand as if to shield himself.

"She wanted to meet this guy Maxwell. Said she wanted to get into the movies and he could help her," he said softly.

"You didn't have to go with her."

"I set it up. I knew someone who could get us an invitation. You can't just crash into a Maxwell party without one. And you can't go alone. Those are his rules." He took a deep breath, trying to contain his misery. "Besides, she promised she would agree to a divorce if I got her inside his den."

After a pause, she said gently, "Why don't we go inside?"

Brent frowned. "Won't we wake everybody up?"

She shook her head and started to walk toward the house. The same dog barked again and he suddenly realized it was Vanessa's new German shepherd, the one she got last week after she found those mysterious footprints in her backyard.

"They're not home. They've gone to the farm in Iowa for the weekend. Paula's mother slipped on her bathroom floor and broke her ribs, and the kids wanted to see the baby rabbits." She stuck the house key in the front door and opened it. "I guess I forgot to leave the light on in the hallway," she said, flipping the switch.

Brent closed the door and pulled her into his arms. He kissed her hard and hungrily, crushing her soft, supple body against his own taut muscles. The despair and frustration of earlier that night exploded in an almost violent abandon at the feel of her, so much in his grasp, so maddeningly real. He coaxed Amanda to respond, and with a sigh she gave in.

Neither one could later recall how they had managed to strip off their clothing, only that the heat of their long separation had taken over their other senses and they had united in feverish surrender. No words passed between them, none needed for the moment.

Brent was the first to stir, reluctant to pull away from her. Part of his mind floated back to reality, and he began to outline his alternate plans. They talked deep into the night, in between tireless breaks of lovemaking. When the first rays of dawn seeped through the living room windows, they were exhausted, both physically and mentally.

Yet they felt rejuvenated by the strength of their love for one another. A bond had grown between them, one that had hung on a thin thread before this day, reaffirmed by their mutual desire to belong to one another. And they knew that somehow, now, they could stand being apart until that goal was reached.

With their arms around each other's naked bodies they staggered into the guest bedroom. She drew the curtains closed, and in the semidarkness and with their arms once again wrapped around each other, they fell into a dreamless sleep for the first time since that fateful afternoon that had brought the other woman to their doorstep and threatened to rip their lives apart.

A couple of hours later the telephone rang. Amanda only moaned, turning sideways and burying her head in her pillow to shut out the noise. But it kept on ringing and finally she reached out and knocked it off the hook.

"What?" Her mind still fuzzy with sleep, she could barely make out the agitated words buzzing in her ears. "Who is this?"

Brent opened his right eye and mumbled, "Whoever it is, we're not home."

Amanda's eyes suddenly flew open and she jerked up in bed, her expression now alert.

"Run that by me one more time, Mrs. Flynn. Slower this time, please?"

At the mention of the housekeeper's name, Brent opened both his eyes, and seeing the bewilderment on Amanda's face, he turned on his back, watching her. Then, slowly, as if in a trance, she put back the receiver.

"What is it? The children?" A cold fear swept over him, but she shook her head and, dazed, turned her eyes on him and just stared.

"Wake up, Manda. Damn it, tell me! I can take it, whatever it is."

"It's . . . it's your . . . wife," she whispered. "There's been a car accident . . . They . . . they found her—" The words choked in her throat.

"Dead?" Brent too was now whispering. It was too good to be true, he thought. All our problems solved . . .

"She's in critical condition. Almost every bone in her body broken . . . including her neck . . ."

Brent stared at her, disbelief in his eyes.

"Her neck . . . not dead . . . ?"

He jumped out of the bed and smashed a pillow against the wall.

"That goddamn bitch! Why can't she die like any normal human being? A broken neck, yet she still lives? Shit, the broad must've fucked Satan himself to cheat death this way."

Amanda sighed. "Wait, Brent. There's more . . ."

But he did not want to listen. She was not dead, what more was there?

"Come on, get dressed. We'll talk to Mrs. Flynn. Then we'll

go to the hospital together and see if we can't help promote some funeral home."

"Brent! Is that a way for a doctor to talk?" She feigned indignation, but the smile in her eyes told him that he had stilled her fears. Last night really had taken place, and they were still together. That was all she needed to know.

On the way to the car, she suddenly remembered that Mrs. Flynn had told her that Amanda had been high on cocaine when they had found her. The driver of the car was dead.

Chapter 43

"YOU NITWIT! CAN'T YOU PUT A SIMPLE SPOON IN MY mouth without wrecking my teeth? It's not as if I can move my head or anything. What is it with this stinking hospital? The service sucks, and they keep sending me assholes like you who don't even know the meaning of professionalism."

The nurse heaved a sigh of relief as she fed Amanda Farraday the last spoonful of her dinner. She was a patient woman, more so than most, but she was rapidly losing her temper and she was glad the ordeal was just about over.

All during the meal Amanda had voiced her displeasure—time and again cursing at the staff's disregard for her comfort, and in less than five minutes the nurse had lost all the compassion she had when she first entered the room. Pity, she thought, looking at the body encased in white sturdy plaster, she should have broken her tongue instead of her ribs, arms, and legs. Had she not been well trained, the temptation to wring that already broken neck could have overruled her sense of morality.

As she poured the prescribed dosage of pain reliever into the patient's throat, the urge to choke her became almost overwhelming and she took a step backward.

Gathering the tray, she swiftly administered her last duty for the evening, pressing her lips together to hold her temper as she helped with the bedpan. Without another word she escaped the room, acutely conscious of the glowering eyes aiming darts at her retreating back. Only after the door closed behind her did she allow herself to take a deep breath.

Left alone, Amanda grinned, her eyes full of glee. Too bad, she thought. The nurse before this one was at least less composed, trembling at Amanda's venom. Well, what else could one do for entertainment? Three times a day was better than nothing. Damn! How long would she have to stay here like this, an invalid at the mercy of others? And no visitors. Brent had come earlier in the afternoon and she doubted he would be back tonight. Perhaps if she was nicer to him next time, he would come more often. Not that he was such a treat, but—

The door gently opened and a ray of hope flashed across her face. With iron self-control that would put the most talented of actresses to shame, she softened her expression and smiled.

"Hello, Amanda."

The tawny eyes widened with surprise.

"You! What are you doing here?" She swiftly recovered and surprise made way for insolent mockery. "Wait, let me guess. You missed me. You couldn't wait to rush over here, throw your arms around me, and tell me how much you love me."

The visitor viewed her dispassionately. Her eyes, cool and devoid of expression, took in the figure in the hospital bed who was held captive by sturdy white casts that left only her hands bare.

Yet if the discomfort appeared devastating, Amanda's feral eyes showed no defeat. They spurned sympathy and spat a malice so fierce, a person with less than steel nerves would back off and seek a quick retreat. But Amanda's guest was not such a person, and she advanced toward the bed.

"Amazing," she said softly. "Some people mellow and mature as years pass. Yet you have managed to stay the same."

Amanda uttered a short unpleasant laugh.

"Admit it," she threw out. "Life was boring these past five years without someone like me to stand up to you, wasn't it? All those mealymouths you call your family wouldn't have the guts to defy you. It takes someone like me to expose you as the manipulator you really are."

"I was wrong," Louise Farraday said. "You've become more vicious and more crude."

Amanda's face flushed a hot red.

Louise moved closer still. "Pity this isn't your funeral I've come to tonight. But as you're still among us, we'd better talk."

"We're all talked out, you and I. Years ago. There's nothing more you could say that would possibly interest me." Amanda clenched her hands, pain flashing across her face at the movement.

"You're wrong again. What I have to say may very well be of great importance to you. As a matter of fact, it just may save your hide, whatever is left of it."

Louise ignored the hoarse laugh that mocked her words.

"You came back to get a divorce from Brent. Get it."

Amanda's eyes widened a second time, her expression incredulous at the older woman's blunt statement.

"Or else, what?" she sneered. The corners of her mouth curled into a snarl. "God it's exciting to watch them squirm, that precious grandson of yours and his miserable little hussy. Why, I haven't had so much fun in years!"

Amanda felt triumphant. While it was true she'd come back to get a divorce, the perverse streak in her nature could not be contained. She took malicious pleasure in playing Brent for a fool. She burst out laughing, this time genuinely amused.

"That stupid ass! He'd do anything to get rid of me. If only he knew—" She suddenly stopped.

"If he knew what, Amanda? That you want to marry Giovanni diMarco, count and heir to the Bellini fortune? That you bore him a son who can't touch a penny of all that delicious wealth unless he is legitimate? And you can't stand being an outsider, his mistress to be precise, knowing you could have it all?"

Louise's voice cut through her and she flinched, again amazed at the woman's sources and the thoroughness of the details she had acquired. Always had. What power money had, she thought bitterly.

"So what? It wouldn't change the situation one bit. He wants to marry me, he loves me," she lashed back, yet instinctively she knew there was more, and suddenly she was afraid.

"Perhaps not. But it would make a world of difference to his mother, Contessa Francesca, who I hear is a strong-willed woman and a most proper one in her own right. And *very* Roman Catholic. Now if she were to find out that you're a married woman—and I presume she doesn't know—*yet* . . ." A flicker in Amanda's eyes confirmed her suspicion, and Louise smiled, and calmly continued, ". . . she would, and could, put a stop to the marriage. Which would leave you in the Adriatic cold, wouldn't it?"

A spark of satisfaction crossed over Louise's face as Amanda's eyes narrowed to slits.

"That's really why you came back, isn't it? This New Year's Eve, at the stroke of midnight, Giovanni diMarco legally inherits the Bellini millions. Should he marry after that, his new wife would not get to share his fortune, bound by a rigid prenuptial agreement. Any illegitimate offspring would be cut off as well." Louise paused, waiting for the impact of her words to sink in.

"Your time is up, Amanda. You've had your fun. Now play your cards right, and be a countess by Christmas."

"You fucking bitch. Why should I trust you?" Amanda snarled, her face contorted. "What prevents you from contacting Francesca as soon as Brent has his divorce?"

"You have my word."

"Your word, my ass. You don't even know the meaning of honor."

"You'll just have to trust me, won't you?" Louise looked at her with contempt. "Oh, and one more thing. You will sign a legal document relinquishing your rights, legal and natural, to Brent's children. All of it. You won't see them, talk to them, or have anything to do with them, ever."

"My God, you will stop at nothing."

"Not where my family's happiness and welfare are concerned." Louise flinched suddenly and the color left her twisted face. Her hands grabbed the railing of the bed, holding on until her knuckles turned white.

Amanda pretended not to notice. "Your family? These are *my* children you're talking about, *my* family."

Louise relaxed slightly. The pain had passed and she took a deep breath, her face still ashen.

"Come off it, you miserable fool," she said sharply. "You don't give a damn about *your* children. If you did, you would've been here to raise them all these years. Face it, Amanda, admit it to yourself, you're nothing but a common slut." She flinched again, weaving against the foot of the bed. After a brief moment she looked up, searching for the bathroom.

"Excuse me," she mumbled and hobbled toward the bathroom door in the corner of the room.

Amanda silently watched her go. Anger and rebellion battled in her eyes until they were an almost bright green. Her fingers clenched and unclenched and she welcomed the pain that racked her broken body as she moved them.

The pale gold Mercedes tore into the parking lot across from the hospital, tires screeching as it pulled into an empty spot. The redhead behind the steering wheel leaned back, for a moment, her eyes closed, her hands gripping the wheel hard, trying to stop the shaking.

Oh, God, give me strength, she silently mouthed, *make the trembling stop. If not for me, for Brent, for the children. I must make her understand, make her see how needless all of this is. All their suffering, what can she possibly gain by it? It's so senseless, absurd. And the children, why must they be victims to the whims of adults? It's not fair.*

Fair. A beautiful word. Yet somehow meaningless. For almost a year people had called her Amanda, and now that she believed it to be her name, the nightmare had returned. She was back in that hospital bed at Barrington Memorial— nameless, a nobody. The family she had come to love and cherish were total strangers.

But even as a nameless nobody, how could she suddenly stop loving those who had become part of her life? It wasn't as simple as switching an on and off button. She had not chosen to come into their lives, just as she now had no choice but to cut herself off from them, for their sake.

Wiping the tears off her face, she resolutely opened the car door and walked toward the hospital.

Still fuming at Louise, Amanda glared at her double, her mood suddenly revived at her unexpected appearance. There was only one reason why the twit could be here, and it was not compassion or concern over her condition, of that she was sure. Why, the evening could become interesting after all, she thought, smiling.

Misled by her smile, her visitor took a deep breath and approached the bed.

"Well, well, look who we have here," Amanda drawled. "To what do I owe the honor of your visit, impostor?"

Her visitor cringed visibly. *Impostor.* The connotation was downright criminal, and staring at the immobile woman in the hospital bed, she suddenly felt soiled and branded. To be a carbon copy of this horrible creature was degrading, sickening . . .

"I've come to make you a deal." She felt her throat tighten as the woman in the bed laughed. Her blood pounded against her temples, the buzzing in her ears intensified, but she stood rigid, willing herself not to waver.

"A deal, eh?" Amanda mocked. "One I can't refuse, no doubt. Let me see. You want to go on sleeping with my husband and he'll make sure the doctors here won't break whatever is left of me. Am I right?"

"I want you to let him go. Release him, and the children."

Amanda looked at her in disbelief.

"That's it? Release him? Is that what he told you, that I'm holding him?"

"Give him the divorce he wants, Amanda. Can't you see how unhappy he is?"

"Ah, divorce. So he won't sleep with you until he's a free man. How honorable. And what a crock of shit. Can't you see that's his excuse to get rid of you?"

"Stop it! We're not talking about me—" She stopped, realizing she had raised her voice. "You must've loved him once; please, don't let him suffer like this. And the children, *your* children, don't you at least care about them? They're innocent victims of your whims. If not for his sake, set him free for theirs."

"Bravo, bravo! Forgive me for not applauding, you're utterly superb. No wonder he fell for you."

"Will you do it?"

"You said a deal. So far I haven't heard the trade-off."

"Set him free and I will go away."

"For good?"

"Yes."

Amanda bit her lip to suppress her amusement.

"You will never see him again. Nor the children," she repeated.

"Never. You have my word."

Her face was now pale, but Amanda did not seem to notice.

"You idiot, you stupid little tart! Do you think I'm fool enough to fall for your half-assed tricks? It's my body that's broken, not my brains," she snarled, her eyes spitting fury and contempt. "I'll tell you what I think of your deal—it sucks. Get your ass out of here or I'll have you thrown out. If ever I would agree to a divorce, it's over my dead body!" She was almost hysterical, foam forming around the corners of her mouth.

Her visitor held herself very still, afraid she'd retch.

"I've wondered why people I thought were my friends disliked me. Now I know. They thought I was you," she said, heading for the door. With her hand on the handle she glanced at the woman in the bed one more time. "You've trapped yourself, Amanda. You'll never have him, but as long as you're married to him, you're not free, either. So, yes, I do think you're a fool."

"Get out!" Amanda screeched. "Just get the hell out!"

But she was alone. The door had closed softly.

Louise opened her eyes and looked at herself in the mirror. The painkiller was starting to work, the pain had ebbed away and she could breathe normally now. Slowly she opened the bathroom door as she heard voices inside the room. For a moment she stood motionless and was about to retreat, when she recognized the second voice. As the minutes passed she lost any feeling of guilt for eavesdropping. Cold anger built and her hand clutched the door handle. When she finally heard the door close behind the exiting visitor, she re-entered the room.

Her eyes were hard as she scanned Amanda's face, contorted with rage.

"Well? You heard. That's my final word on the subject. Screw diMarco and his fucking mother. Right now I've got Brent by the balls and I'll enjoy squeezing them, each and every inch of them. That son of a bitch. Too yellow to come himself, is he? I'll make his life miserable, if it's the last thing I do." She laughed harshly. Louise squinted at the horrible sound, disgust threatening to overcome her. "Why should I risk everything by throwing him over? I can't trust you any more than I can trust Francesca. But I still have Brent. At least with him I can have all the money I want and have a fantastic time watching him suffer and knowing you can't do a fucking thing about it!" She suddenly choked. Her breath came in rasps and her eyes bulged out of their sockets. Louise did not move, dispassionately watching her gasp for air, the grabbing fingers clutching the sheets.

"H-help . . . call the nur—"

Louise finally moved, slowly, alongside the bed and approached the choking woman. She took the pillow from under Amanda's head and looked at her for a moment. Then, firmly, deliberately, she placed the pillow over her head and held it there until the smothered gasps subsided and the clenched fingers relaxed their grip.

She ran through the parking lot, the clicking of her heels echoing in the night. God, she had failed. Miserably. What a fool she was to think, to hope, that the woman would be capable of compassion.

What was it Brent had said last night? "It's easier to reason with a rattlesnake than get through to her." She had not believed him. She could not believe that a mother—any kind of a mother—would rationally sacrifice her own children for the sake of self-indulgence. And how anyone could possibly thrive on the unhappiness of a broken marriage was totally beyond her.

She reached her car and fumbled inside her pockets for the keys. Oh, God, she wanted to scream. She must have left her handbag in the hospital room. With her keys in it. She closed her eyes and groaned. Finally, she bit her lip and slowly began to walk back toward the hospital.

Gently opening the door, she peeked in. The room was quiet. She took a deep breath. Maybe the bitch was asleep. She quietly slipped inside and gasped.

A woman stood bent over the bed, and as she straightened her back, she recognized her. Louise whirled around, the pillow still in her hands. Their eyes locked for a long moment and a sudden calm came over her.

Noiselessly closing the door, she slowly approached the

bed. The patient's face looked peaceful, relaxed, as if in deep sleep. For a moment she watched her, motionless, expecting Amanda to open her mouth at any minute and hurl insults at her. But none came and the sheets that covered her up to her chin remained very still.

Louise's eyes fell on the handbag on the chair. She reached to pick it up and slowly handed it to the younger woman, who, still stunned by the scene before her, remained motionless.

"I believe this is yours?" she said softly.

Chapter 44

THE MERCEDES SHARPLY TURNED INTO THE DRIVEWAY and came to a screeching halt in front of the three-car garage. For a moment the driver just sat there, her hands still gripped around the steering wheel, her body shaking.

She did not know how she had made it back to the Willses' nor how she had even made it to the car. Her mind was numb, yet she felt a calm she had not known for months. But there was no triumph, no joy. Only relief that it was all over, the torment, the needless suffering. They were free—Brent, Mandy, Josh, and yes, even she. She was no longer anyone's double, no longer a clone.

Yet, ironically, she felt a void, a sadness she could not quite explain. It was almost as if she had lost someone she had been close to. *But that's absurd,* she thought. *I've hated that woman, resented her presence, wished her gone—why would I mourn her loss?*

She closed her eyes, her hands gripping the steering wheel even tighter. The vision returned—the vision of Louise holding the pillow that had ended it all.

They had walked out of the hospital together, and as Holcomb, her chauffeur, rushed out to get the limousine, Louise had finally turned to her, and their eyes had locked again.

"Go home, child." Louise's kiss had been warm and gentle.

"Go in peace and rest well tonight. A good night's sleep never fails to chase away the ghosts of a nightmare."

Helped by Holcomb, she had disappeared into the limousine and vanished into the night.

Amanda took a deep breath. *Why, she did it for me, for Brent, for all of us, but also for me.* A shiver ran along her spine and she opened her eyes, bewildered at the sudden awakening.

She had always known that Louise was capable of almost anything to protect her interests, and her family, but tonight she had understood to what ends she would go. The knowledge was chilling, yet at the same time it made her feel safe. She took another deep breath, and another one, and another one, filling her lungs as if to make sure she was alive. Quickly opening the car door, she stepped out and walked toward the house.

As she unlocked the front door, she could hear voices.

"That must be her, now." Karen came from the family room to greet her, a smile of relief on her face. "Thank God you're home. We were worried sick about you—do you know what time it is?"

"I'm sorry, I should've called," Amanda mumbled.

"Are you all right?" Karen scanned the pale face, frowning. Amanda nodded.

"Come on, Karen, can't you see she's dead tired? Come, Manda, let me get you a stiff drink. You look like you could use one." Daryl walked toward the bar and fumbled inside the cabinet.

She let herself be dragged into the family room, grateful they did not ask her any more questions. In the sparse light she did not notice the figure of a man seated in a corner chair, almost hidden by the huge plant Karen had placed at the end of the room. He rose as she entered, his mouth open, disbelief in his eyes.

"Samantha?"

Amanda jumped and stared at the stranger with fear in her eyes.

"My God, Samantha! It *is* you!"

They all gaped at him now; Daryl's hand stayed around the bottle of Rémy Martin, the two women merely stared. The man slowly walked toward them, limping slightly, and stopped in front of Amanda, gawking at her as if she were an apparition.

"Jesus, I can't believe it, it's really you!" He shook his head, the astonishment in his dark eyes suddenly turning to anger.

"They told me you were dead. Why did you let them believe that? Why didn't you come forward and tell them you were alive? Why, Samantha, why?" He took a step forward and Amanda instinctively shrank from his reach.

Her head reeled. *Oh, no, not again,* she silently pleaded. *I've just come out of this nightmare, please God, don't drag me into another one* . . .

"Do . . . do we know . . . each other?" she whispered.

His anger frightened her and his accusations confused her. Who the hell was this man? She racked her brain, but she was certain she had never seen him before. Yet his presence made her uneasy. He obviously mistook her for someone else . . . or did he? Suddenly she shivered, a cold dread taking hold of her, yet despite herself, curiosity overcame the fear. She swallowed hard and took a long, deep breath, her heart pounding in her throat.

"Who . . . who are you?" Her voice trembled audibly. But the stranger had heard the question and a look of contempt seeped into his eyes.

"Don't toy with me, Sam, you know damn well who I am. You can drop the charade, it doesn't become you." He frowned impatiently. "If you wanted your freedom, why didn't you just say so? You've never before taken to dramatics and deception. I must say, it's out of character, you've always been such a fighter. Why did you do it?"

Amanda slowly shook her head. Her mind was numb and she felt woozy.

"Humor me," she whispered weakly, "tell me who you are."

The man's face froze. He slowly straightened his tall body, and Amanda forced herself not to back away again, trembling inside as she watched the ominous figure before her take a deep breath.

"I'm your husband," he said.

The sound of breaking glass cut through the deadly silence. Karen gasped. His face beet-red, Daryl mumbled an apology for his clumsiness and went to get the vacuum cleaner.

Amanda felt the room spin and she raised her hand as if to shield herself from the stranger, to erase the impact of his words.

Karen helplessly turned to her husband, her startled eyes pleading. As if this were his cue, Daryl regained his composure, and clearing his throat, he swiftly moved toward the motionless Amanda and put his arm around her rigid shoulders.

"I'm sure there must be a mistake." He laughed nervously. "I'm sorry, I should've done this ages ago. Amanda, this is my buddy from past Vietnam days, Dr. Brandon Farley, Beau for short. And this is Amanda Farraday, my sister-in-law." He looked at his friend triumphantly, but Farley did not move, never taking his eyes off Amanda's ashen face. "So you see, she's not who you think she is, my friend. I'm sorry to have to disappoint you, but she really is not your wife."

For a moment the man called Beau kept staring at Amanda, and if it had not been for Daryl's strong support, she would have slumped to the floor. Finally, he spoke.

"So you call yourself Amanda now." His voice was soft. "What did you do? Seduce this Farraday into marrying you? I don't know about this state, but in California it's labeled bigamy and punishable by law."

"Now wait a minute, Beau," Daryl protested.

"Wait! Stop it." Amanda tore herself loose from Daryl's protective embrace. "Can't we all sit down and talk this over like civilized adults?" Without waiting for a reply, she moved toward the sofa. "You know, Daryl," she said, "I guess I would like that drink now."

"Dr. Farley, what makes you so sure that I am . . . ah . . . your wi—ah . . . Samantha?" Amanda swallowed the cognac too quickly and she almost gagged.

"Nobody could look like Samantha and not be her."

Daryl choked on his Scotch and coughed. Despite herself, Amanda smiled. If only he knew, she thought bitterly.

"But you don't know for sure, do you?" she asked softly.

Beau Farley frowned. Amazing, Amanda thought, struck by the resemblance. The features were different, but in many ways he reminded her of Brent; the same height, the same slimness, the same blond wavy hair, the lean aristocratic face, and yes, the same arrogance. Only Beau was more handsome. His mouth, on the other hand, had a crueler twist, and the look in his eyes was cold.

"Of course I'm sure," he said, emptying his glass. "How long are you going to keep playing this silly game? Damn it, Samantha, I'm not amused and if there's any decency left in you—"

"I'm not playing a game. Please bear with me."

At that moment, Daryl quickly intervened.

"What she's trying to say, Beau, is that she does not remember."

He described the accident briefly, and when he finished, Beau's expression was once more incredulous. The anger had abated, and when he finally spoke, his voice was almost gentle.

"Well, that makes things easier all around, doesn't it? Since you're not legally married to Farraday, you can come home with me now."

"No!" At Amanda's sharp protest, his frown deepened. At his searching gaze, she blushed profusely.

"I mean . . . I can't just . . . walk away—"

"Walk away from what? A surrogate family? A man who's your double's husband, children who are not yours? It's over, Sam, face it. You're back in the real world now, and the reality is that you're my wife and I'm taking you back with me to California."

She shook her head, wringing her hands. "Surrogate or not, I love them. They're my family. For a whole year I've known nothing but them. I can't switch my feelings on and off just because you—" She suddenly straightened, her eyes widening. "Besides, how do I know that you *are* my husband, or that you're telling the truth, for that matter?"

Farley's lip curled. "Why would I make that up?" He frowned, annoyance flashing in his eyes.

"I don't know. But you could, couldn't you? We only have your word and I can't dispute you." She looked almost triumphant, yet she was trembling inside.

"I can prove it," he said softly. It sounded like a threat and she shivered.

"She's right, Beau," Daryl intervened. "Without proof your word is but another fairy tale. She's entitled to that much, don't you think?" He glanced at Karen and they both knew he was merely buying time. The man was far from deranged and who in his right mind would walk up to a strange woman and claim her as his wife, for Christ's sake?

Amanda stirred, her heart still pounding. She had a splitting headache and the cognac didn't help.

"You said we were living in California. What was I doing here?" she asked.

"It's a long story," he said turning away and picking up the empty glass.

"Tell me, I want to hear it."

"No. Airing our dirty laundry in public is not my style." His curt voice carried a note of finality. Amanda opened her mouth to protest, but he raised his hand and cut her short. "I said I would come up with proof that you're my wife. That's enough for now." He took a sip of cognac and looked at Daryl. "You said her double is this man's wife. What's with her? Where is she?"

Daryl briefed him, leaving out the details. "As a matter of fact, we'd better call Brent over here now," he said.

"No!" Amanda raised her hand, her pale face turning a shade paler still. "Please, Daryl, not yet. Let's first have Beau prove that I . . . that I . . . am who he says I am. There'll be time enough after that." By that time we'll all know that the real Amanda is dead, she thought. It would make things much easier. She sighed. One problem in exchange for another. Was there no end to her suffering?

"There is someone else who can identify you as well as I can," Farley said and took another sip. "I'll send him to you."

"Who?"

He smiled and shook his head. "All in due time, my dear. Have no fear. You *are* my wife and I will have you come home with me, take my word for it. Two weeks. That should give you enough time to say good-bye to that family of yours."

In the silence that followed his threat, the telephone rang. It was Brent calling from Mt. Sinai Hospital.

Chapter 45

THE MEMORIAL SERVICE WAS BRIEF. THE LITTLE CHAPEL of the elegant Lake Forest Funeral Home was packed with mourners, as the minister droned his eulogy with the solemn respect that was expected of him. In life, Amanda Farraday had achieved notoriety through a frivolous lifestyle; in death she drew an even bigger crowd, admirers and enemies alike.

Those who had liked her and enjoyed her dazzling company had come to reminisce the good old times. Then there were those who had come to pay their respects to Brent. There were also some who had chosen to attend for the sake of satisfaction that she could no longer do them harm. But more likely than not, most of the mourners were there to see Amanda's replacement, the double who was said to have fooled even Farraday's closest friends.

Seated in the first row was the Farraday clan, all dressed properly in black. As Samantha sat listening to the minister's dispassionate words of comfort, her eyes demurely lowered behind a black veil, she wondered at the sadness that enveloped her. She felt a sense of loss, a void that puzzled her, almost as if she regretted the dead woman's fate. Could it be because they had been so identical in looks? At least on the surface. In a way it was like seeing herself in that coffin . . . She shook her head—what was she saying—there was no body in the coffin . . .

Samantha felt Brent's eyes on her and she stirred. The minister's voice droned on. Now and then someone coughed; a light rustle, a shuffling here and there. The hushed atmosphere began to stifle her, and she was well aware of the covert glances thrown in her direction.

She suddenly remembered Beau Farley and closed her eyes. Why did he have to show up now? Why, when finally, after an eternity of torment and suffering, she was free—yes, free—to marry Brent and really belong to him, to the children, to his family—why did he have to ruin it all? Such lousy timing indeed . . . or was it? She would have committed bigamy, and wouldn't that have been even more messy in the end? Perhaps she should be grateful that he showed up when he did. Not that it made her life any easier . . .

A rustling noise broke the silence as her surroundings came back to life. Voices all around began to speak in hushed tones. The service was over and people rose. The Farradays moved to the door to shake hands and express their thanks to those who had come. They were soon joined by Paula.

"I can't believe how many attended her memorial. Most of them hated her guts, especially the women," Paula observed, keeping her husky voice low. Samantha did not reply, her eyes seeking Louise, who stood opposite Brent by the door, her frail figure erect and steady. A feeling of awe and renewed respect came over her.

There had been no inquest, no whisper of suspicion. A night nurse had discovered the dead patient and the doctor had pronounced the cause of death to be heart failure. The next day Louise had ordered the body cremated, and her grandson had not voiced any objections.

"Samantha?"

She recognized the name now, still, she did not respond, staring silently at the tall stranger in the dark navy suit. His eyes were a striking deep blue; even more striking was the warmth and affection in them as he looked at her.

"Beau Farley told me I would find you here." He remained a couple of steps away from her and made no move to come any closer.

She braced herself. First a surprise husband, now this

stranger who eyed her with a love and tenderness he did not attempt to hide.

"I'm Peter Haydon. Your brother." He smiled an easy, almost lazy smile. "That is, if you are my sister Samantha."

Her heart skipped a beat. Did he say *brother*? *Brother*? She did not know whether to laugh or to cry. *Oh my God.* A sob welled up and caught in her throat. *I'm not alone, I have a brother.*

"Honey, are you—" Brent broke off when he saw her odd expression, and noticing the stranger, his eyes took on a cold glare.

"Is he . . . ?"

"He says his name is Peter—" she whispered hoarsely.

"Peter Haydon," the stranger confirmed.

"—and that he's—he's my . . . my brother . . ."

The two men stared at each other for a moment, neither of them moving. Then Brent held out his hand and smiled.

"Hi, I'm Brent Farraday, Amanda's hus—" He swallowed, and the three of them knew he was not thinking of the deceased woman.

Still, she did not move. She wanted badly to rush to this stranger and claim him as the brother he said he was. He seemed nice, and so gentle; there was a calm about him that drew her instantly, something special that stilled her fears. She wanted to touch him. But she remained where she was and merely stared.

"I'm sorry, I know this is a bad time, but I just had to see you. See for myself that you were . . ." Peter Haydon swallowed, forcing a smile and failing. "Alive. Really alive." He blinked a couple of times. "Perhaps I'd better go now." He turned to Brent, hesitating a moment. "I suppose I should offer you my sympathies, Dr. Farraday?"

Brent did not smile; an odd gleam ignited in his solemn eyes.

"For the death of my wife or the loss of my beloved?" he asked wryly.

Peter shook his head, his smile forming easily this time.

"If you really love her, nothing is lost. Love is a state of mind, not a possession. No legal boundaries have ever been known to sever such a bond, my friend."

For a moment, Brent gaped, taken aback by the unexpected support. Then, slowly, he relaxed and nodded.

Running feet of children approached them and Josh flung himself into her arms.

"Mommy, Mommy, I looked all over for you." He sounded almost hysterical and Samantha instantly held him in a protective embrace and kissed him. Mandy clung to her too, sobbing.

"We thought you'd left us again," she cried.

With her eyes still on the man who claimed to be her brother, Samantha held the girl close, unable to say the reassuring words she needed to hear. Her eyes brimmed and she kept kissing both children, identifying with their fears, and despair filled her.

"We'll be having dinner with some friends tonight. Would you like to join us?" Brent asked Peter. Samantha shot him a grateful look and led the children out of earshot.

She knew Peter would come. She also knew the evening would reveal a past she was not sure she was anxious to rush back to.

Of course, Peter had come, despite her last-minute fears that her instincts were wrong.

As usual, Paula had outdone herself and they all enjoyed the succulent roast, except for Samantha, who merely picked at her food. The conversation, strained at first, began to loosen up after the second bottle of wine, and Brent managed to keep the tone light, while Paula provided the necessary laughter. Then, just after they had finished dinner, the doorbell rang, and in walked Karen and Daryl.

"Peter! Peter Haydon!" Daryl exclaimed, grinning happily, and Peter grinned back. "Why, you son of a bitch, you. I thought you'd gone back East, New York or Boston."

"I did, but New York didn't like me, so I came back."

"Without telling me?"

"I was in Minneapolis for a while, but then the company moved their headquarters to Oak Brook, and here I am."

Daryl turned to the others. "Peter and I were in the same squadron in Vietnam. We shared everything, didn't we, buddy? Even the women." He grinned at Karen, who stuck out her tongue at him.

"With Beau?" Samantha bit her tongue; it just slipped out and she turned red. But Brent put his arm around her waist as though to reassure her that he understood.

"Yeah, him, too."

"That's how you two met, through me," Peter said, smiling at her.

For the next hour, the two friends acquainted the rest of the group with their experiences, leaving out the gory details and making the war sound like a college picnic.

Curled up in Brent's protective arms, Samantha watched her newfound brother, and somehow she no longer felt as devastated as earlier in the day. Things were looking up; she was finally piecing her own life together, and with a gentle brother like Peter, it could not have been such a disaster after all.

"Your name is Samantha Elizabeth Haydon. You're twenty-nine years old, your birthday is May seventeenth. You were married at the age of nineteen to Dr. Beau Farley and lived in Orange County, California, until your separation six months before your accident here."

Peter paused and took a sip of his brandy, looking at the woman in the tall blond man's arms.

"Sorry, I just remembered something," he said with a chuckle. "Mother almost named you Isabel, after some Spanish queen she'd read about. But Dad called you Jezebel by mistake, and that was the end of that. You became Samantha."

"Of course, it would've been silly to name her Isabel," Karen mused. Then, as six pairs of eyes fixed on her, she blushed. "Not when her middle name is Elizabeth. Why, everyone knows that Isabel and Elizabeth are one and the same name, same roots, same meaning . . . you know . . ." She lifted her chin in defiance and pouted her lips. "Like Hans and John and Ian, they're one and the same, too. Used in different countries, perhaps, still, they're the same." At the lack of response, she shrugged. "Oh, all right. I've been reading up on babies' names, okay?"

"Amazing," Brent murmured, absentmindedly stroking his lover's coppery curls. "Truly incredible. Isabel was Amanda's first name; she was named after Chet's mother. But in high school she decided that her middle name suited her better, and I never knew her otherwise." He reached inside his jacket and took out a cigarette. "Oh, ah . . . Amanda's birthday was May seventeenth . . ." He cocked his head, his eyes on Peter. "Are you sure you don't have another sister?"

Peter shook his head and leaned back in his chair. "But that doesn't mean Samantha doesn't," he said.

Samantha sat up, her heart pounding again. "What do you mean?"

"My parents had three boys and my mother pined for a little girl, but the doctors advised against having another baby. So they took the alternate route. You, Samantha, are my adopted sister."

A hush fell. No one spoke. She could hear a loud buzzing in her ears and the room began to spin. Then Brent's arms went around her and she clung to him, drawing from his strength to remain calm. *No,* she screamed silently, *oh, no! Amanda, my twin sister? Could it be?*

"We'll call Jed Hartley tomorrow." Brent kissed her reassuringly and tightened his arms around her. "It's possible Amanda was not Chet's natural daughter. The question never came up. But we'll find out soon enough."

She nodded, then turned back to Peter. "You said earlier that . . . that we . . . Beau and I were separated. Why? What was wrong with our marriage?" *How strange,* she thought, *I accused Beau of conjuring up his story, yet I take Peter's word that he's my brother and I'm the Samantha they're both talking about. How do I know that this man is indeed my brother?*

"You were having problems, and when Beau got that promotion he'd been working on for years, he moved to Pasadena, to be closer to his job." Peter paused, his eyes on Samantha. "He moved alone. You refused to go with him. That was six months before you came here."

"Do I . . . are there any children from this . . . marriage?" Samantha held her breath.

"No. Beau never wanted any. He said his job was too dangerous to have kids."

"Dangerous? Didn't you say he is a doctor?" Brent frowned.

"Not like you. Science. And a damn good one. He is connected to NASA, and the last I heard, considered quite indispensable."

"Amazing," Brent said again, shaking his head.

"What was she, Samantha, doing? I mean, what was her profession?" Karen put in.

Daryl looked at his wife with surprise. It wasn't like Karen to be blustering, but she too was excited. And she had asked the question on a hunch.

"She ran her own business called *Les Mirages*—"

"I knew it! I knew it!" Karen jumped out of her chair. "An interior decorator. She and Amanda have the same talents. There's no question about it, they must be twins, identical twins."

"How did you know about *Les Mirages?*" Paula gaped at her.

Karen blushed. "I read an article about it a while back. It was, still is, I think, one of the most fashionable interior decorating firms on the West Coast. Pretty impressive, if I may say so."

"Amazing," Brent repeated.

Samantha leaned back against him, her mind in a whirl, and closed her eyes. The pieces were all falling into place, one by one. The exquisite decor of Amanda's house, the attraction to the same type of man, her instant attraction to the same friend. And she suddenly understood why she could play that grand piano in Brent's house with such precision.

"Beau mentioned proof." Samantha's eyes flew open and Peter smiled at her. "When we were children, I accidentally left a mark on you, with a Swiss army knife. You should have a scar on your left calf. Mother nearly killed me when she saw all that blood."

Samantha sat very still; then, slowly, she rose and, ignoring the stares around her, lifted her skirt and lowered her pantyhose. On her left calf, just below the crease in back of her knee, was a scar, small, almost invisible, in the shape of a half crescent. She had not even known it was there.

She stared into the darkness of the bedroom, listening to Brent's steady breathing next to her. Just half an hour ago she had been exhausted, falling over her own feet and barely able to change into a nightgown. Yet here she lay, wide-eyed and tense.

Brent had insisted that she come home with him after the funeral and Louise had supported his decision. The children had clasped her hands as though afraid she would leave them again. Too tired to argue with them she had given in, only because she had needed her family as much as they needed her. Once back in the house she had known as home, part of the strain had lifted and she was glad to see Mrs. Flynn and Amparo, and Kavik, who wagged his tail, barking and jumping against her and licking her face.

Her thoughts wandered to the events of the evening, to Peter and the scar behind her knee. She relived her elation at the revelation of her past. A past that had her linked to a husband she did not recognize and a life she did not recall.

What a strange coincidence, she thought, wearily, that the husband should so closely resemble the man she had come to love the past year. But was it coincidence? Suppose she had loved this man, this husband—if he indeed was her husband—could it then be that Brent had triggered a subconscious memory and she had fallen in love with him because of it?

She sighed and turned her head to look at the alarm clock on her nightstand. One-fifteen in the morning. Better go to sleep, Amanda—no, Samantha—nice name, she liked it. She closed her eyes and tried to clear her mind, but more images flashed and the darkness no longer mattered.

Samantha Farley. She had an identity now, not one she remembered, but still, an identity. She was no longer a surrogate, the shadow of another woman, but her own person. Farley, Farley . . . where had she heard that name before? She racked her brain, searching through her present memory—and came up with nothing. She moved her right leg and stretched her arm, careful not to awaken the sleeping man beside her. Her wrist caught in her pillowcase and she tried to yank loose the bracelet. She cursed silently, then smiled.

This morning at the funeral, Lady Madeline had presented her with another bracelet, one that Amanda had accidentally left at her home in London the year before her disappearance. Her mother-in-law had forgotten all about it until last week when she had frantically been looking for an old heirloom necklace and found both pieces in a leather pouch that had fallen behind her jewelry box. Good old Madeline. She genuinely liked her, and she knew the feeling was mutual.

Her eyes suddenly flew open and she abruptly turned around in the bed, her jerky movement causing Brent to stir. That young woman in Cartier who sold her the bracelet—she had called her Mrs. *Farley*! And written out the receipt in that name. Of course. It had not been a mistake, the woman had recognized her as Samantha Farley!

She shivered and took a deep breath. She would call Peter tomorrow and ask him all about herself and her past. And suddenly she did not feel so bad about being Samantha Farley anymore. If only there hadn't been a *Mr.* Farley attached to this new self . . .

Chapter 46

IT WAS ALL THERE. THE MARRIAGE CERTIFICATE, THE wedding pictures, the zillion photographs and snapshots of their lives together—Samantha and Beau, Samantha with people she did not know, Beau among people he said were their friends, Samantha laughing, Beau grinning, a couple of them with Peter. Even newspaper clippings of Beau's career, Beau's promotion, Beau's society successes, and two of Samantha at the opening of *Les Mirages,* and one of Beau and Samantha shaking hands with the mayor of Los Angeles during the 1984 Olympic Games.

Going through the stack, Samantha's spirits sank to an all-time low, and halfway through it she threw the unseen bunch back into the box and buried her head in her hands, shaking. The color had left her face and her lips appeared bloodless.

A little more than a week had passed since that night at the Willses'—and she was still numb. Each morning she woke up hoping that it had all been a nightmare; each morning she knew she was one day closer to saying good-bye to the people she had come to love. She had lost weight, the dark circles under her eyes had deepened, and depression was rapidly setting in.

She felt trapped. Louise had offered to talk to Beau, but he had refused to meet with her. Or with Brent for that matter. Peter had tried to reason with him, yet he had stood his ground, adamant about remaining detached from her new life and the people in it.

He was also determined to take her back to Pasadena by the end of that week. When Samantha told him that he could not take her with him against her will, he had blown his stack.

"You owe me!" he had yelled.

"Owe you what? For not being dead?" she had retorted.

"For this . . ." He stuck out his injured leg. "Thanks to you I've got this limp. And the steel ornaments in my body—all over. And the damn pain that comes with all of that. Not to mention the agony, the humiliation, the sacrifice I've suffered!"

Samantha shuddered at his anger.

"Wha . . . what are you talking about . . . ?" she whispered.

Beau jumped up. "Jesus, do I have to rake it all up again?"

He began pacing the floor, in his agitation the limp more pronounced than usual.

"We went to a party that night. Somehow we wound up having an argument. A real good one, I might add. We'd both been drinking. You never could hold your liquor, but you insisted on driving us home. Actually, you'd intended to leave me behind, and I should've let you. Instead, you drove us off the road and smashed us into a tree. When the fire department dished us out of the car wreck, you were unconscious, and I was more dead than alive."

Samantha blinked in disbelief.

"Well, they sewed me back together, glued the pieces and stuck steel plates in me where the bones were too weak or gone. Afterward, all that remained noticeable was this damn limp." He took a deep breath. "God, it took me months, almost a year before I could function again. A whole year of pain, of agony. Sixteen operations they did on me. Sixteen lousy operations. And that's not all. I lost my position at NASA." He turned his head, as if to hide his expression from her. "I was working on a priority project at the time—heading it, as a matter of fact—and they couldn't wait for me to become normal again. So I got the shaft—they shoved me aside, just like that, and by the time I came back to the job, I was assigned to a menial task force."

Samantha cringed at the bitterness in his voice, and shud-

dered. God, what had she done to this man? Nobody deserved such bad luck. What was the argument about, she
wondered?

"All those years, all that work—down the drain. They gave
my position to some young punk, who'd never even known
what it was to sweat blood just thinking of potential disasters.
And there I was . . ." He looked at her, his eyes filled with
rage.

"So, you see, *my darling wife,"*—she cringed even more at
his sarcastic drawl—"you owe me. Besides, your lover would
not stand a chance in court when I tell the judge that you
killed a man during that accident."

Samantha gasped, her hand clutching at her throat. "No!"

Beau suddenly grinned, sparks in his eyes. "Well, he did
die. Although not exactly by your hand. His car was stopped
in the middle of the road. You saw him too late, swerved, and
rammed his car before running off the road. The police said
he died of a massive heart attack. But you still hit his car, and
he was still dead. And I could say that he was alive when you
hit him."

"You . . . you wouldn't . . . ," she stammered, raw horror in her eyes.

"Oh, wouldn't I?" Beau sneered. "All's fair . . ." He
laughed, a hollow sound that cut through her and made her
shudder.

He was bluffing, she told Peter, but her brother had shaken
his head and frowned. Beau was a prominent figure at NASA,
and having climbed his way back to the top, he had many
influential friends in high places. A scandal of this nature
would not be good for Brent's medical career. Not that Farley
was a malicious man, but he was used to getting his way—
and he wanted Samantha back.

"Ironic," Beau said, gesturing to the box of photographs.
"Just a month ago I put them all away. You were dead, gone,
or so I thought. It's been over a year, mind you. So I took all
these pictures and threw them in a box. I guess I had reached
the point where I had finally accepted the fact that you were
out of my life. And then—" He turned away and in that moment Brent put his arm protectively around Samantha's
shivering shoulders.

He had insisted on accompanying her today, and to Samantha's relief, Beau had not objected. But after the first five minutes she wished he had stayed away; the confrontation between the two men was nerve-wracking.

"She *is* out of your life, Farley," Brent said evenly, ignoring the glaring look. "Face it. Your marriage was fading long before Samantha left you. Dead or alive, she is no longer yours. At least not emotionally. Why can't you just let it be? Cut the bull; it's time you severed those legal ties. She no longer loves you."

"And you think she loves you?" Beau snarled. "Look at yourself, Farraday. See yourself in the mirror and tell me that she does not see me?"

Brent stiffened, forcing himself not to lose his temper. "The resemblance is coincidental, and you know it." His voice was icy, matching the look in his eyes.

"Ah, yes. I forgot. You were her twin's choice, provided your late wife was her twin."

"Why would you want to force a woman—any woman—to stay with you when you know that her heart belongs to another man? You can't possibly gather satisfaction from that, now can you?"

For a moment Beau kept silent. When he finally spoke his voice was quiet and he sounded almost sad.

"For a year I mourned her death. Now that I find her alive, do you think I would—could—let her go? Just like that? What kind of a fool do you think I am?"

"A bigger fool if you don't. She does *not* love you, Farley. Get it through that thick skull of yours. Do I have to spell it out for you?"

Beau rose to his feet, frowning furiously.

"No go, Farraday. My mind is made up. I go back West at the end of this week, and like it or not, *my* wife goes with me. And that's final." He spun around. "Now let *me* spell it out for you, friend. She is *my* wife, you hear? *Mine*, not yours. Where I go, she goes."

"Wrong." Brent's voice, though soft, was laced with deadly determination. "May I remind you that the two of you were separated at the time she left California? You were living in Pasadena, she in Orange County, remember? And—"

"Cut the crap, doctor. It won't hold up in a court of law, and you know it. The separation was physical, and temporary. No legal papers, no official signatures. Besides, we were getting back together and planning a second honeymoon."

"Your word only, with no one to back it up. Convenient." Brent lit a cigarette. "And supposing for a moment it's true— what was she doing in Chicago on that second honeymoon— alone?"

"She wanted to visit Peter. I still had a project to wrap up, so we agreed that she would go see him first." Farley spoke fast, a little too fast, Samantha thought. "Anyway, she's coming with me now and we can have that second honeymoon after all." He saw Samantha wince and turned away. "I already called my assistant. He'll cover for me while I'm gone, so we're all set."

Brent pursed his lips, his jawline as stubborn as his rival's.

"What is it with you, man? Someone took your precious toy away from you, huh?" His eyes narrowed when Farley spun around, his fists clenched and ready to swing.

"Don't fuck with me, Farraday. Big men are supposed to be good losers. And precious—yeah, you got that right. You've had your fun with my precious half, so consider yourself lucky I don't bust your balls for that."

Brent's eyes narrowed even further. "Okay, you son of a bitch, tell me why the persistence?"

"Look, I don't owe you any explanation, what more—"

"The hell you don't—"

"Stop it! Stop it, both of you!" Samantha jumped up from the sofa, startling both men. She held her hands over her ears, tears streaming down her colorless cheeks. "Does it ever occur to you that I should have some say-so in this matter? Does either of you even care about my feelings? You bitch and bicker about me like I'm sort of a . . . a toy . . . a possession, a . . . a thing. For God's sake, I'm a human being, and it may surprise you, but there's nothing wrong with my mind. This is *my* life you're talking about. If there's anyone in this universe who has a right to run my life, it's me— and only me. And right now I wish you both would leave me alone!" Sobbing, she ran out of the room.

The two men looked at each other sheepishly, neither one saying a word. The telephone in the other room rang and Peter went to answer it. Brent was the first to speak.

"She's right, you know. We are so busy thinking of ourselves, and it is really her life."

Beau opened his mouth to say something, but closed it again.

"Why don't we have her make the decision?" He noticed Beau's brooding look and waited. But his opponent did not reply. "Then, whatever decision she makes, we'll abide by it. I promise, I'll be a good loser," Brent said wryly. "Provided, of course, that that's the way it is."

Peter returned to the living room, a grave expression on his face.

"Brent? You'd better—"

Behind him Samantha burst into the room, her eyes wild with fright and her pale face now but an extension of the whiteness of her blouse.

"It's Josh," she said, sobbing. "Oh, Brent, my baby—"

Brent jumped from the sofa and dashed forward, just in time to catch her body before it slumped to the floor.

They raced to Lake Forest Medical Center in Peter's car. Peter had insisted on driving, saying that he was not as distraught as Brent, and to his surprise, even Beau had come along. In the back seat Brent was holding Samantha, who clung to him like a frightened child. She was no longer crying, but her eyes were closed and Brent knew she was praying. She always prayed when she was scared.

How ironic, he thought, Amanda would not have reacted this way. And here was this woman, praying for a child who was not hers and hurting as though he were her own. He closed his eyes for a moment; he somehow could not imagine a life without her. And what about the children? They only knew one mother. It had been hard raising them without one, but it would be even harder if she were to leave them now.

Peter maneuvered the car expertly through the traffic, reducing speed a little as they came off the ramp. Paula had sounded harried, saying only that there had been an accident. And something about a bike.

A bike! Brent tensed. He knew it, he should have bought the boy a new bike months ago, or at least had the old one repaired properly until he had time to shop for a new one. But he had been so busy lately and with all that was happening, so quickly, one thing after another . . . Damn. There were no excuses for his negligence. He should have paid more attention to his children's needs, regardless. He had nobody else to blame but himself and—

The car screeched around the curve and came to an abrupt halt in front of the emergency entrance. They rushed inside and a hysterical Paula flung herself into Samantha's arms. Matt briefed Brent on the accident.

Josh and three neighbor boys his age had been biking— racing up and down the street, using the cul-de-sac as their main target point. Matt and Paula had taken turns to now and then pop outside to check on them, and make sure they were not leaving the safety of their quiet street.

Neither of them had been present when it happened, but one of the boys had run inside and cried for help. An unknown car had driven into the street at unlawful speed, startling the boys. They had been lucky, directing their bikes into nearby driveways, but Josh's front tire had hit a sharp edge and he had slipped and hit his head hard against the edge of the curb. When Matt reached him the boy was unconscious, his head in a pool of blood. The driver had taken off in a hurry.

The doors of the operating room opened and a drenched surgeon walked out removing his cap and gloves. His eyes lit up when he saw Brent.

"Hello, Brent. That tiger cub of yours is some fighter, good strong stock." He shook Brent's hand.

"Does that mean he'll be all right? No internal damage?" Relief surged through him, but he was still worried. Ian Macauley was one of the best trauma surgeons in the state. Josh must have been in pretty bad shape for the hospital to call on someone of his caliber.

"Everything is fine, nothing broken. He was lucky, an inch off and his skull could've cracked." He smiled. "I wasn't paged, I was actually on duty here. No, no," he said, grinning, "I didn't kill anyone or do anything ghoulish. My younger brother had emergency duty tonight and that son of a bitch came down with some exotic flu, so I volunteered, just for today and tonight. I must admit it's quite a change from a regular trauma center."

Samantha had come closer and Brent instantly put his arm around her. She had listened to the explanation and not quite understood.

"Is he . . . my . . . ?" Her face was still pale, the fear in her eyes bordering on hysteria.

"Your son is fine, Mrs. Farraday. A couple of days and he'll be able to show off his twenty-two stitches to his schoolmates. No broken bones, no internal injuries. A clean, simple wound, that's all. It'll leave a scar on his forehead, but it's close enough to the skull, and with the hair your youngster has, he'll have to show it to you before you can see it."

He gave her his most reassuring smile, thinking how strikingly beautiful her eyes were, and she for that matter. Beautiful and attractive, not to mention sexy. A rare combination. And such courage. Any other woman would've been hysterical, crying and wailing. This one wept silently.

"Can I . . . can I see him . . . ?" She tried to swallow her tears.

"All in due time, my dear lady, all in due time. He's resting comfortably now, but as soon as he's out of danger, we'll call you. No, no, nothing serious, just routine. Just monitoring."

He looked at Brent and Brent nodded.

"Thanks, Ian. I owe you one."

"Yeah, yeah." He waved and grinned and walked away.

"He's one of the best, honey. Josh was real lucky to get him. Come on, I'll buy you a cup of coffee." He kissed her and led her in the direction of the visitors' lounge.

Paula and Matt silently followed them, while Peter rushed back to the emergency entrance where he had left his car. From the nurse's station Beau watched Samantha walk away, her eyes clinging to Brent's. They had all forgotten about him.

Chapter 47

IAN MACAULEY WAS AS GOOD AS HIS WORD—JOSH WAS released from the hospital before his family had time to really miss him, and by the end of the week—much to his chagrin, and Kavik's—he was pronounced fit enough to go back to school.

To Samantha and Brent it was more than just Josh's lucky break, or the fact that his brush with death had spared them miraculously—to them it was an extension of time, a godsend twist of fate that had allowed them to once again be the family they thought they were. And they cherished the moments together.

They were floating in an air balloon, outwardly oblivious to the menacing breeze that threatened to blow them off course and onto the threshold of life's unredeemable black hole. But inwardly, the veneer of serenity was shattered by the lurking shadow of separation that was just around the corner, moving in closer and closer.

Lately, Peter had come by almost daily, and Samantha had drawn comfort from these visits. To her dismay, Beau had accompanied him on some of them. His presence dampened her spirits. Yet, to her surprise the situation between him and Brent improved as days went by; oh, the strain was still there, but the animosity had slackened—he was more like an old family friend than the enemy who would soon break their hearts and tear them apart.

It confused her a little, especially when at the end of the week he crushed her hopes and announced they would be leaving in another week.

"I don't understand it, it doesn't make sense," she complained to Peter. "Why the charade? Why the . . . the hypocrisy? Two weeks ago they were scratching each other's eyes out; today he's the fairy godfather bearing gifts who would put Santa Claus to shame. What is it, Peter, what's going on? What is he up to?"

Peter shook his head, his heart going out to her.

"I don't know, Simi, I really don't know." He eyed her sadly, unthinkingly using his pet name for her.

"I thought, I hoped, for a moment, that he had changed his mind and would let me stay. This is where I belong, Peter, it's where I want to be, can't he see that? You do see that, don't you?"

He nodded, listening.

"It's not fair. No, don't tell me that life isn't fair. Life is, it's people who aren't. And to pretend to be friendly when you're not is downright rotten. If he thinks that this kind of treacherous behavior will win me over, he's got another guess coming."

She turned around, hot tears stinging her eyelids. Peter put his arm around her, but she brusquely pushed him away. She did not feel like being comforted. She wanted to feel angry, to fan that anger to its explosion point. Maybe then she would have enough courage to reverse her decision.

"You know, Simi, you could tell him to go to hell. He can't force you to go with him. Stay. File for divorce. I'll help you," Peter said.

Samantha closed her eyes. Oh God, how she would love to do just that. It would be so much easier on all of them. And in the long run, a more honest solution. But was it fair to Beau? She shook her head, unable to shake the guilt. If she stayed, would she ever be absolved of the guilt she felt at having been the cause of the accident?

Last night Beau had asked her to give him another chance for just one year. If they could not work things out in that one year, he would set her free. No hassles. What was one year in a lifetime? And wasn't it, after all, only fair to grant

him that chance? If only he would not make things so unbearable. She shivered. It was going to be the longest year in
her life.

"No," she said softly. "He deserves a second chance. I owe
him that much. It's only fair."

"Fair? To whom? Don't *you* deserve a second chance?"

"I did get my second chance. Now it's his turn. I'll have
mine again."

She suddenly remembered Louise. Was it a year ago when
the old lady had used the same phrase to her? She smiled at
her brother, a little wearily, her eyes clouded.

"My decision stands. It's best for everybody."

Peter started to comment, but she raised her hand. The die
was cast. With a sigh he put his arm around her. This time
she did not ward him off.

Beau looked at his watch.

"May I use your phone?" He looked around.

"In my office." Brent rose and led the way. "It's quieter in
there."

Samantha watched the two men disappear into Brent's den
and sighed. Kavik let out short barks, jumping around Josh,
his tail wagging in anticipation. She smiled at the rolling boy
on the floor, delighting in his laughter. Shortly Mandy joined
her brother and Kavik tried to jump her. Josh grabbed the
dog by his mane and threw him on the floor.

"Easy, Josh. You might hurt him, you brute." Samantha
shook her head.

"What? What did you call me?"

She laughed and held up her arms to ward off Josh's Indian
attack. He jumped atop of her, growling and making scary
faces and shaking her. Instantly Mandy went for Samantha's
legs, lifting them on the couch and relentlessly tickling her
bare feet.

"My sofa, you guys!" Samantha laughed harder as Kavik
barked and licked her face.

Brent came out of his den and watched the fight in progress with amusement.

"Don't kill her off, guys, we still need her." He grinned and
went to the bar.

It was good to hear her laugh again. God, how he would
miss her. He poured himself a drink and gulped it down.

Suddenly he saw Beau standing outside the den, watching the knot of struggling arms and legs on the couch. Samantha and Mandy were shrieking and Josh growled.

"How dare you call your son a brute." He deepened his voice to a menacing snarl.

Samantha only laughed, then with a swift move threw Josh off her and down on the sofa.

"Gotcha!" She bent down and began kissing him.

"Ugh! Help, Kavik! Get this monster off me. Defend your master, you dumb dog!" He wildly waved his arms and accidentally struck Samantha on the cheek.

"Ouch. What are you trying to do, knock my teeth out?" She covered her mouth and pretended to be wounded.

"Steady, boy. She's the only mother you've got," Beau drawled.

His voice startled all of them. They jumped up and stared at him. Samantha's hand went from her mouth to her throat, her fingers touching the dainty necklace and the pendant hanging from it. She suddenly froze.

Beau looked at the tiny pendant in her hand, then at Samantha, his expression cloaked.

"They . . . they found that on me when I . . . had the accident." The wild pounding of her heart almost choked her and she drew a deep breath. "How . . . how do you explain that?"

"Explain what?" Beau raised his right eyebrow and Brent frowned.

"It . . . it has Brent's initials on the back . . ."

He turned the mizpah over.

"B.F.," he read, then looked at the shaking woman on the sofa.

"Mommy." Mandy tugged at Samantha's sleeve. "Can I feed Kitty in the kitchen?"

"Yes." Brent nodded quickly. "And Josh, it's time for Kavik's walk, young man. Come on, fifteen minutes, and put on a jacket."

The children ran out of the room, Mandy with the kitten Beau had brought her two days ago, in her arms and Josh with Kavik on his heels.

"B.F.," Beau repeated. "It stands for Beau Farley, darling. Those are my initials, not Farraday's."

Samantha's heart stopped beating.

Beau's expression softened. "I had them made for our first Valentine's day together. The day I proposed to you." He reached inside his back pocket, and taking out his wallet, produced a mizpah half. "This has your initials on it—see? S.F."

Samantha remained silent for a moment. When she spoke again her voice was but a whisper.

"If we were . . . having prob—If we were separated, why would I still be wearing it . . . ?"

Both Beau and Brent frowned. Then, nonchalantly, Beau shrugged. "Damned if I know. Sentimental reasons?"

He looked at her curiously. Brent too was watching her and she could feel the impact of her question linger in the loaded silence.

"She wasn't wearing it."

Peter's voice startled all of them. In the heat of the moment they had not heard him come into the room. He looked at Samantha, a hint of a smile in his eyes.

"Two days after you'd arrived here, you found it stuck at the bottom of your purse. I saw you throw it in the wastebasket." He now smiled openly. "You always did have a bad aim, even as a child." Accepting the drink Brent handed him, Peter took a quick sip and sat down. "So I found it the next day, on the floor. I don't know what made me keep it—impulse, I guess—but I stuck it in my coat pocket . . . ah"—he grimaced—"my corduroy jacket, rather. And forgot all about it. Until my cleaners gave it to me." He took another sip. "I didn't want to forget it again, so I hung it on my rearview mirror. In the car. The Mustang that keeled over the cliff."

Samantha gasped. Her eyes widened in horror. "Oh, God, Peter . . . the car . . . it was your car? I . . . I'm so sorry, why, you never told me—"

Peter shook his head and emptied his glass. "Forget it. It's only a car. You're alive, for Christ's sake."

Brent stirred and finally spoke. "It must've fallen out of the car," he mused, an odd gleam in his eyes.

Peter glanced at him. How ironic, he thought. Samantha had thrown it away when she knew it was Beau's. And worn it all this time, thinking it was Brent's. And looking at both men, he saw that they too were thinking the same thing.

Chapter 48

O'HARE AIRPORT WAS BUSTLING. PEOPLE WERE EVERY-where, well-dressed businessmen with briefcases and gar-ment bags, vacationers in jeans and overalls, women in suits, women in jeans, shrieking children, crying children, intimi-dated children clinging to the adults. Some were hurrying, others strolling leisurely, chatting animatedly, but all of them seemed to know where they were going. Even the airline staff, airport personnel and flight staff alike, headed without hesitation to their stations.

A normal day, filled with laughter and tears, with joy and anticipation, with anxiety. The metallic voice incessantly droning announcements of incoming and outgoing flights, from time to time intercepted by a more human voice calling a passenger to an airline service counter.

But if the scene was familiar to Samantha, she showed no sign of it. She moved automatically, a zombie steered by the iron hand of the man by her side, her eyes dull due to the tears she had shed the night before and earlier that morning.

She and Brent had not slept much, just clung to each other one last time as though to gather strength and cherish the memory that would hold them together.

She had not seen the children since the night before. At the first rays of daylight, they had taken a shower, together, one last time, cherishing the feel of each other's bodies, touching each other. When they went downstairs, Mrs. Flynn had been waiting for them with hot coffee and croissants, but they could barely sip the dark liquid. The taxi had arrived shortly afterward.

Brent had gone outside while she had said good-bye to the housekeeper. For the first time since she had stepped foot in the house, Samantha saw tears glistening in the old Irishwoman's eyes. They had clung to each other, sobbing. When she finally staggered outside, the cab driver dashed to open the door for her, but just as she was about to get inside she saw Brent and Beau walking from the far corner of the garage toward the car.

They were engaged in a serious discussion, Beau doing the talking, Brent seemingly deep in thought, his hands buried in his pockets. As they approached her, they both smiled, but her mind was too numb to dwell on the amicable handshake between the two men. Then Beau had quietly disappeared inside the cab while Brent kissed her good-bye, his lips warm and gentle, his eyes warmer and his smile almost cheerful.

"Remember what you told the kids, darling," he had whispered. "This is not good-bye. We'll see each other again, soon. I swear it." He kissed her again and again, and she had clung to him, not wanting to let go.

"I love you," she cried as tears blinded her vision.

"And I love you, very, very much."

She had not waved at him and during the ride to the airport she had kept staring out of the window, not bothering to stop the flowing tears. She did not notice Beau handing her his handkerchief, but when they approached O'Hare, she had automatically blown her nose in it and wiped her eyes before putting on dark sunglasses.

She vaguely heard the announcement for first class passengers to board and again Beau gripped her arm and steadily led her toward the jetway. At that moment she spotted the destination on the airline board, and stopped, puzzled.

"But . . . this . . . this is the wrong flight," she stammered. The American Airlines ground hostess looked at her. "Aren't we going to Los Angeles?"

"Ma'am?"

"It's okay." Beau smiled at the girl, handing her their boarding passes.

"Why are we going to Reno?" Samantha tried to squirm out of Beau's grip, but he put his arm around her shoulders and firmly led her on.

"I have some last-minute business to attend to in Reno, darling, and since it's on the way . . . I'm sorry, I should've told you, but I didn't think you'd mind."

He made it sound like a question and she nodded. She did not mind, of course not. Why should she, what did it matter anyway? She had been snatched away from the family she loved and hurled back to a past she could not remember. They could stay in Reno a week, a month for all she cared.

She quietly slid into the seat by the window and stared out at the bleak wintry morning. A flight attendant brought them a glass of champagne mixed with orange juice and she took a few sips, then put down the glass and glanced out of the window again, not seeing a thing. The plane began to move. She did not notice the flight attendant taking her glass away. And when a few minutes later the plane took off, she settled back in her seat and closed her eyes.

The day after the funeral, Brent had taken her to see Jed Hartley, and they had learned what they already suspected: Amanda was his brother's adopted daughter. There had, however, never been any mention of a twin sister, or Chet would have taken the two of them, of that Jed had been sure. Instead, Chet had adopted another child, a boy two years younger, who had died of kidney failure when he was eight. Amanda never spoke of him, and most of her friends had believed her to be an only child.

After hours and hours of searching through his brother's papers—a task he had avoided for years—Jed had finally found the document to confirm it all: Amanda's birth certificate. She'd been born Maggie Timms, daughter of Jennifer Timms, age sixteen, in Racine, Wisconsin, on May 17, 1959, at twenty minutes after ten in the evening, father unknown.

On his own, Peter had called Racine, driven up there and, using his influence as a prominent corporate lawyer for a large company and a letter of introduction from a friendly judge, obtained the document he had come for. Late that afternoon he had returned to present Samantha with her own birth certificate: Jennie Timms, born of the same Jennifer Timms, age sixteen, in Racine, Wisconsin, on May 17,

1959, at five minutes after ten in the evening; no mention of a father.

Suddenly Samantha understood the inexplicable feeling of loss she'd experienced the night Amanda died.

Later that evening, they had spent the time at the Manchiones'.

She had learned of her collapsing marriage to Beau, caused mainly by their separate interests, he devoted to his obsession with scientific research and she wanting desperately to belong, have a family, children, and a husband. She had sought solace in her business and for a while she had lost herself in her passion for interior decor, but in the long run *Les Mirages* had not been enough. She had become restless, and at the peak of its success, she had sold it and fled to Chicago.

Of all her brothers, Peter, ten years older, was closest to her, and when in trouble, she had always turned to him. This time had been no different. She had wanted to start a new life, and near Peter, Samantha had felt she could make a go of it again. Only, she never got the chance to try . . .

The plane shuddered. Within seconds the Fasten Seatbelts sign lit up and the voice of the flight attendant repeated the request over the intercom.

Samantha opened her eyes, feeling the shocks rip right through her body. She suddenly felt cold and lonely and she shivered.

They were among the first passengers to leave the plane. Samantha moved automatically, guided by Beau's strong arm, her limbs numb, her mind blank. She hardly noticed the peering stares of the faces at the gate, waiting with anticipation to see those they had come to meet. A man at the end of the line waved and she vaguely felt Beau's grip tighten around her arm. Moments later they had passed the queue and, to her surprise, Beau approached the man who had just waved.

"Hi there, John. Glad you could make it." They shook hands and Beau turned to Samantha. "You remember my wife, Samantha? Darling, this is John Phillips, my attorney."

"Hello, Samantha. It's good to see you again." Phillips shook her hand, and despite her apathy, Samantha smiled. His handshake was strong but gentle and his eyes were warm and friendly. He was very skinny, his slightly balding head making his long face seem even longer. It was a handsome face and the freckles around his hawklike nose made it friendly, and when he smiled, his whole face smiled, and she instantly felt comfortable with him. He turned to Beau.

"How was the flight? Not too bumpy, I hope?"

"Quite calm, really. Is everything okay?"

"Everything is fine. The appointment is set for three-thirty this afternoon."

"Great. I knew I could count on you." Beau took Samantha's hand. "Come on, let's get the luggage."

"I've booked you a room at the Hilton. You may want to rest a while." He smiled at Samantha, noticing her pale face.

"You do think of everything, don't you? Thanks, friend. We did have an ungodly early start this morning, but it was the only flight I could get. Besides, we may want to finalize some matters before the meeting this afternoon."

John laughed. "Now who's thinking of everything?"

To their surprise their luggage came off the carousel within minutes and within a half hour of their arrival they had checked into the Reno Hilton and were on their way up to the room.

Shortly before noon Samantha showered and changed and refreshed her makeup. Beau had gone down to the lobby to purchase some shaving cream, which he claimed he had left behind, and John had gone with him. He had urged her to rest a while and said they were going to John's office to discuss some business, but promised they would be back by noon.

And Beau did indeed return a few minutes after noon, clearly in good spirits. He had brought John back with him and announced he had ordered up some lunch.

"I thought you might be hungry but too tired to go out," he said.

Room service arrived and for the first time Samantha noticed that the room was a kind of minisuite with a small sitting area, and they set the table in front of the TV. Beau signed the tab and closed the door behind the waiter.

"How about some wine, guys?" Beau poured three glasses. Samantha was not hungry and picked at her food, but the two men pretended not to notice and kept the conversation going.

"So, Samantha, how would you like to be free?" Beau wiped the croissant crumbs off his mouth and took a sip of his wine, all the while watching her. But Samantha's expression remained blank, the words strange to her ears. What did he mean, free? What kind of game was he playing with her? "Well, would you? You know—free, as in not married."

She slowly sipped her wine and swallowed, and for the first time since they had boarded the plane that morning, she spoke.

"If this is some sort of a joke, it's not funny."

"Darling, do you see me laugh? I'm dead serious. How would you like to go back to your family in Chicago, a free woman?"

She turned to John Phillips, and when he nodded, her eyes widened. She was suddenly alert, her heart jumping wildly. What was he saying? She felt like screaming, waiting to hear more.

"John has prepared some papers for us to sign. That meeting this afternoon at three-thirty? It's a divorce hearing, complete with a judge ready to sign your release from my bondage. How does that strike you?"

She swallowed and swallowed hard.

"D-divorce?"

"Yes, darling, divorce. Final and legal."

"You—you arranged all this . . . and . . . and you never told me? You let me suffer . . . all this time you—"

"Hold it right there." He leaned forward and touched her hand that lay on the table, but she snatched it away from him. "I wasn't sure the judge could fit us into his busy schedule this soon. I only thought of it two days before we left Chicago. John here did a hell of a job persuading the court to fit us in." He suddenly grinned. "Of course, it helps when the judge is one's own brother."

John rose. "Perhaps I'd better leave you two for an hour or so." He smiled apologetically at Samantha. "I'll be back around two."

After he had gone, Beau got up and walked toward the window, his hands in his pockets. He spoke softly, without turning, almost as if to himself.

"We weren't happy, Sam. We were having problems, lots and lots of problems, you and I. I guess it was mostly me. My job at NASA, my ambitions, my need to excel. And through it all, you remained loyal. You stood by me." Beau sighed. "That's just it, you see. You cared. But somewhere along the way the love between us died, at least the kind of love two lovers share."

He was quiet for a moment.

"Sure, we remained good friends, but the spark had died. You were unhappy. I still had my ambitions. So we separated. And then, when you sold your business and left for Chicago . . ." He paused painfully. "I thought at first that you had gone to be with Peter, but when he called three months later and told me you were dead . . ." The silence hung heavy in the room.

"It was an accident," Samantha whispered.

"You had been so unhappy, I thought—"

"You thought I had killed myself." Horror suddenly filled her.

Beau slowly turned around, his face taut.

"I blamed myself. You never did understand my obsession for science, and when I got that promotion and you left . . . well, I . . . what else was I to think? I don't think you ever liked what I was doing anyway, but . . ."

Samantha waited as he rubbed the stubble on his chin.

"There's more, isn't there?" she prodded gently.

Beau sighed. "Yeah, there's more." He began to pace, a deep frown on his forehead. "A week before you left we were supposed to patch things up. To try again, see if we could still make it together. Just then, you found out about Melissa."

The room was quiet once more and this time Samantha took her time.

"And you married this . . . Melissa?" she probed.

"No. I had botched things up badly the first time, so I wasn't about to repeat my mistake. I'm not marriage material. I'm not a good husband, never was, never will be. Lucky for me, she understands that and accepts it."

"So you're still together?"

Beau nodded. He stopped pacing and looked directly at her. "I never planned to marry her. This divorce is for you. You deserve better, some genuine happiness, love, the family you'd always wanted. I owe you that much."

Samantha stared at him, not believing her ears. Was this the man who had threatened her in Brent's house, and refused to listen to reason? How could this be happening after all that had transpired?

"What made you change your mind, Beau?" she asked.

"I guess what I saw back there in Lake Forest," he said simply.

"But you were so determined to take me back with you . . ."

"That was before I saw how happy you were with them. I was angry—I thought we should try again, just like we'd planned."

Samantha wondered.

Chapter 49

THE AMERICAN AIRLINES PLANE LANDED SMOOTHLY AT O'Hare Airport. Again, traveling first class, Samantha was among the first to leave the jetway. She silently thanked Beau for offering to send her suitcase together with the rest of the clothes he had not been able to give away to charity. Her tread was light and her heart sang as she thought of Brent's surprise when he found out. She would call him from the airport, and not wait for him to get her. She would take a taxi, all the way to Lake Forest. Who cared how much it cost? She was free! Free to marry him, free to be a mother to their children.

A familiar face at the end of the waiting crowd at the gate grinned at her and she halted. A man behind her bumped into her, swearing. But she did not hear him, her heart thumping.

She let out a curdling scream and ran the last few yards that separated her from the grinning face. Then practically jumped into Brent's strong arms. He crushed her to him, kissing her again and again. They were laughing and Samantha was crying and she clung to him and they were oblivious of the curious stares around them, aware only of each other and their newfound happiness.

"How did you know?" Samantha finally whispered.

"Beau called me earlier this morning and told me you'd be on this flight."

"He did?" Her eyes widened. "Did he also tell you . . . ?"

"No. Not today. He told me yesterday, before you two left for Reno." She suddenly remembered seeing the two men talk while the taxi waited in front of the house.

"Then . . . you knew?"

Brent nodded. "I didn't sleep a wink last night," he confessed.

A commotion caught her attention and two children ran toward them and she had barely let go of Brent's loving arms when they all but knocked her off her feet.

"Mommy, Mommy, you're back," Mandy cried, kissing and hugging her.

"Daddy said you'd stay this time, for good." Josh nearly choked her, but Samantha only laughed.

"Will you marry me on Christmas Eve?" Brent interrupted.

She could not speak and kept nodding, crushing the youngsters close and kissing them again and again. When she looked up, she saw Paula's beaming face, and her joy overflowed.

"Where are you taking me?" Samantha had been back a week, and with the wedding less than a week away, she had welcomed the opportunity to escape from the house and all the planning, and take a short drive with Peter. As they drove along, she did not recognize the streets or the surroundings and turned to Peter with a quizzical expression in her big tawny eyes.

"This is Lake Zurich," he said smiling, keeping his eyes on the traffic. "I thought you might want to see where I live."

"Is that where we're heading, your apartment?" Samantha asked.

His mysterious behavior piqued her curiosity and Samantha began to wonder why he had chosen this particular moment to show her his abode.

Without answering, Peter expertly swung the red Peugeot into a vacant parking spot alongside the curb and, with a decided click, turned the motor off.

"Come on, there's someone I'd like you to meet." Peter got out of the car and, reaching over to the passenger's side, helped her.

They mingled with the lunch crowd for a couple of blocks, and when he paused in front of a store, Samantha looked up. In gold lettering "Sorel's Art Gallery" identified the large airy showroom she stepped into, and she looked around at the enormous collection of colorful paintings along the walls and on the floor. Samantha gaped. Appreciation filled her and her admiration for their beauty grew as she slowly appraised the talent displayed in the room. A woman approached them, her eyes gleaming.

"Samantha! It's so good to see you again. I cried like a baby when Peter called and told me that you were alive!" She threw her arms around the flabbergasted Samantha and just about crushed the air out of her. "My darling, I never did believe that you were dead. Not for one minute, I didn't. I kept telling Peter, but he wouldn't listen. And see, I was right all along."

"Samantha, this is Vivien Sorel, a good friend of mine." Peter smiled. "And yours. And no, she has never given up hope that one day you'd be back here, alive."

Vivien held her at arm's length. "Peter told me you don't remember much. But you must remember that you were here, helping me, up to that horrible day. You had asked me for a day off, and I've never forgiven myself for granting you the time. You do remember that, don't you?" Her eyes were pleading, and Samantha looked at her sheepishly, feeling guilty and ill at ease. She forced herself to smile.

"If that's how you say it was, it must be so," she agreed and glanced around as if to recapture a memory, a glimpse into a past that kept eluding her, no matter how hard she tried.

"Come on, Viv. Close up for lunch; I'm paying," Peter said, glancing at his watch. He had promised Samantha she'd be back home before Mandy and Josh got out of school.

"Goodness, I can't pass that up, now can I?" Vivien laughed. "Give me five minutes to freshen up."

Peter turned to Samantha, his expression solemn. "I'm sorry, I had hoped . . ."

But she quickly put her fingers on his lips and shook her head. "Thank you," she said softly. "At least I know Samantha had a friend. She's super, and I could always use another friend."

Vivien returned, keys jingling in her hand.

"Here." She handed Samantha a small box. "This is yours. You left it on the desk that morning you disappeared."

Puzzled, Samantha opened the tiny box. A pearl-drop earring blinked at her, and she stiffened.

"You must've taken it off when you made that phone call, the one that got you to ask me for the day off." Vivien searched for the key to the front door. "You always take those things off when you're on the phone. So do I. Why do we bother to wear them? Silly, really. The things we do for ego."

Samantha kept staring at the trinket in her hand, her mind in a whirl. It was the mate to the one in her vanity drawer—the one she was said to have worn when she had the accident.

Chapter 50

AT THREE O'CLOCK IN THE AFTERNOON OF CHRISTMAS Eve the Farraday residence in Lake Forest was buzzing with people. Guests had come from all over Cook County and some even from Europe to witness the Farraday wedding.

Spirits were high despite the absence of alcoholic beverages, which, befitting the occasion, were rumored to be held back until after the ceremony. Instead, as was the Farraday tradition for a Christmas Eve, eggnog flowed freely all across the crowded room. And as the hour of four drew near, anticipation began to mount and some of the more daring guests took refuge outside.

Temperatures were mild for a Chicago winter day and to those on the patio the crisp air came as a welcome breather. And the chatter and laughter continued, drifting through the barren branches of the neighborhood trees. The noise did not bother the neighbors, for they too were at the lively party, enjoying the rich eggnog and relishing the gourmet hors d'oeuvres catered by Stouffers, special courtesy of Louise Farraday.

At precisely four o'clock the musicians began to play Tchaikovsky's *Nutcracker Suite,* and as if this were their cue, the guests began to gather inside the living room, eager for the long-awaited moment to unfold.

* * *

Upstairs in her bedroom, Samantha stood in front of the bathroom mirror and stared at her reflection. She held herself very still while Paula, on her knees behind her, feverishly worked on some last-minute finishing touches to her bridal dress. Her face was calm, the expression in her enormous tawny eyes tranquil and quiet, and only the clenching and unclenching of her hands alongside the smooth, soft lines of her long gown betrayed her inner emotions.

It's finally here, she thought, it's finally happening. The nightmare had turned into a beautiful dream, and in a few moments, the dream was to become reality. How wonderful life could be; how intricate the webs of fate. Her eyes viewed the slender lines of her body, her almost elfinlike face that was so like Mandy's. They had done their utmost—Paula and Mrs. Flynn and even Brent—but they had not succeeded in getting her to gain back the pounds she had lost the last couple of months.

"There. All done." Paula groaned as she rose from her kneeling position. She made a face as her back creaked, then seeing Samantha's questioning look, grinned. Reaching for the tiara of white orchids on the dresser, she glanced at the bride's reflection in the mirror.

"Get down for a second." She held up the tiara and pinned it on Samantha's copper curls. "There." Paula took a step backward. "Jesus, you look fabulous! If you were not my friend, I'd be jealous."

How fitting that she should choose a tiara of white flowers rather than a bridal veil, Paula mused. Nestling on her head like a crown, the white orchids brought out the fiery sparks in her dancing hair, making her look more like a queen of nymphs than a blushing young bride.

Samantha slowly rose, her eyes solemn.

"Come on, smile. This is your day, remember? And it's a wedding, not a funeral."

A smile brightened Samantha's face and her expression softened.

"Now, that's better."

"The sound of the *Nutcracker*'s overture reached them and Paula let out an excited little shriek.

"Shit, it's started." She grabbed the short woolen jacket from the chair in the corner and held it up for Samantha. "Come on, cara, it's time to meet with destiny."

Obediently Samantha slid into the jacket and viewed herself one last time in the mirror. Too pale, she thought. Paula was right, why look so somber? The silver glitter of the jacket's exquisite hand embroidery made her seem even paler, and she reached for the drawer and picked out a soft-cinnamon lipstick.

"Where is everybody? Come on, you guys, they are waiting for you down—" An agitated Karen burst into the room, her cheeks flushed. Then seeing Samantha she suddenly stopped, the words dying on her lips. For a moment she just stared. "Ohhh . . . Holy Madonna, Sam, you're . . . beautiful . . . simply, absolutely breathtaking." She swallowed and shook her head, blinking her eyes as if to make sure she wasn't dreaming.

"Brent will devour you alive!" Karen whispered, moving in a trance toward Samantha's still figure. She slowly reached out and touched the soft wool of her bridal gown, and sighed, a long drawn-out sigh.

"Where is everybody? What the hell is the holdup here?" Lady Madeline strode nervously into the tableau, Louise on her heels, and like Karen, they stopped and gaped.

"Oh, my," Lady Madeline mumbled.

"World, eat your heart out," Louise murmured, smiling.

Samantha stirred, suddenly made uneasy by all those staring eyes.

"We'd better go downstairs," she said, carefully lifting her dress. She was just about to head for the door when Mandy appeared in the doorway.

"Where is everybody?"

Everybody laughed and the girl's eyes widened, startled at the reaction to her question.

"It's allright, darling. Where is Josh?" Louise straightened the floral wreath in the child's hair.

"I left him at the bottom of the stairs." Mandy sounded hesitant.

"Good. Why don't you go back to him and wait for us there, hm? What did you do with your bouquet?"

"Josh has it. I told him to hold it for me until I got Mommy." She turned to Samantha, and her eyes brightened. "You look so beautiful, Mommy. You're the most beautiful bride ever!"

For the first time that afternoon a genuine smile flashed

across Samantha's face. The look she gave her little girl was warm and tender. "You don't look so bad yourself, princess," she said softly and touched Mandy's cheek. "Go, now, darling, we'll be right down." Mandy smiled and quickly left the room.

"I'm ready," Samantha whispered hoarsely. She waited a few minutes for everyone to make it to the living room before the musicians began to play the Wedding March from *Lohengrin*. Then, slowly, she headed for the stairs, and as she reached the top step, the conductor looked up and the music came to life.

Chapter 51

RIGHT AFTER THE NEW YEAR THE NILLSONS MOVED INTO their new home. Nicole was ecstatic about how the house had turned out, calling all her friends to tell them about it. And as soon as the Farradays had returned from their honeymoon cruise, she had called Samantha to tell her how everyone was dying to see the house. She even threw in a few words of praise, although not once did she clearly thank her. But Samantha understood. She had not expected anything else from Nikki, nor did she want anything more. Thankful that the house was finally done, she felt that Nikki's uncharacteristic enthusiasm was thanks enough.

She was glad that she had worked so hard on the Nillson project before Amanda had shown up. And that the independent contractors had been so cooperative and expeditious, even for an off-season. Afterwards, preoccupied by turmoil and grief, the job had suffered a brief stand-still. Yet, once more it had preserved her sanity, for determined to finish what she had started, she had pushed herself to concentrate on its completion and thrown herself into her work.

Oddly enough the time she spent working on the project had brought a better understanding between her and Nicole. Not friendship perhaps, but a mutual perception of each other's temperament and a tolerance that was clinched by the death of Amanda Farraday. Then, at the wedding, Nikki had presented her with the infamous videotape, and together, they had watched it burn in the fireplace.

And tonight, she was actually looking forward to the grand opening of the Nillson's new home.

Putting the finishing touches to her make-up, Samantha viewed her reflection in the mirror. She opened a drawer and took out a pearl necklace. Her hand suddenly stayed in mid-air; a similar vision flashed through her mind.

Had it really been over a year ago that she had stood here readying herself for her first party as Brent's wife? It somehow seemed like only yesterday, and yet—so many things had happened since then . . . And tonight, what was so special about tonight? she wondered. She had stood here many times since that evening a year ago, why was tonight any different?

It must be the dress, she thought, she had worn the same cream colored woollen dress that night and Brent had given her the pearl necklace to wear. Amanda's necklace.

"Come on, Mrs. Farraday," Brent's amused voice was deep and warm and he smiled at her flushed face. "Stop admiring yourself, you sexy nymph. You look absolutely ravishing. What are you trying to do, have all the men at the ball fall at your feet, begging you to leave me?"

His eyes caressed her, and Samantha felt the blood rush to her face at the dark passion. A familiar tingling spread throughout her slim body and her knees began to tremble. She watched him come closer and when he stood tall behind her, she could almost feel the strength of his lean hard body touch hers.

"Here, let me." He took the necklace from her and fastened it around her slender neck, and as his fingers brushed against her skin delightful sparks riveted through her body, and she shuddered.

The party was forgotten; all she wanted right now was his touch, for him to take her, to be made love to. Her flesh tingled at the thought and the urgency of her need soared. Their eyes met in the mirror and for a moment they were suspended in time.

Slowly he bent down and kissed her neck, her bare shoulders, her pulsating throat. Lingeringly, deliberately, his lips burning, searing her flesh. Samantha's lips parted, her breathing coming through in heavy rasps, and she closed her eyes, trembling. Relentlessly he went on and as his hands found her swollen breasts she opened her eyes and turned around, facing him. And she pulled his head down to her breasts, wanting him to take them, her body now taut with flaring need.

"Come, we'd better go," Brent tore himself from her throbbing breasts, his voice husky, "or we'll be late for the party."

"It's only seven o'clock," she whispered.

He looked into her wistful eyes and saw his own desire reflected. And wordlessly, he unzipped her dress and carried her to the bed.

"You ought to be ashamed of yourself, Mrs. Farraday," he drawled, and hungrily covered her mouth, his hands fondling her firm breasts and down the silken flesh of her thighs. "It's one thing to seduce a man, but to make your very own husband lust after you?"

And taking a nipple in his mouth he heard her throaty laugh as she encircled his wiry body with a long bare leg.

It was one huge bash.

"Are you enjoying yourself?" Brent smiled into her sparkling eyes, loving the mischievous dimples that seemed to be a constant feature tonight. Samantha grinned back, feeling light and frivolous and warmed by his caressing looks.

"Stop that," she whispered, and then, as he raised an incredulous eyebrow, she giggled, happily allowing him to steal a kiss.

"Hey, you two, the honeymoon is over." Niels slapped them on the shoulder, grinning. "Of course, for a fee, I'll be happy to let you have the upstairs bedroom." He lowered his voice conspiratorialy.

"You're wrong, my friend." Brent returned the grin. "The honeymoon is just beginning."

"And may it never end." A boisterous voice behind them boomed.

"Have you met my father-in-law? Nikki's dad, Dr. Thomas Webb, Brent and Samantha Farraday." Niels introduced them.

"We've met. How are you, Dr. Webb?" Brent said, nodding.

"Of course we have," Dr. Webb responded. His face was

ruddy, red from the Scotch, and he looked past Brent at Samantha. She stiffened, shifting uneasily under his direct stare.

There was something vaguely familiar about him and it was not because he was Nikki's father, for she had never met him before and he did not look anything like his sophisticated daughter. Perhaps she had sensed Brent's change of mood at the man's presence, the subtle coolness in his voice when he addressed him . . .

"So this is the genius behind this house's success." Tom Webb took her hand and she felt Brent stiffen. "My daughter is lucky to have you for a friend."

"Good grief, do I have to make an appointment to get an audience with you?" Paula all but yanked Samantha away from the old doctor, and relieved, Brent put his arms around the two friends and the three of them laughed. The conversation quickly drifted back to the honeymoon and before long they had forgotten all about Webb.

Listening to the endless chatter, Samantha glanced around the room. It was a lovely party, but after a while the jokes became repetitious and the conversation nothing more than rambling gossip. She forced herself to show interest, but her eyes roamed and once in a while she caught Brent looking at her from across the room and her eyes lit up and she smiled a genuine smile.

The crowd had finally managed to separate them, and mingling politely, Samantha felt lost without her friends. To her chagrin even Paula had deserted her, if only for the moment, to get another drink, and she forced herself to listen to the mindless jokes of the people around her. She was bored, yet careful not to show it, and her mind began to wander.

"Now look, young lady," a blustery voice clamored, silencing someone who was trying to get a word through. "No, you listen." Dr. Webb sounded impatient. "Seems to me, little lady, you might've botched up your own life here. Pinching money isn't always a savings, you know. Like I always say, you get what you pay for."

Samantha froze. A chill crawled up her spine and she suddenly knew why Dr. Webb had looked so familiar. The room began to spin and through her blurred vision she saw the women around her weave, their curious glances oddly grotesque. A sudden wave of nausea surged, and the lights faded to a dim shadow.

A woman gasped, another screamed, but she did not hear them, nor did she see Brent elbow his way through the crowd. She no longer felt anything, and embracing the darkness she noiselessly slid to the floor in a dead faint.

Chapter 52

SHE SLOWLY OPENED HER EYES, HER BLURRED VISION trying to focus on the outlines of a man's face, and as the fog began to clear, they widened in horror. An echo rang in her ears, drowning out the buzzing.

That voice, those words. Terror seized her and threatened to knock her back into dark oblivion. The man's lips moved. God, what was he saying? Why couldn't she hear him? She pressed her hands over her ears. Make the buzzing stop, she cried. That noise, she had to stop that horrible noise! She sat up, still sobbing, and the room began to spin again.

"Samantha! It's me, Brent." He grabbed her arms and shook her, gently at first, then when she did not respond, harder and harder still. "Samantha, you must pull yourself together. Can you hear me?"

He knew he was shouting, but he had to get through to her. He shook her again, hard, and just as he raised his hand to slap her, her eyes flew open and he held his breath sharply. The pain in those enormous eyes—raw, intense—carved deep into his soul, and he shuddered.

"Samantha, can you hear me now?"

She did not reply, but the lines of his familiar face began to take form and the sobbing stopped. Her body was still shaking and the tears were now streaming down her pale face.

"Brent?" she whimpered.

Wordlessly he took her in his arms, and gradually the trembling ceased. He held her gently. Something nagged at him and he wondered what had happened that caused her to faint. He felt her stir against him and he loosened his embrace.

"Darling? How do you feel?" he asked gently.

"A little shaky, but I'm all right now." She felt miserable, but managed to force a watery smile. "Can we go home, Brent?"

"What happened, Samantha? You must tell me, I must know."

"Please, Brent, please take me home."

He was silent for a moment, then rose to find their host.

"Brent?" It was barely a whisper, but he heard it.

Taking their leave, they had driven home in silence. He had not pressed her for an explanation and they had gone upstairs immediately. He had briefly looked in on the children, and finding them fast asleep, slid quietly into the big bed, next to the motionless Samantha. And he had lain in the dark, wondering.

"Brent, are you asleep?"

Her hand touched his and he instantly gripped it tight. Shortly he moved to reach for the light.

"No, no light, please," she pleaded, crawling into the warmth of his arms. "It . . . it's better this way." He waited, patiently.

Samantha began to talk, softly, hesitantly at first, stumbling over her words, pausing more than once. Her mind, no longer groping, let out the memory that had blocked her from plummeting over the edge . . .

Brent stared into the darkness, his arm protectively around Samantha's still body, listening to the even breathing. He felt numb, still partly in shock, the turmoil he had felt earlier gone. The quiet of the room had gradually sucked up his anger and only the hollow echo of her revelation hung in the air, spinning around in his mind, pounding against his aching temples.

Raped. God! His poor darling. No wonder she had suffered all those nightmares. Blurry recollections of an ugly memory buried so deep it had manifested itself in ogre hauntings within her subconscious.

It had happened a month after she came to Chicago. She couldn't remember much about that day. Or night. Nor about what had triggered the assault. Only that there was darkness, and an ominous figure silhouetted against the light at his back—faceless, and evil. And a crippling fear. Consuming her, rendering her helpless.

She couldn't recall if she had fought to get away, or struggled to free herself. All she had retained were blurred images of violence, soiled blotches of terrifying agony. And above all, humiliation—raw, mindless humiliation. As she relived the horror of that moment, her body began to tremble, and the shaking wouldn't stop. She squeezed her eyes shut, tightly, as if to obliterate the ugly cobwebs from her mind.

She had never reported the incident, anxious not to compound the turmoil she had brought with her from Los Angeles, but six weeks later she had found herself pregnant. Frantic, she had told her brother about her decision to have an abortion and Peter, infuriated and worried sick about her, had tried to talk her out of it.

But she had not listened to him and had gone ahead anyway. Yet when they had asked her all those questions about herself and who had fathered the baby, she had panicked and left. Two weeks later she had gone to another place in Joliet where she knew no questions would be asked.

It had been quick and almost painless, but on the way back to Lake Zurich she had hemorrhaged. Frightened, she had stopped at a phone booth. There she had found Dr. Webb's name in the Yellow Pages and, in sheer panic, had gone to him for help. And he had stopped the bleeding.

"God, it was awful," she said now. "He told me . . . it served me right if I'd never—" Samantha's breath choked.

"Shhh, it's all right now, it's over." Brent rocked her and kissed her wet forehead.

"He said . . . I would never ever have any babies again . . . they had butchered me, my insides . . . and—" She buried her face in his arms, her fingers clawing into his flesh.

* * *

Anger surged as he held her tighter against him. The son of a bitch! He had no right, no right at all. Even if it were true, it was highly unprofessional to upset a patient's already unstable condition with such a blunt verdict. Shit! That would explain her reckless driving during that thunderstorm . . . a woman who otherwise squirmed at anyone driving over the speed limit . . .

"Shhh, hush now," he said softly. "We'll get a second opinion about that, so let's not worry about it tonight."

They were silent for a moment and gradually he felt her body relax.

"Samantha? You haven't answered my question, what happened that made you faint?"

"I recognized his voice."

"Whose?"

"Dr. Webb's. He was saying something to someone and the words were so similar to the ones he had used that day. To me, when he told me about . . ."

Brent lay very still, his mind in turmoil.

"You remembered." The quietness in his voice touched her and the realization that had hit her earlier surfaced again, stronger than before, and she pulled away from him.

"Yes, I remembered." She said it as if on cue, without emotion, the fact overshadowed by the impact of her recollection.

He reached out and gathered her back into his arms, holding her firmly. "That certainly was worth fainting for," he said tenderly.

But he knew that the wound had been ripped open. And when it would heal—if it ever did—it would leave a scar. He could only pray that the scar would not leave any visible marks.

"Are you sure?"

Brent forgot his burning cigarette as he listened to the voice on the other side of the telephone, his eyes bright with intense interest. Daryl, who had knocked but received no response, walked into the office and seeing the ash about to drop on the mahogany desk, quickly shoved an ashtray under it.

But Brent hardly noticed his presence and after a moment's hesitation, Daryl turned to leave when his brother-in-law suddenly looked him straight in the face and impatiently gestured him to sit down. "You're absolutely, positively sure? There can't be any room for error, you understand? Not this time, not now."

He listened again, still looking at Daryl, and sighed. Deeply. Then he nodded. "All right. Yes, I'll drop by tomorrow. And Roger, thanks. You've made my day, old boy. I owe you one."

He gently replaced the receiver, his expression pensive for a moment. Then he sighed again. And smiled.

"Roger? As in Weinstein, *the* computer-brained gynecologist?" Daryl frowned.

Roger Weinstein was one of the best in his field, but he knew how Brent felt about him and that he would not refer him to his patients unless they needed someone who excelled in his skill, without expectations for human sympathy or emotion.

"One and the same." Brent extinguished his cigarette and lit another one.

"Must have been important." Daryl narrowed his eyes, his curiosity up.

"It is. I had him check out Samantha." He looked away, suddenly regretting having asked Daryl to stay. He needed to get home to Samantha, talk to her. He bit his lip trying to suppress his emotion that threatened to bubble over and looked at Daryl, his embarrassment now showing.

"Is she all right?" Daryl asked, now anxious.

"Yes, yes, she's fine." Brent rose and stubbed out his second cigarette. "Look, Daryl, do you mind? I've got to go home, I promised Samantha I'd be early today. Tell you what. Why don't you and Karen drop by the house tonight, hm? It's Friday and we haven't seen you guys since the party." Which was only two weeks ago, Daryl thought wryly. "After dinner, okay? Samantha will be delighted. We'll have drinks, and we'll talk. All right?"

"I'll have to check with Karen. The twins . . ."

"Bring them along. Eight o'clock?"

Daryl got up, sensing his friend's eagerness to leave. "Eight o'clock," he nodded.

"See you then."

* * *

"Are you sure? Are you absolutely sure?" Samantha looked at his sparkling eyes, wanting more reassurance. "There's no mistake? I can have babies?"

Brent took her into his arms, his face close above hers, an odd smile around his lips. "Absolutely. As a matter of fact . . ."

"As a matter of fact what? There's more, tell me!" She tried to wriggle herself out of his strong embrace, but he held her even tighter, grinning boyishly.

"As a matter of fact, Mrs. Farraday, you are about to have one."

Her eyes widened, puzzled. "One what?"

"A baby, silly. You're about to have a baby."

"Brent, stop fooling around. What *are* you saying?" Her heart was suddenly pounding and she held her breath sharply.

"Yes, my love. You are expecting a baby. You are about to be a mother again. You are p-r-e-g-n-a-n-t."

He felt her body stiffen, then she began to tremble and he held her, firm and steady, until the shaking subsided. Her enormous eyes softened and tears began to brim. "You're not joking?" she whispered.

"Would I lie to you? Have I ever?"

"Oh, Brent . . ." She started to cry and buried her head in his shoulder. Suddenly she looked up, tears on her face. "But Dr. Webb? He . . . said . . ."

"Never mind Dr. Webb. He's a drunk and a quack. No better than the one who performed the abortion, I'd say. Roger Weinstein is one of the best, if not *the* best in his field, and he should know. Anyway, I trust Weinstein's opinion a hell of a lot more than I believe Webb's." He kissed the tip of her wet nose and gently brushed away her tears. "Those are happy tears, I hope?" he teased.

"Oh, Brent . . . you *are* absolutely sure, aren't you?"

"Absolutely." He kissed her again, and again, and again.

Samantha leaned against him, feeling dizzy. Then, suddenly, she giggled, and simultaneously began to cry again.

"That fainting spell could be due to your condition, you know. Besides the shock of getting your memory back. Double dose, quite heavy, I'd say." Brent grinned.

"Oh, Brent . . ." she said again, and hiccuped. And they both burst out laughing.

"I love you," she offered her lips and he kissed her, long and deep.

"And I you," he muttered in between kisses.

Chapter 53

THE DOORBELL RANG. SHE HEARD MRS. FLYNN OPEN THE front door. Voices from downstairs floated upward, the housekeeper's soft brogue calling up to her. Frantically she scrambled out of bed and hurried toward the door.

"Up here, Paula." Leaving the door ajar, Samantha went back into the room and hastened to straighten the bedsheets. God, how could she have allowed herself to sleep in this late —her alarm clock showed two minutes after eleven! She grabbed her robe from the chair by the wall and hurriedly put it on, just as the door creaked.

"I don't know what came over me, I've never—" One pillow in her left hand, her right brushing away the curls from her eyes, she whirled around and the words died in her throat. The figure in the doorway was not Paula's.

The curtains were still drawn and with the light from the hallway shining at the stranger's back, she could not clearly see his face. Samantha froze. The pillow slipped to the floor and her hands clutched around her robe, her knees suddenly weak.

In the dimness of the room the apparition loomed, menacingly, deceptively taller and darker as the shadows gathered around him. A vision flashed inside her mind, bringing back a horrifying familiarity to the scene before her.

"Paula wanted you to have this—" Matt stopped in his

approach, arrested by her terrified stare. The silence between them grew and for a while they just stared at each other. He was the first to move.

"Samantha . . ." He cleared his throat. He took another step forward. "I—"

"You!" It was a whisper, but that one little word cut through the room and Matt winced. "It was *you."*

The hush in the room was deadly and for a moment time stopped. Then, with a sigh, Matt lowered his head.

"You remembered," he said, his voice sad. "I wondered how long it would take before you remembered . . ."

"You knew. All along, you knew." Her voice trembled.

"All this time I've agonized about this moment. A whole year. I've paid my dues, Sam, believe me. It's haunted me, tormented me, you have no idea—"

She felt her chest constrict and she gasped for air.

"Haunted *you,* tormented *you* . . . hah! What about *me?* What about my torment, my pain, huh? Did you ever think about me? How dare you talk about *your* suffering? My God, Matt, you *raped* me! I almost died trying to undo what you did to me, and you talk about *your* discomfort. You . . . you bastard! Damn you!" She spat the words at him and he cringed at the harsh sounds.

"Why, Matt, why? Why me? Why did you do it?"

He shifted uneasily, avoiding her eyes. "I was drunk. I really didn't mean to . . . hurt you. It just . . . happened."

Samantha was silent, the horror of that night coming back to her in vivid color.

He had walked into Sorel's Art Gallery the week before that horrible night, a stranger seeking her counsel on modern art. She had spent the next hour with him, discussing the different aspects of oil paintings versus watercolor. In the end, they had gone out for dinner. And he had come back the next day and the next, and they had spent more time together.

He had seemed nice and she had enjoyed his company. After two more dinners she had felt comfortable enough to go out dancing with him. Never once had he mentioned that he was married. Nor had she cared, for she had not looked for anything more than a casual dinner or two.

She had liked him, trusted him. Enough to celebrate Labor

Day's at the Marriott Hotel bash with him. Enough to ask him up to Peter's town house afterward for some coffee. She had known that he was smashed, and she had worried about him, and with Peter away that weekend, she had felt free to try and sober him up for his drive home. Too late she had discovered that she had misjudged him.

"I really didn't know what I was doing . . ."

He looked up. "Oh, hell. I meant what I said—that I didn't mean to hurt you. But you looked so much like her, and that night . . . well, perhaps I did want to punish her, lash back, make her pay for the times she had teased me, on and on. I guess she didn't think I was human or something . . ." His voice trailed away and Samantha felt a chill seize her.

Holy shit, she thought, stunned, he's talking about Amanda! He confused me in his head with that bitch!

"Please, Sam, forgive me. I was so drunk that night, and you looked so much like her. It was wrong. I knew it as soon as it was over, but by then it was too late. I called you the next morning, but you wouldn't talk to me. I even went by your place, but you wouldn't let me in, and at the Gallery, Vivien wouldn't let me see you. Then you appeared here as Amanda." Matt took a deep breath.

"Why didn't you tell me?" Samantha demanded. "Why haven't you said anything? All this time, you let me think I was someone I wasn't . . ."

"Well, I thought you were, at first. Four years is a long time. Although, the change in personality did strike me, even in the beginning. But I figured something could've happened to subdue even the worst of us, even Amanda . . . I was fooled like everyone else."

He swallowed hard. Then shook his head. "Also, I kept going back to the gallery, and the week after Halloween, Vivien told me that you'd gone back to Los Angeles."

Slowly, Samantha sank down on the edge of the bed and clasped her hands together.

"But you did come to the conclusion that I was not the changed Amanda. Why didn't you say something then?"

"It wasn't until later. Much, much later. There was something in your eyes, something intangible, and there were the other things. Drinks you detested, the kind of music you preferred, the different taste in food. You know. Personalities

can change, but a person's taste usually remains the same."
He ran his hand through his hair and shook his head again.
"So, I did some checking and found out that no one in Los
Angeles had seen you for months. I put two and two to-
gether, but by that time you and Brent had fallen in love. And
I thanked my lucky stars for your memory loss."

The room was quiet once more. Samantha closed her eyes.
Her ears were ringing, a dull nagging rapidly settling at the
back of her head. So he *had* noticed. She suddenly wondered
who else had done the same thing and not said anything
anyway? Perhaps wanting, for reasons of their own, to believe that she *was* Amanda? Opening her eyes, she watched
Matt pace the floor. "So you had an affair with her." She
almost sounded sad.

Matt paused, and stared at her.

"Who? Amanda?" He laughed, a short, mirthless laugh. "As
strange as it may sound, she wouldn't let me as much as
touch her. She said it would be disloyal to my wife. Imagine
that." Bitterness crept into his voice. "The bitch actually
thought of someone else's feelings. But it didn't stop her from
taunting me, leading me on and on, week after week, month
after month, until—"

Until the day you saw me. Samantha turned her head. All
those years she was married to Beau she had wanted a family, children. Ironic. The last two years of her marriage, although unbeknownst to Beau, she had ceased practicing
birth control, hoping for the child that could possibly bring
them back together. Yet it was a one-time tumble, against her
will at that, that had proved fruitful. How disgustingly unfair!

Then, when she had found herself pregnant, she had opted
to abort the baby. Foolish? Madness. Yes, she had wanted a
child of her own, but not that way. The memory of how it was
conceived would have haunted her and she would not have
had the strength to live with that memory. She knew that
now. She must have known it then.

Yes, ironic, she thought, suddenly sad. Just as ironic as
Paula's suspicion; all this time Paula had thought that her
husband had a long-standing affair with Amanda. So much so
that she had instigated all those incidents to punish her and
make her miserable. Had he told her otherwise? she wondered. But she didn't ask, it no longer mattered. Paula
wouldn't have believed him anyway.

Samantha took a deep breath, suddenly feeling her dead twin's ominous presence in the room. A silent scream crept up and choked at the back of her throat. *Is this my fate? To right Amanda's sins?* A sudden pain stabbed her and she gasped. Holding her side she doubled over, her heart pounding wildly.

"Sam . . . my God . . ." Matt paled. In a reflex he charged forward, his arm reaching out to her.

"Don't . . ." She raised her arm to ward him off, and slowly tried to straighten up. Then, with a groan, she doubled over a second time, her face now as ashen as his. Panic seized her. Her first impulse was to scream and she bit her lip so as not to cry out her fear.

"Let me call somebody." Matt rushed to the door.

"No!" She grabbed the edge of the bed. "No. I'm all right." She closed her eyes for a moment. Gradually the pain subsided and she felt the blood rush back to her head.

Opening her eyes again, she looked straight into his, and saw her own pain reflected in the dark eyes, studying her with genuine worry, and she realized the scare had touched him as much as it had her. *Why,* she thought, surprised, *he must've gone through hell, wondering if and when I'd remember.*

Amanda was dead. The past deserved to be buried with her. Am I supposed to relent now? Let bygones be bygones, shake hands with my rapist and smile?

"You're sure you're all right?" Matt's concerned voice seemed to come from afar.

She turned her head, unable to bear the sight of him. *Am I? Can this ever be erased from my memory? Will the hurt ever go away, will the scar fade, the wound heal?*

"Samantha? Say something, please?"

Looking at him again, she watched him wring his hands, his beard twitch. And suddenly she remembered that he had not had a beard or a moustache two years ago.

"God, Sam, I'd get down on my knees if I thought you'd forgive me. I know I can't undo what's done, but for God's sake, don't do this to me. Say something, anything. Call me names, throw knives at me—anything but this . . . this silent treatment . . ."

He's good, she thought grimly, *really good. He could almost bring a listener to tears. And convincing. Oh, yes, above all—convincing. Is his anguish supposed to touch me? Or his remorse?* She could feel the sting of humiliation, the bitterness at his betrayal, the hurt. *And why shouldn't he suffer? I did. In a moment of flagrant despair I almost killed myself . . .*

"Did you ever stop to think about your wife?" she said harshly. "Even for one split second? What about her feelings?"

She blinked at the sound of his laughter.

"Paula? What of her? If it hadn't been for her, this never would've happened." He began to pace again, rubbing his beard now and then. "After the baby was stillborn, she would not let me near her. Not so much as touch her, let alone make love to her." He laughed again, the hollow sound echoing his torment. "Oh, not that I really blame her. It was all my fault. I was . . . sick, and I killed our baby. And she blamed me. Of course. I blamed myself." He sighed and raised his hands. "I guess . . . well . . . it was to be expected. First the miscarriage, then a dead infant. And all because of me . . ." Matt sighed again, his voice breaking. "But I'm a man, of flesh and blood. As much as I tried to stay away from other women, I'm still only human. You're right, I'm weak, and an absolute heel . . . And then there was Amanda . . ."

Samantha shivered. Suddenly she understood. And her anger waned, slowly, and she began to see him in a different light.

"Paula is my best friend," she said, remembering Paula's confession. "For what it's worth, she loves you. And you, Matt Manchione, bastard that you are, you're a lucky man, and a fool not to appreciate her."

She turned away, the tears now flowing. The dormant bitterness threatening to overcome her again. She remembered the countless nightmares that had assaulted her night after night during the past two years, the haunting fear of her unknown past, and the agony when she had regained her memory. She could hear Matt speak again, but she shook her head, not wanting to hear the words.

". . . we were having problems. I tried to make things up to her, God, how I tried, but she turned her back on me. I'm only sorry that I hurt you in the process. It was not fair, to you I mean. It was my problem. I had no right to drag you into it, or make you pay for my pain. For that, I'm really, truly sorry."

She raised her hand to stop him, then lowered it again, realizing his need to verbalize his guilt.

"You're right. Your memory loss was heaven-sent. A second chance for me, too. That night with you sobered me up. I've been clean since then." He looked at her. "But you're wrong. I do know how lucky I am to have Paula." His voice softened and he was almost whispering. "For what it's worth, I'm truly sorry for what happened."

Silence fell.

Matt looked at her uncertainly, then slowly turned and started to walk away. At the doorway he looked back at her, hesitating.

"Are you . . . going to . . . ?" Tell anyone, Brent? he wanted to say.

But she did not hear him, and with a long drawn-out sigh he turned and left the room.

Chapter 54

WAITING FOR LOUISE, SAMANTHA WANDERED AIMLESSLY around the posh living room. It was a bright Sunday afternoon, and after lunch Brent had dropped her off at the penthouse, while he and Jonathan had gone to play a round of golf. Paula had taken the children to a birthday party and they were not expected back until after dinnertime. Seven months pregnant, Samantha had welcomed Louise's invitation to come and see her.

Noticing an unfamiliar ornament on the mantelpiece, she leaned forward to admire it. Cute, she thought, so like Louise. She smiled and, turning, her eye fell on the huge painting on the opposite wall above the grand piano.

As before, it immediately arrested her attention. Slowly her smile faded, and she grew pensive. There was something about the young girl in that picture, something . . . vaguely disconcerting, something . . . familiar. Samantha shivered, suddenly uneasy. Was it the sad expression in those silent amber eyes? The hidden message behind the look, perhaps? What was it trying to convey? Each time she had come here she had been drawn to this portrait, irrevocably, irresistibly, as if—

"Ah, there you are. I'm sorry to keep you waiting so long, my dear, but I didn't like my new hairdo, so I just had to comb it out." Louise paused in the middle of the room, leaning on the cane that had become her constant companion now. Her keen eyes watched the younger woman tear her attention reluctantly away from the painting.

"You look very nice," Samantha murmured, the enthusiasm lacking in her toneless voice.

Slowly Louise sank down on the sofa, carefully hooking the cane on the armrest.

"Why don't you sit down, child? You ought to stay off your feet in your condition." She glanced at the clock above the fireplace. "Brent and Jonathan won't be here for an hour or so."

She nodded to Kam, who handed her a glass of wine, and resumed watching Samantha, who was once again staring at the painting.

"Mrs. Farraday?" Kam handed Samantha a glass of lemonade.

"Thank you, Kam." Samantha forced herself to turn away from the painting.

"You really do like that portrait, don't you?" Louise smiled.

"Yes . . . yes, I suppose so. There's something . . . arresting about it, something . . . I can't quite put my finger on it." She looked at it again, a deep frown on her forehead, her expression puzzled. "Familiar, I would say."

There was more, she thought, something indefinable. She was certain of it. But what? Something about the eyes of the girl? Where had she seen it before? Where—Samantha suddenly stiffened, and turned to Louise.

"I've been here before," she said, her voice tense.

Louise raised a delicate eyebrow and gave her a quizzical look.

"No, I mean *before* . . . before I"—she bit her lip—"before that night of your seventy-fifth birthday . . ."

Still not responding, Louise kept watching her taut face, a vein twitching in her neck.

"That portrait, it has something to do with"—Samantha's eyes changed to a vibrant hazel—"Vivien . . . Of course! The art gallery. I saw it . . . I met you there . . . at the gallery. I . . . I sold you that portrait, didn't I?" She looked at the portrait. "She was shorthanded and had asked me to help out. It wasn't a Renoir, but you bought it anyway. And . . . and . . . you insisted that I personally deliver it . . ." Her face was now pale and she turned to look at Louise with bewilderment in her huge eyes. "You'd wanted me to help you find the best place to hang it up . . . My God, you knew all along, didn't you? All this time, you've known I was not Amanda . . ." Her voice had dropped to a hoarse whisper.

She suddenly whirled around and almost lost her balance at the sudden movement, grabbing the edge of the piano wing, her hip bumping sharply against the polished wood. Louise gasped, and sat up straight as if to come to her rescue.

"Good God, child, do be more careful!" She clutched her glass and gulped down the wine, the hand that held the glass trembling. She looked up, startled at the stricken look on Samantha's ashen face.

"It's true, isn't it, Louise?" Samantha gripped the ledge of the grand piano, her voice sharp. "Isn't it?"

Leaning back, Louise let out a sigh. "I always did like that portrait," she said softly. "I fell in love with it the moment I laid eyes on it. And somehow it didn't matter anymore that it was not a Renoir. Those eyes." She turned to the painting. "You're right, it's captivating, isn't it? Such depth, such feeling, there's a strength hidden behind that look that's admirable." She looked at the horrified Samantha. "You are so much like her, you know. There's a quality within you that was lacking in Amanda. Your capacity for love, a deep, warm, giving kind of love." She put down her glass and took a deep breath. "Yes, I knew."

Samantha put her glass on the piano, slowly, as if in a trance.

"Why didn't you stop the charade? If . . . if you knew . . . you must've known also that I . . . was married . . ."

"No, not just then. And when I did find out, it was too late. You were in Brent's life and the children loved having the mother they'd always pined for. How could I take that all away from them? Besides, your marriage was a farce, you were separated and about to divorce." Louise refilled her glass and took a sip, and another. "I watched you that night of my party. The way you looked at Brent—yes, my dear, you were in love with him even then. And he, he was falling for you all over again, and harder this time, for he thought you were a changed woman, and one he liked better. How could I take it upon myself to ruin your chances for happiness? You each deserved it, you both needed it." She paused for a moment. "It was Providence, I told myself, you both were given a second chance in this life."

The room remained silent for a long moment. Then Samantha sighed.

"How on earth did you find me?"

"Daryl found you." She laughed at Samantha's shocked expression. "He saw you at that art gallery and asked me to check you out."

"Didn't he think I was Amanda?" Good Lord, Samantha thought, is there more?

"Yes."

"Well, then . . ."

"You didn't recognize him."

"I could've faked it."

"He said you treated him like any other prospective customer, and Amanda could never have been that courteous or patient. His words precisely."

Samantha's breath came heavily. "Why?" she whispered. "Why, Louise?"

"Please, dear, sit down. I'll tell you why, but please do sit down."

"Everything, Louise. Tell me everything. You'll leave nothing out this time."

Samantha sank down in the chair farthest from the sofa, her face frozen, her eyes cold, and seeing her hostility, Louise sighed and leaned back once more, her shoulders slumping slightly.

"You see, after Amanda's disappearance, Brent stopped living. Oh, he went about his usual business and all, but he merely existed, more like a zombie than a man of flesh and blood. I never did understand why—the marriage was a disaster and Amanda was a bitch in more ways than one, but he just pined away, so to speak. That short-lived fling with Bianca turned out to be a smoke screen, and we all began to despair." She paused dramatically. "Mind you, I knew where Amanda was. I had hired a detective who traced her to the south of Italy, but there was no way I or anyone else in our family would've wanted her back. Then you showed up, and somehow the answer to our problem seemed clear . . ."

"So you staged the accident." Disbelief crept into Samantha's eyes.

"No, oh heavens no. That accident was genuine. Neither I

nor Daryl had anything to do with that. Like I said, it was Providence, fate." A faint smile formed around her lips. "I must admit, it was quite convenient that you suffered from total amnesia and all, and it fell right into our plans to reunite Brent with the woman he'd been waiting to return for four long, agonizing years."

Samantha leaned back in the chair, her heart pounding. "So Daryl decided to identify me as his long-lost sister-in-law," she filled in. The words faded. Her throat felt dry and she suddenly felt weary.

"It was a gamble," Louise admitted, "but it worked. Brent never noticed the difference. At least, not so far as the switch was concerned."

The room was quiet again, with only the ticking of the clock above the mantelpiece breaking the tense silence.

"You used me. You tricked me into becoming someone I wasn't," Samantha said. "My God, Louise, did it ever occur to you that you were playing God? What if it had . . . what if I had regained my memory in midstream? You could've hurt us, you could've hurt Brent . . ."

"But you didn't, and everything did go well. At least, until that wretched bitch showed up unexpectedly." Louise lowered her eyes, studying her nails pensively.

"But what if I had?"

Louise waved her hands. "Heavens, Samantha, you're as stubborn as your dead twin," she quipped. Then, noting the expression on Samantha's face, she hastened to clear her throat.

"Oh, all right. I suppose you deserve to know the whole scenario," she said with a sigh. "At first I had planned to introduce you to Brent—you know, the old-fashioned way, bring you two together. But then you had the accident, and that changed everything. When Daryl saw you in the hospital, robbed of your memory, he acted on impulse and identified you as Amanda. Out of curiosity I decided to play along, to see what would develop. And what I'd hoped for happened —you and Brent fell in love with each other." She reached for the bottle of wine Kam had left on the table and refilled her glass.

"If you'd regained your memory at that point, I would've told you the truth. About my initial intentions, and my hopes for Brent. Your accident, Samantha, was pure convenience. It

made everything so much simpler, and it speeded things up."
She sipped the wine. "And then, of course, there was the
matter of the inheritance."

Samantha tensed. "What about the inheritance?"

Louise sighed, almost sadly this time.

"I loved and respected my husband. But with all his business sense, Justin was a sentimental fool. He wanted to see
all his grandchildren married, and used his will to implement
his wish. I was dead set against that stipulation, but he
wouldn't listen to me. And I was afraid for Brent. I wanted
him to have that money. Charity doesn't need it, he does."

"Money . . . ," Samantha whispered. "You did this all for
money . . ."

"No, I did it for Brent. I want for him to realize his dream—
of having a trauma center someday. And Karen, and Daryl. I
wanted them to have it. If Brent wasn't married or living with
Amanda last year at the reading of that codicil, the three of
them would've lost the money, and with it, all hopes for the
future."

"But . . . but that stipulation wasn't met . . . I am not
. . . Brent wasn't—" Samantha stammered.

"As far as everyone was concerned, Brent was married to
you and living with you. At the time that satisfied the lawyer
who executed the will. And that will had one other stipulation
—that I was to police its execution. Which I did. The execution stands as is." Louise grimaced. "I did encounter minor
opposition from Alison, but I've managed to nip that in the
bud."

"Suppose . . . suppose Amanda had returned earlier? Before the reading of the will? What would you have done
then?"

Louise's eyes widened in surprise.

"Brent would still have gotten his share of the money. He
was married, and Amanda would've been living with him as
she did when she returned. That was the easy part. And I
would've gotten you your divorce from Beau Farley sooner."

"Beau . . . ? I suppose you had that part all figured out,
too?"

"But of course. I dug up enough dirt on him that would've
left him with no choice other than to set you free."

"You what?" Samantha stared at her, stunned.

"I blackmailed him." Louise smiled. "My dear Samantha,

contrary to what you were told, your business wasn't thriving, or at the peak of its success when you sold it. It was heading for bankruptcy. But *Les Mirages* didn't go bankrupt by itself, nor—as you were made to believe—did your manager swindle your company funds. No, my dear. Your precious Beau embezzled them and used the money to cover up the fraud he had committed at NASA. Oh, yes." She nodded when Samantha shook her head. "He had made a grave mistake, an error of judgment, and tried to rectify it by using NASA funds. And he got caught. Lucky for him, he had just developed an important program and NASA needed him to implement it. Or they would've fired him. Instead, they temporarily stripped him of his rank and demanded he pay them back immediately. So, to save his cheating hide, he depleted your business funds. That, my child, was the real reason why he wanted to give your marriage another chance. So he would have access to your bank account."

She emptied her glass and poured another.

"And I thought . . . the accident . . ." Samantha thought of Beau's limp, and swallowed hard.

"You thought wrong. You don't owe him a thing. Did he tell you what the argument was all about? The night you had that accident? You had found out about his mistress, Melissa, and wanted a divorce."

"Melissa?" Samantha whispered. "But Beau said. . . . I found out. . . . only the week before I left to come here . . ."

"He lied. Like he lied about everything else." Louise said crisply. Then sighed. "Beau did not want a divorce. That would've upset his applecart, for at the time, he had not yet had the chance to steal all of your money. You weren't drunk, he was. And he was driving that night, or so the police reports state." She paused again. "He must've panicked. He was probably terrified that you'd also find out about the child."

Samantha gaped, and almost dropped her wine glass.

"The . . . the child . . . ?"

"Beau has a child by Melissa. While he denied your hankering for a child, he fathered one by another."

Louise watched for Samantha's reaction to her revelation, but there was none. Samantha was numb, the words echoing through her mind without impact.

"Yes, I guess I did use you," Louise said softly, "and for that, I beg your forgiveness. Still, it was not done with malice, and as I see it, both you and Brent are the richer for it."

She brushed an imaginary strand of hair from her forehead, her eyes pleading.

"I'd grown to love you, Samantha, just like Brent did. And your children. Yes, they're *your* children, you're the only mother they know, and love. And you . . . Look at me and tell me honestly that you don't love them, or Brent?" She slowly sipped her wine and watched the silent woman before her.

"Who else is in this scam, apart from Daryl?" Samantha whispered. An image of Matt flashed before her and she shivered. She felt weak, drained from the blows of the afternoon.

"No one else, just Daryl and myself," Louise answered her.

"You allowed my brother to worry and think I was dead. And I thought he was Daryl's friend?"

"Yes, that was not kind, and I hope your brother can forgive us for that someday." Louise sighed and closed her eyes for a moment. When she opened them again, Samantha saw the glimmer of unshed tears in the reflection of the light. "Perhaps we did wrong. All we thought of was Brent. He'd been so unhappy for so long, and I felt he deserved better. When you made him happy I thanked God for letting me meddle with your life. Forgive me, Samantha, I really didn't mean any harm to you or your brother." Her voice broke and a tear fell on her lap. "By the way, neither Daryl nor I knew that you and Peter were related. The man I hired to dig up your identity reported you only as Samantha Farley, not Haydon."

Samantha sat very still. Louise's words brushed by her, barely touching her conscious mind. She felt empty inside. Something nagged at her and she forced herself to focus on the feeling.

She talks of Brent's happiness, she thought warily, *and mine. How could she . . .* A vision suddenly flashed from the depths of her memory. *She's killed for me. Or was that also just for Brent?* She stirred and raised herself out of the chair.

"When you . . . when you . . ." She hesitated, hedging, feeling Louise's gaze on her. "Did away with Amanda"—she swallowed—"didn't you remember that I was . . . married . . . ?"

Louise's eyes flickered and she lowered them for a moment, then looked up again, her expression gentle.

"Amanda was an impulse," she said curtly. "And no, I can't say I thought of that right at that moment. Later on . . . everything happened so fast, your husband showed up before I had time to ponder that dilemma." She smiled, a little sad smile. "Just as well, really. It saved everyone a lot of headaches, especially me."

They were both silent now, neither of them looking at the other. Finally, Samantha moved. She took a long deep breath.

"It's done," she said softly, her own anguish subsiding at the sight of the old woman's remorse. "It's over, and you're right. It may have been wrong, but how can I turn away and deny the happiness that your folly has brought me and my family?" Her hand touched Louise's and the next minute they were in each other's arms, sobbing and laughing simultaneously.

"Oh, Samantha, can you ever forgive—"

"Hush . . . shhh . . ."

She's killed for me—it chimed in her. *Perhaps she had her grandson in mind, but above all, she did it for me.* She suddenly smiled.

"There *is* something I don't understand," Samantha murmured.

"Yes, darling?"

"If you knew I wasn't Amanda, why did you try to bribe me to get me out of Brent's life? You did, after all, place me there."

"I had to make sure you were not a golddigger like Amanda. That would've been a worse disaster than planting you in Brent's life."

"So if I had taken the money . . ."

"Prevention is better than cure, and it was still very early in the game." She took Samantha's hand and held it tight between her own. "You have no idea how delighted I was when you stormed out of here that day. Your anger was most refreshing and I began to like you even then."

She smiled. "I must have driven you crazy those first few weeks after I moved into your home. But you came through again, coming after me and telling me to return there. It must not have been easy for you. And it was during that time that I knew you were the right woman for my grandson."

Samantha's eyes widened. "You mean . . . you staged all that?"

"Well, not quite. I wasn't exactly my usual charming self. But I must admit, it did come in handy." Louise's eyes sparkled. "Brent deserves a good, loving woman like you, my dear. You'll agree that he's a good man."

Samantha sighed and shook her head in disbelief.

"How could you play God, Louise? Even if your intentions were justified, at least to yourself."

Louise's blue eyes flickered. "Was it so wrong to want happiness and love for my only grandson? The only sin I committed was that I did not unveil the truth. I merely sat back and let things run their course. Now tell me honestly, was I so bad?"

To that, Samantha could not find anything to say.

During the drive back to Lake Forest, Samantha was pensive, thinking over the revelations that afternoon. They had stayed for dinner, and the evening had passed amicably. At no time had Louise let on that she and Samantha had had a heart-to-heart talk other than the usual friendly chatter.

A sudden wave of pain racked her body and Samantha gasped. She felt a rush of moisture seep between her legs, and as another stab of pain pierced her back, she gasped again. "Oh, God, Brent . . ." she heaved. "I think my water just broke . . ." Samantha groaned as the pain returned.

Brent took one look at her, and instantly stepped on the gas pedal. "Hold on," he said tensely.

And looking furtively over his left shoulder, steered the car toward the expressway.

Chapter 55

THE SILVER JAGUAR FLEW ACROSS THE CITY, TIRES screeching as Brent turned sharp corners and swiftly steered the sleek car through the late Chicago traffic. His hands gripped the steering wheel to steady the trembling, his jaws taut. Every once in a while he glanced over at Samantha, who was lying half across the passenger seat, one hand holding her rounded belly, the other clasping the door handle.

The pains came regularly now, ripping through her body with a viciousness that seemed to tear her inside out, forcing deep, guttural groans from her. Watching her face with concern, Brent stepped further on the gas pedal, his jaws twitching ferociously as he made one last turn before entering the Kennedy Expressway.

"Hang on, darling, we'll be there in no time. Just remember the Lamaze exercises. Breathe deeply, in, out, in out . . ."

He listened for her breathing while trying to concentrate on the traffic, frowning at the sound of heaving.

"Take it easy, Sam, slower, or you'll hyperventilate."

He expertly maneuvered the Jaguar through the slower lanes to the left and cursed underneath his breath. It was well past rush hour traffic, yet the expressway was crawling with cars. He glanced at the speedometer and frowned again. Looking sideways he steered the Jag to the far left lane, barely avoiding a racing Camaro and receiving an angry honking from its driver.

"Be careful, please, Brent," Samantha hissed through clenched teeth. "It won't get us there any faster . . ." She groaned as a wave of pain racked her body.

"Damn! I'm a doctor, why can't I have an ambulance at my beck and call?" Brent growled. Then, suddenly, his eyes lit up. "Hang on, baby, we're going."

And he swerved to the left and onto the shoulder that served as an emergency lane, and switching on his bright lights, stepped on the gas. Samantha closed her eyes, trying to block out her anxiety. As another wave attacked her, she completely forgot her fright.

"Oh, Christ!" Brent glanced in the rearview mirror and his moment of triumph vanished at the sight of flashing red and blue lights behind him. He slowed down and stopped the car.

"What is it, Brent? Why are you stopping?" Samantha hissed, heaving heavily.

"Just stay calm, darling, I'll handle this."

Rolling down the window, he fumbled for his wallet and frantically looked for his medical identification card. Before the policeman could open his mouth, Brent waved the card at him. "Officer, I'm a doctor. My wife here is in labor and I need to get her to Lutheran General Hospital in Park Ridge fast." He quickly switched on the inside light, the policeman took one look at Samantha and the stern expression on his face changed.

"Follow me," he said and rushed back to the police car.

Next a wailing siren cut through the night air, and crawling around stopped cars, went ahead of the Jaguar, leading it through the traffic. The two cars sped along, mostly using the emergency lane to avoid ignorant drivers, and before long they swung up the hospital driveway to the emergency entrance.

A team of green-uniformed orderlies rushed to meet them with a ready roller bed.

"Easy, now, guys. Get her to OB, stat. Come on, move, *move!*" Brent ran with them.

"Dr. Farraday?"

He waved the bewildered nurse aside. "Get Aaron Shapiro over here, *now!*"

In the labor room, he grabbed a white jacket and dashed into the scrub room.

"Doctor, Dr. Shapiro is on his way. Can I do anything?" The nurse looked frightened.

"Come with me. I'm going to examine her myself."

A scream greeted them as they reentered the labor room. He took one look at her and swiftly walked to the end of the bed, parting her legs. After a few seconds he heaved a sigh of relief.

"Try to hold back, darling. Don't push, not yet."

He nodded at the frightened nurse and walked to the side of the bed, stripping the surgical gloves off his hands. Samantha had gripped the steel railings, beads of perspiration pearling down her forehead, her breath coming in short rasps.

"All right, we'll do this together. You're hyperventilating, breathe deeply, in. Come on, love, you can do it, breathe, *in*, deep, *out*, again—*in, out*. Deeply, slower. Breathe in, slower, out, inhale, deep, out. Again."

A wail escaped the laboring Samantha. Brent swiftly moved back to the end of the bed, nodding his thanks at the nurse, who handed him a new pair of gloves.

"Get her into Delivery. We can't wait for Genius Shapiro." He went outside to alert the desk nurse.

"She's dilating all the way. I'll do the delivery myself. When Dr. Shapiro gets here, tell him." He turned to leave, then seeing the waiting policeman, quickly went over to see him.

"Thank you, officer. If you don't mind, please leave my ticket with the nurse. I'm sorry, but the baby . . ."

"It's all right, Dr. Farraday. No ticket. Compliments of the state. Just make sure that baby gets out okay."

Brent grinned. "Thanks again. If you stick around, I'll introduce you to the kid."

He rushed back into the delivery room.

A wail filled the room and Samantha smiled through her tears, her glistening body still trembling from exertion.

"A boy! A healthy son." Brent held up the squirming infant for her to see, his eyes shining with pride and joy.

Samantha closed her eyes, her body beginning to relax. Suddenly, a new wave of pain ripped through her and she screamed. Instantly Brent handed the newborn infant to the waiting nurse and reached inside of her. His eyes widened with profound surprise.

"God, Brent, what's happening?" Samantha heaved.

"Push, Sam, push hard. *Now.*"

With a scream she obliged, and shortly afterward a second wail reached her astonished ears.

"A girl. My darling, twins! I'll be damned, there are two of them!" Brent burst out laughing, and through her tears Samantha began to laugh with him. "Shit, I'd better warn Shapiro to have his monitor checked. Amazing, we never detected a second heartbeat." He shook his head, his eyes shining.

"We'd better check. Perhaps there's a third one." Brent grinned happily, and reaching inside of her once more, ordered her to push again. This time only the placenta came out.

With a deep contented sigh Brent handed the second baby to another nurse and stripped the bloodstained gloves off his hands. A broad smile lit his face as he slowly approached Samantha's side, his eyes moist. The look he gave her was infinitely tender.

"When you said you would be better than Amanda I did not think you'd go this far." He took her outstretched hand and brought it to his lips.

"Not better," she whispered. "Just better for you." He leaned forward and kissed her damp forehead.

"I love you, Samantha Farraday," he said simply.